May 15,

To Holly,

BEAUTY & GRACE

A HISTORICAL NOVEL

Thank you for your
friendship and support.
fondly,
Christina

Christina M. Abt

BEAUTY and GRACE

aBc Publishing and Writing
East Aurora, New York

ISBN: 978-0-9905518-3-6

The trademark aBc Publishing and Writing is registered in the
U.S. Patent and Trademark Office and elsewhere.

Manufactured in the United States of America

FIRST EDITION

To women from all worlds
who have faced unjust judgements and treatments
yet still found the courage and heart to survive.

This book is dedicated to you
with my deepest respect and sincere gratitude
for your courage in lighting the way.

INTRODUCTION

JUNE 25, 1928

THE MORNIN' AIR LAY THICK with layered odors o'fish, seaweed and bilge seepin' from nearby moored ships. The briny smells weaved inta every bit o'me life growin' up in the oceanside village of Queenstown, County Cork.

Me family's heritage was woven through a long line o'Irish seafarers, tracing back ta the first-century life of St. Brendan, the Navigator. As me da was forever sayin', "Never forget me darlin' girl, salt water runs through your veins."

Truth be told, I was always lookin' fer ways ta be on the docks. Whether bringin' lunch ta me da at his shipyard job, skippin' school fer my passion o'paintin seascapes 'long the rocky seaport coast or escaping me bed fer midnight communion with the endless shoreline o'stars, me soul was always bein' pulled by the tides.

"Twas me deepest dream ta one day cross the ocean ta America. Not that I was wantin' ta leave behind me family, mind ya. More I was wishin' ta follow the path o'Bridget Hanlon, the sister of me best friend, Margaret Mary.

Bridget was a poet, celebrated within Queenstown for her work oft' published in the church bulletin and every now and then in The Examiner Newspaper. Everyone said she was born ta follow in the footsteps o'Cork's own Mary Ellen Patrick Downing, whose poems were featured in Dublin's Irish Nationalist Newspaper. Oh, but Bridget had a greater dream, one she shared with me and Mary Margaret on a Sunday after our families had come home from Mass.

Truth be told, Bridget didn't exactly mean ta be sharin her dream. 'Twas only on accounta me and Margaret Mary comin' upon her and Padric Mahoney kissin' in the alley behind where we lived. We was always bein' thorns in Bridget's side, sneakin' around and spyin'. We did it 'cause she always give us somethin' good ta keep us from tellin' what we knew. No doubt, the kiss was big news and me and Margaret Mary was beyond excited o'er what treasure Bridget might be offerin'.

"I've not a sweet nor a nickel ta be givin' the two of ya little devils. And I've not a care what ya be tellin' anyone 'bout me and Padric. It makes no matter as I've got me bag right here and the two of us are leavin' straight away fer America. A newspaper editor there wants ta hire me ta write and that's just what I'm goin' ta do. But if ya promise not ta tell 'til I'm gone, ya can have me lace handkerchief that nanny embroidered for me."

Pushin' the delicate linen and lace square into me hand, Bridget gave a quick kiss and hug ta her sister and off she went. Margaret Mary started bawling on the spot, so's I give her the hankie to dry her face and wipe her nose. 'twas only a few minutes afore her temper replaced her tears.

"I'll only have ta share a bed with one sister now, so good riddance. She was nothin' but trouble 'round here anyhow."

Seein' how Margaret Mary wasn't of a mind ta tattle, I asked if she wanted ta sneak off ta the harbor ta watch Bridget board the ship. I was hopin' ta do just the same one day, so's I could become a famous painter in America. The thing was, I was in need of a bit o'courage. Me hope was in watchin' someone else take the steps, I'd be able ta do the same.

So's off we went and watched, and we made a pact ta never tell all we knew 'bout Bridget kissin' or her leavin'. As for me, I made me own pact that come a year's time, I'd be boardin' a ship, leavin' behind Ireland's green shores for America's gold-paved streets.

As fate would have it, in a few months time a handbill posted on the wire fence surrounding the shipyard. I first noticed the artwork cross the top. 'twas a design I knew by heart. The red flag with a white star belonged ta one o'the finest shipping lines in the world. Yet the bold words below was what I cared most about.

"RMS Olympic Sails to America."

Bein' the daughter of a ship builder, I knew the names and histories o'most vessels come ta port. The Olympic was the sister ship o'the Titanic, itself sailed from Queenstown, April 10, 1912, never ta return. Ever since, no matter when the Olympic come to port I was sure ta be there ta see it. 'twas a never-endin' thrill ta watch the grand ship glide into the harbor and watch the wealthy first-class passengers and steerage-class Irish bein' ferried out ta her gangplank. When I saw the list of sailing dates on the handbill, I set me heart on the final one and went ta makin' a plan.

I STARTED WORK, SWEEPIN' FLOORS at O'Brien's Market and keepin' every bit o'me wages in a leather satchel hid 'neath the mattress I shared with me three sisters. As months passed, I saved enough fer me ticket and the new birthie I'd be needin' from a bootlegger 'long the docks as bein only 16, Irish emigration rules deemed me not legal to be travelin' on me own. I also went ta squirrelin' away a bit o'food from the larder each week and packin' a small satchel so's mam didn't miss a few o' me clothes here and there on wash days. I made sure as well ta pack up me rosary, me drawing pad and pencils and me best sketch o'the harbor, so's I'd never forget from where I come.

As the time fer leavin' drew near, the excitement of startin' a new life began bubblin' up within me. I knew the only way ta ever leave me family would be without word or hug, but still I needed ta tell someone 'afore I burst. Margaret Mary was me only choice.

"Are ya daft, girl? You're not but 16 and certainly not smart enough ta go off on yer own. At least Bridget had the good sense ta sail away with Padric, and knowin' that when she got to America she had a job. I'll tell ya straight. From what Padric's family is hearin', life in America ain't the craic. In fact, I heard Padric's da tellin' that there's people dyin' goin' 'cross the ocean in them lower parts o'ships. Irish like us are bein' crowded tight next ta one 'nother in small spaces, makin' 'all of 'em sweaty and smelly, no better than animals. And mind ya, if they manage ta survive the voyage, they're bein' forced ta go ta work in buildin's with little light and not enough air ta breathe for most all the hours in a day. And another thing 'bout goin' on your own, what's ta keep ya safe from any harm?"

Margaret Mary's words flamed me temper. They also left me thinkin' 'bout goin' away from the only life I'd known and maybe never returnin'. Just the same, I knew me heart was driven by waves of wanderlust, surely the same that sent me granddad to worldly sailing adventures at thirteen years. No matter the fears and homebound pleas of me heart, 'twas no denying the call o'the tides on me soul.

So 'twas one foggy mornin', disguised in me brother Quinn's clothes and me da's woolen cap that I stole off a hook as I left out the back door, I made me way up the Olympic's gang plank as 18-year old Taylor Eagan.

Mam often told the story of me birth and how da straight away named me, Teagan, the Irish word for "beauty". Not wantin ta ever lose that connection, I'd heard tell o' American school teacher Annie Edson Taylor—first ta go over the world's natural wonder of Niagara Falls in a barrel. Her story made up me mind ta take away the T from me name fer Taylor and be leavin' Eagan for the rest.

AS I MADE ME WAY DOWN THE ship's stairs ta third class, I managed ta weave me way inta a small space of a bunk bed among five women and their six beibis, Gatherin' me satchel up close to me chest, I shut me eyes and dreamed o'all that lie ahead.

As I did, I whispered a pray to Mary, Mother o'God, that me new life in America not end up in a place with little light and not enough air, and where I be forced ta be for all the rest o'me days.

CHAPTER ONE

MORNINGS STARTED SLOWLY FOR Grace Reid. The auburn hair, hazel-eyed, mid-forties woman had long ago developed a habit of rising early, to allow time for meditation and a bit of yoga before transitioning her long and lean frame into the world.

Grace developed the pre-dawn routine after a therapist suggested the combined practices as a cure-all for violent nightmares haunting her mid-teens. While the nightmares eventually subsided, Grace continued with both the meditation and the yoga as valued parts of her life, despite teasing from girlfriends, college roommates and the occasional men in her life. Now, some twenty years later, she enjoyed the fact that most all those people were evangelizing yoga as the, "newest" self-care trend.

Grace had always possessed a strong sense of personal awareness. When life got messy she knew her survival depended on taking control of the things she could control. That meant staying in the comfort zone of her regular routines.

With both her body and mind exercised, Grace set off for the kitchen and breakfast, an equally formatted part of her rising ritual. The routine began with the brewing of tea in a green ceramic pot handed down from her mother's grandmother, Hattie Burns. She covered the treasured brewer with a quilted tea cozy made for her with love by her mother's mother, Nana O'Connor. With the tea steeping, she moved on to creating her favorite breakfast treat.

The preparation began by toasting a thick piece of grain bread from a loaf Grace purchased every week, at a bakery located near her city condo. She topped the browned and crunchy slice with a thick layer of almond butter and completed her breakfast masterpiece by nestling perfectly halved red grapes into the melting, nutty base. It was a taste treat she'd first enjoyed on a trip to Ireland with her nana, where they traced their O'Connor heritage and celebrated the traditions of their family's homeland.

Placing the toasted treat on a Belleek china plate, Grace poured a cup of tea and settled into the kitchen nook defining her dining area. The early morning sun streamed through the windows, warming her body like a heartfelt embrace and she absorbed every bit of the energy in preparation for whatever challenges her work day might bring.

GRACE WORKED IN THE FIELD of senior health care. It was a career she began in the marketing department of a retirement home following her graduation with honors from Rosary Hill, an all-female college located in her hometown of Buffalo, New York. Yet it was Grace's natural people skills, along with her Catholic upbringing based on service to others, that launched her into the upper echelons of senior care administration.

Grace found most people aged sixty and older vibrant and fun to be around, much like her Nana and Papa O'Connor. Grace had been the favored grandchild in the O'Connor family and she basked in her grandparent's affections. That was one of the reasons spending time in the company of seniors made Grace feel so complete. It was also what most contributed to her success, as she quickly evolved from an entry-level employee to a well-paid, industry consultant. These days Grace could set her own terms, contracting for jobs that suited her interests as well as her bank account.

The bonuses in developing such specialized job skills included travel opportunities throughout the United States, chances to meet all sorts of new people and formulating creative solutions to senior care issues.

While she loved the challenge and the independence of every job she accepted, Grace's latest freelance assignment was a bit out of the ordinary, even by her standards. The assignment began with a message on her answering machine in early January. The caller identified himself as Jonathan Walsh, executive director of Wood Haven Psychiatric Hospital. Initially, Grace found the message a bit offsetting.

A psychiatric hospital? Why would he want to talk to me?

Only one way to find out. Grace answered herself, picking up the phone and dialing the number.

"Hello, Grace. Thanks for calling back."

By the tenor of his voice, Grace guessed Jonathan to be in the later stages of his career, nearing retirement age.

"No problem, Jonathan, although I am a bit curious. How did you get my number?"

The weary-sounding director replied without hesitation.

"From a friend of a friend who's an administrator at the Fox Run Retirement Home in Buffalo. I hope you don't mind that I'm contacting you directly. I'm in a bit of a bind and really need the help of an expert. From everything I've heard, you're exactly what I'm looking for."

Flattered, Grace remained hesitant. Her field was senior care, not patients with psychiatric issues.

Hear the guy out. You can afford to invest a few minutes on the phone. And you never know how you may be able to connect him to someone else in the industry.

"I DON'T KNOW IF YOU'RE familiar with Wood Haven Manor? We're located in Midland New Jersey, not too far from the New York line and we operate under the jurisdiction of the state. The manor was founded at the turn of the century by an order of religious nuns. Their mission was to care for people unwell in body and mind. Over the years, as the state took charge, Wood Haven's patients and treatments changed according to the ideals of medical industry. Unfortunately, some of those changes were far from ideal and didn't always result in the best care procedures, which is something we're working to change."

Grace was aware of the 1971 formation of The American Association for the Abolition of Involuntary Mental Hospitalization. She had followed the group's progress and read many of the industry-related reports. She also knew stories about such asylums were beyond gruesome. Jonathan's words stimulated the empathetic woman's senses as her thoughts darkened with visions of threadbare sheets covering paper-thin mattresses. Her nostrils infused with the suggestion of sanitizing bleach battling pungent urine odors and bloody stains. Her stomach turned at thoughts of undefinable meals, more mush than food. Her ears filled with echoes of furtive moans and cries blended into one dysfunctional voice of need. And all the while, Jonathan Walsh continued.

"Grace, the reason I'm contacting you is that last year New Jersey's Governor appointed a special panel to undertake a thorough investigation of Wood Haven. Their recommendations are layered, beginning with a shutdown of the treatment portion of the facility. 'Deinstitutionalization' is what they're labeling it. They want to move patients out, into the community when possible. When not possible, they want to relocate them into assisted care facilities."

Grace was overstimulated by the conversation, to the point she had little control over her thoughts. In the space of Jonathan's inhale, she blurted out what was foremost in her mind.

"Jonathan, I really don't know why you're calling me. I have never been part of anything resembling Wood Haven, no less the re-making of such a facility. Truthfully, I don't think I would want to be involved, nor would I be very suitable for the work and all it entails."

The direct nature of Grace's words caused Jonathan to deepen his breath. He was used to negative reactions to his Wood Haven employment offers and he'd become adept at delivering coercive responses. Clearly the director was going to have to be especially convincing for Grace to consider the assignment.

"I CERTAINLY UNDERSTAND, GRACE, and I apologize if I have been a bit blunt. I've been working on this project since last September, when the governor brought me onboard. I know the kinds of thoughts and images that ran through *my* mind the first time I heard about it. It's quite a bit to take in and consider, but before we finish our conversation, I'd like to share one last thing."

Here comes the heart-tugging pitch.

She was used to administrators sharing stories of sadness and even tragedy when trying to compel her to become part of a senior care project. She had also become adept at saying, "no". In fact, the word was already forming in her mind as Jonathan delivered his final plea.

"Grace, the treatment of patients at Wood Haven over the last fifty years has been unimaginable, some might say reprehensible. I realize your area of expertise does not necessarily extend to this type of situation. However, I've been told by fellow administrators that you are one-of-a-kind, gifted actually, in your ability to connect with older people. Grace, our seniors *need you*. Some of them came here when they were young adults, barely more than teenagers. They were forced to spend their entire lives in this institution, in some cases for no rational reasons. Please, don't say no right away. Please allow me to send you information about the facility and the elderly who remain here."

Grace was never quite sure how it happened, but the "no" she had ready to roll off her lips somehow morphed into an, "ok."

The next day, an oversized manila envelope stamped with Wood Haven's logo came hand-delivered to her door. Undoing the sealed flap, Grace extracted a collection of pages filled with inks of black and blue, the same colors of the bruised patient's bodies detailed in line after line of the official report.

Grace was challenged by the decades of documented cruelties and maltreatments endured by Wood Haven patients. She could only process a few pages at a time before feeling physically ill and, at one point, wondered if she would ever be able to complete a full review of the inhumane actions. Yet finish she did and, at the last, the compassionate consultant came to one sure conclusion.

There was really no choice but to agree to Jonathan Walsh's proposal to help his Wood Haven seniors—on whatever terms she could manage, and he would accept.

Chapter Two

WOOD HAVEN ADMITTANCE FORM

Patient: *Teagan Cormick*
Date of Admittance: *January 18, 1930*
Number: *01183017*
Age: *17*
Ethnicity: *Irish*
Marital Status: *Single*
Pregnancies: *None*
Diagnosis: *Hysteria caused by overaction of the mind.*

LIFE IN AMERICA 'TWAS JUST as I'd dreamed. Still, 'twas nothin' easy 'bout gettin' meself settled.

When the Olympic docked, all the well-ta-do's in first and second class left the ship. Then the crew came ta steerage, handin' us all tags with numbers on 'em in big black print. We was gathered inta groups by the numbers—thirty or so led off at a time. Then they started transferrin' us ta a nearby barge where we waited, packed tight with whatever belongins we owned.

When the barge finally made its way and got tied at Ellis Island, the air 'round us filled with hootin' and hollerin'. All kinds o'languages. Everyone o'us excited ta be steppin' foot in America.

Twasn't but a few minutes and we was being herded 'gain, this time up a long strip o'stairs. At the top landin' there was people watchin' like hawks. If one of us be strugglin' or seemin' a bit worn out—as ta be expected after bein' cramped in a small space of a ship fer better than a week—you'd be pulled away right then and there. Word was them's pulled was sent back ta the barge, with no chance ta go further. I only know I never saw any of 'em again.

If a body made it ta the top o'the stairs ya was pushed inta long lines, with others newly arrived. The blended smells of so many traveled far and long wove 'round us like a thick blanket. The only air ta breathe was sour leadin' some ta pass out from the stank.

Fer those still standin', we was herded toward a row o'people, *inspectors* I'm guessin' you'd call 'em. If luck were with ya, there'd be an inspector who could speak your language and help make sense of the questions they'd be askin', and ya had ta answer. If not, men in uniforms come and moved ya. Ta where, I had no idea and I never asked. I was just glad I could speak English and kept movin'.

Next, we got sent ta a huge room filled with doctors. They went ta lookin' at our faces, our hair, our necks, our hands, even our eyes. Each doc had a little piece of somethin', like chalk. Every so often they'd scrawl a big mark on a person's clothin'. Thems with marks was made ta step aside, whiles the rest o'us was kept movin'. As the story went, if you got the white mark, ya was goin' back from where ya come.

There was one family, a mam, da and three little ones, come all the way from Italy, don'cha know. The beibi took sick in the middle of the ocean and was still coughin' and cryin' when we's landed. They whole lot o'em got looked over by the docs and was told the child was too sick ta stay and had ta go back. Every one of us in line wept with the mam and da as they stood and decided which of 'em would stay and which would go.

If they kept ya movin', ya got another card and got sent ta a place where people was handin' out money. Not fer free, mind ya. No, this money was traded fer whatever bits of bills and coin you brung from home.

Finally, after hours of wadin' thru long lines, we was left only ta claim our bags and the box lunch kindly provided. Then, as if some kinda magic, we was landed immigrants allowed ta freely make our way 'bout America.

Most who came stayed close by, but some bought train duckets 'cross country. Fer me own part, I journeyed 'cross the bridge ta Manhattan after hearin' inspectors talk 'bout the good payin' jobs ta be found there.

Much ta me good fortune, I got work as a nanny fer a rich family livin' on Park Avenue. Father Murphy at St. Bridgid's pointed me towards the job a coupla' weeks after I come ta his parish. Engler was the family's name. They was fine English folk who paid me a fair wage o'twenty five cents a week along with me own room in their third-floor attic.

Seein' as I knew no one in America, I'd little need fer the money, so's I saved most of it. Only things I ever bought were paints and brushes, along with some bits o'canvas. Whenever I wasn't takin' care o'the three Engler beibis, I was makin' me way through the city, memorizin' places ta recreate in me paintin's. Life in America was good, and about ta get better.

AS THE YEAR PASSED, Mr. Engler became a member o'the Painters and Sculptors Gallery Association, thems who ran the Grand Central Art Galleries. Whenever Mr. Engler talked ta the Missus 'bout his part in the association I strained ta listen. 'Twas all so excitin' hearin' 'bout art exhibits and the like. The more Mr. Engler talked, the more I was set on creatin' me own paintin's ta show him. I was sure if he liked me art, he could get me work in a gallery. Then I could start earnin' me keep, doin' what I most loved.

Soon every one o'me spare moments was spent paintin'. Yet after weeks of tryin', I was left with more canvas coated over than done. I thought 'bout quittin', but whenever the notion entered me head, I heard da's voice telling me quittin' would make me nothin' but a loser. So's on I went, prayin' ta me granny fer help, as she herself had been an artist and the one ta first gift me a set of paints.

So's it was I went ta paintin' from early mornings and prayin' inta late nights and bit by bit, me vision became clearer, me inspiration stronger. Finally, one day I knew, twasn't scenes o'New York City I should be paintin', but memories o'the emerald greens of me homeland.

'Twas then images started pourin' outta me as if me canvas and brushes were one and I was but caught in the middle. Hills and dales of Cork, barnacled docks of Queenstown, memories o'me beloved ocean shore.

Months went by 'til I had enough art ta make me proud. With me wits 'bout me, I went ta Mr. Engler and asked permission ta present him me paintins. Ta me great relief, he agreed.

It took only minutes fer this fine man ta decree me talent, though his praise was cut when he told me I had need ta improve me skills. Seeing me dismay, Mr. Engler quickly offered that he knew a woman who could teach me art and would sponsor me lessons as well. I was over the moon that me paintin's inspired him so.

Mr. Engler sent me off ta Mrs. Fancher, a widowed lady who'd studied art in Paris. She lived in a flat nearby, so's I could get meself there quick-like on Sunday afternoons, when me nannying was done. Learnin' from her, me head become filled with all sorts o'new ideas and thoughts. No doubt I was on a path ta becomin' a true artist. The thing was the Good Lord had a different idea—one that would change the world fer me and most every livin', breathin' person in America.

The Great Crash they called it and fer weeks after that October day, no matter where you went, 'twas all that was spoken.

I DIDN'T UNDERSTAND IT REALLY, so's at first paid little attention. I still had three beibis ta care fer and me paintin' ta keep busy the rest o'the time. Then come a day when Mr. Engler called me ta his study. He told me the crash had taken all his money. He and the missus and their children were goin' ta have ta leave their fine home fer his parent's farm, midstate. They'd be leavin' behind their life as well, includin' me. The only savin' grace was that he give me 'til week's end ta be gone.

Me last days at the Engler's passed like lightenin' and afore I knew, 'twas time ta be leavin'. In thanks for their many kindnesses, I gifted the family me favorite paintin' of the Queenstown docks. In return, Mrs. Engler handed me a sack o'food, enough ta keep me well for a few days. Then with a round o'hugs, we bid a tearful farewell.

As I made me way through the streets, thinkin' 'bout me finely laid plans of paintins and galleries, I held little fear. After all, I was Teagan Cormick, a girl brave enough ta come ta America on me own. I could find work anywhere, even it if meant scrubbin' floors or walkin' dogs. Surely 'twere other families in New York who still had money and would pay.

Took me but a day of searchin' ta realize hardships was felt by all.

No matter where I went in the city, people was loadin' suitcases onta wagons and leavin'. Others were huddled on street corners beggin' fer food or money, neither of which could be found. I was part of a parcel, includin' the once-rich, all of us now poor and needy.

I wandered the streets fer days, carryin' me carefully tied canvases and a suitcase filled with me sketches and a few possessions. At every shop, there was nothin' but locked doors and out-of-business signs. 'Twas the same at restaurants and bakeries. Only places with open doors were churches and poorhouses.

Losin' hope, I made me way ta a shanty town o'Irish I'd heard 'bout, below the 59th Street Bridge. Claimin' a small space of dirt and rocks, I scavenged a scrap o'wood and some cast-off cardboard. There I set me possessions, figurin' how ta best survive. Needn't have bothered though. 'Twas only a bit afore the whole lot of us under the bridge was rousted by the Gardaí—the police—treatin' us like lazy good-fer-nothin's.

The officers pushed and shoved us from under the bridge, one of 'em grabbin' me canvases and tossin' 'em aside. Another lawman, twice me size, rough-shoved me and me suitcase inta the back of a truck with wooden walls and iron bar windows.

I DID ME BEST TA fight back, tryin' ta get out and reclaim me art, but the burly Gardaí was quick joined by another. Together they gathered and tossed me up and back inta the truck, o'er others already loaded like cattle. Hittin' the back wall, me breath was knocked right outta me. Afore I could gather me strength, the doors o'the truck slammed and locked tight. I could feel the truck drivin' away, ta where I'd not a thought.

'Twas hours afore the driver stopped amid the day's fadin' light. A Gardaí come 'round ta open the truck door and two men stepped outta the shadows, like a coupla ghosts. Without a word the Gardaí began yankin' us out o'the truck, the ghosties pushin' us together, shoutin', "Stand right here. Do not move."

With nothin' ta lose, I lept outta the truck, yellin' and stompin' bout me paintins. I knew twouldn't matter a whit what I said, but I couldn't help meself. I'd put every bit o'me soul inta me art and was feelin' like someone dearly loved had been taken from me.

The louder I fussed, the more I got shoved and herded from the rest. I'd no idea who was doin' the shovin' as me scrambled brain kept me from any sort o'straight thinkin'. 'Twas only when me voice become a single sound that I understood I'd been shoved inta a room with a tiny window and no lights. The floor felt cold and slimy and before me there was a metal door that, no matter how I pushed or shoved, wouldn't give a budge.

Time passed. Hard sayin' how long bein' in darkness. All's I knew was me stomach was raisin' a fuss over bein' empty and I'd pee'd meself. When finally the door opened, I had hope fer some nourishment. Instead, two men wearin' white coats snatched me from the floor and drug me through hallways, scraping me legs along the concrete and bruisin' me with their grips.

Truth be told, 'tween me hunger and me pain, I'm not sure I stayed in me right mind. 'Twas no doubt a blessin'. Next I knew, I was in a room with two chairs and a light above, shinin' like a beam. The men whipped me body 'round and shoved me inta one o'the chairs, takin' their place on either side like statues. Neither spoke so much as a word.

Strugglin' ta get hold o'me mind, I tried takin' a deep breath, but 'twas cut short by a shootin' pain in me ribs. As I felt 'bout ready ta pass from me mind, a man come inta the room, with a woman followin'. They was both wearin' white—herself a dress, himself a coat with big pockets. Somethin' bout the two shot a jolt straight through me, like when mam would smack me fer not payin' attention.

The woman moved ta the back o'the room in the shadows. The man, himself, sat down at a desk 'cross from me, smilin'. Not a look o'kindness mind ya, more an odd grin of havin' ta do a job he didn't like. Shuffling through papers, he cleared his throat.

"HELLO, MISS. I'M DR. JENSEN. Do you know what your name might be?"

"Course, I know me name. I'm Teagan Cormick".

As soon as the words left me lips, I knew I'd gone wrong. Me mind was so jumbled I'd forgot me new name o'Taylor Eagan. The man give a stop, lookin' at the papers in front o'him, lookin' at me, then back ta the papers, where he went ta scribblin'.

"And do you know how old you are?"

"Well, if I don't who will? I'm nineteen." I managed ta speak the lie as a truth.

"Are you married? Any children?"

"No ta both," I answered in a way showin' me disrespect.

"Do you know why you are here?"

"Here?" I spat the word back inta his bearded face. "I don't even know where *here* is. I only know me canvases was ripped outta me hands afore I was forced ta come ta this hell hole. I want 'em back. I'm gonna be an artist, don'cha know."

With the same cold smile, the doctor turned his eyes ta his papers and wrote somethin'. Lookin' back at me, he spoke words I can hear yet in me mind.

"You'll not be doing any painting for a while. Your canvases are gone. *Forever.* You're not well. You need help—treatment to calm your mental excitement. You've been brought here to Wood Haven Asylum and this is where you'll stay until . . . or *if* . . . you improve."

The man's words pushed all fear outta me. With anger risin' in me chest I stood and jumped acrost the wooden desk.

"You've no right ta be takin' away me paintin's and keepin' me in this dungeon of a place, with nary food nor water. You're a no-good animal ya wretch. No better than a murderer."

As I got in reach o'slappin the man's face, the room suddenly turned upside down. The two men been standin' on either side o'me chair had me tight in their grips. Takin' a yank, they pulled me fast and hard, turnin' me body in a summersault.

As they twisted me back ta the floor, the woman in the shadows come straight at me. In one motion her hand went inta and outta her white dress pocket, her eyes never leavin' me arm. 'Twas only at the last I saw the long needle in her hand and felt the burn as it stung me in the arm. I wanted ta cry out over the pain, but me mind and me body were solid. All's I could do was sit and stare inta her cold, hard eyes.

WITH THE DOCTOR'S NOD, the guards yanked me 'gain and went ta draggin' me back 'long the hallways. 'Twas me last recall 'til wakin' in a windowless room, sunk in blackness. Only the stank of beddin' on a metal cot ta guide me as I tried movin' 'round.

Gloom, like an ocean's wave, rolled over me. Without warnin', me knees gave way and I crumpled inta a ball. Lying on the slimy concrete, me stomach began retchin' nary food or drink, only the dry heaves o' me fear. I lie there fer more time than I knew, bruised, starvin', wet and dirty from peein' and poopin' meself. Numb in me mind, I was. Far from home, without a soul knowin' if I be dead or alive.

As God is me witness, I remember every bit o'it, as if t'were only yesterday.

Chapter Three

GRACE WAS RAISED IN A middle-class family with values centered upon simple wants and needs. Yet as her life evolved, her consulting career provided an income for things she had never imagined, like a luxury car with heated leather seats, burl wood interior and an engine that could easily top out at 250 mph.

It wasn't that Grace was a race driver wannabe, or even an auto aficionado. Rather, she traveled extensively in her work, distances more suited to cars than planes. After enduring an early career of used automobiles with lagging acceleration and useless heating and air conditioning, Grace took her first consultant's bonus check and put a down payment on what her papa termed, "a fancy-dan kinda car". From that point she never looked back, trading in and up every two years to sleek and reliable automobiles that invariably served as her home on wheels.

As Grace pondered the parade of vehicles she'd driven over the past twenty years, a passing truck splashed a veil of rainwater across her windshield. The car's automatic sensors commanded the heavy-duty wipers to come alive and clear the view. In that moment, a sense of satisfaction spread through Grace's being. Her professional success played an integral part in her personal happiness, and she was grateful to have found work that fulfilled her *and* paid her well.

Travel on Interstate 81 was the quickest and least scenic route between her hometown of Buffalo and her latest consulting job in Midland, New Jersey. The good news was that she would soon be driving through the Pocono Mountains, a strikingly beautiful and natural backdrop which was a mandate, when possible, in Grace's travel world.

Journeying along the mind-numbing highway, Grace found her thoughts drifting to the circle of seniors that had become part of her life over the last two decades. At the top of that list was Mrs. Fischer, a seventy-two-year-old widow who'd resided at The Towers, where Grace was first employed after college.

Irme Fischer was petite and soft-spoken with a twinkle in her eyes and a playful sense in her being. Grace's initial encounter with the woman occurred at a Towers luncheon in honor of "Dental Health Month."

IT ALL BEGAN WITH A set of wind-up, clacking dentures that someone unknown set loose on the luncheon dessert table. Eventually the clattering teeth fell onto the floor, vibrating their way to the center of the room where they caused raucous delight among the seniors in attendance. Tower administrators were furious over the stunt and quickly discarded the moving mouth into a nearby trash bin.

Although the perpetrator of the denture prank was never officially discovered, on the day in question Grace had been relegated to the back of the lunch room, in accordance with her rank as the newest staffer. That's how she was able to watch Mrs. Fischer discreetly nestle the moving dentures between the tray of bread pudding and the bowl of stewed prunes.

Rather than tattle, Grace kept the secret, ultimately retrieving the dentures from the trash bin. Biding her time until the perfect moment, she conspiratorially returned them to Mrs. Fischer with a wink and a smile. From then on, Grace and Irme became accomplices in anonymous jokes that never failed to frustrate Tower administrators and delight senior residents. Over the ensuing two years, the women's playful bond became a trusted friendship regenerating the special bond she'd been missing since the passing of her nana and papa. When Irme passed away unexpectedly in her sleep, Grace mourned the woman's loss as both a confidant and a cherished grandmother.

Images of special seniors continued to file through Grace's thoughts as her mind unconsciously tracked the exit signs along the highway. Suddenly she recognized the approaching turn off for New Jersey, only an hour from Wood Haven.

Good time to stop, stretch and grab something to eat. Hopefully I can find a diner that's still serving breakfast. I could go for some pancakes and sausage.

Grace glanced at her watch, surprised to realize the time was closer to midday than morning. Thoughts of the special seniors permanently woven into the fabric of her life had made time irrelevant. However, her grumbling stomach was strongly demanding that she take notice of the diner sign straight ahead.

Walking into a highway version of a corner café, Grace slid in to the first convenient counter spot. She picked up a two-sided, plastic menu and immediately saw a neon orange note proclaiming, "Special of the Day: pot roast sandwich with gravy and mashed potatoes." Flipping through the menu, Grace's taste buds lasered her eyes onto a "Breakfast served all day" banner. Scanning her options, she came to pancakes. From the choices of sizes and fillings she kept it simple when the uniformed waitress queried, "What'll ya have?

"I'd like a short stack of blueberry pancakes with a side of sausage, please."

"Links or patties?"

"Links, please. And could I have a glass of orange juice now and a cup of tea with my breakfast?"

"Regular or decaf?"

"Regular. Thanks."

The exchange took less than thirty seconds. The same amount of time passed before her glass of juice appeared. Minutes later the waitress served up Grace's breakfast on two dishes. One large for the super-sized, twin pancakes. One small for the four, glistening sausages.

"Anything else?" The waitress queried as she unceremoniously dropped wrapped butter pats and a squeeze bottle of syrup on the counter.

Grace's manners traditionally bordered on overly polite, another vestige of her Catholic school upbringing. However, the combination of the waitress' brusque manner and her ravenous state encouraged an uncharacteristically, direct reply.

"Nope. All set."

As she spoke the words, Grace was already blotting the grease-laden sausage in her napkin. It was a health-conscious routine she'd learned during travels with her nana. Next, she rolled two of the links into a pancake. "Pigs in a blanket" was the title Nana O'Connor had given the breakfast treat. The first time Grace heard the term she had envisioned an image of little pink pigmies swaddled in—what else—blankets. She was surprised to learn it was breakfast food, as she watched her grandmother encase pork sausages in a cloak of fluffy buttermilk pancakes and coat them with real maple syrup.

While the diner's pancakes were a long way from her nana's, and the overly thick syrup was definitely not real maple, Grace relished the mosh of soft cake and seasoned pork luxuriating in the gooey sugar coating. For one glorious moment she was a kid again, with her only focus being the food on her plate.

"More hot water for your tea?"

The waitress topped off the cup before Grace could respond. She also slipped the check alongside her plate. There was a "Have a nice day" note just below the tally, complete with a smiley face.

Too bad she only smiles on paper, Grace thought as she left a five-dollar bill on the counter. It was enough to cover her breakfast and a good tip.

Maybe it'll brighten her day, like those pigs in a blanket just brightened mine.

Full and happy, Grace returned to the highway and was soon heading traveling the back roads of upstate New Jersey into the state's central core. The early morning rain on her windshield vanished as the sun's rays came piercing through the gray sky. Grace took the weather change as a sign that the day would be a good one. At least that was her hope, contrary to the pit in her stomach.

When Grace contacted Jonathan Walsh to say she would be available for the Wood Haven project, her second-thought meter registered off the charts. It was a gut instinct she had come to know and trust in both her personal and professional worlds. It was also what encouraged her to set modifications to the terms of her consulting agreement.

"Wow, that's great news, Grace. I took the liberty of drawing up a contract for the position using the job title of Director of Wood Haven Deinstitutionalization. I'll put it in the mail to you today. I know you will help us tremendously in reorganizing the lives of the patients here at Wood Haven."

"I'm glad you feel that way, Jonathan, but I do have a couple of conditions we need to discuss before I sign any paperwork."

Grace was not completely secure in the job modifications she'd drawn up, but she trusted her instincts. They always delivered when needed, and they were needed right then and there.

"First, I want to ensure I will only be involved with patients who are seniors. They are my area of expertise. Since I will be undertaking work that is not in my usual domain, I want to at least have some part of the job on which I can rely and have confidence."

"Absolutely," Jonathan replied in relief at the first term.

"Also, from your description of the job, I anticipate I will be spending an extended period at Wood Haven. I would appreciate some help in finding a place to live. Something near Wood Haven if possible. A small apartment to rent or lease, short term."

"That won't be a problem at all, Grace. I have a sister who lives in the area and works in real estate. And my cousin is the mayor of Midland Township, a lovely community near Wood Haven and most likely the area where we will set up the group home for our seniors. Between the two of them, they're bound to know of a place to suit you." Jonathan's relief was quickly morphing into enthusiasm.

"Finally, I want an opt-out clause in this contract."

"Opt-out? You need to clarify that one for me."

"What I mean by opt-out is if I sign on for this job and at any time feel I absolutely cannot accomplish the work or am failing at the tasks, I can take leave with two weeks' notice. Of course, all fees would be pro-rated in accordance with my time already spent on the project."

"I have to say, I've never hired anyone under that kind of term."

The director's hesitation caused Grace's heart to skip a beat. She wasn't sure if the palpitation was relief or fear.

"HERE'S MY CONCERN, GRACE. I realize there is much about this project that is off-putting, disturbing actually. The fact that you are willing to join forces with us to put an end to the distressing practices that have taken place at Wood Haven is truly a God-send. At the same time, I don't want anyone working on this transition team who is not fully committed to the task. Your request for an opt-out clause makes me think that you are ready to quit before you even start. That's not good. Not good for you, not good for me and my team, and certainly not good for the ten senior patients at Wood Haven, who we are ultimately trying to help."

Jonathan's words grabbed Grace's instincts and held them solidly in place. The thoughts and fears she faced only moments earlier began to fade. She knew he was right. She was either, "in for a penny or in for a pound," as her papa would say when encouraging her youthful work ethic.

When it came down to it, Grace knew it was more about Wood Haven's past than its present that was giving her pause. She'd read enough about the cruelties and inhumane treatments in the patient files to wonder if she had the stomach for decentralizing the care facility, or *asylum*, as it had once been known. She either had to get over her worries or decline the job. It was that simple. Yet the haunting stories she'd read about Wood Haven's patients plagued her caring nature.

Ok, put up or shut up time, Grace. What are you going to do? No doubt, you have the knowledge to help transition the ten seniors still in residence at Wood Haven. But can you immerse yourself in a facility that has tortured more than aided people in need? Can you overcome the sick sense that undoubtedly pervades Wood Haven's atmosphere? Can you give enough of yourself to support these seniors who have endured unthinkable cruelties more than kindness or care?

As Grace posed the questions, she knew the answers. It wasn't a matter of right or wrong, staying or going. It was about the ten people who had spent years of their lives locked away from family and friends, isolated from the world and the communities they once called home, tortured for reasons lacking in substance or legalities.

"Grace, if you need more time to consider, I can afford you another few days."

Until Jonathan spoke, Grace had forgotten she was in the midst of a phone conversation. The immediate realization propelled the words from within her.

"No, that won't be necessary, Jonathan. You're absolutely right about commitment being vital to this job. I won't need an opt-out clause. I will draw up and sign a contract and mail it to you today. When would you like me to start?"

Chapter Four

WOOD HAVEN ADMITTANCE FORM

Patient: *Peggy (No Last Name)*
Date of Admittance: *April 16, 1926*
Number: *04162610*
Age: *Ten*
Ethnicity: *Unknown*
Marital Status: *Single*
Children: *None*
Diagnosis: *Feebleness of Intellect / Retardation /*

BEIN' FORCED TA LIFE AT Wood Haven, took a bit o'time fer me ta understand. Learnin' rights from wrongs kept me mind fearful. Missin' me family and friends ta talk with set me heart sad. Sleepin' with so many cryin' out and wanderin' in the darkness wore me body out fer many a night.

Tryin' ta figure it all put me searchin' fer others locked away and already learned ta survive. One that I finally found and who taught me most 'twas the youngest among us.

Peggy was but a wisp of a girl when they brung her ta this horrid place. From the moment she come inta the world, this child never knew family. 'Stead she was raised an orphan by the Sisters of Charity. They called her Peggy with no last name.

Sadly, come a time when money woes forced the good sisters ta close the doors o'their orphanage. Their main worry was what ta do with the children? The bebies and young ones tweren't an issue. Families were happy ta welcome infants ta their homes. 'Twas those ten years and more that people weren't wantin'. When none stepped up ta adopt 'em, the sisters did what needed doin'.

They made a plan with asylums ta take the older ones. The thing of it was, ta make it happen, doctors had ta rename 'em—from orphans ta retards. 'Twas a shameful secret carried ta the grave by all 'cept the children. They never knew how or why they was named.

TA HER DUE, PEGGY BORE such heartlessness with good nature. Truth be told, she'd lived her young life always carin' fer others, watchin' out fer fellow orphans, soothin' their worries and wipin' their tears. When she was herded inta the darkness of this place with twelve like her, Peggy started right off comfortin' others. As time went on, even the most hard-hearted nurses turned a blind eye ta Peggy wanderin' the buildin', bringin' her lightness with every step.

Early on, after I was locked away, I spent time layin' lost and lonely on me dormitory cot. One night Peggy sat down aside me and gently stroked me head. At first I thought I must be dreamin'; this had ta be an angel o'God come ta take me ta heaven. Only when I heard her softly ask me name did I realize whoever was comfortin' me 'twas real.

"Me name is Eagan," Then quickly I spoke again. "Truth be told, me name is Teagan. Teagan Cormick. I'm from County Cork."

"Hello, Teagan. My name is Peggy. I can't tell you where I am from as I have never known, but I am pleased to meet you."

Had been a bit since a kind word come me way and longer since a carin' touch. Peggy's tender ways warmed me ta the core, causing tears ta drop from me eyes. With one move, the child wrapped her thin arms 'round me. In the frightenin' dark o'that night, in the hubbub of a hundred others, sweet Peggy comforted me with her special kindness.

From that day, me and Peggy come ta be kindred souls, sharin' a special greetin' each mornin' just like me and me da. "Top o'the morning, Angel," I'd say. And just like I taught her, she'd say back, "And may the balance of the day be yours."

As days passed inta unknown time, Peggy kept comfortin' me as well as others. The docs and nurses couldn't keep up with them's bein' locked away at all hours o'the days and nights. Some sickly and acceptin', others healthy and angered by bein' forced inta this dark place. 'Twas Peggy's lovin' spirit made it easier fer all.

When women got shut away in cages with lids t'were locked, or chained ta pipes on concrete floors, this sweet child made her way ta 'em, softly singin', tellin' stories and doin' her best to get the orderlies to leave 'em go—treat 'em like less like animals, more like people.

'Twas no surprise then that through the hallways and wards, Peggy with no last name become Peggy Angel . . . most just callin' her Angel. That's why 'twas unimaginable when a time come that Peggy's sweetness was savagely taken.

'TWAS A SUMMER'S NIGHT, after hundreds o'nights since she'd been locked away. A young man took a fancy ta Angel, not the first ta do so, mind ya. O'er the years there'd been men from the other side o' the asylum set eyes on her. But this one, he was different. He wasn't one o'us. He was a worker . . . a janitor with one of them big keys could open every room on every floor o'the buildin'.

'Twas a steamy eve, long after all but one dormitory light went dark and the doors locked tight. This man o' bad intent keyed opened the door where we women was sleepin'. With purpose, he snuck along in search of Angel's cot, aside the entry wall where she always lay. Wakin' her with a whisper, the man enticed the sweet woman-child away, promisin' he'd found a troubled soul in need.

The swine then led the unsuspectin' Angel ta the top floor o'the building where the truly mad people was locked away. O'er the din o'tortured shrieks and murmurs, he went ta shovin' her inta a storage closet filled with mops and brooms. Trappin' the poor thing, the letch locked the door behind himself and forced Angel ta the floor. Over her pleas, beggin' fer mercy, his grubby hands went ta strippin' her clothes. In madness, he tore open her body with the force o'his own, shatterin' every part of Angel's bein', again and again and again.

When finally he was done, the <u>pervert</u> drug Angel's half dead form back ta her cot. There he dumped her like a worthless sack, slinkin' away like the worst snake ever created.

In the darkness o'that night I woke ta quiet sobbin'. Truth be told, 'tis not a night in this hell hole without cryin' or moanin'. Yet somethin' 'bout this sorrow was different. Twasn't haunted by odd thinkin' or night terrors. 'Twas pain, fresh and raw.

Quiet-like, I sat up ta try and figure who it was mournin', realizin' the woman was but a few rows away. I'd learned ta make me way through the darkened space o'cots bolted ta the floor, passin' in and among troubled sleepers and them's wanderin' 'round. So's taking careful steps and extendin' me arms ta push aside anyone tryin' ta interfere, I drew closer ta whoever 'twas bleedin' out her soul. When at last I reached the place where I could feel the person, I knelt ta the floor and whispered words I hoped would help.

"There, there darlin'. Whatever's causin' your pain, I'm here with ya."

As I spoke, I rested me hand upon the nearby body. That's when I knew somethin' beyond bad had gone on. The woman's clothin' lie in shreds. Movin' me hand further I felt the rise o'her skin in hot patches. Though blinded by the dark, me fingers knew the feel of bruises swelling 'cross her body. Bile started risin' from me stomach as me imagination took over. I could smell the rot of rape steamin' out o'her bloodied person.

"Ok, dearie, we need ta get ya fixed up, but we can't do it 'til mornin'. So's fer now, I'll lie down here on the floor beside ya and protect ya through the night. I'll not touch ya, but I won't let anyone else near ya neither. I don't know just what's happened, but I can imagine, and I promise ta do all I can ta never allow it again."

Ta be truthful, I wasn't sure if the woman could hear or even understand what I was sayin'. But I knew this woman needed protectin' from the night walkers who blindly spotted weakness and took advantage, crawling onta a body fer fondlin'.

I lie down on the cold, concrete floor, stickin' ta the drabs of dried blood, pee and poop 'twas ne'er fully scrubbed away. Tryin' ta block the disgust risin' through me, a brush o'warmth passed 'gainst me shoulder. Reaching up, I felt a hand—the hand o'the ravaged woman lyin' above me.

Gently I added mine ta hers and give a tender squeeze, hopin' she'd feel a sense o' safety. She responded with a weak return. So's, we stayed connected, waitin' fer the new day.

Not knowin' I'd drifted ta sleep, sounds o'the morning caught me short. Metal carts was rattlin' down the hallway, the dormitory door was bein' unlocked and nurses loudly demandin' we line up fer washin' afore breakfast. I knew t'were I found on the floor there'd be punishment. Quick-like, I raised up, wonderin' what horrors awaited me on the cot.

Me mind went blank and me body froze seein' the abused woman 'twas

Angel. Reachin' out, I touched her head as she once touched mine and whispered her name.

"Angel. Angel darlin', can ya hear me?"

A soft flutterin' o'her eyes was her only response. Time was runnin' short fer both o'us. If I was goin' ta do somethin' ta help Angel and keep meself from bein' in trouble, I had ta be right quick about it. Risin' from the floor I began searchin' fer the one person I hoped might help.

Nurse Bennett was English by marriage, Irish by birth. She was the day nurse, a woman with a heart o'kindness ne'er shown by others in charge. I come to know that fer meself on me first night in the dormitory. She'd found me on me cot, cryin' silent like. Without a minute o'hesitatin', she sat alongside and soothed me, rubbin' gently on me back. She asked me name, 'bout me family and promised I was goin' ta be alright.

I hoped if I could find the good nurse straight away, she'd bend the rules a bit in takin' care o' poor Peggy herself, 'stead of sendin' her down the hall where tendin' was sparse and treatment cruel.

Movin' meself 'cross the room, towards the loo, I went ta acting as if I'd not a care in the world. Spottin' Nurse Bennett by the last wash basin. I moved meself towards her. Catchin' her eye, I spoke.

"Morning, Nurse Bennett. How be ya?"

"Fine, Teagan. And how are you this morning?"

"As me sainted grandmother used ta say, I be fit as a fiddle, thank ya very much."

With a smile and a wink, Nurse Bennett let me know she enjoyed me answer. Movin' ta the metal bowl filled with' freezin' cold water and a sandpaper wash cloth, I spoke again ta the nurse, this time at a sound meant only fer two.

"Nurse Bennett, please don't say a thing. I need ta tell ya, somethin' awful's happened ta Angel. Somethin' a man o'vile nature has done ta her, if ya know what I mean. She's lying on her cot half dead. Please, Nurse Bennett, don't be sendin' Angel down the hall. She'll surely die there. Please help her in return fer the many she's helped since comin' here, includin' me."

Finishin' me plea I turned and looked ta the nurse, heart-ta-heart. A bit o'tenderness come inta her eyes, letting' me know she'd do whatever was needed ta make sure Angel lived.

Not wantin' ta draw attention ta meself, I laid the washcloth inta the icy bowl and stepped ta the line of woman waitin' ta be herded ta breakfast. Lookin' up one last time, I give a nod ta the nurse which she give back. I took it as a sign of our pact.

'Twas quite a time afore I saw Angel again. I was off in the windowed porch by the ward, a place I oft' sat while thinkin' of Ireland and me family. Lost in me daydreams, a familiar soft touch come upon me shoulder, causin' longin' and fear ta pass through me in opposite ways.

Desperately I went ta hopin' that the touch belonged ta Angel. That hope battlin' 'gainst me dread of seein' someone else, or worse, a hollow bein' o'the darlin' woman.

"Top o' the mornin' ta ye, Teagan Cormick".

Whisperin' a prayer fer the sight I hoped ta see, I slowly turned and come ta a pair o'eyes overflowin' with the kindness that once carried me through and give me the strength ta survive.

"And may the balance o'the day be yours, Peggy Angel".

CHAPTER FIVE

*D*AMNITTOHELL!

Jonathan Walsh sprang from his chair like a rocket off a launch pad. *I can't believe I spilled coffee all down the front of me,* he said aloud to no one.

Attempting to blot the caffeine from his shirt, tie and pants, Jonathan quickly realized the futility of his efforts. The best he could do was put on a clean shirt and tie and hope the polka-dot splatters on his pants would become less visible as the day wore on.

Jonathan always kept spare clothes on the metal coat rack in the hallway connecting his office with the executive bathroom. He laughed as he recalled his predecessor giving him a tour of the office space, pointing out the perk of an attached lav. He felt his stomach churn at the memory of that first step into the grimy half-bath, defined by a chipped porcelain sink and permanently yellowed toilet. At the time, he wanted to disinfect his clothes and body after simply standing in the space. Since that day he never again entered the private rest room, not even to wash his hands.

Upon accepting the appointment as Wood Haven Executive Director, Jonathan quickly learned that everything about the place felt permanently stained and soiled—the buildings the furnishings, even the people. After thirty years of working in institutions and medical facilities, Jonathan thought he was immune to pretty much every challenging situation. Wood Haven, however, was providing him a whole new set of life lessons.

As he buttoned the collar of his clean shirt and knotted his fresh tie, Jonathan thought about the events leading to his current job. When a governor calls, you don't refuse his executive request. Yet in those initial days, walking through the drab asylum hallways and settling into his worn office space, Jonathan wondered what ever had possessed him to say, "yes" to New Jersey's chief executive.

The good news was that Jonathan was a man not easily discouraged.

While the deinstitutionalization changes envisioned by the governor's review committee would take time, Jonathan had his own vision for improvements in both Wood Haven's structure and staff. They were things he knew could be achieved in short order. All that was needed was attention, organization and some good old-fashioned elbow grease.

THE EXECUTIVE DIRECTOR BEGAN by assembling his staff and laying out new ground rules for employment. He went so far as to title his pep talk, "The Three C's: Caring, Cleaning and Communication." It was only as he stood before the gathering of uniformed employees that Jonathan became fully aware of the monumental task before him. These were not average workers who would be easily inspired by rousing pronouncements about teamwork. These people were worn down and worn out by their jobs. Wood Haven was in a state of disrepair both structurally and morally and the staff was human evidence of that fact.

Immediately, Jonathan changed the direction of his talk. Instead of preaching, he welcomed the 134 employees to the "new" Wood Haven. The sea of unimpressed faces before him clearly indicated words like this had been spoken before, with little or no after-effect. Rather than continuing with a meaningless introduction, Jonathan cut short his remarks, and returned to his office where he came up with an alternate plan to allow his actions to speak for him. That very day, and on a continuing weekly basis, hot meals and decadent desserts were delivered from a nearby restaurant for every shift of workers.

Next, Jonathon began working his way through Wood Haven's aging structure, making sure to be present at all hours of the day and night. His goal was to meet each staffer personally and ask for nothing more than their faith in him as an agent of change. While the person-to-person contact wasn't miraculous, it definitely set a different tone among the asylum's employees.

From that point, Jonathan began what he termed his "Tom Sawyer" campaign. Every day he tackled a project to improve the facility. Sometimes it was as simple as scrubbing a floor which for years had received nothing more than a-lick-and-a-promise. Other times it was rolling up his sleeves and clearing away decades of cobwebs and grime from windows, removing worn, neglected furniture from rooms on various floors and painting over dull, grayed walls with vibrantly bright colors.

While he labored, Jonathan engaged those working around him, doing his best to make them feel as if they mattered. He asked questions about their families and chatted about their interests and hobbies. He talked to the staff about his latest list of Wood Haven improvements and how he hoped his efforts would enhance their work environment, as well as their patient's lives. Jonathan then went for the payoff as he asked all employees to find ways to continue the work he was undertaking, with a promise to return and help as he could.

In the end, most of the personnel responded to Jonathan's hands-on style and took up his challenge. Those who did not, left, not always of their own accord. Little by little, the halls and rooms of the long-neglected care facility improved, shedding many of the sensory reminders that had hauntingly defined the beleaguered facility.

Wood Haven had not operated at full capacity for more than two decades. Currently, in the main building, the first floor offered nothing more than a security desk and elevator access to the remaining seven levels. The adjacent first floor hallways and rooms were cordoned off and padlocked. The second floor housed administrative and operational offices while the next level was populated by Wood Haven patients dealing with a variety of mental and physical conditions. The top four floors stood empty and abandoned.

In his initial review of the ten seniors currently under care at Wood Haven, Jonathan was stunned to discover that most had been locked away in the asylum for more than half their lives. Files further showed the average age of the group was sixty-eight. Of those, six were ambulatory and of reasonably sound mind. Four were at varying levels of mobility, from wheelchairs to totally bedridden, one affected by dementia.

In talking to staff and observing patient protocol, it was clear these aged individuals had long ago been isolated from any kind of normal routines. No one had tried to spark their minds or engage their senses other than attendants focused on patient incontinence and distribution of mush meals. It was a disturbing set of circumstances that compelled Jonathan to more fully understand what exactly the seniors had endured and find ways to alleviate their pain.

Jonathan poured over the records of the ten geriatrics, one man and nine women. He wanted to know the medical and/or mental issues that originally brought them to Wood Haven. He needed to understand why they ended up spending their adult lives within the confines of an asylum.

By the end of his reviews, Jonathan understood the tragic reality that these people had been institutionalized for reasons far short of acceptable. Worse yet, over time they had fallen through the cracks . . . overlooked by Wood Haven administrators and forgotten or abandoned by their own families.

Reading between the lines on page after page of various doctor's reports, Jonathan came to understand that even if a physician was concerned that a patient had been unjustly committed, there was no recourse. As a result, these ten individuals came to represent health care nightmares as well as political liabilities. No one wanted to know about them or acknowledge they existed.

Jonathan was aware this scenario had played out incessantly across the United States at the turn of the 20th Century and intensified after the nation's financial collapse in 1929. People from all walks of life were forced into asylums, at times by powerful family members and often through circumstances beyond the "patient's" control.

He also knew that the vast number of post-crash admissions had overwhelmed the care system. Administrators and medical staffs were incapable of handling the human overload. As a result, patients endured brutalities designed to control rather than cure, often suffering unspeakable neglect instead of needed care.

Wood Haven had been a core part of that heinous medical system, until the day Betty Ferguson's fascination with the asylum's architecture detoured her daily travels.

Betty worked as a bookkeeper at a steel casting plant, ten miles from her Midland Township home. For seven years, Monday through Friday, she drove by Wood Haven to and from her job. The massive facility and its gothic-style limestone walls intrigued Betty from first glance. They also concerned her when she began to notice the crumbling entryway pillars and unkempt grounds surrounding the expansive Wood Haven property.

One day, on her way home from work, Betty decided to take a turn off the highway to pass through Wood Haven's decaying entryway and drive along the overgrown road to the main entrance. Her stomach twisted in nervous tension over entering the property without permission. Yet something kept pushing her forward, encouraging her curiosity about this place that had fascinated her for so many years.

Parking in a paved area, Betty exited her car and began wandering the grounds without challenge. Being able to draw close and run her hands over the stone buildings she'd seen only from afar sent a chill through her arms and into her body. The reality of trespassing on Wood Haven grounds also delivered shudders of fear, but she'd come too far to turn back.

Emboldened, Betty decided to actually go in one of the buildings. The closest entrance was inscribed with a sign that read, "Chestnut Hall". Presuming the doors to be locked, Betty tucked herself into the lengthening afternoon shadows of the structure and waited. It was only a few minutes before a groundskeeper came along and passed through the entry. The slow close on the door return gave Betty the opening she needed. Before losing her nerve, she slipped inside.

Again, wandering without interference, Betty passed doorways of empty rooms and lengths of darkened corridors. The atmosphere felt haunting, disturbing, to the point she was about to turn back. Then she reached a corridor filled with people. By their institutional dress and their place in wheelchairs and on benches, she had no doubt these were Wood Haven patients.

Standing in the dimly lit hall, Betty was stunned then sickened by the sights before her. Men and women were littered through the hallway, some sitting, some moving. All were dressed in clothes, more stained and tattered rags, reeking of personal odors that infested the air. Of those sitting, some were chained in place, seemingly to keep them from tumbling onto the floor. Others rocked back and forth in rhythm to a beat playing only in their tortured minds.

The patients who were able to walk sifted through the hall in random patterns, stopping and starting, ranting to unseen people on subjects unknown. Some quivered uncontrollably, arms or legs moving in discord with their core, heads twitching in continual motion. From all she was witnessing, Betty could see the decay of Wood Haven's buildings fully reflected in the patients within its walls.

The focused woman was suddenly startled away from the scene by the sound of voices behind her. Tucking her body more closely into the shadows, she turned to see two men in matching green uniforms walking along the main hallway. To her relief, they were completely engaged in conversation about the latest sports scores and had not noticed her . . . yet.

Looking around, Betty realized there was no place to hide. The only thing she could do was flatten her body completely against the wall and hold her breath. With any luck, the men's preoccupation with their conversation would keep them unaware of her presence.

Inhaling deeply, Betty pressed herself as far as she could into the cold stone hallway, trying to imagine herself invisible. Seconds later, amid a heated argument over the New York Yankees, the men passed her by without a glance.

Dizzied by a lack of oxygen and a fear of discovery, Betty moved stealthily out of the building to her car. As she drove back to the security of her Midland home, the sights and sounds of her unofficial Wood Haven tour continued to assault her senses. What she had witnessed was not only disturbing, it was wrong. No matter if those people were ill in their minds or their bodies, they deserved to be treated humanely.

Through a restless night's sleep, Betty churned over all she had witnessed at Wood Haven. Finally, as the winter's sun rose, she became fully aware of what she must do. She would go to the local newspaper and start a campaign . . . a public outcry . . . aimed at restoring Wood Haven and rescuing its patients.

WITHIN MONTHS, BETTY'S PLAN snowballed into a national cause. Television crews and newspaper reporters from around the United States lined up outside Wood Haven's iron gates, all railing against the newly-padlocked entry that prevented their cameras from capturing images of the patients Betty had so movingly described in interviews.

From there came a call for state investigations of the atrocities taking place at Wood Haven. A task force was formed, investigations ensued, reports were issued and committees charged to effect permanent change. That, indirectly, was how Jonathan Walsh came to occupy the worn wooden chair of the asylum's executive director.

Even before accepting the challenging responsibility, Jonathan knew this job would be his last. He was scheduled to retire at year's end. It was the prime reason he'd agreed to tackle the deinstitutionalization—it would only be for one year. He could do anything for that amount of time. Yet once he arrived, once he began engaging with the staff and experiencing the heart-rending fate of the remaining senior patients, Jonathan's attitude changed.

He was still slated to escape the nightmare of Wood Haven in December, but that wasn't good enough anymore. Somehow Jonathan had to make up for the heinous conditions that had been allowed to define the lives of all the Wood Haven patients, as well as those who had done their best to care for them.

Jonathan's immediate reaction was to ensure better living conditions for the ten elderly individuals who had been treated so inhumanely at Wood Haven for most of their adult lives. In order to do that, he needed someone with power and credentials in the senior care industry to join his staff and classify these patients, not by name, but by accurate diagnoses of their conditions and true mental states. With that information, Jonathan could ensure each senior's relocation to a place where they could live with dignity, a place worthy of being called *home*.

His first step was to reach out to a professional acquaintance who had crafted a successful career in matching medical facilities and administrators—a medical head-hunter, so to speak. It was a bit of a cloak-and-dagger operation as care facilities traditionally would not telegraph their staff was in transition, and individuals in the industry would not want their employers to know they were considering a job change. Whenever Jonathan consulted with this corporate matchmaker he was reminded of the Catholic ritual of confession, where any information shared was sacred and protected—at least in theory.

Jonathan proceeded through the steps required by the headhunter in registering the terms of the job and the qualifications required of the potential employee. The employment specialist returned with a list of leads, eight in all. Reading through the resumes, none reached out and grabbed Jonathan's attention.

Though each was "paper-qualified", the sum total of their professional experiences left him uninspired. Whoever was going to become part of Wood Haven's "de-centralizing" would need something extra, something more than desk-bound administrative experience.

Frustrated and short on time, Jonathan changed his tact. He telephoned an old friend, Craig Wilkins. Craig was a former boss and a from Jonathan's early health care days and he knew the man to be insightful, direct, compassionate and professionally respected. Whenever Jonathan faced a career dilemma, his solution always included a consultation with this knowledgeable man.

"Craig Wilkins speaking".

Just the sound of his name settled Jonathan's mind. While the tenor of the retired man's voice had ebbed with age, no doubt there would be helpful wisdom in his council.

"Craig, Jonathan Walsh here. Good to speak with you. How are you enjoying retired life?"

"To tell the truth, I don't know how I got anything done when I was working, Jonathan. I am busier than ever these days with all sorts of projects and consulting work. I do miss the people, though. My work now is pretty much done from home, studying statistics and writing summaries. It's important and I know it matters, but interaction with others is where I'm best. So, I make sure to attend government meetings in Trenton, when the senate and the assembly address pressing senior health care issues. And I still meet once a week for lunch with George and Peter. They're both retired from their directorships at Greystone and Overbrook, so we're like a trio of old work horses. We just don't know how to quit. But enough about me, how are you and *where* are you? Thought I heard rumors you were retiring?"

"You heard correctly. I was all set to clear out my desk and start playing golf, but the governor called and made me an offer I couldn't refuse. I'm at Wood Haven actually, helping with the deinstitutionalization. That's why I'm calling, I was hoping to pick your brain a bit."

"With the little I know about Wood Haven, picking my brain might be a long way from the help you need, Jonathan. Nevertheless, fire away.

The director undertook a thumbnail summary of the situation with full confidence Craig would be able to fill in the details. At the end of the explanation, Jonathan asked if his mentor might know of anyone particularly well-equipped to deal with the multi-layered Wood Haven challenge.

Silence on the other end of the telephone caused Jonathan to break into a cold sweat. Craig was his ace-in-the-hole. Jonathan never doubted that the man would ably deliver some sage advice or a recommendation to solve his dilemma. In fact, it never occurred to Jonathan that his long-time advisor would even hesitate with a reply.

Finally, Craig spoke.

"I think I may know of someone who can deliver exactly what you need."

Jonathan's reflections on his conversation with Craig were interrupted by the buzz of his office phone. Jolted from memories of the past to the present, he grabbed the receiver.

"Jonathan Walsh here."

"Hello, Jonathan. It's Grace Reid. I've arrived at Wood Haven. I'm downstairs at the security desk."

CHAPTER SIX

WOOD HAVEN ADMITTANCE FORM

Patient: *Kathleen McNamara*
Date of Admittance: *January 1, 1921*
Number: *01012138*
Age: *38*
Ethnicity: *Irish*
Marital Status: *Married*
Children: *None.*
Cause of insanity: *Intemperance and Business Trouble*

WHILE MANY COME TA THIS place after meself, there was many here afore me as well. Them's here the longest 'twas usually worse off. They was touched in the head, railin' 'gainst everything, or sometimes sittin' and rockin', or walkin' 'round and 'round in odd patterns.

That bein' said, there was those here a while that were right in their minds. Thems the ones I kept near—like Angel and, fer a time, Kathleen.

The woman was Irish through and through, which was part of what brung us together. The other part 'twas a scoldin' given me by an orderly after I went ta try openin' a window on the porch by the ward. 'Twasn't that I was trying ta get outta the place, mind ya. I was just wantin ta feel the outside on me body. 'Twas only a minute o'me tryin' ta push through the metal bars and reach the window latch afore a giant of a man come throwin' me ta the ground, yellin' ta get away from the window.

The wind was knocked clean outta me as I hit hard on the stone floor. Made no never mind ta the orderly as he drug me up ta me feet, yellin' and actin' like he was goin' ta hit me, or worse. That's when this woman comes up and start goin' on, sayin' things like, "Aw, doncha know this one's a bit off her mind," and "She's just a wee bit o' a woman. Turn her loose and I'll see she doesn't do it 'gain."

Ta her credit, the things she was sayin' worked. The brute went ta shovin' me ta the floor, sayin' 'twas lucky he was havin' a good day, or he'd be draggin' me down the hall. With a turn, he glared at the woman who'd come ta me rescue, shoutin', "She better keep quiet, or next time I'll make sure she gets needles to keep her quiet."

As the woman bent ta help me stand, she spoke words quiet but strong.

"There, there. You're doin' just fine. Get up now and we'll find a quiet place ta sit fer a bit."

She led me like a mam carin' fer a child, and I was grateful ta follow her to a bench in the ward. I sat not sayin' a word, as much outta fear as shock. Twasn't long though afore I had the need ta pee. Knowin' there was no sense askin' ta go ta the toilet. I turned ta the woman who'd rescued me.

"Missus, I have ta pee and no doubt, the orderly won't let me outta here. I don't want ta sit and wet meself, but I don't know what else ta do."

" If you'll be brave, I've got a way fer ya ta pee, but you have ta do just as I say."

With a nod of me head, she laid out a plan.

"Alright now, you're goin' ta sit here and watch me as I walk away from ya, like we's done talkin'. In a bit ya need ta move ta a spot on the other side, over there by the long table and benches, can ya see it now?

Again, not wantin' ta miss hearin' a word by speakin', I nodded me head.

"So's when ya get ta the table, have a look-see in the corner. They'll be a pile o'rags, all of 'em smellin' like pee. Them's the diapers the orderlies go ta changin' all day. They put 'em there 'til the janitors come ta haul 'em off at night. All's ya have ta do is sit yourself on the bench, puttin' your knees under the table. Wiggle your panties down a bit so's ya can pull 'em off ta one side, but keepin' em so's they don't show 'neath your skirt. Then go stand over them pile o'rags and pee. There's plenty there ta keep it from runnin' 'cross the floor. When you be finished, sit back down and pull up your undies under the table, so's no one'll notice. Then move yourself off from the bench as best ya can. I'm goin' ta leave ya now but 'member, do 'xactly as I told ya, or ya may end bein' caught."

While I'd listened close-like ta the woman, me stomach was churning with worry o'er not takin' each step just so. But the need ta empty me bladder was outweighin' me fears. So's, I begun.

Gettin' ta the bench was the easy part. Sittin' with me legs under the table and wigglin' outta me britches was a bit on the tough side. Prayin' ta Mary, Mother of God, I got 'em pulled off enough ta pee. Up I stood and with a few steps was stradlin' the pile o' stinkin' rags. The stench was such, the orderlies kept 'em far from their own smells, so's I was protected in that way.

When at last me bladder was empty, I made me way back ta the bench. Tuckin' me legs 'neath the table again, I wriggled back inta me undies. Ta say I was worn out from all the going's on would be far short o'the truth. Still, I had ta make me way back ta the ward, ta a place where's I could sit and be safe.

Rising up, I made me way ta a chair on the other side o'the room, kitty corner 'tween the pile of rags at one end and orderlies at t'other. I sat, nappin' fer a bit. When I woke, the woman who'd helped me was right there alongside.

"Ya did fine lass and now's ya know what ta do when you have ta pee. But I wouldn't be doin' it often, mind ya. T'is a bit o'luck ta not get caught."

Listenin' ta the woman, 'twas clear she was smart and had figured ways ta stay safe among those wantin' ta hurt us as much as help. Made me curious as ta just who she was.

"So Missus, me name is Teagan. Teagan Cormick. Who might ya be and how is it ya come ta bein' locked up here?"

"T'is a bit of a story how I came ta be in this god-forsaken place, so's I'll start with the easy part. Me name is Kathleen McNamara. I'm the sixth daughter of Padric and Siobhean O'Neill, born in Ballymena, County Antrim."

Realizing we was from opposite ends o'the Isle, I wondered what 'twas made Kathleen leave her people. I only had ta wait fer me answer.

"I decided ta come ta America after me granddad wrote home, sayin' he'd bought a large parcel o'land and was willin' ta give five acres ta any who'd make the voyage. I'd been lookin' fer a chance ta set off on me own. 'Twas the perfect way, as me mam and da couldn't raise too big a fuss, as 'twould be my granddad meetin' me at the end of me voyage."

Listenin', I found meself thinkin' o'me own trip 'cross the ocean—the long lines and the longer questions tryin' ta get inta America, with not a soul ta meet me. I imagined it easier fer Kathleen with her granddad waiting.

"When at last I made me way through the long immigration lines, me granddad and me found each other outside the Ellis Island buildin' where all newly-arrived pass. 'Twas never so glad ta see me family, as was he. We set off fer his land, 14 miles from Ellis Island, in a farming colony on Staten Island.

Granddad borrowed a horse and wagon ta fetch me and, truth be told, the ride was a bit rough. Seemed we'd never get there and most o'the trip I kept wonderin' what sorta mess I'd gotten meself inta."

"We got ta the house o'the man that owned the horse and wagon just as the sun was just beginnin' ta set. We had only a bit o'daylight left ta walk the two miles ta granddad's. So's we give our thanks, quick-like, and set off on a pace. The moon was risin' as we walked the steps up granddad's porch. 'Twas a moment I'll ne'er forget, seein' stars of such brightness. At sixteen, I'd begun me new life in America, with hope fer all good things ta come me way."

Lookin' at the woman, still young in her beauty, 'twas clear she was o'sound body. Listenin' ta her tell her story, no doubt her mind was strong as well. Made me go ta wonderin' just how and why she ended up in this madhouse.

"One thing 'bout me granddad, he'd give women no quarter. They was ta work the same and earn the same as the men 'round 'em. So's when he handed me a deed fer five acres o'land with me name at the top, 'twas not a doubt I would be farmin' on me own. 'Twas a dauntin' task at the start, but I watched the work o'me granddad and followed the same. Afore I knew it, I was raisin' a few head o'cattle and growin' enough crops ta feed 'em and me both. Five years down the road I'd managed ta carve out a decent life."

The woman was a grand storyteller. I could almost feel her worries 'bout managing' the land with no help. Yet twasn't an ounce o'feelin' sorry fer herself. As me mam used ta say, she'd made her bed and she had ta lie in it. And so's she did.

"'Twas six years later when granddad passed, leavin' me the 100 acres he'd bought when first he arrived. While's I respected my granddad's plan fer the land, bit by bit I went about makin' changes, growin' new crops, addin' livestock ta sell fer meat more than dairy. Twasn't long afore me ideas made me a wealthy woman, able ta da anythin' and go anywhere I liked."

Not knowin' the ways of America, I couldn't help wonderin' if Kathleen struggled atal on her own? So's I asked.

"Bein' a woman workin' in a man's way, was ya ever scared or did ya get hurt?"

"Ay there was times when I cried meself ta sleep with worry o'er how ta get crops in the ground or off ta market, or hows ta keep me cows from getting one o' them diseases goin' 'round. But I had me faith in God ta see me through. I prayed every night and always said an extra prayer ta me granddad ta not punish me fer changin' his plans and ta watch over me."

"Kathleen, it seems ta me we'd be cut from the same cloth in that we be right in our heads and healthy in our bodies but locked away just the same. The reasons fer me bein' here are none but unjust and I'm thinkin' the same be true o'you. So's thank ya fer carin' fer me today and keepin' me from bein' drug down the hall."

"You're more than welcome. Women here been punished fer less than good reasons, so's we need ta figure ways ta keep the bad from happenin'. As fer why I'm here, it come down ta simple greed. A man ownin' the land next ta mine wanted it. He tried ta buy from me granddad many's a time but could ne'er make the deal. On his deathbed, granddad made me swear on the Bible that I'd ne'er sell the land—always keep it and farm it—as he'd dreamed. When I kept refusin' ta sell, farmers 'round started doin' mean things. They went ta playin' tricks ta make it seem ghosts was comin' ta the place. I knew better, but me farmhands got fearful and up and left me, mid harvest. I managed ta get me crops in, but 'twas a quick fight won, as the farmers round me started doin' more. They went ta settin' fires on me property, turning loose me cattle, puttin' rats in me cabin. When I'd go ta town, complainin' ta the sheriff, other landowners went right along, swearin' up 'n down 'bout me crazed mind. With none ta say different and hefty bribes paid ta the sheriff and the town doc ta swear me unstable, they locked me away. Once I was gone five years, they could claim me land as abandoned."

There was nothin' I could say t'would help. I couldn't imagine being locked away so's someone could steal somethin' belongin' ta me. And here we sat, the two o'us, rotting away in body and soul fer no reason other than we was strong and determined Irish women.

From that day, Kathleen and me sought each other out so's we could share memories of our homeland, north and south. We talked 'bout our families and all the reasons we had ta leave and why we'd give anythin' ta return. Once in a great while, we'd have a cry o'er this life where we was trapped, with no hope of escapin'. 'Twas a trusted friendship meanin' the world ta us both.

That's why one morning, when Kathleen was nowhere ta be found, I felt a pit o'worry growin' in me. I sat at our bench and kept lookin' fer her smilin' face, but ne'er she came ta the ward, the dining hall or the dormitory.

The second mornin' when she was nowhere ta be found, I looked ta Nurse Bennett at the toilets and asked where Kathleen might be.

"Actually Teagan, she came down with a high fever, late, two nights ago. Dr. Neville didn't want whatever was causing her fever to spread, so he quarantined her, down the hall."

Hearin', them words made me feel sick ta me stomach. No doubt me face showed fear as Nurse Bennett reached out and patted me shoulder.

"There's nothing to worry about Teagan. Although Kathleen's fever was high, Dr. Reveille is experienced in a new treatment for such temperatures. I'm sure you won't understand this, but he has injected her with malaria to battle whatever is causing her fever. I am sure she will be back in the ward, fit as a fiddle, soon. We just need to wait for the malaria to do its job."

I knew Nurse Bennett wouldn't be lying ta me face. She was too good a woman. I also knew 'bout malaria. Me grandad come down with a case in Australia when he was travelin' the world. He near died from it and every year 'round the same time, his shakes and fever would come 'gain. Each time he fought, the weaker he got, 'til he could fight no more and passed. I couldn't imagine a doctor purposefully makin' Kathleen sick with the awful disease. Made no sense ta me atal. Made no sense ta Kathleen's body as well, as the poor woman died without ever recoverin'.

Kathleen's passin' stayed with me a long time, thinkin' how bein' smart and hard-workin' lost her everythin'. Why was it, I wondered, a woman be punished fer doin' well in life while a man be rewarded fer the same. The only thing crazy thing 'bout Kathleen McNamara was the way she was locked away and died. And here I was still alive—on accounta she was smart enough ta save me.

CHAPTER SEVEN

GRACE SAT AT HER OVERSIZED WOODEN desk, absentmindedly passing her fingers over the words and numbers long ago ingrained into its surface. The action kindled a consciousness within her of the endless paperwork once required of Wood Haven administrators. It also fueled imaginings of the lives impacted by the patient diagnoses and treatment reports forever etched into the office desktop.

Earlier in the day, Jonathan had led Grace through the multi-building facility, wing to wing, floor to floor. While walking, the executive director delivered a comprehensive overview of Wood Haven's history. Even for an organized thinker like Grace, the details were overwhelming. On top of it all, she felt a continual darkness permeating the buildings.

The massive limestone exterior of the asylum set an impersonal tone, fully amplified by interior mazes of windowless hallways, flickering fluorescent lights and permanently marred and stained walls. Yet Grace felt something more. A gloom, like a heavy drape, smothering the air and preventing any sense of lightness.

What am I doing here?

Unaware of Grace's concerns, Jonathan continued their tour through the Wood Haven labyrinth of buildings, complete with remnants of archaic medical equipment that she silently assessed as diabolical and excruciating. Adding to Grace's discomfort was her boss's continual reference to the asylum complex as, "the campus."

Her body stiffened when Jonathan first spoke the words. She had known two types of campuses in her life. The first was her alma mater, Rosary Hill College, where she marked the end of her teens and embraced womanhood. It was a time she treasured for the ways in which the educational experience helped her grow and evolve.

Grace's other association with a campus came through her job at the upscale Fox Run Retirement Community. In working to create a positive life experience for their residents, Fox Run administrators decreed that the buildings and grounds be referred to as, "the campus." At first Grace assessed the title as a shameless PR ploy, but as she settled into her job, she realized the marketing spin actually made a difference in the atmosphere and mindset of the community.

BY THE END OF THEIR TOUR, Grace recognized that Wood Haven's worn buildings and pervasive atmosphere stood in complete opposition to either of her campus ideals. Even comparing the extremes felt wrong. She also knew that to remain in her new job, she was going to have to find ways to shake off the foreboding sense that the former asylum infused into her being.

Looking around her office, Grace considered the room. Large. Oversized, actually. She had packed only a few personal belongings for her short-term stay, meaning office décor-shopping would be in order. Years of freelance experience taught Grace that creating a conducive work environment was essential to her wellbeing.

She began envisioning.

For starters, perhaps an oversized chair and an ottoman with a soft-woven throw. She'd need it for the long workdays-into-nights that always become her pattern. A small refrigerator and a hot plate were definites along with her special brewing pot and china cups for those meetings best served by what her nana called, "a spot of tea." Turning her view, she would want translucent white sheers for the oversized window behind her desk, to allow full daylight to flood the room while softening the hand-carved wooden framework.

The rudimentary oak book shelves against the right wall would improve with a few well-chosen knick knacks and some personal photos. Grace always defined her work space with pictures . . . collections of family and friends interspersed with favorite images from work assignments and vacations. All memories of people and places that filled her heart.

The only remaining areas to address were her office walls. The four were painted ordinary white, which Grace deemed a blank canvas in need of colorful salvation. While she desperately wanted to take paint brush in hand, she knew the six-month term of her employment precluded the investment of such time and labor.

Struggling between her senses and her sensibilities, Grace decided to purchase artwork to enliven the vertical spaces. The shopping task would not only brighten her surroundings, it would help fill her leisure time in Midland, where she was about to become a temporary resident. And, the artwork might even add to the décor of her real home, once she completed her Wood Haven assignment

With her vision of an improved office space fully imagined, Grace turned to the file folders on her desk. They were divided into two groups. The first numbered four files and represented the Wood Haven seniors with physical and mental challenges. Looking through Jonathan's summary notes, Grace reviewed the information. The patients ranged in age from fifty-four to seventy-six. Three women, one man. Two use walkers, one is bound to a wheelchair and one, the man, is bedridden. The woman in the wheelchair also exhibits early signs of senility. All are candidates for skilled and long-term care.

Moving to the larger stack of files, Grace glanced through Jonathan's summary on the six remaining seniors. All women, ages 62 to 80. Three dependent on walkers or canes. Three fully ambulatory. All mentally competent.

This is my mainstreaming group. Although after a lifetime at Wood Haven, they are going to require counseling to prepare them for community-life situations. I think it will best to start here.

Grace organized the six files alphabetically according to first names. It was an unusual filing system she had adopted long ago as a way to personalize the individuals. She then decided to title the group for ease of reference. Doodling names related to Wood Haven and deinstitutionalization, Grace was frustrated by the overly clinical tone of every possible choice. Then a name clicked. She thought of it based on her nana's favorite reminder to always, "have faith".

The Faith File.

The designation made Grace feel as if her nana was somehow with her and would guide her work as she helped these six women move on to new lives.

Grace's professional success in the senior care field was founded upon her organizational skills and her strong decision-making abilities. Yet it was her boundless compassion for those facing advanced life challenges that propelled her into the expert realm. The advisor's empathy for seniors was rooted in her childhood experiences, growing up in the care of her devoted grandparents.

By the age of eight, Grace was spending every summer with Nana and

Papa O'Connor on their dairy farm, where her mother was born and raised. The annual ten-week hiatus from the latchkey home life she endured with her career-driven, attorney parents evolved into the happiest years of her childhood. Early mornings in the barn milking cows with papa, summer afternoons riding the hay wagon with nana, evenings on the porch with all three sharing ice cream and watching magical fireflies light the twilight sky, all of it encapsulated a world where Grace was the cherished center of her nana and papa's affections.

As an adult, Grace fully appreciated the ways in which those summer vacations forged her strong sense of self-worth. Every day she was influenced by some life lesson learned from her grandparents. The time also provided her with an unusual life perspective on the aging process. That's why It became Grace's professional goal to ensure that all seniors were fully respected, particularly when their lives reached the stage that they were no longer able, or allowed, to make their own life choices.

Reflecting on the Faith File group on her desk shifted Grace out of her childhood reverie. Fanning out the manila dossiers before her, she chose one at random.

MAEVE MULHERIN DEMPSEY, admitted to Wood Haven on December 29,1931. Suffering from general conditions of depression and grief bordering on insanity, uterine derangement and domestic trouble. At the time of admittance, Maeve was thirty-years old, married and mother of three children.

Running the numbers through her mind, Grace realized that in a few short months this woman would mark her 47[h] year at Wood Haven. She was stunned by that realization.

That's more years than I've been alive.

Continuing through the ten-plus page report, Grace discovered that Maeve had been institutionalized by her husband, with a supporting evaluation from their family physician. According to the notes, Maeve's fourth child was stillborn, causing her to sink into a dysfunctional depression.

While the paperwork used all the appropriate medical terms, Grace suspected the underlying element to Maeve's admission was her husband's inability to care for his grieving wife four months after the loss of their child.

What really tore at Grace's heart was that Maeve's file notes showed that in 47 years, no one had inquired about the woman, nor come to visit her. Nowhere in her file was there even a glimmer that her husband, or her family, or the Wood Haven staff believed or cared that she might be able to recover or improve.

Forty-seven years.

The number kept running through Grace's consciousness as she continued reading Maeve's files.

How does a family walk away from a loved one like that? What about her children? Did they ever wonder what happened to their mother? Did they ever beg to see her? Cry themselves to sleep with the wish to once again be comforted in her arms?

Subconsciously, Maeve's story triggered a tearful reaction within Grace. It was only as her salty drops stained the report pages that she recognized her empathetic sorrow. Grabbing a tissue from her purse, Grace blotted the watery tears from the official paperwork. She then dabbed at her face to keep further waterworks from falling.

Ok, I need to take a break. Maybe get outside of these buildings, inhale some fresh air. Enjoy Mother Nature's beauty that originally earned Wood Haven its name.

Without Jonathan as a guide, Grace tried to imagine the maze-like layout of the administration floor. It was only in stepping out of her office and seeing a red exit sign down the hallway that she felt a sense of direction.

Choosing the obvious, Grace made her way to the signed doorway. Pushing on the exit door's heavy metal bar, she discovered a concrete stairway with a painted number 2 on the farthest wall. Feeling encouraged and slightly more confident, Grace moved through the doorway and began descending the stairs.

Halfway to the first floor, a thought popped into her mind.

I wonder if the main floor access door is locked from the outside?

The possibility caused her heart to pump a little quicker. Upon reaching the first-floor landing, Grace yanked on the exit door's handle with a force intensified by her entrapment fears.

While the door didn't budge, Grace did, ricocheting like a rubber ball. In seconds that played out in slow motion, she lost her sense of balance, bounced off one wall into another and slammed into the concrete floor. The impact forced all air from her lungs, leaving Grace paralyzed in mind and body. Then like a bellow on a fire, oxygen suddenly burst into her being. The shocked woman sucked in air and gasped for more, all the while thinking, *I'm going to die in this stairwell.*

As her blood flow restored and rational thought returned, Grace managed to roll to one side and sit up. Checking her body from head to toe, it was clear the most damaging injury she suffered had been to her self-esteem.

Alright, Grace, get a grip. This is not an impossible situation. Look around, assess, act.

The effect of her pep talk was lessened by the realization that the safety-lock door in front of her was the only way out. Unless of course the second-floor door, where she entered the stairwell, might somehow be accessible.

I assume that every door is an automatic lock, Grace's logical mind chided.

Without thought, a reply often spoke by her papa came to mind. "Well you know what happens when you assume, little girl. You make an ass out of you and me!"

Okay, okay. I'll try it.

Trudging up the two flights of stairs between the floors, Grace felt the full effect of her fall in painful tweaks between her back and hips. None of it really mattered, if she could just break out of this accidental stairwell confinement.

Approaching the second-floor door, Grace cautiously pulled on the handle. Nothing. Not even a centimeter of movement. Between the aches in her body and the fear in her mind, Grace felt herself on the verge of a full-blown meltdown. Even worse, she was hallucinating, as she began to hear echoes of ghostly voices calling through the stairwell.

"Grace? Grace?"

Ghosts in this place know me by name?

"Grace, it's Jonathan. Are in here, in the stairway?

"Jonathan? Jonathan! Yes, I'm here."

Grace determined the voice to be rising from the lower level and quickly began descending.

"Stay right there, Jonathan, I'm on my way".

As she reached the first floor, Grace saw her new boss flanked by a security guard and another man in work clothes. More importantly, she saw the door to the outside world fully open.

"Thank goodness you found me, Jonathan. How did you know I was in here?

"Grace, meet Bob Jeffries. He is one of the janitors here at Wood Haven. He saw you enter the stairs on the second floor. He had no idea who you were, other than a stranger. So he knew you wouldn't have a security pass to scan in order to exit the stairwell. Only administrators have passes. I happened to be coming in the building as Bob was at the security station with Pete. This is Pete Herr, one of our security guards. Bob was telling Pete about some strange woman roaming the building. I had a feeling it might be you."

While Jonathan's tone was kind, Grace could feel a red embarrassment flood her body and spread to her neck and face. How could she have not have anticipated a one-way, security exit door in an asylum? Kindly, Jonathan immediately tempered her humiliation.

"Actually Grace, this is my fault. Our protocol is to walk through all building procedures during an employee's final hiring interview. Your hire was unusual in that it was all done by phone, so I am a bit out of form in following procedure. Quite honestly, by the time we'd finished walking through the buildings and reviewing patient details this morning, I felt as if I had given you more than enough information. I am sorry my lack of organization led to this unnecessary incident on your first day."

Looking at the sympathetic trio of men before her, Grace was no longer concerned that she appeared foolish. She simply wanted to exit the stairway and get out into the fresh air.

"It's all good, Jonathan. Truly, I understand. I'm just grateful that you, and Bob, and Pete connected the dots and found me. Now if you don't mind, I'd really like to get out of this stairwell."

Chapter Eight

WOOD HAVEN ADMITTANCE FORM

Patient: *Maeve Mulherin Dempsey*
Date of Admittance: *December 29, 1931*
Number: *12293130*
Age: *30*
Ethnicity: *Irish*
Marital Status: *Married*
Pregnancies: Four *(three alive / one stillborn)*
Diagnosis: *Depression and grief bordering on insanity, uterine derangement, domestic troubles.*

'TWAS THE MIDDLE OF THE NIGHT when the new woman arrived. An orderly drug her roughshod inta the dormitory and, like a worthless bit 'o nothin', shoved her ta the cot next ta me own. The space had been empty since Rose Jacobson passed away. Took half a day fer anyone ta notice the poor thing was dead and come take her away.

As the woman stood by Rose's old cot, a look of shock and fear went ta fillin' her face. The narrow metal bed was covered with nothin' but a stained sheet hidin' a paper-thin mattress. The stank of urine hung in the air all 'round. After a bit, ya got used ta every breath burnin' your nose and lungs, but bein' new, this woman was far from familiar with the smell. All at once, it seemed she was goin' ta pass out right in front of me eyes.

"Now see here, missy, don'cha be fallin' over on me," I ordered as I jumped up and wrapped me arms about her. The woman was a rail 'neath her sweater and cotton dress and was shiverin with little protectin' her from the cold night air.

"Sit down here. Go on with ya now. 'Tis alright. Smells worse than it feels and the sooner ya get used ta it, the better you'll be."

Truth be told, I knew just how she felt walkin' inta this mad place. I could still remember me own fear bein' dumped on a dormitory cot, missin' me family and my home and cryin' meself dry. Nurse Bennett and Angel had made it better fer me. 'twas my turn now ta be makin' it better fer another.

"What is this place?"

Them's were the first words outta her mouth and they struck me as sad, like a child beggin' her mam ta prove what she already feared true.

"My guess is you'd be callin' it an asylum, more than a hospital. Truth be told, it's a madhouse."

I felt badly tellin' her straight out like that, but there was no sense sugarcoatin' it. What she was seein' in the shadows was only gonna get worse in the full light o'day.

"What's your name then, darlin'?"

The waif of a woman looked up at me, eyes receedin' with pain and overflowin' with tears. I wondered if she had enough wits about her ta even know who she was. Standin' in the middle o'the oversized room with a hundred or more cots o'women snorin' and moanin' in their sleep, she started rockin', to and fro. 'Twas a motion I'd come ta know well in this place of unwell minds and bodies.

"Maeve Mulherin Dempsey," she whispered

"Well, Maeve Mulherin Dempsey, it's good ta meet ya. Me name's Teagan. Teagan Cormick. Where are your people from?"

Again, a long pause and more rockin' afore an answer come. 'Twas is if the motion was pushin' the words from her mouth.

"Me family was from Cork. I come ta America with 'em, ten years past, but don't right know where most of 'em are anymore."

'Twas in that moment a feelin' come inta my heart long ago forgotten. 'Twas a sense o'loss fer life I'd known as a child and fer me family left behind. Then and there as if a spell was cast, Maeve Mulherin Dempsey became me sister, sure'en as if we'd been born from the same mother.

I drew me arms around her shiverin' body and brought her onta me cot, nesting her 'gainst me fer warmth and comfort. If found we'd be taken down the hall, but I was willin' ta take the chance. Maeve was in great need of bein' held close ta another human bein' and ta tell the truth, I was as well.

It'd been more time than I could imagine, since I'd felt the touch of me mam and da, me brothers and sisters. The kind o'touch goes clean through a person's soul. As Maeve's breathin' got deeper and her bony frame went relaxin' inta mine, tears welled up in me eyes spillin' over onta her hair. I wanted ta reach up and wipe away the salty lines stainin' me cheeks, but I didn't dare move fer fear of wakin' the exhausted woman lying in me arms.

Next I knew, the morning sun was pushin' its way through the iron bar windows of the dormitory. Maeve was still soundly sleepin', but I knew t'would be best ta wake her and get her moved onta her own cot.

"Maeve. Maeve, you've got ta come awake, darlin'. Come on now. Open those eyes."

A soft moan and a stirrin' o'her feet and fingers were the only signs she'd heard me voice. But the clankin' of the nurse's carts was growin' louder. For sure, Maeve and I had ta separate or there'd be holy hell ta pay. Gently I moved me arm from 'neath her fragile body, forcin' her away. The motion caused the woman ta wake and up she leapt in a sleepy muddle. Happened all the time with the new ones, not knowin' where they was those first few days.

"No worries. You're fine, Maeve. Look ta me. I'm Teagan, 'member? We met last night when they brung ya here. I know it's a bit confusin', but you're alright."

A tiny smile creased Maeve's lips showin' she took comfort in me words. Yet 'twas only a moment's relief as Nurse Haggerty come paradin' through the dormitory, clangin' her mornin' bell and demandin' us all ta, "get up".

"Alright ladies, it's time to go to the bathroom and move to the dining hall. Get your shoes and let's go. You all need to eat breakfast."

Followin' orders was important and the sooner ya figured it out, the better off ya be. The doctors set 'em and the nurses and orderlies did what it took ta make sure they was followed. Fer meself, twasn't such a bad thing. Me mam had kept us kids in line settin' all kinds o'rules and rue the day we weren't doin' exactly as she planned.

Still, there were those who railed 'gainst routine. Some on account they didn't want ta be here. Others 'cause their minds didn't work right and they couldn't understand. No matter, anyone not followin' orders was punished by getting' took down the hall and forced ta take medicines ta dull their brain.

It happened ta me, early on. I spoke out ta a nurse about not havin' ta go ta the toilet 'ccordin' ta her schedule. I refused twice ta join the line ta the lav afore she called the orderlies. Bein' new, I wasn't sure o'what was comin', but when the orderly grabbed me like a rag doll and carted me off, I knew any sense o'fight within me was better left still.

Next thing, I was in a room with no windows, by meself, save fer the nurse who come regular-like with cold mush and a long needle. The woman ne'er said a word. She just dropped me food on the floor and stuck the needle in me arm. I've no other recall o'the time, how long it lasted or when they finally drug me back ta me cot. All's I knew was once outta that room, me mind came back ta me, along with a desire ta never lose it again. So's, I started obeyin' rules and smilin' at the nurses when they spoke, even when it went 'gainst me grain. Tried me best ta help others do the same, I did. 'Specially when they was newly arrived.

"Maeve, if you're smart you'll do just as they say, even if you're not wantin' ta do so. I'll tell ya more as the day goes on, but fer now, stay close and do the same as me. You'll be fine."

"What are you whispering about, Teagan?" 'Twas Nurse Haggerty. She had a way of sneakin' up quiet-like and hearin' what you didn't want her ta hear.

"I was just sayin' good mornng' ta the new woman, Nurse Haggerty. That's all."

"Well see that you don't cause any trouble, because you know what will happen. As for you," she said pointing to Maeve, "You're to come with me, now."

The look on poor Maeve's face was pitiful. I wanted ta grab her and run so's nothin' bad could happen ta her. But I knew 'twas foolish thinkin'. So's, I stood and watched the nurse take hold o'Maeve's arm and force her ta the hallway. No tellin' where they was goin' or why. All's I could do was say a prayer ta Mary, Mother o'God, ta keep the sweet woman safe from harm.

"Alright, the rest of you pay attention to the orderlies and get to the dining hall. And if I have to send an orderly back here because any of you are lagging, everyone will be punished."

The group o'us standin' and watchin' Maeve being drug away started movin' like cattle in a herd. None wanted ta be pointed out as wrong-headed, so's, we made our way 'ccordin' ta Nurse Haggerty, ending up in the dining hall, on the opposite side o'the buildin'. There we sat silent-like, eatin' our daily breakfast of cold porridge and a mug o'warm water.

After breakfast they moved us ta the ward. Meself, I went and sat in the nearby porch where I could feel the sun as it shone. I had a need ta be alone with me thoughts, most o'which were 'bout Maeve and what might be happenin' ta her. Each imagining come worse than the last, 'til I come ta a place where I had ta change me thinkin'. So's I stood and went ta movin' inta the ward.

Just as I turned, I come face ta face with Maeve, standin' afore me. She looked like a wounded animal, trapped and now set loose. Not a word come outta her.

Understandin' her need, I moved to a nearby bench in the ward and motioned fer Maeve ta do the same. Took forever fer the woman ta take the steps. 'Twas all I could do ta keep from jumpin' up and huggin' the poor thing, she was lookin' so forlorn.

When at last she sat, 'twas with the same rockin' motion from the night before. I understood it ta be her way o'comfort, so's I stayed quiet, allowin' her ta settle herself. In a bit, her movin' slowed and her words began.

"Me beibe died in me arms. 'Twas a girl. A beauty she was with the greenest o'eyes, the fairest o'skin and a hint o'deep black ta her fine downy hair. She never cried, mind ya. She was born with a peaceful soul, smilin' as if she knew some special secret all ta herself."

I'd not a thought 'bout all Maeve was speakin'. I understood her words clear enough, but 'twasn't sure if she was talkin' 'bout a real child born and dead, or if t'were some kind o'made-up tale from her scattered brain. No matter. Least she was talkin'.

"Me other children was happy ta welcome Erin Maureen, Erin after me gran and Maureen fer me husband's mam. Me three boys had been hopin' fer another brother, but deep in me heart, I'd been wishin' and prayin' fer a little lass. I know she's with the angels now and I know God's goin' ta help me through this terrible pain, but me husband says he's tired o'me sadness and me tears. He says I'm nothin' but a reminder o'the loss of our baby girl and I need ta stop me cryin'. I've tried. Lord knows, I've tried. But me heart just won't heal."

Maeve stopped rockin'. In her stillness her face turned pale as the whitest moon and her eyes sent a stream of tears washin' down her cheeks like a gully. 'Twas heartbreakin' ta see her in such a state. I wanted ta do somethin' ta help the poor woman. Not knowin' any other way, I began rockin' 'longside her, like we was two in one. The movin' of our bodies connected and her words began again.

"I begged me husband fer a bit more time, but he said was done with me—that him and the boys needed ta live. So off he went ta our family doctor, gettin' a letter sayin' me mind's gone twisted and will ne'er be right. Next thing I know, I'm sent off ta this place, losin' me boys as well Erin Maureen. No one and nothin' ta live fer."

As Maeve talked, the walls felt like they was closin' in 'round us. The stank and the filth, the meanness o'the orderlies and the odd ways o'the other women. 'Twas like me worst dream, as if we was buried alive in this hell on earth. I didn't know how, but some way, me and Maeve had ta escape.

Closin' me eyes, I imagined me home and me family. I started prayin', askin' fer mercy on our all our souls. As me thoughts turned ta heaven, a peaceful calm come o'er me, and I knew 'xactly what needed doing.

Movin' closer ta Maeve, soft and easy I went ta sharin' stories of me family and me memories o'Ireland. And as she listened and I talked, the two o'us went imaginin' and travelin', far away from the horrors of this terrible place. Far away to the shores of our homeland and those we loved.

CHAPTER NINE

GRACE WOKE SLOWLY in her temporary bedroom within her temporary home. Drifting through her early morning thoughts, she gradually fell into the awareness that it was Saturday.

Thank God. The weekend.

By the end of her first week at Wood Haven Grace had realized two things. One—pouring over and assessing the asylum's patient files demanded a greater personal investment than any freelance work she'd ever tackled. Two—she was more than ready for a break.

The six patients Grace identified as her Faith File priority cases were all women and their latest medical reports assessed them as mentally and physically age-appropriate. Yet details of their institutionalizations, coupled with whispered stories of asylum life that Grace regularly overheard in the Wood Haven corridors, made the file reviews deeply troubling. One hour of reading the files at any one time was about all she could manage. Yet it was nightmares about the cruel treatments and brutal punishments suffered by the ten seniors that were truly exhausting her.

It had been years since night terrors had invaded Grace's sleep. They began in her mid-teens, haunting her to the point that her parents insisted she see a psychiatrist. Grace could still remember every sight and sound of that first visit to Dr. Foley's office. It was the dead of winter, a generally depressing time in Buffalo. Grace had already been out of school for two days because she couldn't think—couldn't function—after continued weeks of nightmares.

At first, she didn't tell anyone about the nightly tortures, primarily because her recall was so fragmented she really couldn't make sense of any of them. It was only after a particularly intense screaming frenzy one night that her mother even became aware of the terrorizing dreams. The next morning, against Grace's vehement protests, her mother made an appointment with a psychiatrist recommended by their family doctor. Grace dreaded talking about the nightmares almost as much as going to sleep and experiencing them.

On the appointed day, her parent's demanding law careers made it impossible for either of them to accompany their daughter to Dr. Foley's office. Instead her mother dropped her off an hour early with a $20 bill and the number of a taxi service to call for a ride home. Before sending her on her way, Grace's mother gave a quick squeeze to her daughter's hand along with a, "You'll be fine Gracie, you'll see". The pit in her stomach told Grace otherwise.

Surprisingly, the nervous teen found the office waiting room more comforting than sterile. After a few moments, she determined it was the soothing ocean sounds drifting out from the room's stereo speakers that set the tone.

Grace's sense of calm continued as the receptionist guided her down the short hallway to Dr. Foley's office. Soft colors, comfortable furniture and a collection of blooming plants gave a lift to the young girl's spirits. The beauty of flowers in the midst of a subzero Buffalo winter felt like a breath of spring.

When Dr. Foley appeared, the woman seemed to reflect the tranquility of her surroundings. She was tall and willowy, graceful in her movements. She wore her hair long and perfectly styled in harmony with her well-tailored slacks and designer blouse. In welcoming her to the office, Grace felt a sense of genuine care in the psychologist's manner and being.

From that point, doctor and patient spent the winter meeting and talking. Grace never felt that their time was about counseling sessions. Rather Dr. Foley seemed more like a kind aunt intent on nurturing her favorite niece.

As for the nightmares, they subsided and eventually ceased as oddly as they'd started. Dr. Foley explained their existence as rooted in Grace 's sense of abandonment—an anxiety that became clear as the two discussed the young teen's latchkey home life with her career-focused parents.

Dr. Foley advised that until Grace was old enough to control her own world, there were simple things she could do whenever loneliness overwhelmed her, like getting out with friends and listening to upbeat music. The therapist also suggested meditation and yoga as means of strengthening Grace's mind and body and potentially controlling the nightmares should they reoccur. Since her arrival at Wood Haven and their nightmare's return, Grace was relying on every one of Dr. Foley's suggested therapies.

Refusing to let the day spiral, Grace climbed out of bed and spent the next 20 minutes practicing her most challenging yoga poses. The mental and physical discipline required by the ancient practice was exactly what she needed to clear her mind and de-stress her body.

Feeling revived, Grace wandered through the unfamiliar surroundings of this place she would call home for the next eight months. Jonathan's sister, Karen, had located the short-term rental in Midland Township. The forty-something realtor was a spark plug of energy and Grace wondered if her friendliness reflected the community-at-large.

Since the place is pretty much furnished, there's not much I need to feel settled. There is that empty space above the living room mantle that would be nice to fill, if I can find something affordable. And I need some art for my office walls.

Grace looked forward to spending her Saturday shopping her way through Midland's downtown. It was one of her guilty life pleasures to stroll through stores and check out window displays. Papa told her it was a family curse passed down from her nana. Grace didn't really care about the genesis of her passion, she just loved shopping. And after the last five days, she was primed and ready for some retail therapy.

Grabbing a quick shower and tossing on some comfy walking clothes, Grace was ready. With purse in hand, she headed down the steps of her Victorian rental and exited through the gate anchoring the yard's white picket fence. Thanks to a map provided by Karen, Grace confidently turned right and began strolling toward the Midland business district.

Grace's job at Wood Haven required workdays of very early mornings and late nights, so her drive between home and work happened pretty much in the dark. As a result, Grace had only seen her new "hometown" through some website links Karen had shared early in their long-distance rental process.

Initially she'd planned on renting a studio apartment or a small flat, which was more than enough space to accommodate her six-month needs. However, Midland was a historic town, dating back to pre-revolutionary war times. The community and its people prided themselves on maintaining renovated buildings, according to the style of the day. As a result, there were only a small number of apartments for rent, most rarely available.

With Karen's encouragement, Grace finally surrendered her apartment ideal and agreed to rent a house. Not just any house, mind you, but the domain of one of the town's founders, Asa Warren. Grace's strongest hope was that old Asa was not territorial about his homestead and wouldn't be stopping by for a late-night visit anytime soon.

The walk to town was half a mile but seemed much shorter as Grace became entranced by the beautifully restored turn-of-the-century homes that defined each block. When at last she reached Main Street, Grace found herself standing in wonder, as if she'd been transported back in time to a colonial village of shops and merchants. Had it not been for the flow of cars along the blacktopped street, Grace was sure she would have been searching for men in breeches and waistcoats and women in bonnets and long capes.

Taking a few moments to fully appreciate the panorama before her, Grace became entranced by the summer flowers cascading over the oak barrels along the sidewalks. Colorful flags promoting Midland as a town, "Where History is A Way of Life," fluttered like butterflies on old fashioned lamp posts.

In the distance, Grace could see a vintage, double-sided brass clock that landmarked the central intersection of the five-block downtown district. An assortment of business store fronts ran along both sides of Midland's Main Street, each ornate and charming in their own way. Oversized store windows presented merchant wares, accented by posters of upcoming community fundraisers and summer concerts. Through every bit of her view, Grace felt magically transported to a "once upon a time" shopper's paradise.

Deciding her day could be no better spent, Grace began at the first store in the five-block stretch. The sign over the doorway read, "Schulz's Fine Paper and Exquisite Cards." From her earliest memories, Grace had loved everything connected to hand-written letters. Whenever she got close to a store featuring notepaper or cards, her world pretty much came to a stop. Per usual, it was almost an hour before Grace re-emerged through Schulz's Main St. door.|

By midday, Grace had reached the halfway point of the town's commercial district. At every stop on her shopping tour she purchased a small trinket or needed utensil to make her temporary housing feel more like a home. Moving along to the second half of her five-block journey, Grace strolled the Main Street crosswalk without a care in the world.

Reaching the first shop on the far side of the street the window display was filled with antiques and collectibles. The hand-crafted sign spanning the building front read, "Jewel's Attic". Grace entered, hopeful that Jewel would have just what she wanted to enliven her office walls and the space above her living room mantle.

A brass bell attached to the top of the entry door jingled her presence. From an unknown source, Grace heard a friendly greeting.

"Welcome to Jewel's Attic. Feel free to look and touch all you like."

Unable to locate the person connected with the voice, Grace politely responded, "Thank you so much."

The shop was well-named as its shelves and aisles were cluttered, much like an attic in any home. However, Grace's organized brain demanded a path through the disarray to avoid missing anything she might value. She began by turning right and aiming to work her way to the far wall.

Moving through the store, Grace discovered a number of treasures that reminded her of her nana and papa—a piece of china from their familiar pattern, a brass and glass chandelier like the one that illuminated their farmhouse dining room, a framed photo of the Sacred Heart of Jesus exactly like the one hanging above their bed, a hand quilted coverlet matching those nana made from scraps of material and bound with white yarn tied in knots.

Approaching the back wall of the store Grace came upon a display of artwork—paintings, sketches, lithographs, prints—everything from flowers to landscapes to portraits. Wandering through the mini-gallery, she was intrigued by the various styles of art. Some looked to be antique while others appeared more modern, in subject and style. Sifting through the artwork, Grace identified a collection of water color, framed prints that detailed the change of seasons.

These will perfectly suit my office and together they're sizable enough to fill the large wall, directly across from my desk.

Continuing to sort through the remaining artwork, Grace selected three more framed paintings of varied sizes, one watercolor and two smaller oils.All were modern works that intrigued her and, as she noted, were remarkably affordable.

That should do it for my office. Looks like the spot over the fireplace is going to have to wait.

As Grace was about to turn and make her way along the opposite wall, something on the floor caught her attention. It was a partially rolled canvas filling a gap between two boxes of empty picture frames. The only part of the painting Grace could really see was an edge of vibrant orange that faded into burnt copper. She had no idea of the subject. Rather it was the colors that attracted her.

Carefully extracting the work of art, Grace moved to a nearby antique oak dining table. Gently she unwound the canvas, praying it wouldn't crack as she did. Unable to keep the curled edges from retracting, Grace reached over to a nearby display of coffee mugs selecting one at a time to anchor the painting's corners. Achieving her goal, she took a step back to survey the artwork, becoming so entranced that she never heard the store owner as she approached.

"It's lovely, don't you think?"

Startled, Grace jumped, but managing to rebalance before doing any damage to herself or the surrounding antiques.

"Oh my, I'm so sorry to have alarmed you. My name is Johanna, Johanna Styles. I'm the owner of the store.

Although a stranger, the warmth radiating from Johanna's soft brown eyes encouraged Grace to offer a friendly return.

"So nice to meet you. I'm Grace Reid. Yes, this painting is lovely. I especially like the way the artist captured the reflection of the sunset on the water. It's quite remarkable. Watching the sun rise and set over water is one of my favorite things in the world. And it can be any water—ocean, lake, river, creek—doesn't matter. This painting makes me feel as if I am sitting on an ocean shoreline. Do you know anything about it, or the artist?"

"I'm sorry, I don't. All I can tell you is it came out of an attic in an old farmhouse in New York State. I go to a lot of estate sales and auctions where, sadly, the owners are no longer alive or residing on the property. Rarely do I get to know much of the history of what I bring back to the store. The only thing I can tell you is that there is an inscription on the back of the canvas with a date of 1928 alongside the word, Eire. It's the Gaelic word for Ireland."

"Interesting, but also a pity. Whoever painted this had talent. The artist could be a master, a Van Gogh or a Monet, but we'll never know since it's unsigned." Grace offered an impish grin to go with her words, to which Johanna smiled and nodded.

"No doubt. So, take it, frame it and display it as a valued piece of art."

"That's exactly what I'm going to do. And I know right where I'm going to hang it.

Chapter Ten

WOOD HAVEN ADMITTANCE FORM

Patient: *Dimitri "James" Ardonis*
Date of Admittance: *February 25, 1923*
Number: *02252925*
Age: *25*
Ethnicity: *Greek*
Marital Status: *Married*
Children: *Two*
Diagnosis: *Intemperance and Business Troubles*

'TWAS A WHILE 'FORE I REALIZED them's in charge was keepin' us apart in separate buildin's, women from men. From all's I could figure, the reason was just what me da had warned me—boys wantin' ta get inta girls bloomers.

Bein' I was young leavin' Ireland and got settled straight away with the Englers, I'd not been close enough ta any man ta figure if me da be tellin' the truth. Twasn't long at Wood Haven afore I knew.

No matter we was separate by orders o' the docs and by force o'the orderlies, them's who wanted found ways ta come together, if ya know what I mean. Mind ya, there was nothin' special 'bout any of it. There was men droppin' their drawers and women liftin' their dresses when and where ever they could.

I saw such things when men was brought over ta do buildin' repairs, or when groups worked mixed in the sewing room—women mendin' cloth and men re-toolin' leather. Even when both was let outside for a bit o'fresh air, there was couplin' goin' on. As God is me witness, there was times when orderlies with the strength o'Samson could hardly pull the deed doers apart.

In me own mind, there was no need fer all the fuss. Mam told us men and women coupled fer only one reason, ta make beibis. Believin' that, I'd no interest in bein' with any man, no less the sort locked away. Never occurred ta me mind, or me body, that there was anythin' else mattered 'bout couplin'.

SO 'TWAS, AFTER BREAKFAST ONE MORNIN', a nurse pulled me from a line o'women shufflin' ta the ward. She told me ta stand 'gainst the far wall where some was already in place. Lookin' over I could see Maeve and Angel. The two bein' there made me feel safe 'bout whatever was goin' on.

I stood meself close ta Angel, so's our arms touched. The warm from our skin kept me nerves from shakin' me body. Not a word was spoke. We all just leaned 'gainst the wall, waitin' fer whatever the nurses was goin' ta tell us.

"Alright pay attention," Nurse Stewart snapped, sharp-like. "You are going outside to clean up the yard. There are leaves to be gathered and tree branches and sticks to be collected. The men will rake the leaves into piles. Your job will be to pick up those leaves and put them into the large push wagons. The guards will empty the wagons when they are full. When the leaves are done you are to move on to the branches and sticks."

No doubt, by the look o'some in line, Nurse Stewart's words confused their minds. Many had no sense about 'em and spent days doin' nothin' but sittin' and starrin'. 'Twas only as the right-minded started doin' that the rest followed along, like sheep in pasture.

"For anyone who might be thinking about trying to wander away from the grounds, the orderlies will be watching. Should you do anything other than work on the leaves and sticks, you will be immediately brought inside and taken down the hall."

All among us knew if we did somethin' displeasin' ta the nurses or docs, they'd do somethin' hurtful back. That's what I'd come ta learn 'bout goin' "down the hall." Them's that went and could still talk when they come back told stories of tubes bein' shoved down their throats ta force down pills and nasty needles o'medicines bein' jammed inta arms to dull the brain. Then there was them been jolted with electric ta keep 'em from thinkin' and talkin'. There was even stories 'bout docs takin' bits and pieces o'brains outta skulls . . . all ta make sure none o'us would ever again think of goin' 'gainst their rules.

As the nurses went ta herdin' us out a back way o'the buildin' I could feel me heart beatin' faster with every step. I was goin' outside for the first time since they'd trapped me in this place of filth and misery. Had no idea how many days, or weeks, or even months it'd been, but I did me best ta memorize the path, by chance someday I could find the way on me own.

As we went ta funnelin' out the door, a sharp morning air hit me 'cross the face. Walkin' on I could feel the end o'winter, hangin' on, like the flame at the end of a short wick. Then a breeze come up the hillside, o'er the near lake. 'Twas soft and gentle, more spring than winter. Truth be told it felt much like standin' on Queenstown's wharf.

In that moment, an ache rose up inside me like an ocean wave rollin' ta the shore. Tears went ta wellin' in me eyes and 'twas only commotion ahead that kept 'em from droppin'. Comin' outta the dawn there be a crowd walkin' toward us, all of 'em men guarded by orderlies from other buildin's.

As the lot o'em drew near, they started pointin' at us women, laughin' and shoutin', like a bunch o'sailors on leave. Twasn't but a minute 'fore the orderlies circled 'round, bossin' the men ta quit botherin' with us women and get ta work. And there they stayed, like a wall wedged 'tween us, the men rakin' and movin' on, while the women gatherin' leaves inta the wagons.

T'would be lying if I told ya I didn't give notice ta the men. Most were odd in action and not appealin' in body. Yet there was one, a man middle in height and compactly built with hair dark as coal. Not wantin' ta stare, I caught glimpses o'him as I went gatherin' up leaves, each quick look makin' me want more.

Slyly I worked me way 'round the women, movin' debris from pile ta wagon. In short order I was alongside the group where this certain man was rakin'. Each time as I went ta pickin' up leaves, I stole a glance his way. At first 'twas only the strength o' his arms I was seein' as he pushed the rake fore and back. But the more I see him move 'twas clear he was able, takin' neither a lazy step, nor unsure action.

The longer we worked, the braver I become, at one-point lookin' straight inta his eyes. They was green, like the emerald in the pin me ma always wore with her Sunday best. Their color gave me pause, long enough fer the man ta feel me eyes upon him. He looked me way. I quick dropped me head, but not 'fore I saw a small upturn o'his lips.

Was he smilin' at me then?

I could hardly breathe with all 'twas runnin' through me mind. Knowin' the trouble I'd be in fer not doin' work, I quick scooped up more leaves and joined others shuttlin' ta the wagons.

Ya need ta move away from this man, get yerself on ta another group, I scolded meself.

But turn 'round and head right back I did, daring meself ta look his way yet again.

Movin' toward the center o'the rakin' I come 'longside Angel. She was helpin' another less able at bendin' and gatherin'. The young girl's kindness touched me and I stopped ta help the pair. By the time we was done, the man was gone, moved onta another rakin' spot.

I kept workin' and lookin' fer him as we started on the branches and sticks. Afore I could find him though, the guards was callin' the men together, declarin' the work done and Nurse Stewart was claimin' we women. Me heart sank at the thought o'not seein' the handsome man again.

Then he was there, ta the side of me, walkin' the long way 'round ta his group.

Was he doin' it on purpose? Did he walk 'round ta be able to pass by me?

"What is the matter with you? Why are you standing there like that? I told you to line up."

Nurse Stewart's voice echoed in me ears as she come 'longside and grabbed me arm. Takin' one last chance, I turned me body and cast a glance o'er the crowd of men now walkin' away. As I did, I saw him. He'd turned back as well, this time lookin' straight at me, the same small smile passin' his lips

"Listen here, if you don't want to be taken down the hall, you will get lined up with the rest of the women. Now!"

Nurse Stewart's temper got me movin' quick-like. Yet the only vision in me eyes was that o' the man's gentle smile. As I fell inta step, Maeve whispered me way.

"Are ya alright now, Teagan? You look a bit flushed."

"I'm fine, Maeve. 'Tis kind of you ta ask."

Talkin' amongst us was not allowed, so's I thought twice afore saying anymore right then. 'Twas only later when Maeve and I was together in the ward I found the courage ta say what was runnin' through me mind.

"Maeve, you was married. Tell me, what it's like couplin' with a man?"

"Go on with ya now, Teagan! Have you never had a man in your life?"

Maeve's response made me wish I'd kept me mouth shut. I wasn't tryin 'ta seem an idiot. I just couldn't stop thinkin' 'bout the man in the yard.

"Fer your information, Maeve Mulhern Dempsey, I left me family when I was but 16 and went straight ta work fer Americans with not a man 'round, but a husband. I've been here locked away ever since. So's no, I never had a man in me life, thank ya very much."

Ta me surprise, me words put a stop ta Maeve's manner. 'Stead of mockin' me, she turned kind and carin'.

"I was married to me husband for twenty years and we made four beautiful beibes, but he wasn't the love of me life. No, that special place in me heart was, and will always be, held tight by Colin Fitzpatrick. Colin and me grew up together in Cork. We set side by each in school from the time we was five years of age. We shared our first kiss under the old oak tree outside me family's home and our first date at St. Brigid's church dance. There was no doubt amongst family and friends that me and Colin would one day be husband and wife."

As Maeve spoke everythin' 'bout her changed. The look in her eyes, the sound o'her voice, even the shape o'her body, all of it softened as she turned a beauty. I found meself caught off guard by the change in her bein', none of it surprising me as much as the tears that started droppin' down her cheeks.

"Colin and I were close, mind ya. Close in ways that happen 'tween a woman and a man. Yet bein' good Catholics, we always made sure we stopped our passion 'fore it went too far. Sure'n we wanted our weddin' night ta be special. 'Twas a pledge we'd made as ours 'twas a perfect love we knew nothin' but death could change."

Takin' a deep breath, Maeve turned and looked inta me eyes. I could see the pain 'causing her tears and felt the heartbreak runnin' through her as she went on.

"Colin was two years from havin' ta serve in the Irish Regiment when the war started. He hated the age rule, but every night I got onta me knees and prayed ta God that the war would end afore Colin was called. Sadly, me prayers went unanswered as on his eighteenth birthday, the letter come. 'Twas on the eve of his leavin', we made vows afore God that joined us, sure'n as if we'd been blessed in a church. That night, in the loft o'his uncle's barn, our passions made us one."

Maeve's words left strong images in me mind. I could almost feel the heat passin' 'tween their bodies on that long-ago night. Wantin' ta know more, I started ta speak and ask questions, but the look on Maeve's face kept me still. 'Twas out of respect fer what I could only imagine come next that I stayed silent.

"I give a promise ta Colin ta write every day. He promised the same. In the beginnin' he stayed true ta his word, sendin' regular posts o' love and longin'. Then his letters stopped. I kept tellin' meself 'twas a reason. That he was fightin' the Germans in places where letters couldn't be writ. Then one night while sleepin' I fell inta a deep dream. Colin and I were together, makin' beautiful love. As we lay side by each, him runnin' his fingers through me hair, he kissed the top o'me head and told me I needed ta be strong, ta be ready, 'cause he'd not be comin' home. I begged him ta take back the words, ta pretend he'd never said' em. He smiled and held me tighter, sayin' 'You've got ta be brave me darlin' and carry on fer our daughter, soon ta be born. I can still remember lookin' inta his deeply brown eyes and seein' his love. And then, me good, sweet Colin was gone."

A hush came over us. Meself, I was lost in a swirl of thoughts' 'bout livin and dyin' and all goes in between. I couldn't imagine the pain of lovin' and losin' me soulmate. Too, I was wonderin' if Maeve and Colin's love makin' a beibe was real, or just a dream.

Lookin' at Maeve, I could see she was in her own mind, far from the nightmarish place we was trapped. Nothin' ta do but sit and wait, hopin' she'd soon return. No doubt feelin' pain when she did. "The beibe Colin told me 'bout in the dream came ta be. Our night o' love did indeed make a child. Yet bein' preggers was a disgrace ta me family and so's da sent me off ta live with me aunt and uncle in America. In no uncertain terms, he told me as soon as I birthed the child, I'd be givin' it up fer adoptin'. Then I could come home and no one t'would be the wiser. Me da was not a man ta cross and so's I did just as he said."

Maeve's story took me back ta the time she was first brought ta the cot next ta me own. I remember the first thing she told was o'the death of a beibe girl in her arms, and the sorrow o'her three other children o'er the loss. Now here she was tellin' 'bout the birth of another child. Could it be? 'Twas only a moment afore Maeve continued her tale.

"Me time in America passed quick-like and each day I felt a bond growin' with me beibe. Deep in me heart I knew I could find a way ta keep the child.

So's, I kept prayin' ta Colin fer help. With nary a word ta a soul, I began lookin' fer work and figurin' ways ta take care of both me and me child. In me mind, I could stay in America and make us a life, no matter what me da said. So 'twas when me perfect little girl was born and they laid her on me belly, I named her Colleen. I gathered her up and brought her ta me breast and took a vow we'd ne'er be parted. The two o'us fell asleep, mother and child, wrapped in all the love that had gone inta makin' her.

"When I awoke, me chest was cold, missin' the warmth o'me Colleen's tiny body. I started feelin' 'round the bed, worried that somehow she'd slipped away. Me mind started goin' wild as she was nowheres 'round me. I started screamin' her name, callin' out fer me aunt as well. Next thing I knew me uncle appeared 'longside, speakin' a jumble of words of which I had no understandin'. Yet in his face, I could see the truth. Colleen was gone, taken from me in the dark o'night just as me da had planned. I raised me body outta bed and began beatin' on me uncle, ragin' at him and beggin' him ta tell me where they took me beibe. Grabbin' me wrists he held on, knowin' me birth-weakened body could only go on fer so long. No matter, I kept rantin' 'gainst all of 'em, inside dying from the feelin' t'would never again see me darlin' Colleen. Me fury pushed me ta losing consciousness and from there I lie in bed fer days, sobbin' and wishin' only ta die and be with Colin."

THE TWO OF US HAD BEEN GOIN' on fer a bit when the thought o'the orderlies come ta me mind. I took a look 'round the ward, checkin' if we was bein' watched. From all's I could see, no one was payin' us any mind, stashed 'way in a corner as we were. Feelin' a bit brave, I reached out and touched Maeve's arm, offerin' a gentle pat. 'twas me hope the touch of another might ease her pain in some small way. While she ne'er looked ta me, her words returned

"After all was said n'done I had nothin' but love lost fer me da, so's I made up me mind ta stay in America. Leavin' behind me aunt and uncle, I found work in a garment factory and went ta sharin' a flat with three Irish women, them's workin' in the same place. Me life was simple, work, eat, sleep. 'Twas all I could manage after the pain of losin' Colleen. Then come a day the brother of one of me roommates stopped ta visit. He was handsome with the Irish gift o'gab. Twasn't long 'fore we were datin' and soon married. He wasn't me true love, mind ya. More he filled up the holes in me heart. We made three boys and a decent life and 'twas good enough. When I got preggers again 'twas no doubt in me mind that the beibe was a blessin' direct from God and from Colin. That's why losin' that beibe, me Erin Maureen, it made me lost ta me husband and ta me boys. I was wantin' only ta die and be in heaven with Colin and nothin' and no one could change i

So 'twas, in the corner of the ward, without carin' who could see, me and Maeve Mulherin Dempsey joined up our hands and cried o'er the loss of our lives and our innocence, and fer the souls of her two beautiful beibe girls.

CHAPTER ELEVEN

COMPLETELY ABSORBED in the photograph of she and Nana O'Connor at the Cliffs of Moher, Grace could fully identify with the country's nickname, "The Emerald Isle." Sparkling green was exactly the way Ireland's landscape appeared in the picture.

"Grace did you get those notes from the last board meeting?"

"Grace?"

"Hello? Grace, you in there?"

As Jonathan flopped into the chair beside her desk, Grace realized she'd been mentally MIA from her office in a full-out daydream. Embarrassed and unsure how long she'd been absent, Grace quickly shook off her travel memories.

"I'm sorry Jonathan. Yes, I'm fine. And yes, I did get the notes. Thank you. I've reviewed them and will be fully prepared for my first meeting tonight with the board."

To her relief, Jonathan continued as if everything were normal.

"Great. Now don't be nervous. The board is fully aware that this is only your second week at Wood Haven. They really are a good group of people and all are truly committed to helping our patients mainstream as seamlessly as possible. The best part is that unlike a lot of boards on which I've served—and I'm sure you have too—there aren't any oversized egos here. The governor had a strong hand in selecting the eight men and women who will serve with us through the deinstitutionalization process and I think you'll find them intelligent, experienced and helpful."

Despite her best efforts, Grace was only hearing bits and pieces of Jonathan's words.

It's the photograph. Every time I look at it I feel as if I'm traveling back in time, back to the trip nana and I took to Ireland. It was such a special experience, one I'd give anything to recreate. But since nana is in heaven with papa and the angels. I just need to be grateful that we had the chance to share special memories like this morning we spent at The Cliffs of Moher

"So I'll see you tonight. Six sharp. I try to get people in and out of these meetings in an hour, 90 minutes tops. We'll have to start on time to make that happen."

Grace scribbled the word, "sharp" on her oversized desk calendar where she had already noted the board meeting's date and time. Looking up she gave Jonathan a nod and a smile, which she was pretty sure he never saw as he hustled off to the rest of his day's agenda.

Resettled into the solitude of her office, Grace retrieved a yellow pad from a desk drawer and began writing. She had to be laser focused for tonight's all-important first board meeting. Organizing a presentation list for the meeting would make that happen.

At the top of the page she wrote the board meeting title, date and time. Skipping a line, Grace began a list of introductory items to present, followed by subcategories for specific discussion points. The more she wrote the more immersed she became in her subject matter.

While she had yet to meet the six Wood Haven seniors in her "Faith File" and the four seniors requiring assisted care, Grace had reviewed their medical records and assessments to the point she felt she "knew" them. Taking one last look through their information, she realized tonight would initiate the process of a new beginning for each one of the ten.

Throughout her career, Grace had been involved in numerous advisory sessions with families and with companies on senior life progressions. From downsizing family households to selecting a retirement home, making assisted life care decisions, setting personal medical guidelines and preplanning memorial services, none of the stages were easy, as all of them represented end of life choices.

The difference in this situation was that Grace's ultimate recommendations would lead to a revival of lives more than an end. It was a very different situation, one in which Grace was determined to succeed. Her seniors deserved a new start after the decades they had endured at Wood Haven. Even without meeting them, they already held a special place in her heart. That's why she was going to do everything in her power to ensure the support they would need to adjust to and enjoy their remaining years outside these walls that had imprisoned them for so long.

Continuing to refine her presentation, Grace moved through five pages of the yellow legal pad. When finally, she deemed herself prepared, she glanced at the clock.

4:48pm. How did that happen? The entire afternoon. Gone.

A rumble from the pit of Grace's stomach made it clear that dinner before the board meeting was mandatory. With the Wood Haven cafeteria closing at 2pm and nothing else but vending machine options on campus, she would have to make a quick drive to town, grab some dinner and get back before the rest of the committee arrived.

Grace had long ago established a pattern of arriving early to important meetings. The luxury of observing others as they filtered into a board room provided her with a certain confidence. And while she wasn't really nervous about her inaugural presentation to the Wood Haven Board, she wanted to approach it from the most self-assured perspective.

Allowing a final five minutes to take one lasts look at her notes, Grace collected her yellow legal pad and her senior files and deposited them safely into her timeworn leather briefcase. The bag had been a gift from her nana and papa when she was hired for her first job. Flipping open a matching black leather portfolio, gifted by her grandparents upon her first promotion, Grace gave a quick check for blank paper and two pens. Always two pens. It was a backup routine she'd learned in observing her mother prepping for court. Finally, confident that all was in order, Grace slid the portfolio into her briefcase and headed to the car.

The summer day was bright and warm despite the late afternoon hour. Grace opened her sun roof and turned up the music as she drove the five miles into Midland. The fresh air coupled with the strong beat of Donna Summer's hit, "Let's Dance" erased all thoughts from Grace's mind. Suddenly she was a back-up singer, harmonizing at the top of her lungs with the famous Disco Queen.

Blowing by the, "Midland Township, Where History is a Way of Life" billboard in a state of disco distraction, Grace was oblivious to the road sign announcing a reduced speed limit of thirty miles per hour. As she belted out the song's lyrics in pitch perfect tone, she was stunned to look up and see a red light flashing in her rearview mirror. Pulling over, she turned off the radio and gave her hair a quick smooth.

"License and registration, please m'am".

"Certainly officer," Pulling the gray suede tri-fold case out of her glove compartment, Grace removed her car's registration from the clear plastic holder. Digging through her briefcase, she found her black leather wallet and pulled out her New York State license.

"Out of towner, eh Ms Reid?"

For the first time, Grace actually looked at the policeman. He was tall. The only thing she could immediately see was the heavy leather gun belt commandeering her open window space. Craning her neck upwards, Grace was further frustrated by the officer's reflective sunglasses shaded by an oversized black hat.

Hmmppff, obviously not one of the good guys. Ok Grace, just play the new resident card. With any luck it'll get you off without a ticket.

"Yes officer, actually I am from out of the area, but I just moved to Midland."

Without missing a beat, the uniformed man shot back, "Well then, have you filed for your official change of residence license, Ms. Reid?"

Clearly this was not going in the direction she hoped.

Come on, Grace, get a grip. This guy is a small-town cop. Answer his questions and if he writes a ticket, so be it. You've got more important things to do.

Looking up again, this time she noticed the policeman's name badge.

"I'm sorry, officer, um, Healy is it? I wasn't exactly clear when I said I've just *moved* to Midland. I'm actually here professionally, working as a consultant. I'll only be living in Midland for the next seven months, 'til the end of the year."

Grace no more than spoke the words and the policeman dropped down to her eye level. Removing his sunglasses, he broke into a welcoming smile that started in his gray-green eyes and spread through his dimpled cheeks.

"I know who you are. You're that woman hired to help with the senior citizens out at Wood Haven. Word is you are pretty darn good at what you do. I sure hope you can help those folks. I've been on a few emergency calls out there and it breaks my heart to see them wasting away like they've been."

Grace felt as if she was riding a roller coaster hanging on for dear life. One minute she was being rousted by Andy of Mayberry, the next she was being hailed as the savior of the senior citizen world. Either way, she needed to get some food in her belly and get back to her board meeting.

Just as she was about to answer the officer, hunger pangs rumbled up from her stomach, echoing loudly through the car. Embarrassment flooded across her face in a hot red flash.

"Thank you, officer. I am going to do my best to help them. In fact, I have a very important meeting tonight at Wood Haven but first, and most obviously, I have to get something to eat."

"Yes m'am, sounds as if you do," he answered in a sincere tone capped by a slight grin. Close-up and with his glasses off, Grace could see this was a man of early mid-age with an edge of kindness in his eyes.

"You might want to try the Dew Drop Inn for your meal. It's off the beaten path, on Hopkins St., just two blocks up and one block to the right. Good food and real reasonable prices. And do me a favor, please, Ms. Reid. Slow down from now on when you come in to town."

With that, Officer Healy handed Grace her license and registration and replaced his sunglasses in their uniformed place. With a smile and a "Have a good night" he turned and walked back to his squad car.

Maybe there's something to be said for living in a rural town with cops like Andy Taylor.

Tucking away her license and registration, Grace followed the officer's directions to the Dew Drop Inn. Exactly as described, the restaurant appeared at the end of the first block on Hopkins Street. Constructed of wood beams, the restaurant was cabin-like in appearance, with a screened-in porch that ran along the entire front of the building. Parking her car in a side lot, Grace entered through a weathered screen door.

The interior was dark, especially in contrast to the sun-filled day. Grace paused to let her eyes adjust. Within seconds, she realized she was standing on the edge of a dining area. It was a good-sized space with a curved bar taking up the entire far wall. The rest of the room was filled with tables for four, each covered with oil cloth fabric in a red-checked design. Overhead fan lights whirred in sync with rock-and-roll tunes blaring from the juke box. Half-a-dozen patrons were entrenched on bar stools with two tables of early-bird diners alongside. Not a waitress or server in sight. Only a middle-aged bartender refilling glasses

Grace's experience with one of Midland's Finest had eaten into her dinner time. To get back to Wood Haven on schedule, she was going to have to order take out. Assessing her best option, Grace headed to the bar.

"Afternoon. What can I getcha?"

"Good afternoon. I was hoping I might be able to order some food to go?"

Disinterest filtered across the bartender's face as he processed zero bar sales and probably no tip from this woman who was, undoubtedly, an out of towner. Quickly sizing up the situation, Grace amended her request.

"But while I look over a menu, I'd love a glass of wine."

Again, the bartender proffered a less-than-enthusiastic look, this time with a reply.

"I got white or pink. Pick your poison"

Thinking better of her choice, Grace again switched gears. "Let's try a beer instead. I'll have a Bud."

With a tolerable nod, the bartender deposited a menu and an open bottle of beer before her. He then returned to his regulars at the far end of the bar.

Guess there's no chance of a glass for my beer.

Grace had never developed a taste for the brewer's blend of hops and barley and she actually had no idea what she'd just ordered. She'd heard the name "Bud" on commercials during her hometown, Buffalo Bills football games. She watched the Bills faithfully from September through December, and sometimes into January if they made the playoffs.

If it's good enough for my hometown team, it's got to be decent, right?

One big sip and Grace was reminded of her papa's favorite "when you assume" saying. Fortunately, the bartender and his regulars were far enough away they didn't notice her gag reflex as she attempted to swallow a healthy swig.

Ok, let's just move on and pray to God there's something on the menu I can eat.

The rudimentary, single-sided bill of fare gave Grace little hope. Yet as she reviewed the specials of the day, she was delighted to find offerings that actually sounded good. The question was, would their taste match their descriptions?

Grace decided to order the burger of the day. It was topped with cheese and bacon and included a side of fries. While she didn't necessarily need all the calories, she figured she would be safe sticking with the basics. Flagging down the bartender, Grace ordered and then sat back, pretending to enjoy her beer.

As time passed, patrons filled in around Grace's barstool. The tenor and tone of their greetings made it clear pretty most all of them were regulars. Soon, snippets of town business and local gossip filled the room. Grace did her best to appear casual while trying to catch the conversations weaving around her. It was going pretty well until the man next to her started a rather loud group conversation, which suddenly included the bartender.

"Well I don't know what you all think, but I don't want any part of them people out at Wood Haven coming into our town."

Grace froze in place. Had she somehow misheard the man's statement? She became even more paralyzed as the man next to her offered his reply.

"Now Bill, no sense getting yourself all riled up. You know the mayor said nothing has been decided *yet,* and nothing will be decided 'til the town board has all the information. And at the end of the day, they have the right to approve it, or they can fight against it."

"Well they better be fightin', or the mayor and all them town board people are gonna be voted out of office the next election. I'll see to it myself."

Grace tried to calm her thoughts and make sense of all she was hearing. They weren't talking about the mainstreaming plan for her Wood Haven seniors, were they? She wasn't anywhere near ready to formulate or share it with the board members. So how could the bartender at the Dew Drop Inn be discussing it? And why in such an argumentative way?

"Here ya go, lady. That'll be four bucks, including the beer."

Sizzling smells of a juicy burger and crisp fries turned the entire bar area mouth-wateringly pungent. As for the translucent grease stains seeping through the to-go brown bag, it was clear this was going to be a three-napkin feast.

Between her scrambled thoughts on the bar conversation and her growling stomach, Grace struggled to pull out her wallet and pay the bill, adding a $1 tip for her bartender host.

"Keep the change," she said as she picked up her dinner and slid off the bar stool.

"Hey thanks, lady. That's generous of ya. Come back again, anytime."

Exiting the restaurant, Grace stood for a moment in the parking lot to collect her thoughts. Whatever it was she'd just heard at that bar, she was pretty sure it was more about the fine citizens of her temporary "hometown" than she really wanted to know.

Suddenly the thought of food made Grace feel sick to her stomach. Dropping the brown bag in a nearby garbage can, she got in her car and headed back to Wood Haven. After hearing those negative comments, Grace sensed it was crucial to review all her files once more before the board meeting.

If a fight was what it was going to take to help the Wood Haven seniors move on to new lives, then Grace was going to make damn sure she was prepared to do battle.

Chapter Twelve

WOOD HAVEN ADMITTANCE FORM

Patient: *Emeline D'Chantre*
Date of Admittance: *July 14, 1930*
Number: *07143034*
Age: *34*
Ethnicity: *French*
Marital Status: *Single*
Pregnancies: *None*
Diagnosis: *Mentally Deranged with Periodic Fits*

ALL ME CHILDHOOD I SLEPT with me sisters, five o'us spread 'cross two narrow beds. Bein' youngest, 'twas times I struggled fer space and air gettin' squished among 'em. So's havin' me own room in the Engler's attic—me own bed, me own dresser and none pickin' through me things—'twas like bein' rich beyond me dreams. 'Twas also why when they forced me inta this place, draggin' me from a windowless cell and dumpin' me inta a dormitory of a hundred or more women, 'twas like bein' buried without a death.

Twasn't just the number of women sharin' the room, but more the moanin' and sleep talkin' that went on through the night. As well, there was them wanderin' and gropin'. As God is me witness, there was nights when not an hour passed but some woman was trying ta climb onta me cot and steal anything worth havin', including me private parts.

At first, I felt badly 'pushin' 'em off, while tryin' ta make sure they didn't fall onta the floor. But I learned quick-like these women weren't right in the head and usin' anythin' less than me full force kept 'em comin' back.

'Twas a night like that when Emeline first arrived. I didn't see her with me own eyes when they brung her in, but me and everyone else could hear the woman. I didn't understand a word she was sayin', but the tone of her voice let me know she was bein' drug through the hallway 'gainst her will.

"Je suis tout à fait bien. Vous avez das le droit de me garder ici. Je veux communiquer avec mes parents immédiatement afin qu'ils peuvent me virer de l'argent pour rentrer à la maison."

In the black o'night, the woman's fearful sounds went ta echoin' off the asylum walls. Her odd words started me wonderin' 'bout the look o' her and if me thoughts might match her bein'. I lay awake waitin' fer an orderly ta unlock the hall door and shove her inta the dormitory. As it went, I fell asleep waitin,' as she ne'er appeared.

In the light of day, I wondered where they'd taken the woman, but stopped thinkin' as memories of me own solitary nights bolted tight in a cell 'twas more than I wanted. All's I knew was if ever again I were ta hear her voice, I'd know her.

Days and nights passed 'fore the woman was finally brought inta the ward. The orderlies blathered that she was a French woman by the name o' Emeline. They also said she'd been locked away, so's none could bother her. Ta my way o'thinkin' 'twas more they were afraid o'what she might stir up 'in the rest o'us.

Like all who come new, the woman was chained ta a bench. She sat quiet-like, lookin' unsure o'just where she might be and why. No doubt they gave her needles, like they'd done ta me, tryin' ta keep her quiet and change her way of thinkin'. When finally she opened her mouth, askin' fer a bit of water, I was surprised hearin' words I knew. They was wrapped in an accent mind ya, and mixed with ones I'd never heard, but she was most clearly speakin' English.

As time went on and the needles wore off, Emeline kept gettin' stronger, talkin' more every day. She was a direct speaker, if you know what I mean, tellin' 'bout politics and religion and private things that mam always said should be spoke only 'tween a man and a woman. But no matter if ya liked what she was sayin' or not, she made it hard not ta listen.

When finally they left her unchained, Emeline went right after everyone, tellin' all she didn't belong locked away and demandin' ta be set free. Each day she bossed the orderlies ta write her family in France, so's they could send money fer her ta go home. All's they did was laugh in her face and ignore her, or worse, say that her family cared not a whit. No matter, Emeline kept rantin' with her demands and her racy stories.

The thing was, the longer she carried on, the less her words mattered. Still, there was somethin' 'bout the woman 'twas curious ta me. Perhaps the clothes she let wear. Her own, fine in material and design, stylish like Mrs. Engler fancied. Not the rough-cloth rags worn by the rest o'us.

Then there was things she chattered 'bout when she wasn't rantin'—famous people and places she'd known. Fer most, I figured she was makin' it up, but as time went on, Emeline's stories proved real by a small silk bag tucked in the hem o' her knickers. In it she kept folded-up pictures, most of herself and rich people in their mansions 'round the world. Then there was the picture she treasured most. 'Twas her mother and father on their weddin' day in Paris. The woman's eyes misted whenever she showed it 'round.

In time, Emeline quit rantin' and went ta sittin' in the porch by the ward, starin' 'tween the iron-barred windows. Twasn't sure if she was tired from all her talkin' or if she was tryin' ta figure a way out. At first, I left her ta herself, but when she'd gone silent a few days, I pulled a chair 'longside and asked her ta tell me 'bout Paris.

The woman started sharin' tales o'life and her family. How she'd come ta America with blessin's from her parents. She said her da would come get her if he knew where she was. She just needed ta write home.

Tweren't long afore she told how she come ta bein' locked away. Like many o'the day, The Crash had done her in. She'd been workin' at a fancy private school, teachin' French and makin' her way on the kindness of the wealthy, them's who liked her manners and her fancy clothes. Once all the people started losin' their money though, they couldn't afford the cost o'their sons and daughters in private schoolin'.

Emeline lost her teachin' job but got lucky findin' another in a bakery. She went ta decoratin' cakes and the like, as she'd learned from her grand-mère. Then, same as the school, the bakery lost customers and had ta close its doors.

This time Emeline found not a bit o'work. Twasn't long afore she was forced ta go ta the local poor house ta survive. 'Twas there her high-class ways got her pegged as a troublemaker and she got shuffled onta a wagon of troublemakers, all sent ta this place ta be locked away.

One day as I made me way ta the spot on the porch that she favored, Emeline wasn't waitin'. Unsure, I stayed fer a bit afore goin' and checkin' with a nurse. She told me Emeline was sent off ta another floor and wouldn't be back fer some time.

I didn't like it. I didn't like it one bit. People didn't just get moved 'round. There was always somethin', some reason, fer a person ta be disappearin', and 'twas never good. Last time a poor soul had gone, like Emeline, they was odd-like when they come back. 'Twas as if their soul'd been robbed and tweren't nothin' left but an empty shell. That was me fear fer Emeline and it kept me awake thru many a night.

WHEN FINALLY AN ORDERLY BRUNG the poor woman back ta the ward, first thing I noticed was the way she was kinda slumped . . . not on a bench but in a wheelchair. I found meself a seat and pulled it 'longside. That's when I saw the straps keepin' Emeline's body from fallin'.

It took a minute ta get my wits 'bout me, never havin' seen a soul in such a state. As I sat, it seemed the woman was more statue than alive and, as God is me witness, I come ta realize the shock musta happened ta her.

I'd heard orderlies talk that electric was bein' used when people got took down the hall. I didn't understand it all meself, but seein' Emelin like a dead woman made me know that it had happened.

I tried talkin' ta her, sweet and soft-like. I thought maybe me voice might spark somethin' in her brain.

Nothin'. Not even a glimmer in her eyes.

I felt a kinda sickness comin' up from me stomach and through me throat but I didn't dare take ill. Not 'less I wanted the nurses ta be reportin' me, or worse. So's, I did what me mam always did when any of us kids was feelin' poorly. I started singin'. Not loud, mind ya. Only enough fer me and Emeline ta hear.

> "Too-ra-loo-ra-loo-ral, Too-ra-loo-ra-li,
> Too-ra-loo-ra-loo-ral, hush now, don't you cry!
> Too-ra-loo-ra-loo-ral, Too-ra-loo-ra-li,
> Too-ra-loo-ra-loo-ral, that's an Irish lullaby

Singin' by memory, I swore I could feel me mam's arms round me, strokin' me hair and holdin' me hands. 'Twas a bit overwhelmin' and tears began tricklin'. I reached in me pocket fer a rag I kept as a hanky and that's' when I saw it, saw Emeline was still there.

Just like me, she was cryin', gentle tears fallin' on her hands tied 'cross her lap. I took me hanky and wiped the poor thing's tears, no matter if the orderlies would see us or not.

With me last dab, Emeline turned ta me and stared. Not scared lookin', mind ya, but the look of a person tryin' ta *be*, and grateful fer anyone helpin'. I smiled, lookin' right back at her, hoping me eyes would say words her mind could hear. She didn't smile but gave me a bit o' a nod—enough ta let me know she was still in there, somewhere.

'Twas then I knew, Emeline was mine ta save. All's I needed was the courage ta do whatever it was she needed.

I started with somethin' I supposed she might enjoy—tellin' 'bout da and me goin' fishing' off the wharf one summer's eve. Twasn't nothin' all that special 'bout the tale, 'cept that bein one of eight, time alone with me da was few and far between. 'Twas also a funny bit o'somethin' in that we both ended up in the drink, as I hooked a fish too big ta reel, but was too stubborn not ta try. As the fish began pullin' me inta the water, da grabbed me pole ta keep me planted, but he ended up fallin' in right alongside me.

Somewheres through me storytellin' I noticed Emeline tryin ta turn more towards me. Not a movin' of her whole body, mind ya, more a leanin' in ta be sure she didn't miss any bit or piece. Seein' that made me know she was hearin' me words, still wantin' the two o'us ta share stories. So's, I picked it up a bit, adding some commotion here and a bit o' fun there, whatever I could imagine might catch the poor woman's fancy.

When I got ta where da and me fell inta the ocean, I took a tumble out of me chair fer special effect. As hoped, Emeline gave the slightest hint of a smile, don'cha know.

Sadly we didn't get further, as one of the orderlies come barrelin' over thinkin' that a fit or some such thing had unseated me. When he stooped ta gather me up and found me laughin' he got right bent and started fussin'.

"What is the matter with you? Do you think it's funny to pretend you're sick or hurt? Do you know how fast I ran over here? I could have slipped or fallen. And all the time you were playing some foolish game. I should report you for this.'

Them's the words none of us ever wanted ta hear—bein' reported. Once it happened you earned a one-way docket down the hall. I'd learned quick-like ta stay away from orderlies and nurses, so's I'd never get reported. Now here I was, on the brink.

"Sorry, mister," I said in me most sorrowful fashion. "I was just tryin ta make Emeline here smile a bit."

"Well you might as well stop because it's going to be a very long time, if ever, before she will be able to smile, or anything else. Can't you see, she's sick? The doctors are treating her and if you've got any sense, you'll leave her alone."

"Yes, sir. Sorry, sir," 'twas all I could muster in reply. Twasn't sure if I was more scared or angry. Either way, I knew 'twas best ta curb me Irish.

As the man walked away, I looked ta Emeline. She'd pulled herself back inta the wheelchair, away from me. Yet I could still see her face and new tears tricklin'.

"Aw, don'cha be lettin' him upset ya now, Emeline. He's just a crabby old man who doesn't know a thing. You're goin' ta be right as rain in no time, I promise. And I'll come every day ta tell ya stories. Would you like that now?"

Minutes passed 'tween us with nary sound nor motion. Then, in the slightest way, Emeline give a nod. I took her hand up in mine. It was cold, frozen-like, as if there was no blood atal runnin' through her veins. And that's how we sat 'til the night orderlies moved us ta the dormitory.

Next mornin' I went lookin' for Emeline, but she was nowhere ta be found. I went ta the same spot where we'd sat the day afore, and the next day, and the next and the next. Never once was she there. This time I didn't ask the nurses anythin', fearin' me curiosity might make it worse fer Emeline, as well as meself. Then finally they returned her again ta the ward.

Truth be told, I wasn't fully sure 'twas her. She looked so different, her face shriveled in a way. Her eyes set in a squint, like she was frownin' all the time. Worse yet, she was twitchin' in her hands and her arms, in her whole body. 'Twas beyond sad ta see the woman this way. Not bein' able ta stand it, I said somethin' ta the nurse at the ward desk.

"What is it be hurting' Emeline so bad she can't sit still?"

"We're not allowed to discuss anyone's medical issues," the nurse answered in a high and mighty manner. "The doctors are taking care of her and that's all you need to know."

May have been all I needed ta know, but I could see fer meself that whatever they was doin' ta the poor woman was makin' her worse, more causin' her problems than helpin' 'em.

I only saw Emeline once more after that. She was sittin' strapped in a chair, not lookin' at anyone or thing, stayin' silent. There were a stiff smile stuck on her face, as if she were enjoyin' some private kinda joke. Drool ran from a crooked opening o'her twisted mouth and down her chin. Her clothes were soiled and tattered, not atal the finery she'd once wore. Her hair was matted in clumps and her arms bruised from straps that kept her in place durin' whatever evil they was doin' ta the woman down the hall.

No matter how I tried sharin' stories, Emeline's eyes stayed empty. Finally, leanin' close I whispered, "Don't ya worry, darlin'. I'll make sure your da knows where ya are."

With that I slid me hand inta the hem o'her knickers, hopin' 'gainst hope. When I felt the soft silk, I took hold o'the bag and pulled it quick-like, 'fore anyone saw me do the deed. With me heart poundin', I tucked it inta me own private place. Then placin' a quick kiss on Emeline's cheek, I stood and left her.

I went back ta me cot and stayed through the day and night, and the next day to come. No one noticin' or mindin', long as I didn't fuss. I couldn't bear seein' Emeline like that any longer. Lyin' quiet by meself was the only way I could figure ta escape the pain, hers and me own.

When again I made me way ta the ward, Emeline was missin' and not a soul spoke o'her. 'Twas as if she'd never been. That's when I made me vow. Someday I'd get silk bag o'photographs ta her family. Somehow I'd find a way. They needed ta have them, so's they'd know.

Chapter Thirteen

Grace's head was pounding.

The Wood Haven Board meeting had gone well, but like any first-time gathering there were moments of tension within the group.

As she sat in wait for the meeting to begin, Grace reviewed her presentation plan of a direct approach. She had no concern about gaining power or taking command of the board. She simply cared about the future of Wood Haven's remaining patients and wanted the ability to set and administer the deinstitutionalization policies for all ten of her seniors.

My seniors.

Grace was surprised by the strong sense of professional responsibility she already felt toward Wood Haven's elder patients. The connection began when she first read the reports Jonathan sent her weeks ago, documenting the decades of heinous treatments enforced upon the nine women and one man. As she delved more deeply into each senior's file, detailed explanations of the toxic care they'd survived began to haunt her personally in recurring nightmares. Added to that, the strange turn of events she'd experienced at the Dew Drop Inn that afternoon and by the time Jonathan introduced Grace to the board, she was primed and ready. Perhaps a bit too ready.

She began with a thank you to Jonathan for inviting her to become part of Wood Haven's deinstitutionalization operation. She then moved on to a brief summary of her job experience and expertise. From there it was an easy roll into the reasons she had accepted Wood Haven's employment offer and her preliminary plans for working with her six "Faith File" seniors and her four in need of long-term care.

The longer Grace spoke and the more information she detailed, the more forceful she became. It was wasn't until she began thumping on her presentation folder in cadence with her words that Grace realized she needed to take a deep breath. However, by then, facial expressions around the board room table clearly communicated it was too late. She had crossed the line of business decorum into the land of politically incorrect.

"Well Grace, thank you for that, um . . . *powerful* presentation." Jonathan's hesitation reflected the uncomfortable silence that had enveloped the board room. Trying to salvage the moment, he continued, "I know you are passionate about doing the best for our seniors, and that was certainly evident in your words this evening."

Oh good lord. What have I done? In all my years I have never been unprofessional in a meeting. What's wrong with me?

Within the discomfort of the room, Grace tried to quickly assess her most proactive course of action. Should she apologize? Offer an explanation? If she did offer an explanation, what would it be? Maybe the best thing to do was to just lock her lips and slink away from the meeting, hoping for a fresh start the next time the board convened.

In the midst of her panic, Grace received a lifeline. A stylish woman at the opposite end of the meeting table leaned in, as if trying to gap the distance between them. With a smile that suggested a certain wisdom, the woman spoke.

"Grace, I must say I admire your passion. So many times I attend board meetings where people talk about their project, or work to be accomplished, in a completely uninspiring manner. Tonight I think you gave us all a lot to think about in how to best care for these Wood Haven seniors. "

Wait, what? Was this woman . . . what was her name again . . . I can't remember right now . . . was she actually praising my presentation? Ok, maybe this is my chance to make it better. Maybe I just need to be honest and let the chips fall where they may.

"Thank you so much, Melissa," the woman's name came to mind as soon as Grace began speaking. "I appreciate your kind words. Actually though, I need to apologize for my presentation this evening. While I am definitely passionate when it comes to the elderly and their life issues, the circumstances here at Wood Haven are different from the kind of projects I traditionally undertake. Truthfully, I was nowhere near prepared for the case files I have reviewed over this last week. The long-term treatment of these patients is unimaginable and their stories have touched me to the core of my being."

As she spoke, this time in a quietly controlled manner, Grace noticed the board members turning towards her. She read their collective body language as a positive, which encouraged her to continue.

"Honestly though, what fired me up this evening, perhaps to the point of being a bit unprofessional, is something I experienced outside of Wood Haven's walls. Earlier tonight, I went to a restaurant in Midland for dinner. The Dew Drop Inn. While waiting for my food, I was on the fringe of a conversation that took place at the bar. From all appearances, those speaking were town residents. At least in their interactions they all seemed to know each other. While I am not usually an eavesdropper, when I heard them talking about Wood Haven, I couldn't resist."

At this point the entire board became re-engaged. Grace had their full attention and a second chance to effectively state her cause. Not wanting to ruin the opportunity, she took a deep breath, which seemed to reflexively encourage the same in everyone around the table. Heartened, Grace began again.

"What transpired next at the Dew Drop was a pointed and fairly hostile conversation about Wood Haven and our deinstitutionalization plans, led by the bartender, Bill I believe is his name. He went so far as to say that he wanted no part of any of our residents coming into his community. Honestly though, it wasn't as much what the people discussing our seniors had to say, as the way they said it. Almost with a hateful venom. All I could think of was the pain our Wood Haven seniors have already endured for so many years and now to have this kind of nastiness showered down on them, for no reason other than unsubstantiated fears of being around people who have spent time in an asylum—it was heartbreaking. I was so disturbed that I left the restaurant and came directly to this board room to wait for our meeting. I guess in that time, I got pretty worked up over the whole thing. So, I want to apologize if my presentation was a bit intense ."

At the last of her words, a collective chuckle circulated around the boardroom table. The uncomfortable silence, which only moments earlier had chilled the room, was melting into a cascade of relief. The board members leaned back in their chairs, most of them smiling over the positive impact of Grace's unrehearsed speech

"Grace, thank you for telling us about your experience in Midland." The speaker was an older man, sitting to the left of Jonathan. She recalled his name as Driscoll. Henry Driscoll. His dress of a suitcoat and tie led Grace to imagine him as a former corporate executive, now donating his retirement time to volunteer work. In the early part of her presentation, Henry's demeanor had been ramrod straight, his expression stoic. Now looking directly her way, a warm smile crossed his face.

"I have been part of the not-for-profit sector for more years than you have been alive, most of that time working with challenged adults. I know first-hand the kind of behavior you experienced at the Dew Drop today and how disconcerting such negative attitudes can be. My best advice is to put those kinds of individuals and their reactions to the side—don't focus on them. Rather, work to create a public message that will help educate people about the benefits of our residents becoming part of their community. It won't be easy. In fact, I'd hazard a guess there will be moments you'll go so far as to write resignation letters to all of us gathered here tonight. But based on the fire in your belly that you just showed, I don't think any of us doubt you are up to the task."

As Henry delivered the last of his words, a heartening round of applause filled the meeting space. Stunned, Grace cast her eyes around the room, seeing admiration and support in the actions and appearances of every board member. Clearly, they believed she could lead Wood Haven's seniors to new lives.

Jonathan wound up the meeting by opening the floor to questions. When none were raised, he adjourned those gathered to his adjacent office for the board's usual refreshments of beer, wine and popcorn.

Grace wanted desperately to grab a glass of wine in each hand and gulp them straight down. However, having just regained the support of the board, she decided to bypass the potential for any further mishaps. Instead she made the rounds, saying good night and thanking each one of the eight members for their understanding and support.

Back in her office, Grace set her meeting notes and files on the desk, next to the stack of folders she'd spent the day reviewing. Normally, she would put everything away in its proper place for the new day to come.

"Not tonight, Gracie Mae."

The words echoed through her mind as if papa were standing beside her. It was his favorite phrase and one he used whenever she begged for one more horsey ride or one last cookie before bed. She didn't know where the name came from. Her middle name was Elizabeth, after her mother's younger sister. Added to that, her mother absolutely hated the name Gracie. Any time anyone used the shortened version, Grace's mother would pointedly correct them in a manner that always embarrassed her daughter. Thankfully tonight, there was no one to interfere with her enjoyment in recalling papa speaking his special name for his favorite granddaughter.

Oh papa, I may be in over my head this time. These seniors have been so abused and they deserve so much better in the time they have left. But I'm not sure I'm up to fighting the community battles it seems I'm going to have to face. And what if I can't reach the seniors themselves? What if I can't connect with them and help them know they can trust me? How I wish you were here to talk with and advise me.

As if in the room, Grace heard her papa's voice echoing through her mind.

But I am here, Grace, just as I've always been. Nana too. You're just tired. It's been a long day. Leave your work on the desk, turn off your office lights and go home. And have sweet dreams, Gracie Mae. Dreams with no worries. Nana and I will be watching over.

And that's exactly what Grace did, without further care or worry. As she snuggled down into her bed, thoughts of Nana and Papa O'Connor filled her mind as she drifted off to sleep and into dreams that were sweet and comforting.

Chapter Fourteen

WOOD HAVEN ADMITTANCE FORM

Patient: *Gabrielle Liberty Filipek*
Date of Admittance: *September 12, 1932*
Number: *09123232*
Age: *32*
Ethnicity: *French Canadian*
Marital Status: *Single*
Children: *None.*
Diagnosis: *Political Excitement, Vicious Vices in Young Life*

'TWAS ONE THING 'BOUT bein' locked away. Ya was ne'er sure o'the day or the time. Early on, 'twas was hard on me soul, 'specially when it come ta thinkin' 'bout home and me family. I was but a young woman o'seventeen when I was carted off ta this godfersaken place. Truth be told, I've not a clear idea how old I might be at this point, as there's nary a way ta trace the passin'o'time.

I remember birthdays when me mam would bake me favored apple cake with custard sauce. Me da would light the candles while me brothers and sisters went ta singin' "Happy Birthday" at the top o'their lungs. Now I haven't a clue when me birthday comes 'round. No sense o'months or years since bein' here, locked away.

Me sadness over such things changed when Gabrielle Liberty Filipek come along and made herself welcome as family.

Liberty was drug in one early mornin' afore lamps was lit and doors unbolted. None of it kept her from raisin' a ruckus though, loud enough ta raise the dead.

"Get your filthy hands offa me. You've got no right pushing me around like this."

Her words echoin' through the building was what woke me from a sound sleep. Unsure o'what I was hearin' I sat up, listenin and tryin' ta imagine all 'twas goin' on. That's when I heard noises soundin' like a crashin' o'bodies on the other side o'the dormitory wall and more shoutin'

"I don't care what you do to me. You'll not break the spirit of Gabrielle Liberty Filipek."

Next I know, the dormitory door come flyin' open. A coupla burly orderlies come tossin' a woman inta the room, right acrost the cots where bodies lie sleepin'. As they slammed shut the door I could hear 'em laughing evil-like and one of 'em saying, "That ought to take care of the bitch for a while."

Hadn't a clue who the woman might be, but 'twas angry o're the way she'd been treated—mean and hurtful—like meself and others here, bound 'gainst our will

Maeve and me and a few others made our way over ta the floor where the woman's body'd bounced and landed. She was layin' odd, like a ragdoll been pushed and pulled too many ways. Takin' a look 'round fer anyone might make trouble and seein' none, I bent down ta the woman and stuck me fingers 'longside her neck. Sure as I was standin' she had blood coursin' though her veins.

I put me hands under her arms while Maeve took hold o'her legs and we moved the poor thing over ta a row o'cots 'gainst the concrete wall. About the time me arms was ready ta give out, we come ta an empty cot and raised the woman up onto it.

The two of us stood and watched her fer a bit, wonderin' what best ta do. She was long and lean and looked like it'd been a month o' Sundays since she'd had a bath or a clean set o'clothes. Then again, most locked away in the filth of this place weren't lookin' much better.

Decidin' it be best ta let her rest, we started back ta our own cots. That's when the woman give a moan and a'movin' o'her arms. 'Twas only a few seconds afore the poor things eyes come halfway open. Then, as me da used ta say, all hell broke loose.

The woman shot offa the cot like a bullet from a rifle. Spinnin' 'round like a dervish she started yellin', "Where am I? Where is this place?"

I did me best ta talk ta her, but 'twas as if her brain was too filled with fear ta hear me.

"T'is alright now dearie, settle down. You're in a dormitory with only us women. No one here's gonna hurt ya now."

I kept sayin' the same thing over and over ta her, keepin' me voice quiet-like, while Maeve was doin' her best to keep others around from getting' too stirred up. Finally, saints be praised, the woman slowed down her spinnin' and shoutin'. When at last she stopped dead, she took a deep stare inta me eyes. 'Twas a bit frightenin' and, truth be told, 'twasn't quite sure whether ta stay or ta run. Made no never mind as before I could choose she quick took hold o'me hand and pulled me close, nose ta nose, her sour breath chokin' me own.

"Who. Are. You?" She said, spittin' out each word out in a forceful whisper.

"Me name's Tegan. Teagan Cormick."

"Where am I?"

"Locked up in a dormitory in an asylum. What place and where, I've not a clue."

"How did *you* get here?"

"Tossed in a paddy wagon, carted off and locked away. How long ago, can't rightly say."

Me answer seemed ta give the woman pause as she quit talkin' fer a bit and loosened-up her grip.

Straight away I stepped back, feelin' a bit woozy from the heat o'her stinkin' breath on me. I felt Maeve come up next ta me and together we stood watchin' and waitin' for what might come next. Seemed the woman was tirin', like a child wearin' down and needin' a nap. Then just as quick, she went ta talkin' again.

"My name is Gabrielle Liberty Filipek. Gabrielle is for my grandmother who came to America from French Quebec. Liberty is from my mother's love of her adopted American homeland. Filipek, well Filipek was the last name of my father from Poland who left my mother before I was born and never returned."

'Twas surprisin' the woman went ta sharin' bits n'pieces 'bout her life right off. 'twas as if she was needin' the words outta her mind. As she finished speakin', she moved back ta the cot 'gainst the wall and gave way. I took steps toward her, watchin' ta make sure she wasn't goin' ta spring up again in some kinda rage. The closer I got, the more I could see any bit of energy she had remainin' was helpin' her breathe, in and out.

"Gabrielle?"

She moved not a bit.

"Gabrielle? Can ya hear me?"

At last her eyes opened and her head turned ta me just a piece. Still not a word passed o'er her lips.

"Ya need ta stay here on this cot and be quiet-like. Gather your strength so's you can manage ta get up when the orderlies come 'long. Me and Maeve here will help ya get through ta breakfast and the ward. Then we'll make a plan ta keep ya safe from the nasty things that can happen ta a body 'round this place."

Whether she heard me words I can't rightly say, but stay on the cot she did, not movin' as much as an inch. When the orderlies come 'round in the daylight, Maeve and me made our way over ta the woman and helped raise her onta her feet. Together we got on, through the toilets and inta the dining hall where's we sit down by Angel. The three of us acted like a bit of a shield around Gabrielle as she made short work of the watery gruel.

WHEN THE TIME COME, we guided Gabrielle ta the ward, settin' her down on a bench in a far corner, out o' the way from the nurses and orderlies. She'd not much ta say. I'm guessin' 'twas a bit of a shock tryin' ta reclaim her mind and body. I'd been the same in me first days. Me mind ragin' 'gainst not knowin' where I was, while me body was too tired ta do anythin' about it.

Still, I imagined the poor woman might enjoy a distraction from those in front o'her, walkin' 'round in circles or rockin' back and forth on benches. So's I moved closer and started doin' what I knew best. Talkin'.

"Gabrielle, let me tell ya a bit 'bout me and me family. I hail from County Cork, Queenstown ta be exact. I grew up there with me mam, me da and me seven brothers and sisters.

"Don't call me that."

The words come quiet, but strong. All the same, I didn't 'xactly get what she was sayin'

"Beggin' yer pardon?"

"Don't call me that," she said again, this time a bit louder and agitated.

Her boisterous words brought Angel and Maeve closer. Formin' 'round us, they made a wall keepin' the orderlies from seein' the woman. All the while I did me best ta calm her fury.

"Well now, sorry if I misunderstood, Gabrielle. What t'is it you'd like me ta call ya?"

"Liberty. My name is Liberty and I won't answer to anyone who calls me otherwise."

As she spoke, a single tear run down her cheek, makin' it clear the name held great meanin'.

"Liberty it is then."

The group o'us, Liberty, Maeve, Angel and me, started visitin' together every day and right quick we become thicker than thieves. We was a good blend, becomin' family ta each other, sharin' our sorrows and hangin' on ta the few joys come in-between the sufferin' and madness. And all was peaceful for a while.

As Liberty's body and mind got stronger, she went back ta railin' 'gainst the rotten ways all o'us was bein' treated. She sassed the orderlies and complained ta whoever'd listen 'bout the bad food and stinkin' beddin'. She even went so far as ta get others, more than me and Angel and Maeve, ta try and figure a way ta escape the tortured world where's we was all trapped.

The thing was, tweren't many of a mind could even understand what the ragin' woman was sayin'. Fer the most part, they ignored her rantin', no matter that she kept on.

"Why is it ya feel the need ta fuss so, Liberty? Do ya not get tired of fightin' with nothin' changing?"

"That's the problem with you, Teagan. You don't understand that if we would band together and fight back, it could get better."

"I luv ya like a sister, Liberty, but your way o' thinkin' is wrong. Them orderlies and nurses can hurt ya in ways ya don't yet understand. There's even been those died tryin' ta fight."

"The thing is, if some are going to be punished or murdered for fighting, then the rest should get something in return. Better food, less cruelty or punishments. I know these things for a fact as I helped organize protests with women fighting for the right to vote. I was arrested for my actions and physically abused in jails and those dangers endured by me and hundreds of others are what made it so women in America can now vote."

As Liberty went on talkin' that day, her passion kept growin'. Afore long, a group o'women was gathered 'round with Liberty coaxin' 'em ta stand 'gainst them's makin' the rules. Nothin' Maeve or Angel or me could do would quiet any of 'em.

Tweren't but a fast minute afore two orderlies come right at Liberty, one of 'em takin' her by the arm and draggin' her away, the other bossin' the rest gathered ta, ". . . quiet down or you'll go down the hall as well." As it happened, most went back to their pacin' and rockin' while the three o'us offered up silent prayers fer Liberty's safety.

'Twas a while afore any of us again saw Liberty. The outspoken women showed up in the ward one mid mornin' as I was goin' ta meet Maeve on the porch. She was set inta a corner of odd tables and chair, on a bench, leanin' 'gainst a grime-filled wall. When I realized who I was seein', I took me time goin' towards her, knowin' orderlies would be keepin' their eyes her way.

Wanderin' close, she looked like some I'd seen been taken down the hall for more than needles and tubes. 'Twas no doubt in me mind that the docs delivered jolts o'electric straight inta Liberty's brain ta change her way o'thinkin'.

"Bet you thought I wasn't coming back."

Her words were weak, but still held a spark.

"Truth be told Liberty, I wasn't sure just what was happenin' ta ya. Mostly I prayed you had angels watchin' over."

"I'm tougher than any of you know. It will take more than some prodding and pushing of electric rods to break me. I've only started."

Liberty's words put fear inta me soul. She'd not been in this place long enough ta know how nasty it could get. I'd seen women drug down the hall and come back mute. Not ta mention ones close in me heart that ne'er returned. I dinna want ta think o'losin' Liberty the same way.

"Listen here, missy. No doubt you're a force when crossed, but this place ain't like others. They'll do more than hurt ya here. They'll kill ya fer speakin' out like ya done. Ya got ta simmer down, stop rilin' up the others with minds not sound as yours. If'n ya don't, next time ya might not come back from down the hall."

She give no reply, but Liberty's eyes showed that me words meant nothin'. So's I stopped talkin' and sit down by her, sharin' the warmth o'me body.

"My mother raised me to fight against injustices against women, but there's something more that pushes me. Something I've never shared and not a soul still alive knows. I fight so that women in the future—the next generations-—will have better lives. So that my daughter would have had a better life had I chosen differently."

When she finished talkin', Liberty struggled ta sit up and turn ta me with a stare so strong it forced me ta look back. When our eyes met, I could see fear and anger goin' all the way ta her soul. She was waitin' fer me ta be shocked or disprovin' o'the words she'd just shared. I had no thought one way or t'other. Liberty had quick become a friend in this hell-forsaken place and that's all that mattered ta me.

"I don't know 'bout you havin' a daughter. What I do know is that you're a strong, smart woman and makin' friends with ya has been a gift. If you're a mam, or not, doesn't change ya better or worse ta me. It's just a part of who ya are."

"I'll tell you who I am. When I was twenty I fell in love with a man who promised me the world and I believed him. When I ended up pregnant with his child he left me. Just like my father left my mother. I was unmarried and alone. Yet unlike my mother, I didn't have to pack my bags and sneak away from my family in shame. Instead I told her and she understood. From that point, my mother took care of everything. She found a Chinese woman, not a doctor but an herbalist, who guaranteed her medicines had helped other pregnant women. Pawning the diamond lavalier given to her by her grandmother, my mother paid for the herbs and steeped teas from the powerful plants for me to drink, every day for a week. Finally I began to bleed, slowly at first, then a powerful flow. My mother put me to bed and in two days time, it was done. My baby was no more."

"Alright you two, time to move on to lunch."

Me mind was so focused on Liberty I'd not heard the orderly come upon us. Takin' a bit of a jump, I stood and stepped away. Movin' inta the space, the orderly rough-pulled Liberty ta her feet and went ta marchin' us both along ta the dining hall. Once there we sat 'longside Maeve and Angel, the four o'us come together again as family.

I ne'er again spoke to Liberty o'that time in her life. 'Twas enough she talked of it once. But from then, whenever she went ta fightin' 'gainst how we was bein' treated, I did me best ta calm her passion and keep her from being punished. I understood 'twas her carin' heart that caused her ta speak out. And Gabrielle Liberty Filipek been punished enough in her life, fer doin' nothin' more than sharin' her heart and givin' her love.

Chapter Fifteen

THE JANGLING telephone pierced the morning silence. The unexpected sound startled Grace halfway off her chair.

She'd gone in to work early. Getting locked in the stairway on her first day and her shaky meeting with the Wood Haven Board four days later made Grace determined to get her second week off to a better start.

Weaving her way through the behemoth building that now housed both Wood Haven patients and administrators, Grace felt an eeriness within its walls. Walking with an awareness of re-tracing steps of those who had come before, she reached her office and settled in behind her desk. There, working in the solitude of the breaking dawn, Grace found herself half-listening for echoes from the past.

There were none. Only the jarring ring of the telephone.

"Good Morning. Grace Reid."

"Good Morning, Grace, glad I caught you." Jonathan sounded particularly business-like.

"Can you clear your schedule for a meeting with Mayor Jenkins? I happened to run in to him this morning when I stopped at Cuppa Joe for breakfast. I mentioned our board meeting last week along with your concerns over the attitude of Midland residents. He was concerned as well and agreed to meet with us to discuss."

Ok, girl, pull your head out of your paperwork and get onboard. Jenkins, must be the mayor of Midland. Meeting with him, while it may be playing politics, is clearly important.

"Certainly, Jonathan. What time and where?"

"Actually he'll be here in ten minutes. It was the only free time on his schedule today. We'll meet in my office. See you then."

As Grace heard the click of the receiver, she glanced at the clock. A few minutes before 9am, just enough time for a quick freshen-up. Grabbing her purse from the drawer and her portfolio from the desk, Grace whisked out of her office and across the hall to a door imprinted with the outline of a female figure.

Grace took a deep breath before entering the ladies room. On her first day, she learned the hard way that the antiseptic smell of the lavatory cleansers failed to conceal the decades of bodily waste and stains permanently infused into the room. She also discovered that the only way she could withstand the odors was to inhale deeply before entering and hold her breath until she was back out in the hallway.

As Grace pushed open the door, she took heart that her bladder held only a morning cup of tea. A quick pee, a wash of her hands and a run of her fingers through her hair, it was a short list to accomplish, hopefully on one breath.

Grace was within seconds of a perfect escape when she heard her mother's personal hygiene sermon.

One of the most important things you can do is keep your breath fresh. No one likes to talk to a smelly Ned.

Annoyed and at the same time feeling oddly obliged, Grace opened her purse and pulled out the travel toothpaste and brush she always kept handy. Drawing a line of paste along the bristles, she realized in opening her mouth she would be forced to exhale, reflexively followed by an inhale.

Okay, I can do this. When I can't hold my breath any longer, I'll gradually exhale. Then if I have to, I'll inhale slowly as I finish brushing and make my escape out the door.

Part one of her plan went off without a hitch. It was only as she started to inhale that things went awry. The flow of the bathroom's odored-air into her body caused Grace to start gagging. Immediately toothpaste began foaming and overflowing her mouth. That, in turn, triggered waves of saliva, which doubled her choking reflex.

Gasping for air, Grace's body automatically tried to take another breath, this one loaded with a swell of saliva-enhanced peppermint slush determinedly focused on exiting her body. With her throat now fully constricted, the growing minty tidal wave had only two possible escape routes —through Grace's mouth or out her nose. As the gooey tsunami crested at the back of her throat, it spewed out through both.

With minty residue burning its way through her throat and up her nose, Grace's eyes teared into full blurriness. Using her hands as a guide, she felt her way along the bathroom wall to the door. Flinging it open, she lurched across the hallway and stumbled into her office. Coughing and retching, Grace collapsed onto her desk chair, waiting for the raging storm in her body to subside.

Within minutes, her coughing waned, her teary eyes cleared and her throat and nose calmed from enflamed to raw. However, every part of Grace's head felt as if it had been worked over like a punching bag. All because she wanted to brush her teeth before a meeting.

The meeting!

Looking at the clock Grace saw that her "few minute" time frame had passed. If she zipped to the bathroom and grabbed her purse and portfolio, she would be only a couple of minutes late.

Grace breezed into her boss's office just as the two men were sitting down on opposite sides of Jonathan's oversized wooden desk.

"Ah Grace, there you are. Mayor Jenkins, I'd like you to meet our deinstitutionalization consultant, Grace Reid. Grace, this is Mayor Jenkins."

"Nice to meet you, Grace. Please, call me Carl."

"Hello, Carl. Nice to meet you as well." As she spoke, Grace extended her hand, which the mayor latched on to with all ten of his perfectly-manicured fingers. Suddenly he was heartily shaking their three hands in unison, like a well-primed pump.

Yep, a politician for sure, always trying to make that extra impression. At least the handshake wasn't a bone-crusher.

"Shall we get down to business, Mayor?" Clearly, Jonathan was on a mission. "I know you are a busy man and we really appreciate that you made time to discuss our issue, before it turns into a problem."

Releasing Grace's hand, the mayor refocused his attention across the desk. "Certainly, Jonathan".

Grace and the mayor sat down alongside one another. Without turning her body, she gave the government official an extended side glance. The forty-something man was tall with a strong hint of toned muscles beneath his perfectly-tailored suit. As if feeling her attention, the mayor turned into Grace's gaze. Immediately she felt a body blush beneath her business-perfect white blouse that spread up her neck and across her cheeks. Everything about Carl Jenkins' appearance was appealing, from his gray-blond hair and ocean blue eyes to his broad shoulders tapering into an athletic torso.

This guy probably won the election on looks alone

"Grace, are you alright?" Jonathan queried.

"I'm fine, thank you. Had a bit of a coughing fit in my office. Swallowed some water the wrong way and it's still settling. I'm good now though. Let's get started."

For the next hour the trio discussed potential problems and concerns related to Wood Haven residents mainstreaming into the Midland Community. Jonathan began the conversation by summarizing Grace's experience at the Dew Drop. While he didn't present the details in precise order, he effectively communicated the important parts.

"Grace, what's your take on this? After all, you were the one who overheard the conversation."

As the mayor turned fully toward her, his eyes focused on her mouth as if willing words to exit her lips. In response, Grace began a checklist of issues she'd been working on since her early morning arrival.

"Well Mr. May . . . Carl, from my perspective there is one main issue—the well-being of the six Wood Haven women who will be moving into general society, some after lifetimes of institutionalization. Our plan is to transition these women to a group home somewhere in the Midland Community and no doubt, into life situations foreign to them. I believe we can all agree that their actions and reactions in these situations may be unorthodox."

Both men sat intensely listening to Grace's feedback. Something about their attentiveness encouraged the consultant to move away from her prepared notes.

"If I may speak freely, my true concern is that those who cannot comprehend the senior's behavior, or are frightened by it, may respond by lashing out. To try and avoid such situations, I have started defining areas of common need where some of our seniors may be capable of interacting and forming relationships with Midland residents."

As if waiting to pounce, Jonathan interrupted Grace. "Of course we are aware, Carl, that we have to be responsible for our seniors who end up living in Midland. I want to assure you, we will do everything to manage their interactions so that they will be controlled and reasonable.

Grace was never sure if it was the lingering after effects of her bathroom fiasco, or simply her frustration over Jonathan's response, but the next thing she knew she was on a passionate rant—much like the one she'd undertaken at the previous week's board meeting.

"Jonathan, not to disagree, but the onus of controlled and reasonable interactions should be on the Midland Community. Generally, the people of Midland have lived normal lives, not been locked away in an asylum, and should act accordingly.

The longer she spoke, the more Jonathan fidgeted in his chair. Looking across the desk, Grace could see that her words were lighting him up like a firecracker. Before he got the chance to explode, Mayor Jenkins intervened.

"Grace, I agree one hundred percent. The people of Midland have a responsibility to make sure that the establishment of a senior home and the transition of Wood Haven's residents into that home goes well."

Jonathan settled back into his chair, respectfully deferring to the mayor.

"That being said, the town has yet to vote on approving any kind of housing for Wood Haven's seniors. Currently, there's no zoning for such a facility and that's a looming issue. And, as you have already heard, there are a vocal group of Midland residents who do not want a senior home like this in our community. Further they are much more active than the majority of our Midland citizens who are fine with the home but won't go out and publicly support it."

Listening to his carefully chosen words, Grace understood how Carl Jenkins had been elected to public office. He was intelligent, reasonable and excelled at explaining things you didn't want to hear in ways that seemed reasonable. As she caught herself halfway agreeing with him, Grace answered the mayor, one point at a time.

"I'm glad to hear you say that the town needs to be responsible in welcoming Wood Haven's seniors, Mayor." Grace decided she needed to be on more business-like terms with this guy, until she was sure he was truly invested.

"And I certainly understand there is a legal process involved in establishing group housing in Midland. Where I beg to differ is in the way the vote on this issue can turn out. I happen to think if the town government—your government, Mr. Mayor—will stand in support of a senior residence in accordance with your ordinances, this could be an open and shut issue.

"Now Grace, I think the mayor knows his town better than either one of us and certainly he is not saying that he won't support our group housing cause." Jonathan appeared red in the face and excited in his speech, a reaction that made Grace realize perhaps she had crossed a line with her righteous words and attitude.

"Actually Jonathan, Grace is exactly right. My public endorsement of your project would make it a sure bet."

Jonathan's chin dropped in shock while Grace turned toward the mayor. She sensed a hammer about to drop and knew it would be best to face it head on.

"However, I was not elected to tell the people of Midland what to do. I was elected to listen to their concerns and administer their majority decisions. Which, in this case, is exactly what I am going to do."

A knockout punch, just as she'd anticipated. The good news was that Grace was a fighter, especially when it came to causes she cared about. And she definitely cared about the women in her Faith File.

"Mayor Jenkins, I am very pleased that we had this chance to meet and talk today. I know Jonathan mentioned you have a busy day ahead, so I'm going to call an end to this meeting. I have a long list of items to address in preparation for our Wood Haven seniors transferring to their new lives—new lives they deserve after years of being locked away beyond their control. Please know I am determined to do all within my power to ensure that happens, even if it means taking on the Town of Midland zoning board, the citizens and you, Mr. Mayor. Thank you, gentlemen, for the meeting. Have a good day."

With a flourish, Grace swooped up her purse, grabbed her portfolio and exited the office. While she might pay for her rude behavior, at the moment she was savoring the righteous feelings fostered by her words and actions. That singular focus is what kept her from noticing another person in the semi-dark hall, lurking outside her office. As she turned into her doorway, Grace felt the force of a body against her own. Grabbing on to the person for balance, she spoke to the unknown individual.

"I'm sorry. I was completely preoccupied and with such little light in this hallway, I just didn't see you. I apologize for walking into you."

Without a word the person took a step back, disengaging their bodies. As if an apparition, the individual then disappeared into the shadowy hall, leaving Grace with a sense of unease.

Taking steps toward her desk, Grace looked up at the clock. It wasn't even halfway through Monday.

Chapter Sixteen

WOOD HAVEN ADMITTANCE FORM

Patient: *Regina Wilson*
Date of Admittance: *Original date June 14, 1933; subsequent dates noted in file.*
Number: *06143331*
Age: *31*
Ethnicity: *English*
Marital Status: *Married*
Children: *3*
Cause of insanity: *Deranged Thinking. Suicidal Tendencies*

'TWAS HARD, PEOPLE COMIN' and goin' all the time. We was never told when a body might be comin' inta this terrible place. They was just sent straight away with the rest o'us. 'Less o'course they was troubled. Then they was chained and locked away in a room on their own. Worse was when ya started knowin' a soul and all at once they take sick in mind or body. Next thing they're gone. Sometimes fer a bit, sometimes forever. None o'it close ta a decent way o'livin' 'twas still understandin' such things when Regina come 'long. She was a tiny bit of a thing, short like me mam, with a frame could blow 'way in a strong gust o'wind. I first come upon the woman sittin' on a bench in the ward, quiet like a church mouse, stayin' ta herself.

Ya never knew if a new one was goin' ta welcome company, so's I sat and watched her fer a bit. Not a muscle did she move. Finally I got up and walked meself over ta her bench, takin' a spot on the very end. Seemed she had not a thought o' me bein' there, so's I stayed still, waitin' ta see if she would look me way or speak. Not a word. So's I decided t'would be up ta meself.

"Afternoon. Me name is Teagan. Teagan Cormick. What be yours?"

No answer.

"Well, I'm pleased ta meet ya."

No answer 'gain.

I was on me way ta movin' along when me ears caught the soft sound o'her voice.

"You need to be careful who you talk to, you know."

The wisp of a woman twasn't lookin' me way, but no one else was near. So's I answered with the first thing come inta me brain.

"Why's that, if ya don't mind me askin?"

Silence built 'tween us. Many locked away here did the same, their minds bein' unwell in one way or 'nother. There was no makin' 'em talk. Ya just went ta waitin' or give up. As she'd spoke once, I decided ta wait.

"There's people wanting to hurt you and me because we know things."

"What kinda things?"

'Twas at this point the woman turned and looked ta me with her deeply black eyes. Seemed as if she be ponderin' somethin'. What, I'd no idea. All's I know is when next she spoke her voice was loud and angry-soundin'.

"Don't try and fool me. I know you have seen them and heard them. They're everywhere. Everywhere I tell you. And if we do the wrong thing or say the wrong words, they're going to punish us. I'm too smart to get caught, but you, you are foolish and will get in trouble if you are not more careful."

Not havin' a clue what the woman was thinkin' I couldn't help but ask.

"How is it ya know 'bout these people? How might I get ta be smart like you 'bout such things?"

The words no more than left me mouth afore the woman was flyin' at me face. Her quickness pushed me flat onta the bench. Orderlies come runnin' and I was hopin' they'd get ta us right quick. 'Twas 'almost in the woman's full when two o'the men latched on, pullin' us back, from one ta two.

"Alright, settle down," the larger of the two white-suited orderlies barked. "You don't want us to call the nurses and have them take you down the hall, do you?"

Fer me part, I stayed still, makin' sure 'twas no doubt I'd not started the trouble. But the woman, the more she was held the worse she got. Nothin' good was going' ta come o'her fight and I wished in me heart ta quiet her.

"What exactly is going on here?"

'Twas Nurse Stewart, who stood not a whit o' nonsense.

"These two were in a scrap. We were trying to get them to settle down."

"Well it doesn't appear you're doing a very good job. Take the quiet one and chain her to a bench by herself. Make sure no one comes around her for the rest of the day. As for the other one, take her down the hall and put her in a room. Leave her chained. I'll have a doctor come and attend to her."

As the orderly went ta claspin' chains 'round me ankles, me stomach turned as if tainted by the sourest milk. Twasn't I was scared fer meself. I'd been chained afore and lived ta tell. 'Twas more fer the woman. Much was goin' round in her brain but none o'it seemed ta be set in meanness. More she was used ta bein' hurt and wantin' not ta feel such anymore.

Days passed and I found meself lookin', hopin' ta see the odd woman yet again on a bench or lyin' on a cot. The longer it went without her, the louder the woman's voice come inta me head, warning o'people always listenin' and wantin' ta punish.

Whatever was it made her think that way?

Worse, could her words be tellin' truths?

'Twas only when she back in the ward that I come ta understand

At first glance, I had not a clue who she was, smilin' and talkin', movin' through the room as if a nurse, not one locked away. As she drew near and her black eyes looked upon me, I knew 'twas her.

"Hello, my name is Regina."

"Nice ta know your name, Regina. I'm Teagan. Teagan Cormick. We met before, a while back."

"Oh, I'm so sorry, I don't remember. That happens to me sometimes when I'm not feeling well."

Unable ta deny her charm, I invited the wisp o'a woman to sit on the porch and chat a while. Not once did she speak 'bout those watchin and wantin' ta harm us. 'Stead she went ta sharin' stories o'her husband, Eddie, and her three children, Eddie Junior, Margaret and Frances. A proud mother she be, with a grand desire ta get back ta her beibis.

Truth be told, twasn't somethin' happened, bein allowed ta leave once ya was locked away. But this one, she was determined. She kept on talkin' o'her husband's promise ta come back and take her home. I would have felt sorry for her, if it hadn't gone on, just as she said.

One morning I woke ta Regina's cot sittin' empty. Quick-like I sat up and looked 'round, thinkin' she might be wanderin'. Ta me disappointment, she was nowhere ta be seen. Like a church mouse, I rose up and made me way ta the dormitory door. 'Twas locked but with voices I could hear on the other side.

Talkin' was going on, and a bit o'laughter, somethin' not oft' heard in this god-awful place. A man's voice strong and clear echoed through the walls. In return a woman spoke and with every fiber of me bein' I knew 'twas Regina. There was no way ta hear the words they was speakin' but the tone was clear. 'Twas no anger, no fear. Then, in a bit, all was quiet. They were gone.

Makin 'me way back ta me cot, I lay waitin' fer the orderlies ta unlock the door. When at last they came I went off like a flash inta the hallway, lookin' fer Nurse Bennett. 'Twas me hope she'd tell me 'xactly what happened ta Regina.

I found the good nurse down aways, by the door ta the dining hall door. Afore anyone could stop me, I went up ta her and asked me question.

"Nurse Bennett. I found Regina's cot empty this mornin'. Was wonderin' if ya could tell me where she's gone? I know doin' such goes 'gainst the rules, but t'would mean a great deal if you would. I'll not tell a soul, cross me heart."

With a quick look 'round, Nurse Bennett turned herself towards me so's nothin' she said could go further.

"Because of the good care she got here, Regina has gone home. Early this morning her husband came to take her back to their three children. Now Teagan, take yourself into the dining hall and I had better not hear a word of this anywhere."

Grateful ta be knowin' the truth, I reached out and give a hug ta the good nurse. Hard ta say which one o'us was more surprised, but me quick step back kept Nurse Bennett from doin' anything but smilin'. I turned meself away and moved ta the dining hall, just as she'd ordered. Nary a word did I speak 'bout all I was told, nor that Regina was gone. Rather, 'twas happy she hadn't again been taken down the hall.

Me thoughts turned ta Regina fer long after. The way she went ta worryin' bout them's listenin' and goin' ta hurt people. Then actin' as if none o'it come outta her mouth. Instead only carin' 'bout her husband and her beibis. I'd never known someone ta behave such a way and kept tryin' ta understand. It troubled me mind so much and so long that one day I went ta imaginin' her standin' afore me.

She was appearin' a bit older and a bit rounder, but no doubt 'twas Regina. I rubbed me eyes, tryin' ta clear the imaginin', but when I looked 'gain, 'twas still seein' the woman.

While it made no sense, I was past trying ta make it right. Takin' steps towards her, hopin' 'gainst hope she wouldn't disappear, nothin' before me changed. Not even the look in her black eyes.

"Regina, t'is it really you?"

Not a sound did I hear. Not a move did the woman make. Another few steps and we was standin' toe ta toe.

"Regina, t'is me, Teagan. Come on woman, ya must know me."

At last, an answer returned from the depths of her bein'.

"Get away from me. I know who you are and what you're trying to do. I know they sent you to watch me. I'm not stupid. You are not going to see me do anything wrong.

A sadness washed over me like a cold fog on a damp Irish morn'. 'Twas Regina afore me but not the woman who loved her family so. Rather 'twas she whose mind had twisted and betrayed her before and so's it seemed, done again.

I wanted ta reach out, wrap her in me arms and untwist her mind, but I knew t'would be fer naught. Nothin' in me power was strong enough. So's I walked away, with hope that whatever the doctors would be doin' down the hall might bring her back.

That's how me and Regina carried on. Her husband bringin' her here ta treat her mind and givin' us back our friendship, 'til off she'd go home again ta her beibes. Got so I could set the seasons by the woman's return—winter ta spring seemin ta be her time ta struggle.

One early winter's day, as I was sittin' on the porch lookin' at the world through iron bar windows I saw Regina on the porch o'the building straight 'cross. She was with a man I guessed ta be her husband.

She was back.

I started watchin' fer her, in the ward, the dormitory, the dining hall. Nary that day nor the next did she come. 'Twas a time of days afore I again saw me friend and when so, I hardly knew her.

An orderly brung her ta the ward and sit her down on a bench, nary pausin' ta chain or tie her. The woman's long brown locks was cut short like a man, her bein' seemin' less than half well, covered as it was in clothes fallin' off her body. Her feet was bare and purple in color. And there was her face, pale and lined.

As I walked nearer, hopin' against hope 'twasn't Regina, she raised her head just 'nough fer our eyes ta meet. Hers was black as always, but now blank, as if taken from her head and replaced with a coupla stone cold marbles.

'Twas no way ta keep meself. Me heart began breakin' and me eyes tearin'. I knew better than ta let anyone see me cryin'. Last time a woman went ta blubberin' she stirred up a hornet's nest of others cryin' and carryin' on, all through the ward. The orderlies was fit ta be tied as they couldn't make 'em calm. Next thing ya know, the nurses was roundin' us up and lockin' us inta the dormitory, even tyin' some ta cots. I dinna want that happenin' again. Not knowin' what else ta do, I turned meself and walked 'way.

I kept seein' Regina that same spot every day and on a cot near me at night. N'er once did the look of her change, ne'er again did we speak o'her returning home ta her beibis.

All she could tell me was that people was wantin' ta hurt us, cause we knew things.

Chapter Seventeen

SUNLIGHT STREAMED THROUGH the paneled board room, transmitting the feel of late spring into the formal office space. It was Grace's first meeting as an official member of the Wood Haven staff and she was a little unsure what to expect.

Employees could be territorial when faced with a consultant hired to advise on a project. Grace had faced her fair share of hostile work environments over the years, but she took heart in that she had a track record of winning over any adversaries before her job was done. As she took a seat at the far end of the oval table, she prayed Wood Haven would be no different.

"Grace. Good, I'm glad you're here early. I wanted to touch base about our meeting this morning with Mayor Jenkins."

The reminder of her earlier sparring match with the Midland politico set Grace's nerves on edge. It had taken her the better part of the morning to settle down after the tirade she'd rained down upon the mayor. Anticipating that Jonathan would follow up with an official reprimand didn't help her jumpy mood. When lunchtime came and went without consequence, Grace thought she might be off the hook.

Apparently not.

"Grace, I understand your dedication to ensuring the successful mainstreaming of our Wood Haven seniors into the Midland Township. I also fully understand your frustration with the politics that will assuredly define exactly how and where we are able to integrate your "Faith File," as you call them. But the reality of our situation is that we are a publicly funded facility. The elected officials in charge of mandating and distributing those funds have a strong say in everything we do here."

Grace had never really been involved in politics, nor did she ever have a desire to be part of a campaign or run for office. For the most part, she viewed government as a profession gone wrong, since the "public service" ideal she remembered from her high school and college days had devolved into a profession based on money and power. Regardless, Grace had to admit, Jonathan was probably spot-on with his assessment of their political situation.

"If you are going to succeed in this job, Grace, you are going to have to learn how to accept terms dictated by those who fund us. That's not to say we won't find ways to work around political road blocks that could detour things we believe are right for our seniors. We just have to be a bit less blunt, a bit more collaborative than you were this morning with the mayor."

Jonathan's words continued to ring true in Grace's mind. No doubt, she was going to have to polish her negotiating skills and turn up her Irish charm to get what she wanted for her Faith File. Thankfully Jonathan seemed willing to accept her tirade against Mayor Jenkins as a misstep and continue to support her work.

"I understand, Jonathan. I apologize for my outburst this morning. I appreciate your willingness to discuss and advise me on the political ins-and-outs of this process, as I am uninitiated with the strings attached to government funding. That's of the reasons I hesitated to accept this job. At the same time, it's a challenge I look forward to meeting and conquering."

As Grace was about to tell Jonathan an idea she'd been working on since their morning meeting, members of the Wood Haven staff began filtering into the room. Within minutes the board table was fully ringed with men and women of varied ages, all armed with portfolios and pens.

"Afternoon, ladies and gentlemen," Jonathan's voice silenced the group's chatter. "We have a full agenda, so let's get to it."

For the ensuing hour, Grace sat and listened as administrators of the various Wood Haven departments reviewed their achievements, challenges, lists of needs and wants and general observations on the facility's overall progress. There was Joe Bush from maintenance and grounds, Mary Burke from nursing, Janine Skelley from dietary, Jeff Goodwin from finance, Gloria Day from marketing and Craig Jennings from government relations. Each individual gave Grace a layered overview of Wood Haven, providing her with a clearer perspective of her role in its overall workings.

"Ok. Before we finish up, I want to formally introduce the newest member of our staff," Jonathan's announcement caused Grace to straighten up against the back of her wooden chair. "Some of you may have already met her informally, but today I want to make sure you all are aware of her background and the integral skillsets she brings to Wood Haven."

During what seem like an endless monologue, Grace listened to Jonathan summarize her resume and focus on the consulting work that had earned her national repute among senior care executives. While Grace was proud of her professional achievements, she rarely talked about them with anyone outside her family, and never publicly. Jonathan's continued litany of her success made Grace halfway wonder who he was talking about.

"So, as you have just heard, Grace Reid brings experience, expertise and, as I have witnessed in her first week at Wood Haven, a great deal of passion for the well-being of our seniors. Please, do your utmost to work with Grace, communicate with her and to support her as she learns the ropes."

With a pause, Jonathan swiveled in his chair, turning in her direction.

"Grace, welcome. We are pleased you have joined our staff."

A round of applause echoed off the paneled board room walls. Feeling a slight flush up her face, Grace turned toward each of the seven seated around the table and gave a nod of appreciation, ending with Jonathan.

"Thank you, Jonathan, for that glowing introduction and I thank each one of you for the warm welcome. I don't believe I have ever received a round of applause before!"

Grace's gentle humor spread a comfort level through the room. From her various consulting jobs, she knew the impression made at a first meeting like this would set the tone for her entire Wood Haven tenure. She also knew it was vital that she be open, honest and real.

"As Jonathan stated, I have worked with senior care administrators across the United States. While I am proud of the list of facilities I have served, no matter where I've traveled the really important part of my job has always been doing the best I can for the seniors. Please know that any advice or ideas you want to share with me will be welcomed and appreciated. Also, I look forward to your individual insights on our senior's abilities as far as needing long term care or being able to mainstream into the Midland Community. The more information I have, the better I can do my job of providing these special individuals with the lives they deserve."

Looking around the table, Grace could see the commitment of each supervisor in their body language and the warmth of their eyes. The staff was clearly engaged in their work and in the well-being of those living at Wood Haven. Grace could feel the sentiment of the moment filling her heart and it took every bit of her self-control to reign in her emotions before they welled into tears. Thankfully, Mary Burke, from the nursing department, spoke up.

"Thank you for sharing your passion for your work, Grace. Everyone at this table feels the same way. We've been hand-picked by Jonathan, not only for our professional skills, but for our deep devotion to caring for seniors, particularly these seniors who have been at Wood Haven for so many years. We all understand that their lives were stolen from them, some by medical or mental conditions, some by the unjust social systems of the day. Knowing that you bring a proven ability to make change and provide better lifestyles for them is the best news we could hear."

What Grace had hoped would be a comment to lighten her mood ended up encouraging emotional responses from all in attendance. Men and women alike were brushing back tears for those whose lives had been defined by the brutalities of the Wood Haven asylum.

"Well, I would say that our meeting is ending on a good note. As always, your positive outlooks are what make us a strong team. Don't ever forget that. And now, if you will step into the reception room next door. Janine has provided us with refreshments to celebrate Grace's arrival. And please take this opportunity to personally introduce yourself and make Grace feel welcome."

Moving enmasse, the administrators made a beeline to the reception table laden with cookies, a fruit and cheese tray and a metal cooler of assorted drinks. With every attempt she made to fill a plate, Grace was waylaid by conversation.

First came Janine, who encouraged Grace to stop by the kitchen anytime she was hungry. Judging by the array of cookies set out on the table, Grace had no doubt she would be following up on the offer.

Joe stepped up next wanting to share a couple of hideaways on the grounds where he assured Grace she could claim a few tranquil moments when in need. His list included a grotto area at the far end of Wood Haven that she would find by following the maintenance road leading from the parking lot to the back of the property. Then there was what Joe described as "the creepy but interesting" hilltop cemetery with a breathtaking view of a nearby man-made lake.

Mary and Gloria approached as a duo, like girlfriends as well as fellow administrators. They made offers of a girl's night out and social activities in Midland. They were especially enthusiastic about a disco on the outskirts of town, which they promoted as THE nightspot. Grace nodded in appreciation while internalizing the culture gap between their early 30s's and her mid 40's.

As she again went to reach for a plate to fill, Grace felt a movement along her side. It was Jeff shyly standing by. His slight build coupled with his thick-lens glasses seemed to personify the stereotypical appearance of an accountant. That image was fortified as Jeff spoke in a tone that required Grace to lean in closely to hear his words. The effort, however, was worthwhile as he made an offer to work up financials on cost of living statistics in Midland. Such data would be essential to Grace's plan for her Faith File.

Looking around, it seemed everyone was engaged and feasting. Finally, Grace thought, she would be able to fill a plate and enjoy. As she took a bite of a particularly dense and chewy chocolate chip cookie, a voice spoke behind her.

"You better watch those cookies. Whatever Janine puts in them is addictive."

Startled, Grace whipped around to find herself face-to-face with Craig. At the board meeting they were seated at opposite ends of the table, preventing Grace from noticing his piercing blue eyes and the attractive curl to his blond hair. However, up close-and-personal, Grace became fully and embarrassingly aware as a blush crept up her neck and spread across her face.

"Hello, Craig is it?" Struggling to control her voice, Grace took a step back from her fellow administrator, but not before noticing the matching deep-set dimples on either side of his engaging smile.

"Craig it is. Glad to know I made enough of an impression for you to remember my name."

Grace took yet another step back to increase the personal space between them, all the while trying to decide if his response was flirtatious or friendly.

"Seriously, just wanted to say hi and offer my help. This place is definitely a political landmine and it's easy to step on toes without realizing it. Feel free to stop by my office anytime. Third door down the hall from you, last room before the exit sign, on the right."

Before Grace could reply, Craig was on his way out of the reception room.

Well, apparently I don't have to waste time wondering if he was flirting with me.

Immediately Grace realized she'd said the words out loud. Panicked, she looked right and left, but to her relief everyone was focused on their own conversations.

Ok. Perhaps it's time for a quiet exit.

Grace made her way to Jonathan who was digging heartily into the cookie tray.

"Great meeting, Jonathan. Thank you for your introduction to the staff and, again, thanks for your counsel about working with Mayor Jenkins. I appreciate your guidance."

"No problem, Grace. I understand your passion. We just need to harness it into words and actions that will benefit us most. We'll make it. I have no doubt."

With a smile that communicated her appreciation, Grace slipped out of the room and returned to her office. And to the Faith Files of the six women whose lives she was determined to change.

CHAPTER EIGHTEEN

WOOD HAVEN ADMITTANCE FORM

Patient: *Michael O'Connor*
Date of Admittance: *November 11, 1934*
Number: *11113436*
Age: *37*
Ethnicity: *American*
Children: *None*
Cause of insanity: *Soldier's Heart*

TWASN'T OFTEN WOMEN AND men locked away in this hellish place come together. Mostly it happened when the men was repairin' the buildin's or we was workin' in the out o'doors. Twas an outside project one sunny day that had the orderlies bring out both women and men and where I first laid me eyes on Michael "Mick" O'Connor.

He was a fine strappin' man catchin' the notice o'most any woman, whether she be o'sound mind or not. The thing was, the man paid no attention, always walkin' and workin' as ordered. Yet there was somethin' 'bout his way that kept him in me mind and in me dreams. Twasn't a passion fer 'em, mind ya. 'Twas more his sad way o'goin' 'bout things that made me know he had a need for a bit o' kindness.

Come a day when this man and me had a chance ta chat. 'Twas no more than a few minutes, don'cha know, but still I come ta better understandin' his sorrowful soul.

We was outside in the vegetable garden which, saints be praised, put something more than crusty bread on our plates and watery broth in our bowls. I was on me hands and knees with other women, weeding 'round the plants. He was with the men driving stakes fer fencin' ta keep deer and such from strippin' it all ta the ground.

As I worked me way through the peas and over ta the lettuce, I come near enough ta the man ta speak. Havin' noticed his quiet ways, I made up me mind ta start easy.

"So's does ya think you'll be able to keep them animals from eatin' the garden?"

He give not so much as a nod or a look me way. So's I tried again.

"Fer sure'n these vegetables will make a fine supper one night. I'm hopin'your stakes and fencin' do the job."

"They will."

'Twasn't much but I knew I'd made me start inta his mind. Havin' a look-see 'round fer orderlies and noticin' none, I kept movin' me weedin' closer 'til a whisper 'tween us could be shared.

"Me name is Teagan. Teagan Cormick. Seen ya 'round a bit and truth be told, ya remind me o'me brothers back home in Ireland. We'd work in our mam's garden just like this and that memory is tuggin' at me heart today."

This time the man quit his hammerin' ta give me a look. 'Twas as if he was tryin' ta pick his words. As I was about ta turn inside out from waitin, he spoke.

"I did the same gardening with my sisters in our backyard in Jersey City. I miss it as well, and them."

I chose me next words careful-like, knowin' full well what I said could stop the man from chattin.

"Me mam's favorite veggies was pole beans. She'd get me brothers ta cut switches from the nearby trees and tie 'em inta triangles fer the beans ta climb on and bloom. Then she'd have us pick and clean 'em fer a dish she'd make with just-dug potatas and loads o' butter and cream. As I'm kneelin' here in this garden I can smell it now, warmin' on the stove."

The brawny man returned ta his fence stakes, sharin' neither look nor word. 'Twas only as he hammered a stake inta place afore me that I saw a trail o'tears flowin' from his eyes. 'Twas a painful sight, his face showin' sadness. Whatever tragedy put the man in this place, 'twas no doubt he carried it still, deep within him.

Seein' an orderly comin', I knew time ta be short. Quick-like, I moved ta the place the man was diggin' fer the next post and spoke direct-like.

"I can tell ya be carryin' a deep sorrow and I'm most sorry fer your pain. Ya remind me so much o' me brothers and if they was locked away in a place like this and hurtin', I pray ta Mary, Mother of God, that some kind soul would help 'em. So's I'm goin' ta share with ya a secret sign me and me brothers made fer times when our mam punished us fer gettin' inta mischief. When e're we'd be in sight o'each other, we'd give a tug on our ear, a bit like scratchin' an itch"

Reachin' up to me ear, I give it a tug so's the man could see what I was sayin'. He watched me hand pull on me ear but gave no sign o'wantin' ta do it himself, so's I kept talkin.

"Whenever one o'us give a tug, we knew we was thinkin' o'each other and all would soon be well. So's anytime ya see me, I'll be giving ya that sign, so's you'll know you're not alone. That someone in this horrid place is thinkin' of ya."

"Weeding time is done. You women need to go back to your building now. Move along."

The orderly'd come closer than I knew. Still, I was sure he'd not heard a word. But had the man? Was he understandin? All's I could do was have faith and pray

As I moved away from the rich soil and sprouting plants, I heard a gentle callin' o'me name. Turnin', I seen the man, look at me with a yearnin'. Afore I could answer, he spoke.

"My name is Michael O'Connor. My family and friends call me Mick."

With that he reached up and give a tug ta his right ear.

"Good ta meetcha Mick," I shot back, tugging at me own ear as well, the two of us like brother and sister.

From then on, I did me best ta be sent fer outside work. When luck come me way, me and Mick would cross paths and we never failed tweakin'our ears in secret communion. As God is me witness, in such moments, I could see Mick as a happier lad. Not ta say he was jumpin' fer joy, mind ya. Rather his face held a peaceful look, his eyes not near as empty. 'Twas only after not seein' him fer some time, and wonderin' why, I come ta know different.

Nurse Bennett was makin' her way inta the ward, givin' a look-see over those o'us sittin' and those wanderin'like lambs lost from their flock. As she passed me by I give her a nod and a smile, as we oft' did.

"Hello Teagan. How are you feeling today?"

"Well, thank ya, Nurse Bennett. And yerself?"

"I am well also. I've noticed you've been outside quite a bit this summer.

It's served you well. You look healthy and strong."

Thank you, missus. I've taken a fancy ta workin' in the garden outside the buildin' here. T'is something me mam taught all o'us kids ta do and it feels good havin' me hands in the dirt again. I'm hopin' too that the fence put up by the men will keep the animals from eatin' the vegetables afore we have a chance."

"I hope so as well. Although one of the men who was especially good at protecting the gardens is no longer working on them. Hopefully the fencing he put up stays in place without his attention."

Nurse Bennett's words gave me stomach a turn. Fer sure there was nothin' in what she said ta exactly describe Mick. Still me mind went ta racin' in wonder and a bit o'fear if something had happened ta him.

"A man dedicated ta the gardens, ya say? Is it the tall, fine-lookin'one you'd be describin'? "

"Actually, Teagan, I never pay much attention to people's appearances, but his name was Mick."

I knew instinct was ringin' true. Mick gone missin' from the gardens was more than a simple thing. I needed ta find out where he'd gone. Nurse Bennett was not one ta be talkin' 'bout such things and none o'the orderlies spoke unless makin' demands or hollerin'. Who could I ask? Who would know?

I got meself up and made me way over ta the porch, off the ward. 'Twas as much fer the sun streamin' in that I went. Bars scored the windows, but no matter. I could still see the blues o'the sky and the greens o'the land that kept me dreamin' 'bout me paintin' days on Queenstown's shore.

"Teagan, are you alright? You walked away so quickly."

"Fer sure, Missus, I'm doin' fine. Just found meself in need of a bit o'sunshine, doncha know."

"Certainly there is benefit to those golden rays. I was looking for you to let you know that one of the orderlies just told me that the fence around the vegetables has been fortified by the man who works as our gravedigger. He has tools that can put the stakes in the ground more deeply and attach the wire much tighter, which he believes will keep the wildlife on their own side of the fence through growing season. He also attached some cloth strips all along the fence to scare away the birds."

I could hear the words the kind woman was sharin', but the only thing passin' through me mind was Mick. Where'd the man gone to?

"Thanks fer lettin' me know, Nurse Bennett. After all me weedin' work, I look forward ta tastin' the fresh-grown foods. By the by, I was wonderin' if ya might be willin' ta take a walk 'round the garden so's I can see the new fence, bein' it's such a nice day and all."

"Truthfully Teagan, we're not supposed to take patients outside without an orderly, as much for your protection as mine. But I know how much you love being outdoors and working in the garden. Let me see if John at the main desk can spare someone to accompany us. But it can only be for a few minutes as we all have work waiting."

I hadn't the faintest why goin 'outside mattered in tryin' ta find Mick. I was just followin' me gut in that I needed ta get near the garden ta dig fer the truth.

"Fer sure, Missus. 'Twould put me mind at ease bein' close-up ta the garden and all."

'Twas only a bit afore Nurse Bennett took me from the ward and inta the hallway. There we met with a stump o'a man, more wide than tall, but powerful built. She called him Frank the orderly and told him ta lead the way as we followed close behind.

Frank was a chatty sort. Words kept flowin' from him the whole time we was makin' our way 'long the corridor and out the door. I strained ta listen hopin'ta hear Mick's name. T 'was only as we reached the fenced garden and went ta circlin' 'round all four sides that the man's words caught me ear.

"Yeah, that gravedigger really did a job building this garden fence. I'm hoping to maybe grab a vegetable or two for myself when it's time. But you know it's too bad the fellow who put so much into this garden won't be around to enjoy it. Did ya hear about that, Nurse Bennett? About that Mick guy?"

His words hit me brain like a brandin' iron. Waitin' fer Nurse Bennett ta answer, I could feel the heat of Mick's name burning inta me mind. What did the orderly mean, sayin' he wouldn't be 'round ta enjoy the garden? Had Mick got well enough ta go home? At this very minute, was he was buildin' a fence 'round a whole new garden in Jersey City?

"I do know about Mick. Actually I was with Dr.Bentley when he made the call to the O'Connor Family. And I was in charge of preparing his uniform and his medals for them."

"Oh yeah. I heard he was some kind of honored army guy. Since I'm always assigned to the women's wards, I was never around him, but talk from other orderlies was that he'd seen some tough battle action. That's what put him here."

"Yes. When Mick was admitted, he brought a suitcase with his full army uniform and a valise of medals and ribbons for bravery in combat. He didn't want to show them to anyone or talk about what he'd gone through to earn them, but he didn't want to be without them either. In the end, that's what completely tortured his mind. He was terribly troubled by his war experiences and the fact that he survived when so many of his platoon did not. It was quite a shock for the supervisor who found him here in the garden."

The two o' 'em was talkin' as if I weren't even there, clearly caught up in the sadness o'the story. 'Twas so much more I was wantin' ta know, but when Nurse Bennett said Mick was found in the garden, I stayed still and quiet, hopin' they'd go on with what was yet ta be said.

"Yeah, talk is somehow he snuck out here with a tool from the garden work that he'd kept hidden away. Musta been really bad for him to bludgeon himself like that

"I can tell you that Dr. Bentley completed the official certificate with the cause of death being, 'Soldier's Heart' and I would say that was exactly why he died."

Me ears went ta ringin' as the words passed 'tween Nurse Bennett and the orderly. That sweet Mick had done himself in was more than I could bear. All the same I could now understand the sorrow in his eyes and the sadness he was always showin'. Heard tell o' men come back from war not able ta talk 'bout the terrible things they'd seen and done. Never known such a man afore.

"Teagan, we need to go in now."

Movin' slowly, I stepped close ta the garden, as if in me own little world.

Lookin' up ta the heavens I give one last tug on me ear.

Prayin' your soul is now restin' in peace, Mick. It's what ya deserve.

Chapter Nineteen

GRACE WASN'T A COFFEE DRINKER. She'd never developed the need or desire for a jolt of caffeine to jump start her day. However, something about this particular Monday required a jolt. That's what led her to stop at Cuppa Joe on her morning drive to Wood Haven.

Once inside the popular Midland diner, Grace felt the intensity of the restaurant regulars assessing her appearance and whispering about her identity.

From youthful summers spent on Nana and Papa O'Connor's farm, Grace learned small towns functioned as close-knit communities. Everyone knew everyone, as well as everyone's business. That's why she understood her arrival in Midland was cause for diner gossip.

Too tired to care, Grace moved with purpose to the take-out counter where a fresh-faced young woman welcomed her.

"Good Morning! How are you?"

The query interrupted Grace's focus on the coffee she was about to order. Momentarily blank, she recovered with a smile and an appreciation for the friendly greeting.

"I'm still waking up a bit, but overall pretty good. Thanks for asking. How are you?

"I'm great. My name is Suzy. You must be new in town. I don't think I've ever seen you at Cuppa Joe before."

"Actually, I *am* new. I'm in town working on a contract job. My name is Grace."

"Well, welcome Grace. What can I get for you this morning?"

"Can you, by any chance, make me a to go of half coffee, half hot chocolate? I'm happy to pay an extra charge if there is one."

"Hmmm, no one's ever asked me for that before, but I'm sure I can make it. It'll just take a minute. If you'd like to sit at the counter, I'll bring it to you as soon as it's ready."

Grace wasn't thrilled about moving to the counter area of the restaurant, but most of the swivel stools were empty and her time there would be short.

Not much risk of early morning interaction. Why not?

As she lowered herself onto a stool, Grace heard the ring of the brass bell attached to Cuppa Joe's front door. The next thing she knew there was a person was claiming the stool beside her.

"Well good morning, Miss Reid. Nice to see you again.

Turning a half swivel, Grace came face to face with the Midland police officer who had stopped her for speeding her first week in town.

Oh no. What's his name?

Grace could envision the officer's nametag attached to his uniform shirt, just above the pocket.

Officer Haley, Harley, Healy. That was it! Healy.

"Good Morning, Officer Healy. Hope you're not here to give me a ticket for being illegally parked?"

"No m'am. I stop at Cuppa Joe every morning about this time. We policemen have to have our daily coffee and doughnuts, you know!"

The man's gentle humor soothed Grace. Since arriving in Midland her consulting work had kept her pretty isolated. Other than her day of retail therapy and her unfortunate experience at the Dew Drop, Grace had little feel for the overall nature of the town. Officer Healy's friendly manner was encouraging.

"Here's your chocolate coffee," Suzy interjected into the conversation. "That'll be 80 cents. I had to charge just a bit extra."

As Grace pulled our her change purse, Officer Healy put in his two cents.

"Chocolate coffee? I never heard of such a thing, Suzy. What is it?"

"Actually, it's a special request of mine," Grace replied. "I really am not a coffee drinker, but I felt the need for a bit of caffeine this morning. I asked Suzy if she could mix coffee with some hot chocolate to make the flavor a little less bitter. Here's your 80 cents plus a bit extra for your efforts this morning. Thanks so much, Suzy."

"You're most welcome. I'm here every weekday, so anytime you want to stop in for another chocolate coffee, I'll be happy to serve you. Actually we should add it to the menu."

"Hey Suzy, that's a great idea," Officer Healy jumped back into the conversation. "Why don't you name it after Miss Reid, since she's the one who made it up?"

"We should," the enthusiastic waitress replied. "We could call it Cuppa Grace. People would love it!"

Grace felt a flush flood from her toes to her hairline. Having her name on a diner menu was something to which she had *never* aspired. She absolutely had to put a stop to this idea before it went further.

"Actually Suzy, I think a more generic name would be better. Something like cocoa java or choco coffee. That way people would have some idea of what they were ordering."

"Oh, we name things after our customers all the time," Suzy bubbled. "We have the Hardy Marty sandwich, named after Marty Walsh, one of the town highway guys. Then there's the Suzy Q, a salad named after Suzy Morgan, a Midland bank teller. And we have the Mighty Mike, a burger loaded with cheese and fried onions and served with a big side of french fries and pickles, for Lt. Healy here."

Grace couldn't help herself. The idea of the Mighty Mike caused her to burst out with laughter. As she swiveled again toward the Midland officer, she could see his discomfort over his hamburger celebrity. Still, the moment was too perfect to let go.

"So, the Mighty Mike, huh? Sounds like a pretty manly menu item. Is it popular?"

Without missing a beat, Suzy chimed in, "Oh yeah. We sell a ton of orders every day. It's been on the menu for five years. Actually, anytime we talk about taking it off, people get mad and threaten to go down the street to that new McDonald's place."

Doing her best not to laugh directly in the squirming police officer's face, Grace realized there was no way to conclude the conversation graciously. With little fanfare she picked up her chocolatey java, thanked Suzy for creating the morning pick-me-up and turned to make her exit. However, a last glimpse of the local cop caused her to take pity on the poor guy.

"Nice to see you again Lt. Healy. And one of these days I'm going to have to try the Mighty Mike. I love burgers, and it sounds delicious. Have a great day."

The officer gave up a smile of gratitude as he and the rest of the diner patrons watched Grace walk out the door.

"Well she sure seems nice," Suzy chirped.

"Yep, I think she is," Officer Healy agreed. "Now can I get one of those chocolate coffees things and a couple peanut sticks to go?"

As GRACE SETTLED INTO HER Wood Haven office, she drained the contents of her to-go cup. *I really enjoyed this cuppa Gra . . . ok, blot that thought out of your mind right now. Don't want any part of that becoming a reality.*

With a last gulp of the mocha combo, Grace turned her attention to the Faith Files. So far, she'd made her way through the records of Maeve Mulherin Dempsey, Rebecca Odera Washington and Gabrielle Liberty Filipek. Three files still to go. Grace set a goal of working her way through all of them by day's end.

Studying the files, Grace was learning that although the life circumstances of the six women were different, they had all endured the same experience of being locked away in an asylum for most of their adult lives, often for reasons completely unfounded. It was also clear, in reading through the reams of documentation, that the men legally responsible for some of these women made purposeful decisions to commit them and never looked back.

Depression following a miscarriage, mental instability due to political involvement, hysteria caused by loss of home and family, poverty. Any one of those things could cause serious emotional issues for men or women. Even if the diagnoses were correct and treatment was required, generally such conditions are temporary. Every one of these individuals should have been able to return to their lives, not been forever imprisoned.

Grace diligently continued working through the files, taking notes and writing questions about the various treatments. She also jotted down personal details about each woman. Knowing their individual life stories would be crucial to building trusted relationships and helping each one transition from Wood Haven to Midland.

"Good night, Grace."

The words cut through her concentration like a buzzsaw. Looking up, Grace realized it was 5pm and Jonathan was standing in her office doorway.

"I'm sorry to startle you. I did knock."

"Not a problem, Jonathan. I've been working on these files all day and completely lost track of time. You headed home?"

"I wish. No, I have a board meeting for the local Boys and Girls Club and then I promised I'd stop at a fundraising meeting for the St. Michael's Hospital Gala. *Then*, I can go home and make myself a peanut butter and jelly sandwich and eat it standing up while falling asleep." A hearty laugh escaped the executive director's weary body. "Who says men can't multi-task!"

Grace smiled at her boss's self-deprecating humor, at the same time sensing the sadness masked by his joke. Jonathan's wife of more than 30 years, Mary Beth, had passed away eighteen months earlier. Grace learned of his loss from Janine Skelley one day while buying lunch in the Wood Haven cafeteria. Janine told her that the couple married out of high school and raised a family of four. Their last child had just graduated from college and Jonathan was all set with his retirement date. They were getting ready to follow their lifelong dream of traveling across the United States with no plan other than to stop in new places and meet new people.

Two weeks before they were scheduled to start on their adventure, Mary Beth developed stomach pains. Jonathan later found out, his wife had been dealing with a throat issue that made it challenging to swallow—something she never mentioned. As she apologetically explained, she didn't want to worry him over something that was nothing more than an annoyance. However, the pains in her abdomen raised even Mary Beth's concern.

Quietly, on her own, she scheduled an appointment with their family doctor. Whatever was wrong, she planned to find out and explain it to Jonathan in a calm and controlled manner. She was sure she would just have to fill some prescriptions and adapt her doctor's orders into their travel plans. No way was her health going to interfere with this dream trip they'd imagined for more than thirty years.

As it turned out, MaryBeth never got the chance to explain anything to her husband. Less than an hour after she entered her doctor's office, she was on her way to a local oncologist. An hour after that she was admitted to a hospital specializing in cancer treatments. By the time MaryBeth called Jonathan and he rushed to meet her at the hospital, she had been diagnosed with esophageal cancer that had metastasized to her stomach. Three months later she died.

Jonathan never mentioned his wife's passing and Grace never inquired. She was grateful, however, that she knew the circumstances of his widowhood and always kept that information in mind when they were together.

"Well, don't stay too late, Grace. I know you are trying to get up to speed, but work will always be there in the morning. You need to take a break. Get rest. Do something fun."

"Thanks for the reminder. I can get so wrapped up in my work, and I've learned it's not the best thing for me, professionally or personally. I just have this one last file to go through and then I'm on my way. Promise!"

During her first week on the job, Grace found the after-hours quiet of Wood Haven's' administrative offices unsettling. Now that she was more accustomed to the unidentifiable sounds of the vacated floor, she felt reasonably comfortable.

One last file. Come on Grace you can plow through this in an hour.

Despite her self-encouragement, Grace had her doubts about the time it would take to review the final Faith File. She had left it last for good reason. The stack of papers housed in the thin manila folder measured over two inches high. Grace assumed that the woman's extensive mental and medical struggles were responsible for the reams of medication and treatment reports. Instead what she discovered was that this woman had been confined at Wood Haven longer than all but one other person in the group.

Patient: *Teagan Cormick*
Date of Admittance: *January 18, 1930*
Number: *01183017*
Age: *17*
Ethnicity: *Irish*
Marital Status: *Single*
Pregnancies: *None*
Diagnosis: *Hysteria caused by overaction of the mind*

She was admitted almost fifty years ago? And she came here when she was only 17? So this woman . . . what's her name? Teagan Cormick. She has spent more than half her life locked away. And for what? Having an overactive mind? If that were truly a harmful mental condition, almost everyone I know would be locked away, including me.

While the thought initially amused Grace, in a quick moment she realized the seriousness of the circumstance. A fury began to flow through her body and increased as she read through decades of doctor's evaluations and disciplinary reports. What became clear was that during Teagan's life at Wood Haven she had established a role as a protector of others. More often than not, reports about her rebellious actions were related to situations where she was aiding women.

Grace found details of forced isolation, questionable medical practices and punishing maltreatments morphing into disturbing visions. Her thoughts became so realistic that she imagined women in the hallway outside her office—where Wood Haven patients had once lived. Unsettled, Grace called out.

"Is someone there?"

Holding her breath, Grace waited for a response. All that returned was silence. Then she heard it. A quiet sigh. Someone *was* right outside her office.

Cautiously, Grace left her chair, making her way around the desk and across her office to the door. As she leaned into the hallway, she felt a burst of energy on her left side. Turning quickly, Grace called out, "Wait. Stop. Who are you? What do you want?"

The shadowy figure never slowed down along the hall to the exit stairs. With a determination overriding her fears, Grace set off on a run. It took her only a few strides to get close to the person clearly struggling to go faster. Catching up, Grace managed to latch on to an edge of the person's clothing.

"Stop, please. I mean you no harm. I just want to know why you are outside my office?

Leveraging her grip Grace rotated the person into her view. In the dim hallway light it was hard to see the details of whoever was before her, other than it was a woman, none too young in age. It was also apparent she was heaving with need for the oxygen she'd used up, trying to escape.

"Look, I don't know who you are or why you were standing outside my office, but I can see that you are struggling for air. Let's sit on this hall bench so we can both catch our breath. Then we can talk."

With no options, the woman allowed Grace to lead her to the nearby wooden seat. Lowering in unison, Grace was relieved to see that the woman's breaths were becoming less labored, more evenly spaced. Clearly this person was unused to physical activity. Grace also guessed that her age was more advanced than she first imagined. A pang of compassion pushed any remaining fears from Grace's heart. This intruder was no threat. Whoever she was and for whatever reason she was standing outside her office, Grace was quite sure she had no evil intent.

"Ok. Let's start over. I'm Grace Reid. I work here at Wood Haven helping people here. I am not going to harm you in any way. I just want to make sure you're ok and help you get back to where you belong."

The woman finally turned and looked directly at Grace. Her eyes were a beautiful shade of green, overcast with shadows of sadness. For a moment she searched Grace's face, giving no clue to her thoughts or intent. The silence between them built until Grace wondered if the woman had perhaps suffered a stroke and was no longer able to speak. She was about to reach out and touch the woman to try and communicate in another way when she heard the unimaginable.

"Hello, Missus. Me name is Teagan. Teagan Cormick."

CHAPTER TWENTY

WOOD HAVEN ADMITTANCE FORM

Patient: *Janna Mazury*
Date of Admittance: *May 3, 1939*
Number: *05033931*
Age: *25*
Ethnicity: *Polish*
Marital Status: *Married*
Children: *Six*
Cause of insanity: *Involutional melancholia*

BEIN' IMPRISONED IN THIS nighmare of a place caused a deep longin' fer me homeland. Time spent with with Maeve 'twas a blessin', as we'd sit and chat 'bout our families and our villages—every word keepin' all o'it close in our hearts. Truth be told, there was times when I lay sleepin' I was sure me mam and da was with me, 'til I woke and tears went ta streaming knowin' 'twas nothin' but a dream.

Janna was of the same heart as Maeve and me. Though she be Polish, her love o' home and family matched our own.

I first met her in the ward. She'd been chained ta a pipe which forced her ta sit on the hard, cold floor. Watchin'as she kept movin' ta get comfortable, 'twas clear the poor soul had no strength 'gainst the heavy metal chains. I went and sat close by in case she might be lookin' fer comfort. While sittin', I went ta imaginin' me childhood and the lessons taught me by me mam. No matter if I come ta her whinin' or cryin', she always said the same.

"Now, Teagan, t'is not so bad. You just need ta offer it up."

Me child's mind could ne'er understand me mam's words, but I knew better than ta open me mouth with questions. Still, I was in great need o'comfort 'gainst the things makin' me sad, or mad, or whatever was hurtin' me young heart. So's one day, after being teased unmercifully by Tommy Dempsey in the school lunch room, I started a bit of a game 'tween God and meself.

I bargained if God keep Tommy away from me, I'd offer up three Our Fathers, three Hail Marys and three Glory Be's. And if he happened ta find a way ta punish the bloomin' eejit fer bein' so mean, I'd pray the Apostle's Creed fer good measure.

The next day at school, Tommy Dempsey wet himself in front o'the whole play yard, a rough game of football squishin' the pee right outta him. His blokes started pointin' and laughin', causin' Tommy ta turn all shades of red as he shouted, "Bugger off ya bloody scabs."

As it happened, the principal, Mr. Donoghue, was in the school yard at that very moment. Upon hearin' the swear words comin' outta Tommy's mouth, he sent the lad home for a week as penance. From then on, God and me was regular players o'the "offer it up" game, even after I was fully grown. So's it was, sittin' next ta this woman in need of comfort, the time seemed 'bout right for a round.

Morning Lord. T'is Teagan. Guess I'll start off by thankin' ya fer the sunshine I can just see through the bars o'the windows in this nasty place. While I'd be much happier outdoors, feelin' the sun and the wind doncha know, I'm havin' faith you've a plan for me life. And, as me mam always preached, I'm keepin' faith in that plan.

Had a mind ta ask if you'd be willin' ta play a game of "Offer it up" this fine day? Ya see, there's this woman here, well, I don't quite know her name or such, but as you can see, Lord, she's in sort of a bad way. I was hopin' ya could help her.

If ya might get the orderlies ta set her loose, let the poor thing sit on a chair or a bench. Then I'd have a bit o'time ta talk ta the woman and maybe do somethin' for her. If ya can do that Lord, I'll say a full rosary this very night. Now mind ya, I'm not tryin' ta tell ya how ta run people's lives. It's just I can't hardly stand ta see the woman chained ta a pipe, sittin' on the concrete like she is.

So's give it a thought, Lord and I'll be waitin" and watchin' fer a sign. Oh, and if ya could please, remember ta keep blessin' me mam and da and all me brothers and sisters as well, I'd be most grateful.

Makin' a quick sign o'the cross, I blessed meself as well as me "offer" ta God. Then I sit in wait, ta see if Himself was in a game-playin' mood. 'Twas only a bit afore I knew. Nurse Bennett come by where I was sittin'. Without so much as a glance me way, she bent down ta the woman in chains.

"Janna, I'm Nurse Bennett. I'm in charge here today. I'm going to have the orderlies unchain you and bring you down the hall to see the doctor."

Hearin' them words, "down the hall" put the fear o'God clean through me. Takin' a quick look at the poor woman, her body movin' no more than in shallow breaths, there was no tellin' what the doctor might be goin' ta do. 'Twas more than I could manage, fearin' fer this woman's life. So's I gathered up me courage and spoke ta the go nurse.

"Excuse me Nurse Bennett. I know ya got your plans and all, but is there anyway ya could just unchain the woman and leave her? I'd be happy ta help her onta a bench and watch o'er her 'til we're sent ta the dining hall or the dormitory. I know it's not usual, but I'm feelin' sad she's bein' sent down the hall, bein' here just a day."

"I'm afraid I can't do that, Teagan, although your offer is very kind. You see this woman has some problems in her mind and in her body. That's why her husband has sent her here, away from him and their six children. I don't know if the doctor will be able to help her, but I do know that if we don't try she will never get better."

"Six children? Fer sure'n that's a brood. How is it she gave birth ta 'em but isn't home carin' fer 'em?"

"You know I can't talk about such things, Teagan. All I can say is she gave birth to those six children in five years and the strain on her body caused her to develop a deficiency disease. Or as women in my family have called it, The Change.

"The change, ya say? Exactly what kinda changing da ya mean? Me da used ta say that mam change in that she twasn't the same lass he married after all us kids come along, While's I can't say t'is true or not, she ne'er gave up takin' care o'us."

Nurse Bennett looked ta me as if I'd two heads. Givin' a quick laugh she turned straight towards me ta answer.

"I think the change your father talked about was something different than what this woman has gone through, Teagan. Her change is something that all women experience as they get older and their bodies are no longer able to make babies."

"Not make beibes? How is it that kind o'change can happen and how can it hurt a woman's mind?"

I'm sorry Teagan, I don't have time to explain right now. I have to get this woman down the hall."

With that, the nurse turned on her heel and made her way ta the orderlies. Givin' 'em directions on what ta do with the woman, she set off ta her other nursin' chores. 'Twas only a moment 'til two o'the oversized orderlies was unchainin' the woman and draggin' her along the concrete floors inta the hall, with no never mind o'the pain they might be causin'.

I could feel anger risin' in me. 'Twas bad enough the woman be shut away in in this dark, nasty place, but ta be taken down the hall ta suffer God knows what awful kinds o'things, twasn't right. Me brain got so addled I couldn't think straight. So's I went lookin' for Maeve, hopin' she could calm me down. When I found her on the porch, I asked if she'd seen the new woman?

"Aye, Teagan. As they was draggin' her down the hall. Seemed like she'd not an ounce o'life in her."

"That's what I thought as well, doncha know. So's I asked Nurse Bennett all polite-like if she could let the woman go unchained and just let her set fer a bit. As God is me witness, she only talked 'bout how the woman was here 'cause o'some *change* that made it so she couldn't care fer her beibes. Six of 'em in all at home with their da. Can ya imagine?

"Sure'n, I can imagine Teagan. I meself suffered with the change and 'twas part of the reason me husband and me doctor put me here."

"How can changin' give people the right ta lock a woman away, Maeve? I just can't bring meself ta understand it."

"Ya see Teagan, the kind of change that's bein' talked 'bout isn't the same as you're thinkin'. It's the way a woman's body changes as she grows old. Ya know, when your time o'the month stops and ya can no longer make beeibes in your belly."

"Aw, go on withya, Maeve. Never heard such blarney in me life. Women quit havin' beibis just 'cause of that, they're tired o' it. Has nothing ta due with some changin' o' their bodies."

"Ah but t'is exactly that. You've just not been old enough ta know fer yourself. Not only can it matter in a woman's body, but in her mind as well. So's this woman may get well again. Whether they let her go home, that's another thing all together."

'Twas many a day afore I saw the woman again. This time she was tucked in the corner o'the ward, tied inta a wheel chair by rags knotted 'round her body. I was drawn ta her like a moth ta flame, hopin' she was better now than afore.

"T'is good ta see ya, missus. If I rightly recall, Nurse Bennett said your name was Janna. So's, Janna, how'd ya be feelin'?

Hearin' her name, the woman's eyes come alive. She sit up a bit and turned her head, clearly tryin ta figure who I might be.

"I saw ya your first day here. Me name is Teagan. Teagan Cormick. There's no reason for ya ta remember me. Ya was feelin' poorly last time we was near one 'nother."

The waif of a woman nodded, not speakin' but surely breathin' and hearin'. That's how Janna and me come ta know each other, sittin', talkin' and listenin', me doin' most o'the talkin'. Janna doin' most o'the listenin'. Thanks be ta God, Twasn't long afore Janna was sittin' on her own, eatin' and walkin' as well. Even Nurse Bennett said she was comin' along.

THEN COME A DAY WHEN Janna went ta talkin' more than listenin'. She started with memories in bits n'pieces, tellin' stories 'bout comin' ta America from her village o' Zarnow in Poland.

"I was happy when my parents chose to leave Zarnow. Moj tata and moj mama's meager incomes earned not enough. So, they made up their minds to emigrate to America for a time of ten years. Their plan was to work hard and save every penny earned so that they could return home with much money. As for me, unknown to my parents, I made up my mind to work and save for my own new life, where I would stay in America and marry and make many dzieciuchs— babies. It was that plan that led me to my husband, Otto Kutzner. He was a good German man I met at an Easter Service at St. Stanislaus Bishop and Martyr's Church on New York's East Side, where he and I married and settled nearby."

The tellin' o'her comin' ta America was tirin' ta the woman and so's she stopped talkin'. That didn't keep me from sittin' with Janna mind ya. I wanted the woman ta know I was waitin' fer more. So's I told some o'me own family stories, sharin' memories about me trip ta America, 'til she had strength ta begin again.

"My parents stayed ten years, as planned, and a few months more to see me married. Then off they went to Poland, while Otto and I began our life in

America as Mr and Mrs. It wasn't but ten months before our first child, a son, was born in January. In that same year I gave birth to twin girls, followed twelve months later by a boy. Another set of twins came in just a year. It seemed Otto and I could make babies by wishing them. It was much to manage. But I gave every part of myself to our family, making life all Otto and I dreamed. Life was good until I reached my 40th year. Overnight I found myself sad, unable to rise in a strong mind each morning. Worse, I would shout at my children for the feeblest of reasons. Scared and confused, I wondered if it was brakuje domu i rodziców—a sadness for my home and my parents. I wrote to mama, telling her of the dark feelings in me. She returned a letter where she explained many women in our family had felt and acted the same, even herself. She assured me in time, the darkness would go away."

The pain o'Janna's words was reflectin' in her eyes. The more I listened, the more I began wonderin' if this sad time might be the change Nurse Bennett had told me. Not bein' sure, I sat quiet-like, lettin' Janna put together her thoughts and words.

"A time came when the sadness made me unable to leave my bed. Frightened, Otto went in search of a doctor. When the two men returned and entered into our bedroom, they spoke about me as if I were not there. Otto told of the births of our children and the doctor explained the toll their close arrivals took on my body. The doctor declared the need to examine me and told Otto to leave the room. Deeply frightened by being alone with this man I did not know, I closed my eyes and held my breath, waiting for what he was about to do."

Bein' 'round doctors was not somethin' I knew. Me mam always had neighbor women help when she was feelin' sickly, and meself, I'd always been strong. 'Twas only when forced ta come ta this awful place I learned 'bout the nasty thing's doctors could do ta a body. So's I was understandin' Janna's fear as she kept on with her story.

"I felt the doctor move to the end of the bed where he pulled up the covers, exposing the lower part of my body. Commanding me to bend my legs and set my knees apart, he began pushing and prodding sharply through my private parts, causing pain to shoot through me. Had I not been so frightened, I would have called out in discomfort, but my dread of this man and all he was doing kept me silent. After what felt like forever, the doctor withdrew his hands and pulled the sheet back over my body. He asked if I was still menstruating. When I replied infrequently, he moved to the doorway, commanding Otto to return. He addressed my husband stating that I was suffering from a deficiency disease that he imagined was brought on by the number of children I bore so closely. He said not only had I reached an early end of my child bearing years, but this disease could cause me to be mentally unstable and capable of anger that was a threat to our family."

Speakin' the doctor's words caused a flush o'tears from Janna's eyes. Listein' ta her story, I was sure she was far from crazy with not a mean bone in her body. "T'is alright Janna. Go ahead. Have yerself a good cry and be lettin' your sorrows drain 'way through your tears."

"Oh Teagan, it was heartbreaking to listen to the doctor fill Otto's head with such terrible things. But at that moment even I was not sure if what he was saying might be true. The only ray of hope came when the doctor offer three choices of treatments that might cure me. The first was simplest in the form of medications—belladonna, cannabis and opium. He also explained a new treatment that could be blended in to my morning tea called Ovariin, which he described as pulverized cow ovaries. The third was to remove my baby-making parts from my body, but he warned, none were guaranteed, and that the only way to be truly sure I would never hurt our children was to have me committed."

As I come ta understand how Janna and Maeve been forced inta this madhouse and 'bout "the change" Nurse Bennett been tryin' ta explain, seemed to me none o'it was 'bout women no longer havin' beibes. More, 'twas 'bout men misundstandin' the natural way o'women's bodies. And the high price women paid for them men's mistakes.

CHAPTER TWENTY-ONE

GRACE GENTLY LED TEAGAN back to her office and settled her into her comfy oversized chair. Wrapping her favorite mohair shawl around Teagan's shoulders she encouraged her to put her feet up on the nearby ottoman. All the while Teagan kept a questioning eye on this woman who was offering such unusual kindnesses.

"I was just going to make myself a cup of tea. Would you like some, Teagan?"

Making the offer was second nature to Grace, but she could tell it was clearly out of the norm for the wary woman. Rather than wait for a response, she began transferring water from her oversized lunch thermos into a pan on her hotplate. Next she set out her grandmother's green teapot alongside two cups and saucers and two bags of Irish tea. While waiting for the water to boil, Grace placed a small bowl of sugar and a carton of cream from her utilitarian refrigerator on the table next to Teagan. The addition of two spoons and two napkins rounded out their service. Through the entire process, Teagan's eyes monitored Grace's every move.

When at last the pot boiled, Grace poured a bit of steaming water into the uncovered teapot, swirled it around and poured it out into a nearby potted plant. With the ceramic brewer properly warmed, she placed two tea bags into the pot, filled it with steaming water and replaced the top.

Carefully, Grace set the two cups on the table near Teagan and pulled up an office chair for herself. It was only then she noticed tears filling the woman's eyes.

"I've not been where tea was proper brewed since sittin at me mam's table, many years ago."

The idea that such a simple act could inspire intense emotions within this woman caught Grace off guard. Her heart beat through her chest as she poured tea into each cup and watched Teagan reverentially add in cream and sugar, like a sacred ritual.

"Did your mother often make tea for you?" Grace hoped the question would not be too painful for Teagan to answer.

"Aye, all Irish drink tea, doncha know. It's the next best thing ta mother's milk."

With a quick wink and a smile, Teagan brushed aside her tears, revealing a playful nature. It was a character trait Grace found remarkable considering the woman had spent 48 of her 65 years locked away in an asylum. Rather than unwittingly lead Teagan down a path of painful memories, Grace decided to try and keep their conversation light by talking about the here and now.

"So Teagan, I think perhaps you've been outside my office a few times before. In fact, now that I think about it, I believe we bumped in to each other in the hallway one morning last week. Do you often walk in this hallway or was there something special you wanted to talk to me about?"

Grace's gentle prod brought an immediate reaction from the Irish woman.

"Now missus, twasn't spyin' on ya, exactly. I'd just heard some nurses talkin' 'bout this new woman come ta Wood Haven and I was curious. That's all. So's if you're thinkin' 'bout lockin' me away fer it, I'll ask ya please ta think again. I meant no harm."

"I certainly understand your curiosity, Teagan. I would feel the same if I were in your place. As for locking you away, for any reason, those days are over. Never again will you, or any of the others here, be locked away as punishment."

Looking at the woman, Grace could see doubt running through every bit of her being. Teagan had no reason to trust her and even less reason to believe anything she said. If Grace was going to help this woman and the other Wood Haven patients like her, she was going to have to come up with some meaningful ways to connect with them.

"Ya know, this blanket o'yours, it reminds me of a favored shawl o'my own. Me granny knit it for me, don'cha know and it's been a bit o'time since I've thought o'it. Makes me feel good, havin' it wrapped 'round me."

It was as if Nana O'Connor was whispering in her ear, as she listened to Teagan talk about the special shawl. The soft coverlet had been a gift to Grace from her nana, purchased on their long-ago trip to Ireland. While it wasn't a huge connection, it was a start.

"Interesting you would say that, Teagan. My nana gave me that blanket, as you call it. In fact, she bought it for me at a lovely woolen shop in Cork, when we visited Ireland after my high school graduation. So it seems as if we already have a bit in common."

"Cork, did ya say now? Where 'bouts were ya visitin'?"

"Well we traveled quite a bit, going to Kinsale and, of course, Blarney to visit the Blarney Castle. But I distinctly recall that we found the shawl in a lovely wool shop along the harbor in Cobh."

Grace didn't anticipate talk of her travels bringing any special reaction from Teagan. So when the older woman jumped up and grabbed Grace by the shoulders, she was unsure how to respond, other than to wait for Teagan to explain.

"Ya don't say! Cobh along the seaside is where me da worked and straight up the hill, by the Catholic Church, was where me family lived. It's been many a year since I've seen me hometown. Tell me, what did it look like? Was there men workin' the shipyard? Did ya stop by Fitzgerald's Pub right 'cross the road from there?

Grace felt confused as if her brain were clouding over. She'd just finished reading through Teagan's file and there was no mention of Cohb as the Irish woman's hometown. In fact, Grace clearly remembered reading Queenstown as Teagan's place of birth. Unsure of whether this was an issue of dementia or just a touch of forgetfulness, Grace answered thoughtfully, trying to minimize any confusion.

"Well, Teagan, I'm not sure exactly what to tell you. First of all, it's been almost thirty years since my nana and I traveled to Ireland. Second, in all the paperwork in your file, your hometown is listed as Queenstown, not Cobh. So perhaps I have misunderstood what you are asking?"

Without pause, Teagan answered back.

" 'Tis a bit confusin' I know, Missus, but the towns we're talkin' 'bout are one and the same. When I was but a mite, me village was known as Queenstown. As time went on, them's in charge decided ta change it up ta Cobh. None of us liked it much, so's for years, we still called it by the name we'd known for so long. We Irish tend ta stick with tradition, doncha know."

A sense of relief enveloped Grace as she processed Teagan's logical explanation.

This woman is far from demented. In fact, she's mentally sharp and physically fit enough to force me to have to run to catch up with her.

"I can understand how you feel about the changing of the name of your town. I come from a close-knit community of Buffalo in nearby New York State. I think if government officials ever tried to change the name of our city, they'd have a riot on their hands."

"Sure'n t'is a slap in the face when they go ta changin' the name o'the place ya call home."

The conversation encouraged Teagan to share more details and stories of her Irish heritage As she did Grace realized their common devotion to family and home would offer ways for the two women to connect and build trust. It was a comfort that made Grace smile.

"You know, Teagan, I think we're going to become fast friends. I'm so glad you came to share a cup of tea and I hope you'll come back again. But now I need to go home and have some dinner, and I imagine you need to return to your room as well. Can I walk with you?"

"No need, Missus. I'm used ta findin' me own way. But I will take ya up on your offer fer tea again. Would ya mind if I brung me friend Maeve along? She's an Irish gal as well and I'm thinkin' she'd enjoy your fancy china cups and the way ya steep the tea, just like home."

"I tell you what, Teagan. You are welcome to bring Maeve and any of your friends. I'll be sure to have plenty of Irish tea and china cups on hand. I may even sneak in a scone or two as well."

"Oh, that t'would be grand. I'll be sure ta tell those still able ta move 'round. We're not so young anymore don'cha know, but we're still hale and hearty! Thanks again fer your kindness, Missus. I'll be on me way now."

The thought of Teagan walking away caused a catch in Grace's breathing. Already this woman was etching her way into her heart. She couldn't let her go just yet.

"Teagan, would you do me a favor?"

"Sure'n I would, Missus. What's your pleasure?"

"It would mean a great deal to me if you would call me Grace. I'd like to be more than just a 'Missus' to you."

As the words left her, Grace stepped closer to the petite woman. Enfolding Teagan in her arms, she received a heartfelt embrace in return. It was more than a physical reaction to touching and being touched. It was a connection that felt like a reunion of souls, as her Nana O'Connor often described such special moments.

Finally releasing each other, Teagan took a step back and stared powerfully into Grace's eyes. Clearly the woman was searching for something.

Perhaps answers to a half century of questions.

If that were the case, Grace was going to do everything within her power to provide Teagan with answers.

"I'll be honorin' your request and callin'ya just as I did one o'me best friends in Queenstown. G'night, Gracie girl."

With that, Teagan Cormick disappeared into the shadows of the hallway, back into the darkness that for so long had shaped her world.

Chapter Twenty-Two

WOOD HAVEN ADMITTANCE FORM

Patient: *Rebecca Odera Washington*
Date of Admittance: *August 10, 1941*
Number: *08104121*
Age: *21*
Ethnicity: *German African*
Marital Status: *Single*
Children: *None*
Diagnosis: *Mental Excitement, Feebleness of Intellect*

TWASN'T A DOUBT WHEN Rebecca come ta be locked away with the rest o'us. Right off she was different in the looks o'her dark skin and coiled hair. Then there was her constant jabberin' 'bout life bein' unfair and deservin' better—usin' words that somes I knew and somes not. Ya might say 'twas impossible ta shut her up.

I didn't begrudge the girl, mind ya. As I come ta discover, she'd more than her share of reasons ta fuss. That's how we connected straight away.

She'd been raisin 'a ruckus in the ward and while the orderlies said not a word, 'twas clear they were 'bout ready ta tie her down and use a needle ta quiet her.

After so much o'me life wasted in this wretched place, I was carin' less 'bout the rules and more 'bout the hateful things bein' done ta people, often fer no good reason. Not wantin' Odera ta know the punishment of a needle, I stepped up ta the girl and placed me hand on her shoulder. I told her I understood she was havin' a struggle and asked what I might do ta ease her mind. Quick-like she stopped all she was sayin' and doin' and stared inta me. While bein' a bit fearful o'how she might go, I gently led her ta the porch. There's I sat her and meself down, side by each. Thinkin' back ta when me and me own sisters mended our scraps, I decided ta start easy.

"There now, what's your name?"

The answer she returned softened both her voice and her manner.

"Meine nahe ist Rebecca Odera, but Odera is what I was called as a child. In das Hebrew language of meine mutter it means one who ploughs or makes the way in life. In das African language from the people of mein vater it means one of destiny. That is the meaning I chose and why meine full nahme I proudly wear."

"'Tis a beautiful story, Rebecca Odera. Nice ta meet ya. Me name is Teagan. Teagan Cormick. Don't have a middle name as I was the last o'eight and I'm thinkin' me parents run outta ideas by the time I come 'long. As fer the meanin' o'me name, when I was born me da chose to christen me, Teagan, as he believed me ta be the most beautiful beibe. And 'tis 'xactly what me name means . . . beauty."

"I too shared ein bond with mein vater, Amara Botha. He was ein African soldier to das Great War sent to fight for the das English Army. In that way he and meine mutter, Rivka Abramson met. She was only eine maiden when to her village das Englishe Army came. Das villagers hid inside their houses and shops in secret and fear, but as time went on friendships arose. For meine parents it was more.

It was not easy for meine mutter und mein vater as they spoke different languages. Worse, mein vater was ein African Black und meine Mutter was eine white Jewess."

Meself bein' Irish and Catholic, 'twas little I knew 'bout Jewish people and their ways. 'Twas only in America that I come close enough ta Jews ta get a bit o'understandin'. Same o'black people. Me first time bein' 'round anyone o'color was durin' me ocean voyage 'board The Olympic. Deckhands in the lowest levels was black men, forced ta work like animals. From that little bit o'seeing both peoples, I could only imagine such a different man and woman joinin' together. Tellin' their story, Rebecca left little ta me imagination.

"Meine parents found places to meet—behind Heir Schulz's butcher shop, in the alley of Berkowitz's mercantile, among back lots of the Königsbacher brewery—always because of their attraction to each other. As their love stronger grew, family and friends warned them apart to stay as white and black together were not allowed, but determined to marry they were. In a Jewish temple in Kowelenz meine parents stood, amid bomb rubble and before

God. A fellow soldier from mein vater and a Jewishess already in the holy space praying witnessed the promise of Rivka and Amara to forever love and honor."

In describin' her parent's weddin' 'twas as if Rebecca drifted away. Not in body, don'cha know. 'Twas in her mind she was no longer with me. Tho' anxious ta hear the rest o'her story, I was wishin' wherever she'd gone, I could go as well. By the light in her eyes, it seemed a most magical place. I found meself tryin' ta imagine where she was and what it looked like. As if seein' inta me mind, Rebecca began tellin' 'xactly what I was wishin' ta know.

"Meine parents in the forests outside of Kowelenz settled. Together eine small cabin they built and for their own farmed. They had enough for themselves and eine bit left to barter for clothes and goods. Quietly they lived, remembered by none. Not even the army of England, which mein vatter deserted and was for him looking. In that cabin born and raised I was, in meine parent's ways and beliefs, both African and German. A rich life for all of us it was.. But when ten years of age I became, our lives forever changed. German soldiers for meine parents came."

Rebecca's story started me thinkin'. Life inside these dark hallways and stained walls 'twas simple. We heard nothin' o'the outside world. Truth be told, anything happenin' beyond ourselves made no matter. Most was troubled enough in their own lives, no less lives o'others. Rebecca's tale o'the government punishin' people fer who they was born ta be, 'twas beyond me way o'thinkin.'

I found meself wonderin' if she might be imaginin' the story and that's how she come ta bein' locked away in this rotten place. Yet as the young woman kept on, the strength o' her words made 'em near impossible ta deny.

"We, in the woods, invisible were. Sometimes to market mein mutter would go, but never mein vater. Yet as we settled to sleep each night, mein Vater our cabin door bolted und slid across a heavy chest. Beneath his pillow, a knife he kept, ready for what could be. Then too soon the day we dreaded arrived. Eine night at our door we heard pounding and the shouted demands,"Offne die Tür." As we had practiced, meine mutter beneath floorboards mit mein blanket and mein doll, hid me. While louder their pounding grew, meine mutter the floorboards replaced and ein chair over them set. Meine vater then das bolt unlocked und handle released. Die Beutche Soldaten into our home burst und arrested mein vater and mutter. They demanded alle kinder—all children—to come out, but mein vater in calm voice said, 'No kinder are hier.' Das soldaten then mein vater started beating, calling him 'schwarze lügner'—black liar. I heard meine muttter scream und then above me a loud crash came."

"Alright, let's go you two. It's time to move to the dining hall for dinner."

'Twas a nurse passin' by and orderin' us. Her words cut thru straight me. In me mind I shouted back, *No! Not yet. We're not done talkin'. Leave us be.* Yet I knew better than ta say such things or ta try try and stay put. With any luck t'would be another few minutes afore she'd come 'round 'gain, so's I spoke encouragin' words ta Rebecca.

" 'Tis alright. Finish your story. No worries."

The dark-skinned girl took a look into me eyes. As I returned her steady gaze, she thoughtfully faded back ta Germany.

"Above me I heard die stomping feet of meine mutter as she was shouting at die soldaten. Ignoring her, they pushed meine vater und he fell and hit his head. Blood through cracks in the floorboards dripped onto meine face as I could see meine vater on the floor, laying injured. Die soldaten through our cabin ripped, while mutter tended the wounds of meine vater. When no kinder were found, two soldiers yanked mein vater to his feet and another meine mutter grabbed. From our home they dragged both and the cabin became quiet. I knew meine parents were forever gone. Until I was sure that safely I could come out, I stayed silent in das dirt and gravel, holding tight to mein blanket and doll. I could, in mein head, hear meine mutter say this was their wish—*ihr Leben für meins*—their lives for mein. When I out of the space crawled, it was night. I slipped on a dress in which mein mutter had into the hem sewn gold coins, hidden for mein safe passage to Belgium to pay. Mein blanket und doll into a satchel I put and as mein vater had told me, I to Heir Dutweiller's house went."

Rebecca's voice dropped ta nothin'. Everythin' 'bout her seemed suddenly weak, as if she might fall inta a faint. I was about ta reach out and give her a good shake, when her words begin again, this time coming from a place deep within her.

"When to Herr Dutweiller's I came, he to the back of his house and an outside door took me. I through das door und down musty steps into ein root cellar followed. Quickly inside he closed us to keep us unknown. As a candle he lit, silent I stood. Then five steps more onto ein muddy floor and through a trap door, beneath which were rations of glass jarred foods. *Geh hin und bleib ruhig Bis die Tür wieder geöffnet ist* was his order—enter and stay quiet until das door is again opened. For some time hidden I stayed, waiting for someone unknown, to come. Dark was the cellar but still I could feel snakes und spiders, so wrapped in my blanket and close to my doll I stayed. When hunger came, jars of fruits und vegetables I chose blindly. I in those same jars myself relieved when emptied they became."

I could see the nurse returnin' ta the ward, getting' closer and closer as she come lookin' for those laggin'. No doubt, there was two choices. The first ta raise up and walk away from Rebecca, hopin' she'd follow. The second ta sit right still and hope in the short space o'time left, the child could finish the tellin' o' her story. With one look at the sorry state of this sweet thing 'longside me, I made me choice. Sayin' a silent prayer ta Mary, Mother of God, I sat and listened.

"Forever it seemed until ein hooded man yanked open the trap door. From the darkness he pulled me and money demanded. I from the hem of my dress offered coins that meine mutter had so carefully sewn. He das money grabbed und then up the cellar stairs und behind the barn dragged and shoved me. He into ein wagon bed tossed me und under piles of straw did bury me, warning, *lüge still und schweige--* lie still and stay silent, no matter what happens. It was 320 kilometers to Belgium the distance, to the freedom of which meine parents had dreamed. When at last there we arrived, only black-skinned immigrants were willing to harbor me because of the color of my skin and the look of my hair. A family from Morocco, mutter, vater und vier kinder, under their roof took me. I found work as a seamstress and in the hem of mein own hand-sewn blue dress, meine money I saved. Slowly a life I built, tucking away wages for mein dream of life in the great freedom of America. When sixteen I became, guided by memories from meine parents, I finally to New York City journied. There people saw only my dark skin and so I with three colored women an apartment in Harlem shared. I as a seamstress in a factory, long hours again worked and die memories from meine mutter und vater kept close".

"Alright you two, this is your last warning. Move on to the dining hall this minute!"

'Twas was no longer a choice we had, so's I stood. The warmth of me body drawin' away from Rebecca shook her mind. Though confused, she knew 'twas time ta move and trusted ta follow me. As we made our way ta the dining hall, Rebecca softly finished her tale.

"Eire nocht I was late the factory leaving, the darkness hiding dangers. I was blocks from mein apartment when a man before me jumped. He scared me and I tried to run, but faster he was and he to ein alley dragged and raped me. Meine mind can only parts of that night recall, as for dead he left me. I was by a beggar found and to the police brought. I could neither meine name nor my address tell and so I to a poor house was sent. When my memories I recovered, I no longer had work or a place to stay. I was to here forced to come and locked away."

Rebecca and meself fell silent as we entered inta the dining hall. We settled in at a long wooden table, amongst Maeve and Angel and Gabriele, all o'us swallowin' the tasteless food and drinkin' the sulphur water.

Fer the first time since bein' trapped in this nightmarish place, I understood in me soul things could be worse. More, I come ta understand that Rebecca herself knew much worse and deserved ta rant 'bout life bein' unfair anytime she pleased.

CHAPTER TWENTY-THREE

GRACE'S WORK WEEK FLEW BY, most of it taken up in meetings with Jonathan, and the Wood Haven staff, along with one important phone conference with Rebecca Whitford, the New Jersey State Secretary of Senior Services. Then there was her run-in with Teagan Cormick that had jump-started her week.

Meeting the plucky Irish woman made the Faith Files come alive for Grace. Teagan's stories and observations reenforced the trauma suffered by so many unfairly locked away. The encounter also boosted Grace's determination to improve the lives of the six Wood Haven residents slated for deinstitutionalization. That's what she focused on in her Friday conversation with Secretary Whitford.

Following the agenda she'd drawn up on her trusty legal pad, Grace provided the state administrator with a summary of the ten Wood Haven seniors and their various housing and medical needs. She then separated them into two groups, one capable of mainstreaming and the other individuals in need of long term care, and the options she envisioned for both. The teleconference had gone well until the secretary asked Grace one very straightforward question.

"What have these seniors said when you've asked what *they* want?"

Grace sat momentarily stunned by the query. To date, she had developed her plans and made her determinations by studying stacks of patient files compiled by various doctors over the last fifty years. There was so much material to review and process, other than Teagan, Grace had yet to speak directly to any of the other nine people whose futures she was deciding.

How has this happened? From the very start of my career I've made a difference in the lives of seniors by treating them as real people, not aging case studies. Now, because the circumstances of these seniors are outside my traditional caseload, I've distanced myself? Treating them as words and numbers on impersonal medical reports?

"Hello, Grace. Are you still there? Have we lost our connection?"

"Yes m'am, I'm still here. I apologize for not responding to your question. Actually it set me back a bit.

You see, I have built my career on supporting seniors as they make choices about housing, downsizing, retirement and end of life decisions. In that role, I have always taken a direct and personal approach no matter the individual or their circumstance, treating all as equals in everyway. For some reason in my first few weeks here at Wood Haven, I have been focused so strongly on reports and data about these seniors slated for deinstitutionalization, I seem to have forgotten the most essential element of my job, that being the people."

"Thank you for your honesty, Grace. I can certainly understand how the perameters of this job require new ways of approaching and tackling your case load. At the same time, I think you have just reminded us both that while the deinstitutionalization of Wood Haven offers a wide range of professional challenges, the essence of this project is the same as all of our social service work—the people we are striving to help."

"Absolutely, Secretary. And thank you for allowing me this misstep. I pledge it will not happen again."

"Grace I have seen your resume and talked to people who have been a part of your career. The only misstep you could make in this job would be to walk away before completing all the tasks. After speaking with you this afternoon, I have full confidence that you will do all within your ability to find the best future for every one of your ten Wood Haven seniors. Know you can reach out to me anytime you have a concern or question. I may not always be available, but I will get back to you as soon as my schedule permits."

"Thank you again, Secretary Whitford. I appreciate your support."

"Actually before we hang up, can we agree to a monthly phone call to talk about Wood Haven and, what is it you call them, your Faith File?"

"Yes m'am. The Faith File, and I'd be pleased to update you regularly."

"Sounds good. Give Janie a call, she's my AA here in Trenton. Nothing gets on my calendar without her say-so. Use the number you called today. Thanks."

With a click, their conversation ended, leaving Grace with a page and a half of notes and a headfull of thoughts to process.

But not at 5pm on a Friday, she chided herself. *Time to take a break. Get something to eat and plan some fun for the weekend.*

Grace locked her Faith Files in the bottom desk drawer, knowing if she packed them in her briefcase, she would work through the weekend. The idea of catching up while the rest of the staff was out of the office greatly appealed to Grace's sense of dedication. However, she was also trying to adopt the advice Jonathan had shared about finding balance in her life. The challenge was that in living in a new community, Grace had no set patterns, no circle of family and friends, no favorite hangouts to keep her occupied with things other than work.

Well then, it's pretty obvious I need to start finding some of those people and some of those things!

By the time Grace finally left the office and arrived at her rental home, her growling stomach was demanding dinner immediately, if not sooner. While pondering her meal preference, Grace realized she hadn't eaten since breakfast.

I really do need to start keeping better track of myself. I won't be able to do anyone any good if I end up sick on the job.

Having only patronized Midland's Dew Drop Inn and Cuppa Joe, Grace turned to the weekly Sun Journal Newspaper, delivered free of charge to her porch every Friday, for dinner suggestions. Inside she found a centerfold restaurant section.

Perfect. Let's see, Italian? Not really in the mood for cheese and sauce. Pizza? Ditto. Diner? Looking for something a little more. Steakhouse? A big slab of beef, not too appealing at the moment. Chinese? Thinking more homestyle. Café? Hmmm, maybe.

Grace read down the short list of café choices. There were two: Le Café and Welcome Home. While she loved the ideal of Paris suggested by the first name, there was something about Welcome Home that struck a cord. With a quick change from her business professional "uniform" of a suit, white blouse and sensible heels to jeans, a lace-trimmed peasant blouse and platform sandals, Grace flipped on the front porch light, hopped in her car and set off for the Main Street address of Welcome Home.

This was her first Friday night in downtown Midland and Grace was surprised by all the activity. Unsure of the street numbers and not wanting to be "that driver" who slows traffic while searching, Grace decided to leave her car in one of the municipal lots and walk to the cafe.

As luck would have it, her parking spot ended up just a block away from Welcome Home. She saw the classy hand-painted sign highlighted with white sparkling lights the moment she reached Main Street. Strolling up to the beveled glass, wood frame entry door, Grace noticed a menu in the oversized picture window completing the restaurant's façade.

Every appetizer made her mouth water. Every entrée made her stomach growl. And the desserts sounded as if they would definitely be worth the calories.

Now if they offer a decent selection of wines, or a top -shelf bar, I may just have found my new home away from home.

Once in the rustic entry, she paused to allow her eyes to adjust to the soft lighting. In that moment, Grace heard her name spoken by an unfamiliar voice.

"Hello, Grace. Nice to see you this evening."

Turning toward the greeter, Grace's eyes focused on the person of Mayor Jenkins.

"Hello, Mayor. Nice to see you."

"I know we got off track a bit in our meeting the other day, but I think it would be nice to dispense with formalities. Can we go back to you calling me Carl?"

The intensity the man displayed in their discussion of Wood Haven had receded. In its place was the charm that had made a first impression upon Grace and, no doubt, won over many voters.

"Of course, Carl. And I agree, our meeting did get a bit off track. So, I look forward to meeting again and finding positive ways to solve the challenges of your town and my seniors."

Grace was not going to give the guy the satisfaction of an apology for calling him out the other day. At the same time, she could hear Jonathan's words of wisdom, that they needed the mayor on their side. She needed to imprint that into her brain.

"Agreed. Perhaps we should seal our pact over a drink at the bar?"

Grace held a strong resolve against mixing personal with professional. Something about the mayor strengthened that instinct.

"Thanks Carl, but I just stopped by for a quick bite to eat. It's been a very long week and I wouldn't be great company. I'm sure I'll see you again soon though. Enjoy your weekend."

Extending her hand, Grace offered her most charming smile and hoped it would be enough to keep the mayor at bay. As in their initial meeting, the man wrapped both his hands around hers and clasped them more than shook them, lingering longer than Grace felt necessary.

"Another time then." The mayor withdrew his hands and, with a nod, walked out the door. His abrupt departure left Grace feeling as if she were in a vacuum. It was only the voice of the Welcome Home hostess that brought her back into the moment.

"Good evening and welcome home."

The woman's greeting matched the restaurant's comforting design of soft lighting, warm colors and uniquely framed images detailing the 200-year history of the town.

"Thank you. Do I need a reservation for dinner tonight?"

"I think we can find a table. How many?"

Grace knew the question was coming and had gotten comfortable with her answer.

"One."

"Name please."

"Reid."

"Thank you Ms. Reid. If you'd like to have a seat in our bar area, perhaps at one of the hightops or at the bar itself, it will be just a few minutes."

There was a time when the prospect of dining solo kept Grace tethered to the basket of take-out menus set alongside her home phone. She was forever grateful to Mary Wilson, a lovely widow she met through one of her senior consulting jobs, for helping her realize that worrying over social mores, such as a table for one, would short-change her life.

"My dear, if you let the way other people think determine your standards, one day you will wake up old, like me, and wish for the chance to do all the things everyone else said you shouldn't. And trust me, there will be nothing you can do about it then. The key is to experience every moment to the fullest. Remember, in life, there are no do-overs."

While the wise woman's words didn't immediately change Grace's single lifestyle choices, she did find herself using Mary's "no do-over" mantra as a guiding force. Little by little, Grace thought less about the judgement of others and more about her own passions. That's how her proviso against dining out alone became replaced with the fun ideal of sampling restaurants she'd never frequented and cuisines she'd never experienced. In short order, Grace lost her self-consciousness about society's "table for one" stigma.

Strolling into Welcome Home's bar area, Grace considered her seating choices. Both the bar and the bistro tables offered seats amid a sea of unknown faces. Deciding she had nothing to lose, Grace slid onto a bar seat of black leather fastened with decorative brass rivets and a mahogany wood frame. A friendly bartender came by within minutes. Confirming she could add her drink to her dinner bill, Grace ordered a glass of the house red.

Taking a deep breath of the burgundy liquid before sipping, Grace relaxed fully into the comfortable bar chair. Glancing around, she reviewed Midland's citizen medley surrounding her. There were couples and groups of varied ages and families gathered primarily at the high tops. The constant among all was the mood . . . easy and fun. Just what she needed after a long work week.

"What new drink have you concocted tonight?"

The voice in her ear startled Grace as much for its proximity as its personal tone. Turning towards the smooth speaker, she was surprised to find Officer Healy. Grace hadn't seen the deputy out of uniform before, and her body's response to the good-looking man was a lovely blush across her cheeks Fortunately she was able to pull back from her instinctive reaction and offer a reasonably intelligent reply.

"Nothing too creative tonight I'm afraid. Just a glass of red wine."

"Sounds good to me. Mind if I sit down?"

For the first time, Grace noticed a glint of gold highlighting the policeman's blue-gray eyes, adding his own personal twinkle to the dimly lit bar room.

"If your week has been anything like mine, then you need to pull up a chair."

Grace wasn't sure why she'd shared anything about her work week with this man, pretty much a total stranger. Then again, if life balance and fun was part of her new agenda, maybe Mike Healy was just what her executive director ordered.

Chapter Twenty-Four

WOOD HAVEN ADMITTANCE FORM

Patient: *Elizabeth Engler*
Date of Admittance: *October 9, 1936*
Number: *10093648*
Age: *48*
Ethnicity: *American*
Marital Status: *Married*
Children: *3 (2 living and one deceased)*
Diagnosis: *Grief, Feebleness of Intellect*

I KNEW THE WOMAN FROM HER first step inta the ward. Her dress was far from the elegant frocks she'd once worn and her look was pale and thin. No matter. 'Twas fer sure the woman who'd once taken me inta her home and helped start me new life in America.

An orderly come and set Mrs. Engler on a nearby chair. I couldn't help but be starin' at this once-elegant lady, now seemin' so lifeless.

What in the world was she doin' shut away within these terrible walls? What sadness had come inta her life that she was bound away in this misery?

As 'twas time ta be movin' ta lunch, I made up me mind ta be her guide. Seein' no one 'round ta lead her, I moved 'cross the room ta her side.

"Mrs. Engler, mum, it's me, Taylor. Taylor Eagan. It'd be time for lunch and I need ya to come with me now. Can ya do that?"

Takin' hold o'her elbow I kept her close by and steered her gently. As she followed me lead, I knew as she once protected me in startin' a new life, I now held the same duty in return. I aimed her to a seat at the dining table alongside the women who'd become like family ta me, knowin' they'd treat Mrs. Engler the same. Introducin' her 'round and tellin' of our connection, she was warmly welcomed by Maeve, Angel, Liberty, Regina and Janna, even though she gave no response.

The lineup of lunch tables and benches was already set with wooden bowls of watery broth and a few carrots floatin'. Alongside were plates of stale bread. No spoons or nappies. If ya was hungry, you figured how ta use the bread ta soak up the weak broth or ya just picked up the bowl and drunk it down. Some was only able ta drop their heads and slurp, like dogs. Mrs. Engler did none o'it. She just sat, starin'.

"Mum, ya need ta eat somethin'. If ya don't, the orderlies will end up tellin' the nurses and next thing ya know, you'll be locked in a room with nasty needles getting' stuck in ya. Please, eat a bit o'somethin'."

'Twas no use. The woman had no bein' left in her.

I couldn't just let her be taken away like so many, n'er ta return. She was once a kind and lovin' woman who deserved the same.

Lookin' round, there was no orderlies and no one payin' attention ta anythin' but their food. Quick-like I switched me empty bowl with the Missus. A few quick gulps and the tasteless liquid was gone. When time came fer us ta return ta the ward, no one was the wiser that Mrs. Engler had taken nary a sip. Fer that day, at least, I'd saved her from needles and such.

From then I kept on as Mrs. Engler's protector. Ne'er so close orderlies could take notice, but near enough ta keep her safe. Blessedly, the woman did what need be, moving from place ta place like a puppet. I did me best ta get her ta eat a bit and cleaned her plate when she didn't. When 'twas clear she wasn't gettin ta the toilet. the orderlies put her in diapers, leavin' little need fer them ta notice her atal. That's how the woman began wastin' away afore me very eyes, with not a soul but me carin'.

I was desperate fer a way ta reach Mrs. Engler and kept tryin' ta unlatch her mind that was so soundly shut. As I thought and thought more, images of the Engler beibis passed through me mind. Suddenly, I had no doubt what would reach the ailin' woman. Her children. The three had filled her heart. Surely, memories of 'em would wake her.

When next we was in the ward, I took me place 'longside the fragile woman. Prayin' ta the Holy Spirit fer guidance, I began tellin' a story from me time with her family.

"I always loved bein' nanny ta your children, mum. Each was special in their way. Edwin was the quiet soul, always thinkin'. But he had a way of expressin' himself in his drawin's and his piano playin'. I remember how he loved the classical music ya favored so much. He'd practice and practice 'til he'd get the notes just right. Then off he'd go ta find ya so's he could play fer ya. His reward was the kiss on the head ya always gave. Kept him smilin' the whole day.

"Ella was the sweet one. Ne'er a moment passed she wasn't doin' somethin' kind. She 'specially loved animals and would spend hours in the garden listenin' ta the birds, fillin' their feeders and scrubbin' their water baths. And the youngest, Ernest, named fer your da. He was the child most determined ta stay by your side. 'Twas a special relationship the two of ya had—always stirrin' memories of me and me own da."

As I spoke I kept watch ta see if even a bit o'life returned ta the Missus. Sadly, none. Even so, I couldn't give up. Each day I'd start again, tellin' stories o'the children and the ways they loved her. Truth be told, I could only hope the tales might be as comfortin' ta her as they was ta me.

As time went on Mrs. Engler lost the strength ta even get off her cot. The orderlies paid little mind changing her diapers once a day, but other than that, leavin' her. Sores soon began breaking out 'cross the poor woman's body. When the stench o'the oozing and the rot in her diapers got bad enough, a nurse took notice. Straight away she got two orderlies ta gather up what was left of Mrs. Engler onta a stretcher and wheel her away.

I tried followin' 'em, but a nurse shouted me back. So's I stood in the dank corridor doin' me best ta watch where they was goin'. Ta the end of the hall and a turn ta the right. Then I could see no more.

I knew that turn led ta the back o'the buildin'—"down the hall"—that we all feared. Twas off limits fer all but the docs and nurses. Anyone else found wanderin' was pushed back, told ta stay out or be punished.

I'd only made the turn twice. Once when they took me ta stick needles in me arms. There was the time I could hear troubling' sounds' comin' from that way. Twasn't words exactly. More like moanin' and carryin' on in ways that caused me curiosity ta rise. So's, I collected me courage and set off ta see what I could.

Makin' me way 'long the dark corridor, I reached the end where I had no choice but ta turn right. "Twas there the odd sounds grew louder, feelin as if they was headin' directly at me. Takin' a breath, I realized they was comin' from behind each o'the hallway doors.

Every entry was solid metal bearin' a doorknob, a keyhole lock and a small, square window with a slidin' flap. I moved ta the first door and listened. There was a steady clankin', metal on metal. I knew the sound. 'Twas a chain hittin' 'cross a cot's iron frame. No doubt, the person on the other side o'that door was shackled. Goin' ta the next door, I held me breath, tryin' ta be sure what I was hearin'. With me ear pressed tight ta the cold metal, I heard a woman's voice singin'.

My feet are here on Broadway this blessed harvest morn,
But oh! the ache that's in me heart for the spot where I was born.
My weary hands are blistered through work in cold and heat!
And oh! to swing a scythe once more through a field of Irish wheat.
Had I the chance ta wander back, or own a king's abode.
I'd sooner see the hawthorn tree down by the Old Bog Road.

As the woman kept on, I knew she was singin' "The Old Bog Road", a song oft' shared among the Irish come ta America. Me heart broke as me mind conjured a person chained ta a bedframe, both hands and legs, tryin' ta find comfort in an old verse. I'd no idea who 'twas on the other side of that thick door or why she was locked away. I did wish ever so deeply ta be able ta see and talk ta her.

"Alright, I'll check the doors in this hallway while you collect the charts and deliver them to Dr. Neville's office."

"Yes, Nurse Stewart".

Me ears heard the voices afore seein' the people went with 'em and, as luck would have it, afore they saw me. I had just enough time ta scurry inta the murky corner where the two hallways met afore the nurses pass me by. While the one kept walkin', the other went where I'd just been standin'. I wanted ta see who it 'twas on the other side o'that door, but me mind was insistin' I get away while I had the chance.

I stayed still 'til the nurse went inta the room. Then, betwixt and between shadows cast by bare hangin' bulbs from the ceilin', I worked me way from the forbidden space back ta hallway outside the ward.

Just as I was feelin' safe, a nurse come along, walkin' as if on a mission. Seein' me on me own, she stopped.

"What are you doing out here in the hallway by yourself? Where have you been?"

Twasn't often I got meself inta scrapes where a nurse could scold me. Punishment fer wrong doin' was too great a price ta pay. So's I always tried me best ta keep me nose clean. Standin' like a wayward child, I knew me answer could get me locked away, or worse. Lines of sweat went ta formin' in me armpits and me stomach knotted.

Mary, Mother of God, help me.

"Sorry, nurse. I got lost somehow tryin' ta find me way ta the ward. I just want ta get ta me bench and sit quiet-like. Could ya help me?"

The look cross the face of the hard-hearted woman showed she had no faith in me story. That bein' said, she was holdin' an armful of files needin' attention. 'Twas that bit o'luck saved me. 'Stead of questionin' me further she grabbed hold o'me shirt with her free hand and shoved me through the double doors ta the ward. Like a rotten child, she went marchin' me straight ta an orderly.

"I don't know how this one got out. I found her wandering the hall on her own. Says she got lost. Cuff her to a bench for the rest of the day to be sure there's nothing else going on with her."

As she turned ta leave, the nurse gave a good hard stare right inta me eyes.

"I suggest you not be found wandering again. If you can't be trusted to stay where you belong then we'll lock you down the hall. Remember that."

Without waitin', I slunk ta the bench wheres I always sat and plunked meself down. An orderly followed close behind with a chain and clip ta lock me. I didn't look up or talk fer the rest o' the day. I knew I'd been saved by the skin o'me teeth and wasn't about ta give anyone reason ta think further.

Twas the memory o'that long ago threat kept me from goin' down the hallway where they'd wheeled Mrs. Engler. I wasn't lookin' ta put meself in harm's way. All the same, I knew I couldn't let a fine woman like herself be taken away without a soul knowin' her whereabouts.

I spent me next days watchin' the nurses—seein' how they come and go— tryin' ta figure me way back down the hall. The last time I'd gone by chance, almost leadin' ta harm. This time, I was needin' ta be sure. From all I was seein', me best time o'slippin' away was last thing at night, when them's in charge was leadin' us from the dining hall ta the dormitory.

Givin' it a few tries, it seemed stayin' in the middle of thems movin' was the smart thing ta do, then droppin' off where there was no windows and little light so's I could move on ta the hallway, quiet-like. If by chance I was noticed, I'd decided ta do me best ta act confused and sorry. The rest I'd leave God's hands.

Evenin' come and I went 'bout me business as planned, movin' ta the middle o'the group bein' herded from dinner ta bed. As the orderlies moved us, a few began wanderin', as was their way. 'Twas all just enough distraction ta let me fall off inta a dark space where I held me breath and stood statue still. Twasn't long afore the only sound was me own breathin'. Wantin' ta be extra sure, I counted ta ten 'fore steppin' outta the darkness. Lookin' both ways like a kid crossin' the road, me path seemed clear. I flattened meself along the wall and began tiptoein' ta the forbidden hallway ahead. Ta reach it felt like a journey miles long.

Comin' ta'the juncture o'the two halls I took a look 'round. There was two nurses was in the hallway where I was headin'. They was talkin' and ne'er saw me, but I knew me luck wasn't lastin' forever. Tucked in the shadows I stayed still as a church mouse.

"I've called for the doctor. It usually takes an hour or more before he gets here. By that time she'll be dead and all he'll have to do is sign the certificate. Then James can bury the body."

Twas the taller of the nurses talkin'. I knew her as one o'the important ones in charge, not oft' 'round the ward. She stood ramrod, every bit o'her in perfect order from her cap ta her starched white uniform. The other nurse spoke as if they be friends more than co-workers.

"She certainly didn't last very long. I remember the day she was admitted with that suitcase full of gorgeous clothes. What was it, a month, six weeks ago? I looked at her chart that day. The notes said she'd been in an accident with one of her children who ended up dying. Guess I might feel like nothing mattered if that happened to me and one of mine."

"Can't say. I never really knew anything about her. Just one more to process through and manage. If I became involved in their stories, I'd never get my job done. Which, speaking of my job, I have to get back to my office. Leave her door open for now. She's not going anywhere. And while you're waiting for the doctor, go over to the cemetery and let James know he's going to have a grave to dig tonight."

As the two begin walkin' me way, I leaned inta the wall, wishin' it could magically swallow me up. 'Twas only their talkin' kept 'em lookin' straight ahead, with no notice o'me atal. With the one nurse comin' back, I knew I had but a short space o'time. Holdin' nary a thought o'the best way ta find Mrs. Engler, I headed ta the door I knew 'twas open.

Warily I pushed through and 'cross the threshold. The space was bleak with nary a glimmer, save fer a danglin' bulb overhead. Took me eyes a bit ta make out what me nose knew straight away—the stench o'death was fillin' the room. I spotted the shadow of a body tied ta a cot. The stank of pee and poop mixed with the rottin' flesh kept me back. Whoever this person, they was clearly voidin' all life from their body. 'Twas no hope of helpin' 'em.

Truth be told, I'll never know what kept me from turnin' and leavin' the deathly scene. Maybe 'twas a glimpse o'somethin' familiar in the dark outline? A curiosity o'the most human kind? Then again, maybe 'twas the hand o'God pushin' me deeper inta the room. Whatever 'twas, I moved closer ta the body, now barely risin' and fallin' in breaths. Leanin' toward the person, more corpse than bein', I laid eyes on a mark, a mole set just ta the side o' the nose on the right side o'the person's face.

Woe gripped me, twistin' me gut. I knew by that mole, 'twas Mrs. Engler lyin' here on death's door. Me next thought was of the conversation between the nurses. ". . . she'd been in an accident with one of her children who ended up dying".

I felt meself sinkin' ta me knees, slidin' inta the sticky pool o'fluids streamin' from the woman's body. At last I knew her reason fer bein' locked away and why me stories 'bout the beibis never reached her. No matter which child had gone ta the angels, the smilin' faces of Edwin, Ella and Ernest musta haunted her to death.

Leanin' 'gainst the cold metal table on which she lay and tryin' ta get me wits about me, I felt a thud 'gainst me head. Shoutin' in fright, I reached up ta swat away whatever was bangin' 'gainst me. 'Twas the lifeless hand o'Mrs. Engler. The true sense of life inta death come upon me. With nothin' ta do and not a way ta help, I needed ta go fore I was found out.

Ignoring the stank and mess 'neath me, I knelt and whispered a prayer fer Mrs. Engler's perpetual soul. Rememberin' somethin' me da done when his own mam died, I took me thumb and made a sign of the cross on her forehead.

Grabbing the table edge so's I could stand without slippin' in the slime, I took one last look at the remains of the woman who'd been so kind and lovin' ta me, as much as me own mam. Brushing a kiss cross her cheek, I turned and fled the room, not once lookin' back.

I've not a clear thought how I made me way through the hallways and inta the dormitory where I slunk onta me own cot. There I lay sick ta me stomach and brokenhearted, in a state of neither bein', nor carin'—and no one carin' in return.

As darkness wrapped 'round me, I understood the reasons Mrs. Engler give up and died. And I was quite sure as well that a bit o'me died right along with her that night.

Chapter Twenty-Five

GRACE FOUND HERSELF GULPING rather than sipping her wine, grateful for the almost immediate spread of warmth through her body. The slight tipsiness helped take the edge off her nerves in engaging with Mike Healy.

As it turned out, Grace had no need for worry. Mike was surprisingly good company as he guided their chat through movies, books and even a touch of sports. When the hostess appeared with the news that her table was ready, Grace felt a wave of disappointment. In retrospect, she imagined it was that unexpected emotion that caused her spontaneous reaction.

"You're welcome to join me for dinner, Mike. That is if you're not already meeting someone."

Seriously? Could you not sound like you're fishing to find out if he's dating?

"Actually I was supposed to meet someone, but she had to cancel at the last minute. So I was just going to order take out and eat at home."

Ok, you really need to get a grip. What are you doing thinking about spending time with this guy when you don't even know him?

As if reading Grace's thoughts, Mike broke into the same charming smile he'd flashed the day he'd stopped her for speeding.

"But I have to admit, sharing a table with you sounds much more agreeable than staring at the four walls of my apartment."

It took a moment for Grace's mind to catch up with Mike Healy's words. It was more his movement off the bar stool along with the hostess's question that confirmed her new dining plan.

"So there'll be two of you now?"

Without pause, Mike replied, "Yep. That's not a problem is it, Belinda?"

The body language and tone of the woman's voice made it clear that pretty much anything he suggested would be just fine with her.

"Not at all, *Officer* Healy. Right this way."

Grace sat fascinated as Belinda turned on her spiked heels and walked away, swaying her tightly-clothed hips in a clear, "come get me" message. The interesting thing was Mike Healy seemed to be paying no attention.

"Shall we?"

Emphasizing his words with a gentle touch on Grace's elbow, Mike guided her off the bar stool and into the wake of Belinda's path. When they arrived at the table, the hostess again extended herself toward Midland's finest, brushing her hand across his torso.

"I'll be right back with another place setting. Don't go away."

The obvious flirtation made Grace uneasy. Clearly the two had some sort of relationship, in which she had no desire to become a third player. Keeping it light and easy seemed the best course to get through the evening.

"So, it seems you're a regular here. What do you recommend?"

"Actually, I don't come here that often, only when a certain lady in my life is in need of a special night out. As for my favorites on the menu, I'm a pretty meat and potatoes kind of guy. I almost always order the meatloaf dinner with a salad."

Grace never heard most of the man's dinner recommendations, as her brain got snarled in the image of the officer and his mystery lady tucked away at a romantic table for two. It was only as Belinda returned and began setting a placemat and silverware in front of the good-looking cop that Grace realized she'd been temporarily MIA from the conversation.

"Here you go. Everything you need to enjoy your dinner. And if you decide you need a little dessert later, just let me know. I get off at ten."

Looking over to Grace, the hostess brusquely added, "Your waitress will be with you shortly."

Again, with nothing to do but stare at the woman's firmly molded derriere swaying off into the darkened restaurant, Grace realized her jaw had dropped and her mouth was hanging open. Taking a quick glance at Mike, she was relieved to see he was busy studying the menu. With any luck, they would order, be served promptly and say their good-byes. Grace could return home, and Mike would be free to enjoy his late night "Belinda" dessert.

"Decide what you want?" Mike's eyes reflected a genuine quality that attracted Grace. "I've looked through the whole menu, but I really don't know why I bother. I order the meatloaf everytime."

The charm of his smile coupled with his open nature seemed to belie the suggestive exchange Grace had just witnessed. To be fair, he hadn't started the flirtation, nor did he really engage. It was more that Belinda continually inserted herself beside him, as close as legally possible. The thought of Mike having to arrest her for bodily interference sent up a chuckle from Grace's chest.

"What's so funny? I can't have spinach in my teeth already. I haven't even eaten my salad yet!"

"Sorry, I was just thinking about the hostess, and how if suggestive behavior were a crime, you'd be forced to arrest her in the middle of this restaurant."

The look on Mike's face was one of surprise, followed by a hearty laugh.

"Yeah. Belinda has a way about her. She doesn't mean anything by it. She had a rough time growing up and got in with a bad crowd in high school. I kind of stepped in, like a big brother, and helped turn her life around."

"Well, I'm an only child, so I don't know much about brothers and sisters, but I'll tell you this. I've never heard a sister talk to her brother like that woman just spoke to you."

"I know. And I tell her about it all the time. The thing is, she was abused so badly as a kid that she thinks the only way someone can show love is through physical expressions, most of them inappropriate. She's in counseling and doing a lot better, but I think when she sees me she's grateful and wants to thank me and falls into old patterns."

The look in Mike's eyes and the earnestness of his words caught Grace off guard. Her life had been filled with the protective love of her grandparents. She couldn't imagine being abused as a child and how that would have changed her.

"I'm sorry, Mike. None of this is really my business. I was just surprised by the way she approached you. I guess I should have been a little more thoughtful and a little less judgemental."

"No problem. I'm used to her and don't think twice when she says some of that stuff."

"Good evening. My name is Jessica. I'll be your server tonight. Can I start you off with something to drink?"

The waitress' arrival was perfectly timed, allowing the uncomfortable topic of Belinda to fade away.

"Since we both drank red wine at the bar, what do you say we order a bottle to share over dinner?"

Grace had a rule of one glass of wine a night when dining out. It wasn't that she couldn't handle more. She just always wanted to be sure she was fully sober when driving home. However, something about the restaurant and being there with Mike made her willing to bend her one glass rule. After all, she could always say no to anything more than a second glass.

"Sure. You pick."

Mike chose a french red and followed with an order of his usual appetizer.

"Hope you don't mind. I got in the habit of enjoying crusty bread and a mix of cheeses with wine before dinner. It's something I picked up in Paris a few years ago and I try to keep the memories fresh by continuing the tradition. John Wilkins is the chef here at Welcome Home. He is a friend and keeps a private selection of cheeses on hand, just for me. "

Listening to this man, she'd initially categorized as Barney Fife, talk about Paris and French culture surprised her. At best, Grace imagined Mike occassionally traveling to the New Jersey state capital on official police business with maybe an extended overnight added for a college basketball game. Yet here he was talking about vacationing in one of the most sosphisticated and glamourous cities in the world. So far tonight, she was two for two in unfairly judging people.

"It's lovely. Thank you for being willing to share your private reserve. I love taking time for a nice meal, especially after a long week."

"That's the second time you've said that, Grace. What made your week drag?"

Grace's first instinct was to brush off the question with a simplistic answer like, "Too much paperwork and not enough time," or "Still getting settled in the new job." But she wanted to share some of her work week. Actually, she needed to talk about her job. She needed to tell someone about the heinous treatments that so many at Wood Haven endured and share her ideas of ways to help make life better for those who still remained. Mostly she wanted to tell Mike about meeting Teagan.

Before she could start, however, Jessica returned with their wine and a large wooden board filled with beautiful cheeses, red and green grapes, a variety of sliced apples and a gorgeous loaf of artisan bread. Although she had never been to Paris, as Jessica filled their glasses with a deep burgundy wine, Grace imagined they were sitting in a bistro along the Left Bank, with all the time in the world to sit and talk, eat and drink.

"Santé," Mike spoke with a sexy French flair. as he raised his glass. Grace immediately returned the toast, bringing her glass to eye level and mimicking his pronunciation.

"You have to clink!" The words sparked out of Mike's mouth like oil on a hot griddle.

"Ok. Ok. We're clinking," Grace responded, wondering what was so important about the ritual.

"Sorry, I guess maybe that came out a little too passionately," he said with a laugh that exposed his dimpled smile. "It's just that the French consider it bad luck if you don't clink glasses when you toast."

"Really? Somehow I didn't take you for a superstitious kind of guy."

"Well, generally, I'm not, but in this case, I'm not taking any chances. As the French tell it, when you toast, you must maintain eye contact, you must clink glasses with each person in your group and you must not cross anyone else's arm as you do it."

"Wow. That seems like a lot of rules just to be able to drink some wine."

"Oh, it's much more than that. The French believe if you don't follow each step, you will suffer the penalty of seven years of bad sex."

Grace couldn't believe her ears as she processed the final part of Mike's explanation. In the past hour she'd been exposed to more suggestive conversations than in the last year. It had been that long since she'd been part of a serious relationship with John, her ex-fiancé. The after effects of their rancorous break-up still lingered in her heart and kept her from trusting any guy who'd approached her since. Yet here she was sitting across from a man she found extremely attractive and who was stirring some almost unforgotten longings, and he was explaining how she was tempting the gods with seven years of bad sex. Frustrated confusion spread across her face.

"Hey, Grace, it was just a joke. Well at least on my part, although the French *are* pretty serious about their toasts."

"You know, Mike, I think maybe I need to call it a night. I'll leave some cash to cover my part of the wine and cheese board."

"Come on, Grace. There's no reason to leave. I really am a nice guy, but I am a guy. Sometimes we don't always get it right, especially when we're around someone we're trying to impress on a first date."

"Is that what you think this is? A date? We're a long way off from dating, Mike Healy."

"Ok. Let's see if we can start over here and maybe salvage this dinner. Grace, I am genuinely sorry for anything I may have said or that has happened tonight that might have been offensive. Truthfully, it's been a long time since I've been out with a real lady. Mostly I hang out with other cops, all of them bachelors. To say that our social life is a slight step up from a frat house would be pretty accurate. Then there's the people in my life like Belinda, who because of unimaginably cruel circumstances are not your average neighborhood types. I can't ignore them because they are outside the norm of what people judge acceptable. They need help and I do what I can to be there for them. That's how Belinda got this job. I talked to John about giving her a chance as a hostess and he agreed as a favor to me. Right now, it's all that's keeping her from falling back in with people who will use and abuse her until she's dead. So, please, don't leave. Give me a chance to redeem myself."

Mike's words danced through Grace's mind and amid the mayhem there was one question she had to ask.

"What about the woman you were supposed to meet here tonight for dinner? Is she another one of your special projects, or someone that you spend time seeing?"

Grace hated the way her words sounded, like a jealous woman wanting to be told she was the only one. It made no sense that the question burned in her mind, or that she should feel territorial about a man she barely knew. What made her feel worse was the loopy grin that grew on Mike's face as he answered her.

"No, Grace, she isn't one of my special projects, as you call them, but she is someone I see regularly."

Watching the color drain from her face, Mike quickly blurted out the rest before he lost more ground with his dinner partner

"Her name is Maria. She's an older woman, but someone I have come to love deeply, ever since she gave birth to me 45 years ago."

With a twinkle in his eyes, Mike reached across the table and gently wrapped his hands around Grace's fingers. When she didn't pull away, he knew he'd won, at least the first round of what he imagined could become a very interesting relationship.

Chapter Twenty-Six

WOOD HAVEN ADMITTANCE FORM

Patient: *Maria Rodriguez*
Date of Admittance: *March 18, 1940*
Number: *03184016*
Age: *16*
Ethnicity: *Puerto Rican*
Marital Status: *Single*
Children: *None.*
Diagnosis: *Feeble mindedness, bordering on insanity*

C HANGE O'THE SEASONS 'TWAS the only way a soul could tell the passin' o' time. So's I'd sit meself by a window most everyday ta try and get a feel fer what was happenin' outside. "Twas in those moments I found meself wishin' fer a breath o'fresh air, the feel o'rain on me face, a gust o'wind through me hair. Growin' up as I did on the Queenstown Wharf, outdoors was me way of livin'. Bein' kept inside concrete walls and behind iron-barred windows was akin ta the death o'me.

When I found meself sad and teary o'er such things, I'd hear me da tellin' me ta straighten up. He'd always say, "Cormicks never been a family o'weepers, so quit feelin' sorry fer yerself. There's always worse." That's what come ta me mind when Maria first come ta the ward.

She was different-lookin'. Both dark-skinned and hair, the thick strands hangin' straight below her waist, with a frame too frail ta hold up 'gainst a breeze. The orderlies led her inta the ward like an animal on a chain and when they got ta a bench, they pushed her down ta sittin' and wound the chain so tightly round it, she'd no choice but to stay still.

I kept me eyes on her fer a bit, waitin' ta see if she'd go ta railin' 'gainst the tie down. She made not a move. Some in the ward went close and tried talkin' ta her, touchin' her head and her hands, but still she gave not a bit o'notice.

I'd no way o'knowin what 'twas ailin' her, or what might make her well. As me brain tried ta figure the answers Nurse Bennett come ta the ward. She walked right over ta the girl and sit down, lookin' through a folder she brought with her.

Without bringin' attention ta meself, I made me way closer ta the two, hopin' ta learn somethin' 'bout the poor thing. They sat together for just a bit, Nurse Bennett readin' and writin', the girl still as a statue. 'Twas as if she had no idea anyone was 'round her. Seein' the nurse close her folder and stand up ta leave, I couldn't help but speak.

"This girl is so sad. She doesn't move and she's barely breathin'."

"I understand your concern Teagan, but you must leave her alone. What happened to this girl is none of your worry. You need to pay attention to yourself and avoid making any trouble.

Taking a step closer, the caring nurse dropped her voice to a whisper.

"The orderlies watch you, Teagan. They're waiting for you to do something they don't like so they can take you down the hall. Please, just walk away and find Maeve or Angel or anyone else. Just not this girl."

As soon as the words left her, she knew she was wrong. Nurses was never ta talk 'gainst them like the orderlies. The thing was, Nurse Bennett 'twas made only of kindness and that's how she always treated me.

"T'is not a problem. I'll not say a word. I'm just feelin' sad fer this sweet young thing who's lookin' so lost."

"There's nothing you can do except leave her alone. She's just had a surgical procedure that may help her and that's really more than I should say."

"Alright, Nurse Bennett. Thank ya then. I'll leave her be."

The two of us turned in opposite directions, me ta the window and Nurse Bennett ta the desk where, just as she said, orderlies be sittin' and watchin' me. I kept me eyes on the nurse, tryin' ta hear her words. Bit by bit I drew meself closer ta the desk, doin' me best not ta be noticed.

"She's recently come out of surgery where she was sterilized. After three pregnancies at such young ages, the doctor felt there was a need to control her body. She'll need watching, but don't bother her. Let her rest. I'll see to it that she is fed. It will be some time, *if* she is able to recover."

Sterilized. I'd not heard the word afore and had no thought o'its meanin'.

Seein' Maeve on the other side o'the room, I made me way ta the chair 'longside her.

"Morning' Maeve."

As always, she offered a smile that warmed me heart.

"Mornin' Teagan. Another day upon us, eh?"

"Fer sure and with it another poor soul chained ta a bench. Don't know her name as such, but I heard Nurse Bennett sayin' she'd just been sterilized. Might ya know what that means?"

With a drop in the color o'her face, Maeve took a breath and closed her eyes. I stood by quiet-like 'til she went ta speakin'.

" 'Oh Teagan, 'tis a terrible thing that almost happened ta me and did happen ta some women I knew. They was patients o'the doctor that put me here. A cruel man he was, thinkin' nothin' of robbin' a woman o'life with her children. Worse, he believes in cuttin' the baby-makin' parts outta women's bodies. He calls it turnin' 'em sterile so's they can ne'er give birth 'gain. But that's only the half of it. One time I laid eyes on a woman he'd turned sterile. She was leavin' the doctor's office where me husband brung me. The poor thing was in a wheelchair, bein' pushed by a nurse, as she was too frail and weak ta walk. In the room where the nurse told me ta go was the table where the woman had just lain. 'Twas dripping with her blood and the insides that had just been cut outta her sat piled on the floor."

As Maeve told her story, I felt meself goin' weak at the knees. Quick-like I sit down next ta her so's not to pass out and draw the orderlies attention. Noticin' me distress, Maeve reached a hand over and give me a squeeze. The warmth o'her skin brought comfort and I did me best ta regain me wits. While sittin' I eyed the girl, chained ta the bench. She appeared dead, though I knew she was livin'. 'Twas no wonder with havin' her insides ripped out and no longer able ta have beibes.

"Maeve, do ya know if the woman you saw lived, or died?"

"Not a clue. I ne'er saw her again as, not long after, me husband and me doctor made it so's I was put inta this place. Truth be told though, I can't imagine how the woman could have survived, appearin' much like herself over there on the bench."

Maeve's words put the fear of God in me fer the dark-skinned girl. She couldn't die. There had ta be a way ta help her. 'Twas as if what happened ta her was as much about meself and others wanderin' around this awful place, none of us havin' any chance fer a real life.

"There must be somethin' we can do ta help the poor thing, Maeve. Have you got any idea?"

"Teagan, ya know the orderlies won't let us near her, and if'n they did, we ain't doctors. We don't know how ta make it better in her mind or her body. So's say some prayers ta Mary, mother of God, beggin fer mercy on the soul o'the sufferin' child. There's not much else ta do."

While I didn't like Maeve's answer, I knew it ta be right. Lookin' at the weakened young thing, I give thought ta all'd been taken from her. The only thing I could imagine helpin' her would be what Maeve said. Prayers.

Last time I remembered truly prayin' was in Queenstown. Like all Irish Catholics, we Cormicks went ta Church every Sunday. But fer me mam, prayin' once a week weren't enough. That's how our family come ta novenas on Wednesday nights, sayin' the rosary, speakin' special intentions fer the livin' and dead and singin' a blessing at the end.

> *Bless this house, Lord, we pray. Keep it safe, night and day.*
> *Bless these walls both firm and stout. Keepin' want and trouble out.*
> *Bless the roof and chimney tall. Let your peace lie o'er all.*
> *Bless our loved ones here within. Keep 'em pure and free o'sin.*
> *Bless us all that one day we, will join ya Lord, ta dwell with Thee.*

The words and melody flowed through me mind as if I was home with me mam and da. Emotions welled up in me heart and pushed through me eyes in salty tears. How I missed me family and me homeland. What was it ever possessed me ta leave?

"Dear Teagan, there be no sense in spillin' tears. This woman is either goin' ta get better or not, and none of it 'tis up ta us. Go on now and dry your eyes. We'll pray the rosary together, a novena fer the woman. Not outloud mind ya, but in our souls, askin' God's will be done."

So's we sat fer a while, appearin' as if our minds were blank, like so many couped together in this gloomy place. Only we was prayin' fer the girl's sorry soul. At the end of the novena, Maeve and me looked ta each other, silently agreein' we'd continue on, askin' the Lord ta heal this youngster we knew only by her dark skin and hair.

Sadly, our prayers made no matter. The woman stayed mute. Orderlies went ta movin' her from place ta place, chainin' her ta a bench or a cot so's they wouldn't be bothered. Maeve and me knew as long as the woman made no trouble, not a one would care. 'Twas a blessing of sorts, but we could see the child getting' weaker as the chains was the only thing keepin' her from tumblin' ta the floor.

Come the day when Maeve and me finished another silent rosary and I got up and moved ta the young girl. The stench o'her filthy clothes coverin' her slowly rottin' body brought a bile up me throat and inta me mouth. Still I couldn't stop. I couldn't let another day go without trying ta reach her.

"Hello, love. I don't right know your name. Mine's Teagan. Teagan Cormick. I've been sittin' by ya here fer some time now and I wantcha ta know that me and me friend, Maeve, we're prayin' fer you ta feel better. But we can't help ya all on our own, doncha know. Ya need ta want ta get well. Ta be sure, you've been hurt in ways no woman should ever know. All's of us here has felt some terrible pain and been locked up with no escape. But ya can't give up. Try just a bit, won't ya?

Me words flowed freely as me tears, lookin' at this young thing trapped in her own private hell. Right then and there I vowed ta take care o'her in whatever ways I could manage.

The next morn', as I passed the young girl's cot, I went ta counting the steps and turns 'tween hers and mine. At the bathroom, I dampened a cloth and wrapped it 'round a bar of soap, quick-slipping both inta me pocket. That night, after the orderlies locked the place, I waited fer sleep ta spread 'cross the room. When all was quiet, I traced me way ta the girl. Chained by leg and arms ta the iron bed rails she was. Kneelin, I softly went ta whisperin' in her ear.

"Hello dearie. It's me, Teagan. I've come ta give ya a gentle wash. No worries."

So's begun a nightly pattern in which I glided a damp and soapy cloth o'er the girl's neglected body, focusing on her face and exposed parts o'her arms and legs. Though she never responded, I was able ta wash away much o'the grime on her body. Accomplishin' that give me courage, ta try and put some food inta her.

I went ta Angel for help and together we started puttin' a bit o'bread crusts in our pockets each day. At night we'd go ta scoopin' the soft middle from the hard outer and rollin' it inta tiny bits. I'd lift the girl's head as far as the chains would allow while Angel held a bit o' bread, softly passin'her fingers o're the girl's lips 'til they parted. Quick-like, Angel'd poke her fingers through the child's teeth and release the bread inta her mouth. Truth be told, I wasn't sure if she might go ta chokin', or swallow, but prayed fer the latter. Movement of her throat give me answer. And so's we kept on with the feedin' the girl all the while I kept talkin'.

"Well done, darlin'. We've got ta getcha eatin' so's ya can get your strength. I don't know as ya can hear me, but if ya can, me and Angel here, we'll be back tomorrow and we'll help ya eat some more then."

Angel and me kept on with her bathin' and feedin' every night while Maeve and me carried on the silent novenas each day. Our efforts were exhaustin' but we couldn't give up. 'Twas like the three of us was givin' the girl our own wills ta live.

ONE NIGHT, BEIN' 'SPECIALLY DISCOURAGED, I recalled the thing that ne'er failed me in times o'need. 'Twas prayin' ta me granny. Me mother's mother held a special place in me heart as in my growin' up years we spent time readin' stories, havin' tea parties with her special raisin scones and takin' walks through the hills and dales outside o' Queenstown. 'Twas a time when I lived as much of me young life with me granny as with me own family and it wove a strong bond 'tween us.

Dearest Nanny, I can't imagine me life has come ta this, or if you're even still watchin' o'er me. But if ya be, please hear me. There be a young girl here whose life has been terrible, worse than mine. She's been tortured and gone ta sufferin'in ways beyond me imaginin'. I'm doin' me best ta help her Nan, but it's no never mind. She's still dying afore me very eyes. Can ya help her? Can ya talk ta the Good Lord and beg him ta spare her life. I know it's not much o'a life in this awful place, but still, I can't bear ta think of her dyin'. Loves ya, Nanny and sorry I haven't been chattin' with ya more. I promise if ya help the poor thing, I'll chat with ya regular like, and the Good Lord as well. Ya can tell him that for me.

The next morning, lookin' ta the cot and the always lifeless body, I noticed the girl's head turned a bit, as if she was tryin' ta find me. Thinkin' I was dreamin', I got meself up and moved towards her. The closer I come the more I could see her eyes was clear and lookin' straight at me. Droppin' down 'longside the chains holdin' her frail body, I could see her lips movin', formin' words barely strong enough ta be heard. Nuzzlin' 'gainst her, cheek ta cheek, for the first time she spoke ta me.

"Thank you Teagan. Thank you."

Chapter Twenty-Seven

GLANCING AT THE OVERSIZED CALENDAR that also served as her desk blotter, Grace was startled to realize she was a full two months into her Wood Haven consulting job.

How did that happen? Seems like I just got here.

"Morning, Grace. How was your weekend?"

Craig Jennings' smooth voice flipped a switch in Grace's body. It was an unusual reaction as she always made a point of keeping her business and personal lives separate. Yet there was no denying the attraction factor of this tall dark and handsome co-worker.

Get ahold of yourself Grace. You've got no business getting into a relationship with someone from Wood Haven.

"Hellooooo! You in there, Grace?"

"I'm sorry, Craig. I've got a lot on my mind this morning. My weekend was great, thanks. And yours?"

"Good. I left a bit early Friday and drove to the shore in south Jersey. I have a cottage in Cape May that was my grandmother's. It's tucked away in a compound of houses with private beach access. I escape whenever I can for ocean time. It's a drive for sure but I always come back refreshed and energized. I actually stopped to ask if you would be able to join me in a meeting with some reps from the state office on aging? They want an update on our progress with the plan for placing our seniors. Jonathan knows about it and has given me the go ahead to include you."

"What time and when?" Grace asked, glancing down at her desk calendar.

"Friday. Eleven a.m. We're scheduled to meet in the board room and then go to lunch in Midland. I thought it would be good to give them a feel for the town after we lay out your mainstreaming plan."

"Good idea. If it's alright with you, I'll put together an agenda that you can fax today to everyone from the state. That way they have time to think of questions or concerns they may have and add information that could be helpful to us.

"Thanks, Grace. You're the best!"

With a wink Craig was gone, leaving her in a vacuum of emotions that ultimately returned her thoughts to Mike Healy and their Welcome Home dinner.

Despite the ups and downs of the night, Grace enjoyed herself in the company of Mike Healy, more than she'd enjoyed any man's company in quite some time. And unless her radar was off, the good-looking cop was taken with her as well. He fairly begged her to stay and have dinner with him for crying out loud. The question was, who should make the next move? In Grace's mind there was only one answer. And it wasn't her.

Looking down at her desk, Grace realized while day dreaming, she'd been doodling Mike's name. *Ok, this has got to stop, Grace. You need to get ahold of your emotions and you know best way to do that is to focus on your work. Plain and simple.*

Pulling out a yellow legal pad from her desk drawer, Grace started working on Friday's meeting agenda. She began with an outline of her proposed plans for the four seniors who would require full time medical care. Next she detailed her Faith File of the six able to live independently with an aide. After a few rounds of edits, Grace felt satisfied all was ready to be typed and faxed.

With the state meeting coming up, she needed to make it a priority to meet personally with all ten of her seniors before Friday. If she got organized, Grace was confident she could make it happen.

She decided to start with the group of four. Considering their various stages of dementia and physical disabilities, it would probably take a full day to meet and personally assess all of them. That would leave two days to do the same with the six independent seniors and Thursday to write up the reports and recommendations for each senior. A perfect plan!

Grace tucked the files of the four seniors into her leather portfolio and added Friday's meeting agenda and a couple of pens. She'd stop first at Jonathan's office to give his secretary the agenda to type and fax. Then it was off to begin meet her seniors.

It was interesting how she felt she already knew them from her intensive study of their medical charts. The thing was Grace struggled between her excitement over the new lives they would soon enjoy and her heartbreak over the tragic life stories they shared. Regardless, she knew it was time to begin.

The rooms of the four seniors were located on the third floor, at the far-left end of the building. As Jonathan had explained on their tour, this section had originally housed the rooms where mental health treatments of the day were performed. While most had either been renovated into patient rooms or storage areas, one room along the hallway still held vestiges of the asylum's torturous therapy equipment. Brass pliers. A corroded silver injection tube. An oversized patient chair with leather tie downs dangling from the head, arm and leg rests. It took all of Grace's determination to push past the gloom incited by their presence.

Time to turn away from the evil and focus on the goodness I can effect in the lives of the four individuals I'm about to meet.

Grace began in the room at the end of the hallway, noted by a worn number 366 outside the door. Knocking softly, Grace heard a strong voice commanding her, "Enter!" Without pause, Grace pushed open the door and became entranced by the person of 80-year old Dimitri James Ardonis.

"Mr. Ardonis, Hello. My name is Grace Reid. I am new here at Wood Haven and thought I would stop by and say hello."

"Good day, Miss Reid. I am assuming it is Miss, as I do not see a wedding ring on your left hand.

"You would be correct, Mr. Ardonis. It is Miss."

"Well then, please call me James, as do all beautiful women."

Grace knew from his file that James Ardonis was perfectly sound of mind, but his body was crippled from years of shoveling dirt and transporting bodies as Wood Haven's grave digger. It was Grace's plan to relocate James to the nearby St. Augustine's Senior Care Facility. There he would receive regular physical therapy treatments for his back and legs that were twisted and gnarled and had become, essentially, non-functional.

"Why James, I didn't read anything in your file about you being an incorrigible flirt!"

"In my homeland of Greece, speaking the truth about a woman's beauty and respectfully admiring her beauty is considered appropriate and encouraged. So you see, Grace, I am not a flirt, as you call me. Rather I am a connoisseur, admiring a beautiful work of God's art."

"Fair enough, James. Thank you for the compliment."

The Greek gentleman broke in to a smile radiating joy from his eyes. Grace was drawn into that smile and the charm of this man whom she knew had buried many who were unable to survive Wood Haven's tortures. In fact, he'd lived and worked for 55 years in the abhorrent asylum was paying the long term physical price for his part. His charismatic personification of his lengthy medical file made Grace more determined than ever to provide the proud man with a better life.

"James, along with wanting to meet you, I'm here to talk with you about some changes that are going to take place at Wood Haven. Changes that I hope will please you."

"If you are involved, I am sure I will be most pleased," James answered with innate charm.

"I am involved to the extent that I am the one making plans for patient changes. Wood Haven is closing this year. I am in charge of making sure everyone living here is transferred to safe residences with excellent care. Have you ever heard of St. Augustine's?"

"I have not, but then again, I have not been out of this room in many years. No doubt much of the world has moved beyond me."

The genuine way this man described his life at Wood Haven caused a ball of emotion to form in Grace's stomach and travel up, through to her throat. Taking a deep breath, she managed to swallow the emotion before it escaped in sympathetic tears.

"James, I can only imagine how it must feel as if life has passed you by, but I think you'll find St. Augustine's a pleasant place in which to step back into the world."

"Whatever is meant to be in the remaining years of my life, Miss Reid, is what it will be. As you see with your own eyes, I will not be taking many steps anywhere. But I do not feel sorrow for myself. I have enjoyed a good life here. I was given a job that allowed me freedom to live on my own and to be out, surrounded by nature's beauty. It was better than many who were kept here. For that I am grateful."

Grace found herself mesmerized by James—by the gentle rhythm of his faint Greek accent, by the contrast of his olive skin against his deeply hazel eyes, by his positive outlook on the vile Wood Haven life he had experienced.

Even at almost twice her age and disabled, the man radiated an inescapable charm that required all of Grace's self discipline to keep her thoughts on track.

"James, we are going to make sure you get regular physical therapy at St. Augustine's. Nothing too strenuous or painful. Just some basic, easy ways to help your legs and hips feel better. Perhaps in focusing on relieving some of your pain you might become interested in the social activities at St. Augustine's. Things like bingo and movie nights and resident parties. I imagine a man of your good looks will have the ladies noticing you from the moment you move in.

"That, my dear Miss Reid, is of no importance to me. Long ago I promised my heart to a woman and have never since cared for another. While I will gladly accept therapy for my body, I am in need of none for my spirit, my heart, nor my mind."

Grace was taken back by James' unexpected declaration. Could it be this man was still engaged in a love more than half a century past?

"Certainly the woman of which you speak was part of your life fifty years ago, or more. Is it not possible that with your move to St. Augustine's you might allow yourself a new friendship or perhaps even a love relationship?"

"Oh, I will have both, Miss Reid, as I have throughout my time at Wood Haven. While I was once married and a father to two children, I lost them all when I lost my business and my money. I was partnered in a construction company with a man who professed to be my friend but who stole from me until our business collapsed like a house with no foundation. My wife and I were in an arranged marriage. She was a younger woman with a great desire for the finer things in life. When I could not provide those things, she no longer had use for me. One day while I was out looking for work, she took our children and disappeared, leaving me not so much as a note."

As James shared his story, his gleaming eyes dimmed behind a curtain of tears that refused to drop. It was as if holding on to them kept the memory of his loved ones forever within his being.

"My family's leaving was a disgrace in my culture. I had failed, which turned me mad for a time. When finally I was able to reclaim my mind, life as I had known it had been ripped away, not only my wife, my children and my business, but my home was sold out from under me, to settle my many debts. I was lost and ended up wandering the streets of Hoboken until I could wander no more."

The story seemed unbelievable. Yet Grace knew from studying his Wood Haven file that James was telling the truth. What differed from the pages of those notes was the increased intensity of the details when spoken by the man who lived them.

"My recall from that time is unclear. What I do remember is waking up in this place unable to go freely or make choices, as if a criminal. That is how I came to life as a gravedigger. My strength allowed me to drag dead bodies from the treatment rooms or the dormitories, where ever people gave up their life struggles. In time, those in charge provided me with a spade and instructed that I give the dead a resting place in the ground. Spending that time in the cemetery allowed me a freedom denied to most and I did nothing to jeopardize that. Eventually I was allowed to live in a two-room cottage at the bottom of the cemetery hill. That is where I promised my heart to the woman that I still love."

Struggling to understand all James was sharing, Grace was left with a question that seemed invasive but necessary.

"Are you saying you fell in love with someone you met after you were committed here, James?"

"Yes, Miss Reid. She was i alithiní mou agápi—what you would call my true love-—and she continues to be the same, even today.

Chapter Twenty-Eight

WOOD HAVEN ADMITTANCE FORM

Patient: *Stephen Andreas*
Date of Admittance: *July 19, 1928*
Number: *07192832*
Age: *32*
Ethnicity: *Dutch*
Marital Status: *Widower*
Children: *2 sons*
Diagnosis: *Depression, lethargy*

TA BE SURE, THERE WAS TIMES when a line o'men would pass through the ward on their way ta fix somethin' in our buildin'. When I went ta hearin' their footsteps I tried me best ta draw near for a glimpse of the dark-haired, emerald eyed fella caught me fancy when we was outside cleanin' up the yard. Twasn't often I'd see him so's mostly I just imagined him and me talkin' and laughin' and doin' all sorts o' things. I pondered me mam and me da and how they always got on, givin' a hug or stealin' a kiss when they thought we snappers tweren't watchin'. But at the end o'the day, such imaginin's made me loneliness worse, so's I stopped thinkin' such thoughts atal.

Then come a day, warmed with the sun's bright glow, when Nurse Bennett gathered up Maeve and Angel and meself and moved us outta the ward. The three o'us stood like statues, not knowin' why we'd been culled from the rest. No doubt, "down the hall" was hauntin' our brains.

When the good nurse finally come ta us, she did so with a softness in her face and a hint of a smile, givin' us all a breath o'relief fer sure.

"We'll be going outside on this fine summer morning to do work in the cemetery. I'll need you to stay close by me and pay attention when I give directions. Do you understand?"

We was each sound in body and mind, no doubt why she picked us three. So's we answered yes ta her question and waited fer what was ta come. 'Twas only a minute afore she was leadin' us ta the back door o'the buildin' and out inta fresh air.

Feelin' warm sun and a summer breeze 'twas a bit overwhelmin', at least ta me. I stopped straight away and closed me eyes, pretendin' ta be in Queenstown, waitin' fer an ocean liner, or better, fer mw da ta come along with his gear so's we could go fishin'.

"Teagan, are you alright?"

I heard Nurse Bennett callin' but couldn't force open me eyes. 'Twas as if they had a mind o' their own, stayin' trapped in the magic o'the sun and the air.

"Teagan, I need you to open your eyes this minute."

The tone o'the good nurse let me know I had ta be both listenin' and doin'. So's I pressed open me lids and mustered me best "sorry missus" smile."

"Ah Nurse Bennett, 'tis sorry I be. No idea what come over me, other than bein' outside on such a glorious day."

In a blink, somethin' went ta passin' o'er the woman's face I'd not seen afore. 'Twas a look far from anger or disapprovin'. More a flash o'somethin' akin ta pity, only kinder. There was no way o'knowin' what was passin' through her mind. I could only hope fer charity from her soul.

"I certainly understand enjoying the gift Mother Nature is giving us today, Teagan, but I need you to do as I ask, when I ask. We only have so much time before Nurse Stewart will expect me to have you back inside. Don't make me sorry I chose you to help.

The idea that stoppin' 'long the way could make trouble fer the kind woman give me pause. Nurse Bennett was the only one who treated any of us close ta human. That alone made me not want ta be the cause o'any trouble fer her.

"'Tis sorry I be, Nurse Bennett. You'll not have a worry 'bout me laggin' again."

Off we four set fer the nearby cemetery. 'Twas a bit away from the buildin's, along a windin' road and up a steep hill. At the end of our climb we was rewarded with a view o'the nearby lake, givin' a special sense o'peace ta the sacred space. The graveyard itself held a surprise in a small gatherin' of men, already workin'. Without pause, Nurse Bennett give us direction.

"We're going to divide up. Maeve, you and Angel will work together on the far side of this section. Teagan, you and I will begin here. We have to clear the overgrown grass and dirt that the men are digging out from around the concrete markers in the ground. Then we have to put it all into the wheelbarrows. They'll be no talking, only work. So, see that you keep your minds on your business."

The vision of the men distracted me brain from Nurse Bennett's voice. Worse yet, when one of 'em workin' the ground looked me way, I 'bout fainted. 'Twas me fella, the one 'bout which I'd been dreamin'.

"Alright, Teagan, let's get started. *Teagan!*"

"Yes, Missus, " I answered, stumbling over a hidden rock while tryin' me best not ta let the man know I'd seen him. 'Twas too late. His sweet green eyes latched onta mine and I could see a grin passin' his lips as he was watchin' me go off balance. All's I could do was put me head down and go ta work on the task at hand. T'would have been a grand plan had not Nurse Bennett called out fer help.

"You there, the man with the dark hair. I need you to better dig out this area of markers."

Fairly jumpin' up from his place two rows over, the fine man dropped himself down 'long side me and started diggin' away.

"Teagan, I want you to collect the clumps of dirt and grass as this man works. It will make for a neater clean-up. I'm going to check on Angel and Maeve. I'll be back."

I near cried out ta Nurse Bennett ta not leave me, but the gentle tone ta the man's voice calmed me straight away.

"Yazoo Koukla. I remember you from when we cleaned the outside yard. It is nice to see you again and this time to be able to speak. My Christian name is Dimitri James Ardonis, but most call me James."

The man had an accent unknown ta me, but fer the most part, he spoke so's I could understand him. Givin' him a glance, I could see what his words tweren't sayin'. 'Twas a man of good intent, no doubt. So's I replied, "Me name is Teagan. Teagan Cormick. Nice ta meet ya James."

We worked in silence, me gathering the muddy clumps o'grass as James was diggin' from 'round the small markers buried 'neath the ground. As we moved 'long the rows, I noticed numbers carved inta each concrete circle. Not knowin' their purpose, I asked James if he knew?

"Ne, these are grave markers, Teagan. Each number is attached to someone once locked away here, as we are, but who has died."

The thought that we was clearin' away gravesites gave a bit o' turn ta me stomach. In Queenstown, when a soul passed, they was buried proper-like with a headstone bearin' their name and their years of livin' and dyin'. These small circles had nothin' more than a number, as if the soul 'neath 'em had no meanin'. I've not a clue if 'twas me temper or me heart, but from somewhere tears started formin'. Without movin' closer, James reached out and touched me hand.

"What is it that is wrong Teagan? Is there something I can do?"

"No, but thank ya kindly. I'm just sad ta know that we're tramplin' on the graves o'people who was forced here, like you and me. Not a soul knows they've been laid ta rest and not a person ta come and pray over 'em. Most likely will be the same fer us, don'cha know. Makes me sad and mad all together."

"I understand, Teagan. In my Greek homeland, graves are considered sacred gathering sites. Family members are expected to visit every month, bringing with them vases of oils, floral wreaths and ribbons to leave in memory. If the deceased should not have children to mourn them, they are required to hire mourners before they die, so that they will always have visitors to their graves. The souls under these tiny round circles have been buried without ceremony and without loved ones. It is hurtful to me as well."

The man's words warmed a spot in me heart, that had long been cold. 'Twas as if he could see straight inta me and know just the right things ta say. Though I didn't dare let him know, I had a desire ta say a bit o'something' in thanks.

"How are we coming along here?"

Nurse Bennett come marchin' 'long the row o'markers, inspectin' our work as she went.

"Seems as if you two work well together. Keep on. I am going back to the other side."

Waitin' 'til I was sure the good nurse had gone away, I whispered me thoughts ta James.

"Your words were just right. We Irish put great stock in proper buryin'. Helps ta know someone else thinks the same bout these poor souls who were ne'er laid ta a proper rest."

"In honesty, Teagan, I should tell you, I am the one who buries people in this cemetery. It is my job. When I was first forced to come here, I could not tolerate sitting in the ward and watching others rot in mind and body. So, I offered to work wherever the orderlies could use me. At first, they ignored me. So, I started doing little things like picking up garbage off the floor, cleaning tables in the dining hall, anything to make the work of the orderlies easier. Then when the first season of warm weather arrived, Nurse Stewart and Doctor Jensen agreed to give me the job of groundskeeper. I worked hard and long through that season, earning the trust of all. Then, Ed died."

"Ed was the gravedigger here for many years until a morning he did not show up. An orderly was sent to the cabin at the bottom of this cemetery hill where he lived. There he found the man stone cold in his bed. As there was no one to take Ed's place, I stepped forward. Dr. Henn, the man in charge of all that goes on here, agreed to let me dig the graves, but not to live in the cottage. I had to prove first that I would not try and escape. It took many seasons before the doctor believed in me, but I earned my way and I have been living in the cottage and digging the graves, ever since. The blessing is that this work allows me to say a few words over each body before I bury them. I always ask God to bless their souls as they pass to heaven using the Greek blessing of my family.

Μήπως ο Κύριος ο Θεός να παραχωρήσει την ανάπαυση ψυχής εκεί όπου οι δίκαιοι εγκαταλείπουν. Για τα έλεος του Θεού, τη βασιλεία των ουρανών και τη συγχώρεση των αμαρτιών τους, ας ζητήσουμε από τον Χριστό τον αθάνατο Βασιλιά και τον Θεό μας. May the Lord God grant their soul rest where the righteous repose. For the mercies of God, the kingdom of heaven, and the forgiveness of their sins, let us ask from Christ our immortal King and God."

I was touched by the words o'the man, but truth be told, knowin' James was the one ta put bodies inta the earth made me feel a bit odd. I couldn't help but ta ask what was on me mind.

"Is it hard to shovel dirt over the body of another bein', even if they're passed?"

James took a few digs inta the grass afore answerin'.

"It is never easy to lower a body into the ground, knowing their time came to an end in a place like this, without family or friend and often after much suffering. But it is only the skin and bones of the person I am laying to rest, not their soul. I take comfort in that."

I understood the words he was sayin'. Still I was sure I'd never be able ta do such a thing meself. As such thoughts kept runnin' through me head, James spoke again.

"There was one time when I did not think I would be able to bury a body. It was early on, after I had been given the job. An orderly came to me in the dormitory. He said a grave needed to be dug with speed, but did not say why. Only that the dead man would be delivered to the graveyard at sunrise."

"I rose and dressed and made my way into the moonlit night. Stopping by the shed alongside Ed's cottage, I chose the spade with the pointed tip, grateful for the mild weather that would ease my struggles in turning the ground. I walked to the top of the hill and stood for a moment, letting the gentle sounds of the nearby lake bestow peace upon me, praying for the unknown soul I was about to bury."

Comin' to the end o'the circles where we was workin' I looked ta James fer where next ta go. Risin' he moved a row and motioned fer me ta do the same. Again, side by each, the thoughtful man went on with his story tellin.

"I accomplished my task well before dawn and moved to a nearby bench where I slept into the sunrise. The sounds of approaching footsteps accompanied by loud talking roused my mind. Opening my eyes, I saw two orderlies swinging a blanket between them, clearly struggling with the corpse trapped within the folds of the woolen coverlet. Wanting to keep them from carelessly dumping the dead person into the grave, I quickly rose and met them at the foot of the site. There they dropped the body, obviously glad to be rid of it, and left without a word. Determined to provide a sacred burial for this departed soul, I slowly unwound the twisted blanket in order to properly cover the corpse before lowering it into the ground."

"Respectfully peeling back the scratchy woolen fabric I felt shock run through my body as I came upon the face of the dead man. His name was Stefan. He was a Dutchman from Holland who was committed sometime before me. Although we did not know each other well, we had much in common, Stefan and me. We both were married and fathers to sons. We both were carpenters in our own businesses. We both worked endless hours to make good lives for our families and we both lost our business through no fault of our own. And that is what caused our wives to leave us, taking our children with them."

'Twas a bit surprisin' hearin' James speak 'bout a wife and children. All's the time I'd been thinkin' of the handsome man, not one idea o'family'd crossed me mind. Now that he told me, a bit o'guilt crawled inta me fer the dreams 'bout the two of us I'd been havin'. Still in all, I was wantin' to be 'round the man, so's I stayed close and listened.

"The deep sorrow Stefan and I felt over losing our families caused our minds to turn black. We could do nothing but search for our families and pray for their return, which sadly led to the same turn of events in our lives. We lost our homes, our tools, our friends—everything of meaning. Each of us was finally arrested as a vagrant, the courts individually determining as, "depressed." That's how we were locked away in this asylum, and how we met. Being held against our wills did nothing to help us. Finding each other and becoming friends did. Everyday Stefan and I would talk about our boyhood memories and share our family traditions, mine from Greece, his from Holland. It was in those moments that we found ways and reasons to survive. When I began working outdoors on a daily basis, Stefan and I did not talk as often. Sadly, he returned to the darkness in his mind and nothing I could say or do when I would see helped."

"Eventually, I was forced to realize I would have to leave Stefan in that dark place. Sometime later, I was told by an orderly that one of the new doctors had taken him down the hall. That was the last I knew of him until that early morning when I experienced the anguish of burying my friend's body."

A crackin' in his voice let me know James was still sad o'er the loss o'his friend. Reaching fer clumps of dirt and grass he'd been digging, I let me hand graze across his own, hopin' me touch might soothe his ache. In turn, the man fixed his passionate eyes upon me and, as God is me witness, I was sure'n me heart was beatin' right outta me body. Turnin' so's he could sit aside me and reaching ta hold me hand, James finished tellin' what he needed.

"The shock of finding Stefan that morning beneath the stained and coarse blanket was made worse by the fact that his face had been disfigured, especially around his eyes. Tenderly, I reached up and drew down his lids, allowing my friend to rest in peace."

"Rewrapping the blanket around him, I began my liturgy of Greek prayer while I carefully lowered his body into the ground and covered him with the earth that had once given him life. It took seasons for me to recover from the shock of Stefan's death and I constantly challenged myself with questions of how he passed. It was only through conversation I overheard between two nurses, as they strolled around the cemetery one day, that I came to know the truth."

"It seems one of the nurses had been working with the doctor treating Stefan after they moved him down the hall. She said they were trying something called a lobotomy to see if it might cure his black mood. The woman went on to describe the treatment in words that are forever engraved into my mind. She said that the doctor used a hammer to give two quick shocks to Stefan's head to keep him from feeling the greater pain he was about to inflict. He then rolled back one of Stephan's eyelids and stuck a device the size of a pencil through the lid and up into Stephen's head. The doctor again used the hammer to strike the device, relentlessly hitting it back and forth, back and forth for several minutes. Finally he removed the device, along with the crushed and oozing front lobe of Stefan's brain."

It took a bit fer James ta be able ta go on. He went back ta diggin', his tears waterin' the grass all 'round him. When at last he spoke, 'twas in a tone that broke me heart.

"That night I returned to Stefan's grave and sat and talked with him, just as we had always done. I talked about our sons, I talked about our lives. Then at last, I stopped talking . . . and wept sorrowfully for us both."

Chapter Twenty-Nine

ALTHOUGH IT WAS ONLY 10:30 in the morning, Grace was starved for lunch. However, she definitely was not interested in the salad and pita bread she'd brown-bagged from home. Instead, a hot fudge brownie sundae with whipped cream was streaming through her consciousness, an indulgence she allowed only in life's most stressful moments.

Her interview with James Ardonis was more emotionally draining than Grace had anticipated. It wasn't that talking to James was depressing. Actually, in spite of an advanced back condition that prevented him from walking, the man was mentally sharp and engaging, with a charm Grace found enchanting.

Ok Grace. There are some nice benefits to this job but romanticizing an 81-year old man is not one of them.

The thought of crushing on James caused her to giggle outloud. Clearly she needed a break before meeting and assessing the three remaining seniors on her to-do list.

"Hey Grace, got a minute?"

Looking up, Grace saw that the voice belonged to Mary Burke, purposefully striding along the hallway in the latest style of pantsuit uniform. Grace recognized Wood Haven's head of nursing as consistently ahead of the curve, in her appearance as well as her methods of organizing and administering patient care. That was the irony of Mary's job these days—her expertise in carrying out her duties would ultimately eliminate her position. Once all seniors were transferred to new sites, there would no longer be a need for any Wood Haven nurses or administrators.

While it was a challenge for Mary and her nurses to work towards closing down the institution, they all fully appreciated the responsibility of providing a better life for the remaining Wood Haven seniors. Grace admired every member of the nursing staff and was grateful to have such a strong medical team as a partner in the deinstitutionalization process.

"Good morning, Mary. What can I do for you today?"

"Actually, it's more what my staff and I can do for you, Grace. We've been going through the archives and old records preparing for Wood Haven's final shut down and unbelievably we came across suitcases belonging to patients who were committed here over the last eighty years."

Grace's curiosity shifted in to overdrive.

"No kidding. What's in them? Do the patients know about them? Are they stored someplace safe?""Whoa, hold on, Grace. One question at a time. I don't know what's in all of them as I didn't feel it was my place to open them. I did check through a couple to identify exactly what we were dealing with and they contained personal items that apparently each patient brought with them when they were committed. I haven't spoken to anyone about them yet because there are hundreds of these suitcases and I am not sure if any belong to the ten seniors still living here. And yes, they are safe. They are in the attic of this building, where they apparently have been for decades. I wanted to tell you about them because I know you are starting to meet one-on-one with the seniors and I was thinking if we do find suitcases belonging to any of them, it might be a good way to return them through you. Depending on what's inside, the contents might help you get to know them better and make it easier to place them in their new living situations."

"That's a great idea, but I think we should make sure of the contents in each case first. I would not want to deliver them blindly.

"Absolutely. I was just on my way to tell Jonathan about them. I'm sure he will have his own idea of how best to handle their return. I'll let you know what he decides."

"Perfect. In the meantime, I'll continue to meet with the seniors on my list for today. They are the four in need of skilled care. I'll be following up with them several times before they are placed. If Jonathan approves, I can take their suitcases to them another time."

With that Mary set off to inform Wood Haven's Executive Director of her discovery, leaving Grace to more fully consider the intriguing news. Images of hand-written letters on yellowed note paper, sachets of faded perfumes, bits and pieces of lace and ribbon, leather covered books with dog-eared pages, black and white photographs permanently creased by cherished years of viewing—all of it played through her mind.

What a treasure trove to discover and hopefully to be able to return to these special individuals who lost most everything from their lives when they were committed here.

The enormity of the circumstance fueled Grace's emotions as she approached the room of her next senior, Maria Rodriguez. Where only moments earlier she'd wanted a break before continuing these interviews, she was now energized by the idea of being able to restore some small aspect of her senior's forgotten worlds. Politely knocking on the door, pushed open the door to the room.

"Good afternoon, Senorita Rodriguez. My name is Grace Reid. I am new here at Wood Haven. I wanted to stop by and introduce myself and say hello."

"I know who you are and you are not welcome in my room. Leave. Now."

Grace was startled by the tiny size of the woman bundled beneath the sterile white blanket particularly in relation to her oversized reaction. Taking a few steps closer to the bed, Grace could see the woman's glossy black hair highlighted with streaks of gray, perfectly framing her soft brown complexion. Without a touch of make-up, Maria Rodriguez was beautiful despite having endured almost four decades of asylum life. It was that realization that encouraged Grace to try and engage the woman again.

"I beg your pardon, Senorita. Did you say that you know of me? May I ask how?"

"You can ask all you want, but I will not speak with you now or anytime in the future. Entonces véte. Aléjate. Ahora!"

Though Grace was far from fluent in Spanish, it didn't take a translator to understand she was being told to get out of the room. The question was, why?

"Senorita Rodriguez, I sincerely ask that you take a moment to chat with me, so I can better understand why it is you don't want me in your room. We have just met so I cannot imagine why you would not like me."

Silence was the woman's only response.

Confused and concerned, Grace decided the best course of action was to honor the woman's request and leave the room. However, before exiting she tried one last time.

"Tengo muchas ganas de conocerte, Senorita Rodriguez. I very much would like to get to know you. In the meantime, I bid you a good day with a promise to return again."

"Espere! Wait! How is it you know my language?"

"I don't really. In college I was friends with a girl from Puerto Rico. She taught me a few phrases like the one I just spoke."

"So you are dishonest in trying to make me believe you speak Spanish."

"No, not dishonest. Trying to relate—find common ground between us."

"Mentirosa! Get out."

Grace had no doubt it was best to withdraw, which she did with a respectful, "Good day, Senorita Rodriguez. I'll be back again." In the mean time she would consult with Mary Burke for suggestions on better ways to approach the fiery senior.

Alone in the hallway, Grace experienced a burning in the pit of her stomach. In all her years working with seniors she'd never encountered such intense hostility aimed directly at her, and for no discernable reason. The enthusiasm she'd felt for her job only minutes earlier was now shattered into shards of self doubt.

The best thing to do when you fall off is to get back on and try again.

The words flashed through Grace's mind as she recalled a special birthday celebration on her grandparent's farm. She was five years old the first time Papa O'Connor set her in a saddle. It was on a horse he'd purchased as her 7th birthday gift. As her loving papa led the horse around the fenced-in pasture, Grace felt a freedom she'd never known. Within minutes, she was begging to ride on her own. Against his better judgement, he allowed Grace full rein, only to watch her slide gracefully down the side of the horse and hit the ground, once they started trotting.

Rather than offer sympathy, papa caught the horse and led it back to where Grace lay sobbing in the pasture. There he shared his, "get back on" wisdom and picked her up and plopped her back in the saddle. Grace was as much angry at her papa as she was scared of the horse, but in the long run, the lesson of facing her fears by trying again became a valued part of her life philosophy.

Ok papa. I'm getting back in the saddle. Still on my list for today are Janna Mazury, age 64, and Regina Wilson, age 76.

Checking the nearby room names and numbers, Grace noticed a sign indicating the two women shared one living space. Checking two residents off her list with one visit held a definite appeal for Grace, especially after her disastrous encounter with Maria Rodriguez.

Unless they're both angry with me as well. No time like the present to find out.

With a knock, and what she hoped sounded like a friendly hello, Grace stepped into the room. Unlike the previous living quarters, a large section of the far wall had been removed, creating an open entry into the adjoining room. From all appearances, the area where she was standing served as a living space and the other area, as a bedroom. Sitting in two over-sized lounge chairs before her were the women she assumed to be Janna and Regina. They were contentedly dozing under matching, hand-knit afghans.

Not wanting to wake them, Grace sat down at a nearby table and opened their files to review. The women were twelve years apart in age and their Wood Haven histories showed that Regina had been admitted and discharged multiple times over the last four decades, while Janna had been locked away since her commitment in 1939.

The common thread between the two women was painful endings of their relationships with their children. Additionally, the loss of freedom these two women experienced in being committed to Wood Haven was inconceivable to Grace. She wondered how to even begin talking to Janna and Regina about their futures, as she imagined that concept had long ago become meaningless to them.

"Hello, dear. I'm so sorry for sleeping so long. Have you been here much time?"

The gentle voice encircled Grace like a kind hug. Looking up she saw the younger-appearing of the two women awake and smiling. Taking a guess, she spoke.

"Hello, would you be Janna?

"Why yes, I am Janna. Janna Mazury. And who is it you might be?"

"My name is Grace Reid. I'm new here at Wood Haven and have stopped by to say hello and get to know you and Regina.

"How lovely. Thank you, Grace, for your interest in two old women. We've been here so long It's hard to imagine anyone cares. Don't misunderstand, the nurses are most kind, but other than our medical care and Jonathan stopping to say hello, we don't see or talk to anyone outside of the ten of us still here.

The woman's voice was absent of any traces of rancor, and Grace marveled at her seemingly compliant attitude. According to her records, Janna had been committed for involutional melancholia, resulting from giving birth to six children in three years and a subsequent shift of her system into early menopause.

"And Regina? How did the two of you come to share this living space that is so different from any of the others I have seen here?"

"Now that's quite a story, my dear. On some of the details I'm a little fuzzy. I do remember it was Teagan who brought us together one day in the dining hall. Regina was still getting her bearings, if you understand what I mean, and sweet Teagan was helping. She led Regina to lunch sitting alongside her on the bench, with me on the other side. From that day we came back to those same places for every meal and from that Regina and I have become been best friends

As Janna pause, Regina stirred slightly under her afghan. Reaching over, Janna tucked the woven blanket under her friend's chin and around her shoulders, much as a mother would do for a child. The moment was tinged with a poignancy that Grace honored with silence, allowing Janna to continue in her own time.

"As you see, Regina can sleep through most any noise or distraction. Though it's not always been that way. Being forced away from her children brought sorrows that kept Regina awake long into most nights. For years she walked wall to the wall in the dormitory, trying to survive the darkness. Often I would walk with her and take naps during the day, when others could keep her company. It was only when Jonathan came and learned of our friendship that he ordered our two rooms to become one. Being together, just the two of us, has made Regina feel safer at night. And while it has been slow in coming, Janna is now able to close her eyes and sleep in peace, rather than in painful nightmares of the children she does not know."

Observing the two women as Janna spoke, it was obvious that being confined together in this asylum for more than forty years had bonded them in significant ways. It was also definite in Grace's mind that no matter what future living situation each might require, Regina and Janna would live together for the rest of their days.

CHAPTER THIRTY

WOOD HAVEN ADMITTANCE FORM

Patient: *unknown female*
Date of Admittance: *March 9, 1946*
Number: *03094645*
Age: *mid forties (estimated)*
Ethnicity: *American*
Children: *unknown*
Cause of insanity: *Softening of the Brain*

BEIN' LOCKED AWAY WAS HARD on both me mind and me body. 'Twas not only bein' shut off from the world that kept me reelin'. 'Twas also seein' so many poor souls chained ta beds or kept in wire cages, most left fer no better than dead.

I oft railed against me loss o'freedom. Yet as I could see me own face and body changin', lookin' more and more like me mam, I come ta understand 'twas best ta just accept the will o'God.

Truth be told, there was some who helped make me days and nights more bearable. Chattin' with Maeve always made me smile, as did watchin' sweet Angel doin' kindnesses o'er the wards. And there was the few times I found ways ta be close ta James. Sure'n those moments kept me heart beatin'. But in this barren place, the one who from me first night and through many days after kept a small flame o'hope in me soul 'twas Nurse Bennett.

The first time ever I seen the good nurse, I'd just been drug inta the ward. Me head was hurtin' and me body achin', some parts gone numb from bein' banged up and scraped raw by orderlies haulin' me 'crost the hellish hallways. But like sun through the blackest clouds, along come Nurse Bennett, makin' her way ta where I was sittin' on me cot. She touched me gentle-like, makin' it feel like me mam were standing right there, 'longside me.

"Hello. My name is Nurse Bennett. Can you tell me your name?"

"Course I can. Why does ya want ta know?"

"Well, it can be a bit scary here at first, and I thought if we knew each other's names, it might make it nicer."

'Twas the first bit o'kindness shown me since the gardia tossed me inta their wagon and stole away me paints. While I hadn't a clue if the woman could be trusted, nothin' in me power could control the tears fallin' in answer ta her kind-hearted question. Wipin' me face on the sleeve o'the rough rag dress they'd put on me body, I pulled in a breath and let loose me voice."

"Me name is Teagan. Teagan Cormick."

I knew soon as the words left me mouth I'd given 'way the secret o'me real name. Truth be told, I'd no sense if life could worsen if'n the woman knew me name be Taylor Eagan when I first come ta America. So's I said a prayer ta Mary, Mother o' God, askin' fer protection—and waited.

"Well Teagan, thank you for telling me your name."

The woman's soft tone matched the feel o'her hands as she lay 'em upon me back, gently give me a rub. 'Twas much the same as me nanny would do when I'd come cryin'. 'Tween the woman's touch and me own memories, I fell ta sobbin' without effort. Nurse Bennett's response was to keep on, her soothin' hands seemin' ta draw the pain right outta me body. When at last I'd not a tear left, the good nurse pulled a cotton handkerchief from the pocket of her starched white uniform and wiped me face clear, like a mam ta her babe.

"Teagan, keep this handkerchief with you for nights to come when you will need comfort and I cannot be here. I promise I will check on you when ever I come into the wards, to see how you are doing. Remember, no matter how it may seem, you are not alone.

With that, Nurse Bennett was gone, leavin' a cold, empty space 'tween where me body and hers had been touchin'. From the damp hankie in me hand, I could sense a trace of her scent and pushed the cotton cloth close to me nose. 'Twas the only way I could think ta be keepin' her near.

As nights come and passed o'er and 'gain, I kept looking fer the gentle nurse. Twasn't wantin' more than ta hear her speak me name . . . me real name. Ta know someone noticed if'n I was even alive. But no matter where I kept watch, Nurse Bennett was ne'er ta be found. 'Twas only one early mornin' as orderlies was passin' through that she come me way 'gain.

I was wakin', sleep still in me eyes, when I had me first glance her way. 'Twas sure I was dreamin' 'til she was standin' 'longside me.

"Good Morning, Teagan. How are you?"

The surprise of seein' the woman after so many days o'searchin' kept me dumb. Not a word come ta mind or mouth. Just a tear run down me cheek. Without thought, Nurse Bennett sit down next ta me. "Teagan, I was here the first night you were brought in and I understand you've had a rough go. I want you to know that I am keeping an eye on you and doing my best to make sure you are alright."

Me single tear burst inta full-out blubberin' as I found me tongue.

"Nurse Bennett, I'm forever grateful ta ya fer carin'. Bein' in this place feels like I'm dead and gone, with not a soul in the world knowin'. I miss me mam and me da somethin' fierce."

Them words was all I could get out, as me tears kept flowin' beyond measure. Me nose soon joined in, runnin' snot over me lips

"Where's your handkerchief, Teagan? You need to use it to wipe your tears and then follow along with the rest to the bathrooms. Then it's on to breakfast. I will keep checking in on you as I can and I need you to remember what I said on your first night. You are not alone."

With a soft squeeze of me hands in her own, Nurse Bennett moved on ta others in need.

I managed ta get meself off the cot and ta the toilet, no matter I'd rather have curled up and died. But Nurse Bennett wanted me ta go on. She wanted me, Teagan Cormick, ta live. So's from that day, each mornin', I rose and did me best.

Nurse Bennett and I become friends of a sort. She'd stop a minute ta speak when she could and when she couldn't she'd cast a glance ta let me know I was in her mind. I come ta love her like me mam and turned ta her whenever I come scared or needy. We went on as such without measure and me devotion ta the woman grew ta no end.

Then come a day came when me world changed.

'Twas a sunny winter's morn in me special window corner o'the porch. I sit watchin' the snows swirl 'round, hopin' fer a chat with Maeve or a stop-by from Nurse Bennett. Ta me pleasure, on this particular day, 'twas the good nurse who not only come by but set down beside me, puttin' a smile inta me heart.

"Good Morning, Teagan. I'm glad I found you."

Her smile was kind, but the good nurse's eyes showed sadness.

"I wanted to tell you that I went to see my doctor recently. He told me I have some health problems that require I stay at home and rest for a bit. Of course, I can't do that and continue to work so, sadly, I'm going to have to leave my duties here."

Me mind struggled ta sort out the woman's words, unsure if the bein' sick or the leavin' 'twas worse. Not able ta choose, I sit still-like, closin' me eyes in hopes I was havin' a bad dream could be blinked 'way.

"You've become very special to me, Teagan, and I didn't want to leave without saying good bye and to tell you I will miss you and our chats."

The more she talked, the tighter I clamped me eyes, squeezin' the pain outta me heart and inta me tears. In the turn of a minute, Nurse Bennett would be fore'er gone from me life—a sorry life that mostly become worth livin' due ta her love and kindness. How ever could she go off and leave me?

Every bit o'me, body, mind and soul 'twas breakin' inta a million parts. I couldn't bear ta look at the woman. At the same, I was desperately wantin'ta throw meself inta her lap and have her hands on me back, rubbin' away the pain spreadin' through me. Finally, I opened me eyes and saw the same sadness starin' back. 'Twas then I knew this leavin' was as hurtful fer her.

As if understandin' each other's minds, we wrapped inta a hug we both knew 'twas needin' ta last a lifetime. Pullin' back, the good nurse whispered, "Forever and always, sweet Teagan, remember you are not alone."

And then she was gone.

There's no way of sayin' how I lived the next bit o'me life. Don't right recall much after that winter's day. Maeve talks 'bout how she found me later on, lyin' on the floor in the ward, still and silent. She says I stayed that way fer quite some time.

The orderlies carted me back ta me cot and tried gettin' me up each mornin' ta pee and eat, but I was havin' none o'it. Maeve says they even took me down the hall fer a bit, but when they brung me back, 'twas just the same. So's they wrapped me in diapers and left me on me cot ta rot. 'Twas fine by me, but not ta others.

It started in the dark o'night. Maeve and Angel come ta me cot. Angel put little bits o'food inta me mouth with Maeve holdin' me nose, makin' it near impossible ta not swallow, just as together we'd done for others. Then the two sit and whispered stories 'bout me family and me beloved Ireland, remindin' me o'reasons ta go on.

Each night they come again. Each night I went ta swallowin' more regular-like. The two next went ta makin' me sit up and givin' me water ta drink. 'Twas all small bits and pieces they kept addin', always in the cloak o'night, so's no one t'would be the wiser.

With food and drink comin' inta me, pee and poop was comin' out, me diapers stinkin' ta high heaven. Knowin' me weakness, Maeve started talkin' 'bout me da bein' disgraced by me diapers and needin ta get meself up and ta the toilet.

The next morning as orderlies come through, I got off me cot, shakin' head ta toe. Maeve and Angel took sides, helpin' make me way ta the toilet. With no shame, stripped me naked they did and cleaned me body like a baby, re-dressing me in bed rags fashioned inta clothes of a sort. That's how it begun. How I managed goin' on without Nurse Bennett.

T'is not ta say that I ne'er took a slide backwards. There be days cryin' on me cot and feedin' me heartbreak by not eatin' or drinkin', don'cha know. On those days 'twas only me cherished handkerchief that brought me back and kept me livin'. But all me melancholy come ta a stop the day Angel come and asked fer me help.

Seems she'd met a woman in another ward. Poor thing was wastin' away o'er her child who'd passed. While the woman's body be sound, her mind was lost in pain. She was doin' nothin' but layin' on a cot, willin' herself the same fate as her beibe.

With Angel leadin', not a soul kept us from goin' ta where they'd kept the woman. Soon as I lay eyes on the poor thing, I knew her mind and her soul as t'were me own. I begin talkin' ta her, much the same way Nurse Bennett had done me early on. From then, little by little, I kept on 'til the woman started comin' back from the dead.

Suppose ya could say helpin' her helped me as well. Sharin' Nurse Bennett's ways made it seem she was still near. Chattin' with the woman, 'twas as if the carin' nurse was whisperin' just what ta say in me ear.

From then, Angel come often ta ask me ta chat with others in need, sayin' I was becomin' me own special angel in the wards. Best of all, she spoke of knowin' in her heart that Nurse Bennett was watchin' o'er me and bein' proud.

Truth be told, I'd me own sense o' pride as well, helpin' others lives ta ga on and me with 'em.

O'er time new nurses come in place o'Nurse Bennett and those who'd worked with her. Maeve and I went back ta our chats. Angel kept helpin'others. I spent time thinkin' 'bout me family and imaginin' how they'd gone on, wonderin' if mam and da were even still with us. I wished too fer a chance ta get outta this place. 'Stead, I just went ta getting' older, turnin' inta a bit of a mam ta them's trapped here, same's me. Some ended dyin' in me arms. Others went on, findin' ways ta survive. No matter, I made sure they's understood a soul knew their name, and cared. That they weren't alone.

Then come a day in a lifetime o' such days. I woke and made me way ta the toilet and on ta eat. Sittin' at the end of able, I felt a motion aside me. 'Twas Angel.

"Teagan, you've got to come. There's a woman in need of help. She was brought in a few days back and the orderlies put her down the hall. I stopped to check on her and she grabbed on to my hand and held it so tightly. I tried talking to her but couldn't get any response. The nurses say she doesn't seem to know who she is and neither do they. She was found wandering the streets. She appears elderly and quite fragile. Definitely confused and scared. You have such a way of calming people, I thought you might be able to help her."

Goin' down the hall after Angel, waves o'fear come runnin' through me. I went ta rememberin' the bullyin' orderlies from me first night—shovin' me onta the damp stone floor and leavin' me ta dirty meself and ta starve. Addin' ta such 'twas a worry of goin' ta see this forlorn woman with not so much as a memory o'herself. So's it was, all of it made me determined ta find ways ta bring her comfort.

Comin' ta a stop, Angel pushed open the door afore us. In the dank room, a tiny form lie tied ta a table close ta a frightenin-lookin' machine. At first glance, the woman appear dead and gone, but drawin' closer I could see a bit o'a rise and fall in her chest.

Covered she was in a long muslin gown with a hood toppin' her head and fallin' o'er her face. I knew it ta be the dress o'one whose brain was bein' filled with electric from the machine. The only body parts ta fully see were the woman's hands and feet. Lined with deep purple veins they were, more bones than flesh.

Stepping right close, I gently folded her hand inta mine. 'Twas cold and lifeless. I added me other hand and begin gently rubbin' 'long the woman's paper-thin skin. As if risin' from the dead, her fingers wrapped 'round me own and I knew 'twas time ta speak.

"T'is alright dearie. I'm here with ya. Me name is Teagan. Teagan Cormick. I was brung here, just like you, so's I know all you're feelin' and I want ya to know, you're not alone."

Nary a moment passed afore the woman give a weak squeeze, as if beggin' ta be heard. Not wantin' ta turn loose her hand, I went ta figurin' how ta be able ta look inta her eyes, ta let her see the care in me heart. Gently, I pulled one of me hands 'way and reached up ta the hood 'ttached ta her gown. Pushin' back the cotton from her head, the woman looked at me with the deepest of longin's, her eyes speakin', as sure'n as if they had words. What's more, I knew just what she was sayin', as if her thoughts were me own. And in that moment, me brain cried out what me lips could only whisper.

"Fer the love o'God. Nurse Bennett—ya come back."

CHAPTER THIRTY-ONE

GRACE CLIMBED THE STAIRS to her rental home feeling as if she were scaling a mountain. Her work week had been emotionally and mentally exhausting, which took a toll on her body as well. All she wanted on this Friday night was to collapse on her sofa and not move, other than to possibly order a pizza—delivered.

The intensity of the four Monday interviews with the seniors she'd ID'd for skilled care, persuaded Grace to scale back the remaining Faith File interviews. She needed to allow more time for each senior to become comfortable talking with her. She also needed to allow herself time to process the poignant stories and memories shared by each one. Equally important, she had to conclude all ten interviews and produce the associated reports by her Friday meeting with the state. Ultimately, she decided on two Faith File interviews per day, Tuesday through Thursday, and then get to her desk no later than 6 am on Friday to complete all ten reports for the 11 am meeting. Busy, doable and draining.

Exchanging her business suit and stack heels for comfy pj's and slippers, Grace called the Midland Pizzeria and ordered a small cheese and pepperoni. She then pulled out a bottle of French Bordeaux and uncorked it to breathe. While most people she knew favored white wines, Grace had developed a taste for the fuller French reds and held a secret dream of taking an extended trip through France's vineyards and their sacred wineries.

Collecting a plate, napkins and silverware along with her bottle of wine and appropriate glass, Grace trudged into the living room and plopped down on the couch. Amid hearty sips of Bordeaux, she mentally wandered through the Faith File and her two days of encounters with the group.

Gabrielle Liberty Filipek. The background summary on the woman revealed that she had been a vocal and tough patient from day one of her asylum admission. What her file did not explain were the reasons Liberty's aggressive behavior continued over the entire four decades of her confinement.

"Hello Gabrielle. My name is Grace Reid. I am a new member of the Wood Haven staff. I've come to get to know you and to chat with you about your time here.

"Well you can start by using my proper name," the woman spat out the words as she raised up from the chair in which she'd been seated. Moving within striking distance, she proceded to lambast Grace, adding a pointed finger at her chest.

"It's Liberty and if you don't call me rightly, you might as well leave now, as I'll not waste my time talking to you."

Grace stepped back from the woman's reach, simultaneously casting a quick glance at the bulleted notes on the front of her file.

Yep. Seventy-eight years old. This woman is not only sassy, she's spry. If it comes down to a battle of wills and/or bodies, I'm not sure I'll win either.

"I apologize, *Liberty*. The files I was given on your Wood Haven history list your name as Gabrielle Liberty. I will make sure to note you prefer being called by your middle name."

"Middle name, nothin'! Gabrielle was only in honor of my grandma. Nobody ever called me that. I've been Liberty since the day I was born and will be 'til the day I die."

"Again, thank you for letting me know. It's frustrating when people fail to call you by your proper name. So, Liberty, tell me about yourself—your family, where you grew up, special details or memories."

"Why should I tell you anything? And why do you want to know anyway? Most times when people 'round here ask questions it ends up leading to trouble of some kind."

"Well that may be what has happened in the past, but I assure you, Liberty, I am here solely to get to know you and find out from *you* what would make your life better."

"I'll tell you what would make a better life for me. Getting outta this place and doing what I damn well please. If you can't make that happen then I'm not talking, 'cause we're wasting each other's time, plain and simple."

Grace was taken back by the direct and forceful impact of the woman's words. At the same time, she was impressed with Liberty's clarity of mind, all of which encouraged her to reply in equally direct language.

"As a matter of fact, Liberty, I *can* make those things happen, to some extent, but in order to do so I need to know more about you. Are you willing to answer some questions?"

Grace's words seemed to score a direct hit and momentarily set Liberty back on her heels. It only took a quick breath, though, before the septuagenarian once again went into verbal attack mode.

"So you can get me out of here, huh? Well what about the rest of the people who have been trapped in this rotten place along with me, for most of their lives? Are you going to talk to them and spring them outta here as well?"

"As a matter of fact, yes. I've already met and chatted with four Wood Haven seniors who were very cooperative and thrilled that by sharing their stories they are helping me help them move on to new lives."

Considering Maria Rodriguez refused to speak to her, Grace realized her claim of "chatted with four seniors" might not be one-hundred-percent true. Still, she figured stretching the truth just a tiny bit to gain Liberty's confidence would be forgiven at the Pearly Gates.

"Ok, maybe I'll talk. But if I find out you were lying about any part of your cockamamie story, all I can say is, you'll be sorry."

Grace wasn't sure what Liberty's threat meant, or if she was somehow capable of following through. All that mattered for the moment was that she had a pass into this woman's life and she was going to tread quickly and lightly before the opening slammed shut.

"So, your Wood Haven file indicates when you were admitted you were not married. Correct?"

"Yes."

"And did you have any brothers or sisters?"

"No."

"And you are the only surviving member of your family, as far as you know."

"Brilliant."

Liberty's rudeness and sarcasm were not lost on Grace. While the woman might be cooperating, she was definitely in adversarial mode.

So, maybe posing questions requiring more than a one-word response will get us beyond this contentious stage.

"What memories do you have, Liberty, of being committed to Wood Haven?"

"Don't want to talk about it."

Well, it was more than one word. Obviously I need a different tact. Maybe playing the honesty card again will work.

"Look, Liberty, I have been hired by the Wood Haven administration to help relocate all ten of you seniors to a residence that will feel like a real home. It will be a place where you can live a more normal life, which you obviously want and deserve. The questions I'm asking will help me determine the level of independence you'll be able to manage and what support you might need. The more you tell me in your answers, the better I'll be able to help you. Conversely, the more you hold back, the harder it will be for me to truly know what will best suit you."

A blended look of disbelief and hope came over Liberty's face. Patiently, Grace waited and watched to see which emotion would win out. It was only a matter of moments before she had her answer.

"I was young and living in New York City, working odd jobs as I could find them. Mostly I was traveling to Seneca Falls and Washington, D.C., as part of the National Women's Party, fighting to earn women the right to vote. There was a whole group of us that traveled together and pooled our money for lodging and food. Mostly we saved our earnings to be able to post bail when we got arrested at protests."

The information amazed Grace. Nothing in Liberty's file indicated she'd been involved in the Women's Suffrage Movement. Stories about those who won the right for American women to vote had been a historical favorite of Grace's, in school and at her nana's knee. Although her grandmother supported the suffragists, she had not been an active part of the revolution. Sitting across from Liberty, Grace realized she was in the presence of a woman who actually helped change the history of the United States.

"Thank you for sharing that story, Liberty. I have to say, the chronicle of American women winning the right to vote has always fascinated me. To meet someone involved in that achievement is quite an honor."

"Yeah, well, there were a lot of us fought for the vote, from New York to California. Then once we got that done, we began working on an Equal Rights Amendment. I was helping write documents to make into law, but then I got arrested at a protest."

Liberty's pause drew Grace's attention away from her note taking and to the woman before her. The mask of fierce intensity she'd worn only moments ago was gone. In its place shown the tender face of her heart.

"After being arrested I got tossed into this rotten place. No one, not family or friend, knew I was locked away here. And nobody—nobody—ever came looking for me."

"Well, I may not be family or friend, but I definitely care that you were locked away here. And as I said, my plan is to help you, and the other seniors, move into a new place that I hope you will enjoy as a home. After all the years you've been forced to live this life, you deserve that."

Liberty stared into Grace's eyes for what seemed like an eternity. Then, with unexpected ease the woman rose off the chair where she'd been glued and moved to Grace, wrapping her in a strong embrace that dissolved into tearful sobs.

"It's been so long since I've seen the outside world or thought that I might once again live in a place I could call home."

Stepping back and meeting her eyes with Grace's, Liberty asked the key question.

"Can you really make that happen, Grace? Tell me the truth."

"Yes. I can, and I will. I promise."

Needing to move on to her next interview, Grace shared another embrace with Liberty, adding a promise to return the following week with more information about moving. The ashen appearance of the woman reflected the intensity of their meeting and what it had demanded of her, physically and mentally.

"For now, I would ask that you rest, Liberty. This has been a big day . . . for both of us."

Smiling weakly in response, the 78-year old woman walked to her bed and collapsed onto the mattress. Grace moved to Liberty, covering her with a cotton blanket that had been folded over the bedframe and caressing the exhausted woman's head until she fell asleep.

Exiting the room, Grace too felt as if she needed a rest, but there was still another senior to visit. Walking down the hallway to the next room, Grace hoped this interview would be a bit less emotional. Realistically, she imagined that to be a false hope.

The sign on the wall outside the door read, *Rebecca Odera Washington*. According to the file, she was about to meet a 58-year old German-American woman who'd been committed to Wood Haven in 1941 for reasons of political excitement.

Like a movie trailer, visions of the 1970's demonstrations Grace joined in protest of the Vietnam War played through her mind. Suddenly she was considering the terms of Rebecca's commitment relative to her own life experience.

Could it be that women who did the same 50 years earlier were committed to insane asylums as punishment?

Preparing herself for another emotional roller coaster, Grace knocked and opened the door to Rebecca's room with a deep breath and good intent.

On the far side of the room, she saw a slight-built woman, Afro-American in appearance, sitting in a chair and knitting.

"Guten Morgen. Oh, I'm sorry, when knitting my mind often to my childhood returns. Good Morning."

The woman's smile enlivened her face, from her eyes to her mouth.

Good Morning, Rebecca. My name is Grace Reid. I am new to the Wood Haven Staff. I've come to chat and get to know you.

"I wish you welcome, Grace. My friend Teagan told me of your presence and of your kindness. I trust Teagan with all my heart and happy I am to share with you what you want to know.

Smiling at the thought of Teagan paving the way, Grace decided to address the most difficult part of Rebecca's story right up front.

"Well to start, I'd like to know about you. From my file information I've read you are German-African and you were committed to Wood Haven in 1939 for reasons of political excitement, politics and war. Those are three things that can be connected but are also very different. I wonder if you would be able to tell me exactly what brought you to Wood Haven?"

"Oh my, this is something about which I have done my best to remember. Still I some parts cannot recall. Plainly put, attacked I was one night when from work I was walking home. All that happened was hurtful and so I like a dummkopf was thinking. Soon gone was mein job and mein place to live. I was to a poor house sent where it was very crowded. Survive I could barely do. Then away one day I was sent from the poor house to this frightening place where now we are."

Grace felt the indignities the woman had suffered through the haunted tone of her words. Further, she imagined the disorientation of being shipped off to an overcrowded poor house, then committed to a brutal insane asylum.

"Were your parents also sent to the poor house?"

"Nein. Die Beutche Soldaten—I am sorry—*the police* because mein parents being different races took them from our home. I saw them never again."

The directness of Rebecca's statement caused Grace to look up from her notes. Making a quick calculation, she realized the woman before her must have been little more than a child when losing her parents.

"Were you with them that night?"

"Ja. They had a plan. I in a hole under the floor was put while mein parents were beaten and dragged away. Under the floor I praying, crying and waiting stayed, but they never came back."

Rebecca spoke of the tragic night in a monotone voice, devoid of emotion. Yet as Grace searched the woman's eyes, she could see that the pain of watching her parents being abused and taken away remained clear and strong. She needed to know more but worried that continued recall of the painful events might be too much for the woman.

"Would you like some water and perhaps to rest for a bit? I know sharing such memories can be tiring."

"Nein. Until you know what you need I will continue. It has been many years since I these stories have told. Perhaps it is time for an old woman of such nightmares to rid herself."

Grace nodded, hoping that proceeding would not cause more turmoil than the sweet woman could manage. Waiting respectfully, she watched as Rebecca appeared removed from the room, her body set in a rigid shape, her face contorted by shadows from her past.

"When I finally out from the floorboards came, I to a safe place journeyed as mein parents had told me. From there I to Belgium was taken. A factory job with long hours I worked there, saving my earnings so I one day to America could travel, to the land of opportunity.

In America I with other women who appeared the same made friends. Together we lived and in a sewing factory worked. It was from that place I was to home walking when that night I was attacked. I have the rest to you already told."

I knew if I dared raise my eyes to Rebecca's, the power of the moment would lead us both to tears. Instead, I pretended to keep writing notes until I had a grip on my emotions. As I was about to close the file and thank Rebecca for her time, she began speaking again.

"There is one thing more. While I to Wood Haven did not chose to come, it has for me a safe place become. Each day my meals I have to eat and at night a bed on which to sleep. A few nurses to me have been kind and I have friendships with others found in Maeve and Angel and Teagan. Once I the rules learned to follow and quiet my thoughts keep, no harm to me has come. For this I in meine heart am grateful and to mein parents ein mein prayers give thanks."

For the first time, I realized that amid the horrible living conditions at Wood Haven there was a routine that allowed people who had seen a darker side of life than most, like Rebecca, to carve out a decent existence. I imagined this was especially true during the years of The Great Depression, when so many in America were claiming cardboard boxes for houses and picking through trash bins for food.

"I am glad to know your life here has provided you a sense of security, Rebecca. That is part of why I am here. The people in charge of Wood Haven believe that you and the others, like Maeve and Teagan, deserve to live in a place where you have more freedom. To be able to spend time outside when you please, or go for a walk, or choose the foods you want to eat but still in a place that is safe and you are protected. So they have asked me to talk to each of you and find out what you think you might like in a home. Once I have spoken to everyone, I will put together all of your thoughts and do my best to find a place where you can live together."

"Oh, no. I to move am not sure I would want. I here know I am happy. So thank you, but no."

This was a twist Grace didn't anticipate. After all the horror stories she'd read and heard about Wood Haven, she never imagined someone would refuse to leave. The question was, how to explain to Rebecca that there was no choice? Actually it seemed like she was forcing her into a life of more of the same, where she was not allowed to determine her own future.

"I understand how you feel Rebecca. I have lived in places where I never wanted to leave. Sadly I had to, each time for a different reason over which I had no control. The thing is, even though I hated moving, once I settled in a new place, I was just as happy because home was really about me and the things

I love to do in my life. I'm sure living with Teagan, Maeve, Liberty and Jane Bennett, will make your new life happy as well."

As she spoke, Grace noticed Rebecca gradually turning away from her. Drawing closer, she realized the woman was sound asleep, or at least appeared so as her eyes were closed.

No doubt her ears as well.

"Pleasant dreams, Rebecca. I'll be back soon and we'll talk more."

As Grace left the room, a smile crept across the Rebecca's lips. Peeking out through one eye at the closing door, she whispered, "Auf Weiderschhen, Miss Reid but I will not leave, no matter what you say."

CHAPTER THIRTY-TWO

MONDAY DAWNED ABOUT THREE DAYS too early for Grace. She'd stayed low-key all weekend, expending energy only on laundry and a few house cleaning chores. The rest of the time she spent reading, watching TV and indulging in a variety of less than healthy food choices, all in the comfort of her PJs. Still, as she drove to work through Midland's Monday morning traffic, she felt exhausted.

Good thing I don't have friends in Midland. I would never get away with a PJ weekend back in Buffalo.

Reflecting on home while driving temporarily Grace distracted from her brain's revolving thought-go-round of Wood Haven Seniors. *Six down, four to go.* It was a silent mantra she invoked throughout the weekend and was now using to guide her morning commute.

Realistically, Grace knew this week would be no easier than the last. While she felt accomplished to have aced every item on her previous week's checklist, including an outstanding meeting with state officials, she was facing an even longer and more intense list over the next five days.

I have to get back to my seniors and keep building on last week's visits. There there's my mid-week presentation to the Wood Haven Board to summarize all my senior meetings. I need to check in with Mary Burke to see where she is with those suitcases and get in touch with Commissioner Whitford's AA, believe her name was Janie, to set up next month's phone conference. Then they'll be the last-minute meetings and odds and ends that pop up every week. Aaaaaand, I think that' about . . . CRAP!, Friday's Midland Town Board Meeting. I need my preliminary deinstitutionalization plan ready to present.

There really wasn't much to do in preparing the town board report. She needed to provide them with information on the basic numbers of Wood Haven seniors who could live independently, with the help of an aide, as well as an outline of her search plans for the Faith File house.

Yep. That's all, Grace thought in a mocking tone.

No doubt there would be road blocks to Wood Haven seniors transitioning into a residential Midland neighborhood. It wasn't just Midland, though. Most towns railed against any kind of "group home" coming in to their community. That is until their own aging parents or loved ones need long-term care. Then like a wave of a magic wand, group housing transformed from the bane of a town's existence to a valued necessity.

Grace could feel her blood pressure rising as she organized and reorganized the millions of thoughts swirling through her brain. That's why she once again failed to pay attention to the speed limit sign on the outskirts of Midland. It was also why, once again, she saw the bright red gumball light reflectively revolving in her rearview mirror.

Pulling over, Grace grabbed her license and registration from her wallet and glove compartment, respectively.

Please don't let it be him. Please don't let it be him. Please, please, please don't let it be him.

Rolling down her window Grace saw that it was *him.*

"Morning Officer Healy," she chirped, doing her best to sound happier than she felt.

"Good morning Grace. Don't think I've seen you since we shared dinner at Welcome Home a few weeks back."

"Really? Could be. Time passes so quickly these days."

Grace was not about to let this guy know that, despite her best efforts, she'd spent every day since their dinner wondering if he might call and ask her out. The silence from his end led her to believe that what she thought had been a lovely evening, wasn't anything special to him

"Actually, I was planning to call you, but right after our dinner I was invited to attend a week-long law enforcement seminar in California as a last-minute speaker. Then when I got back I had to pull double duty to make up for being gone so long. As you say, time passes quickly. That's why when I saw you speeding out of town this morning, I figured I would stop you and kill two birds with one stone.

Seriously? This guy thinks after writing me a ticket, I'm going to want to go out to dinner with him?

"Well, I hate to burst your bubble, Officer Healy, but once you write that ticket, I'll be on my way. Don't want to be late for work, you know."

Well if you only have time for one of my two objectives, and if you promise not to tell anyone on the town board, I will forego writing that ticket in lieu of asking you to dinner. This Friday? At Welcome Home again?"

Grace's mind immediately moved in to full out war with her body. While her responsive bits and pieces were shouting out, *Sure! What time?* Her mind was screaming, *What is wrong with you? You don't have the time or the energy to get involved in a relationship right now. Plus, you're only here through the summer. What is the point of even thinking about getting involved with someone?*

"Grace, don't tell me that the idea of dinner with me is so unappealing that you'd rather get a speeding ticket?"

The devlish twinkle in his eyes and his deep dimpled grin put the brakes on Grace's inner voice.

"Well, when you put it in those terms, I guess I have to agree. Ok. Friday at Welcome Home. I have a meeting with the town board at 4pm. Would 6 be ok?"

"Six it is. I look forward to seeing you. I really enjoyed our dinner last time. You're good company, Grace Reid. You keep me on my toes."

Doing her best to settle the warring factions of her mind and body, Grace decided to smile, say good bye and extract herself from the spell of the policeman's charm. With a wink and one last dimpled smile, Officer Healy returned to his patrol car and Grace set off for Wood Haven.

SETTLING IN AT HER DESK, Grace sorted through the Faith File and decided to start the day by interviewing Angel. The woman's profile showed that she'd been committed to Wood Haven in 1926, at ten years of age.

Angel has been at Wood Haven for 52 years. What a waste of a life. To top it off, according to her file she was raped here at a young age. Yet from all the notes and observations in her file, it appears she has been a caregiver to others the entire time. Considering the strict rules that defined this place, it's amazing she was allowed the freedom to move through the asylum as she did.

Gathering up her files, Grace set off to meet this woman with the intriguing name. Traveling to the cavernous building's third floor she took a turn to the right where the independent seniors were housed, opposite from those in skilled care. Monitoring numbers along the shadowy hallway, Grace arrived at the room assigned to Angel. A hand drawn image of a heavenly guardian taped next to the number provided further confirmation of the room's resident.

Knocking to announce her presence, Grace walked through the doorway to find a lithe woman lying upon the bed in the room's far corner. She was wrapped unevenly in a cotton shawl allowing glimpses of the coarse Wood Haven-issued hospital gown she wore. Her upswept white hair touched with streaks of gold appeared as a crown on the woman's head, with willful wisps cascading down and around her neck. She was resting so peacefully that Grace hesitated to speak, but knew she had to try.

"Angel?"

A slight move of the woman's head encouraged Grace to try again.

"Angel. Are you awake?

This time the woman turned fully towards Grace, casting the most brilliant cerulean eyes upon her. The effect was immediate as Grace felt pulled to Angel as metal to magnet.

I now understand what that phrase means, 'the eyes are the window to the soul'.

"Hello, Angel. My name is Grace Reid. I work here at Wood Haven and I've come to see you in the hopes that we might visit?"

"Oh yes, I know who you are. Teagan told me all about you. She said you are someone who is very kind and you are going to invite us all to tea in your office."

"Well, I'm pleased that Teagan would say such nice things and I do look forward to sharing tea with you. But today I am here to learn about your time at Wood Haven and see if you might like to talk about a new place to live. I know you have been here for most of your life, so you may have strong feelings about moving. So I thought we could chat a bit, and perhaps sort things out.

"Oh, I have very strong feelings about where I want to live. I am going to remain right here. You are right about me having lived most of my life in this place. It is my home. I have been treated well here. The nurses and orderlies have been kind to me. I have been able to help others and they have helped me as well, especially when I was hurt shortly after I arrived. I have no thoughts or desires about moving to any other place."

Grace was startled by the strength and passion with which the woman expressed herself. She was also surprised by Angel's attachment to a place that was not only branded by cruel and inhumane treatment of others, but where she had been brutally raped.

What was it about Wood Haven that so strongly motivated Angel to want to remain?

"Angel, everyone has their own definition of home. Based on all I have read in your file about the many ways you have helped patients and staff at Wood Haven, I understand why you are comfortable here. But do you think it's possible that some of those feelings are connected as much to the people as the place?"

Grace held her breath in anticipation, wondering if her words would have an impact. The thoughtful expression on Angel's face gave Grace hope.

"I've never thought about it like that. And yes, I suppose it would pain me to lose my friendships with Teagan and Maeve and the others, much more than with this building."

Relief spread through Grace's body, easing the tension she hadn't realized she was holding. Like it or not, everyone in the Faith File was going to be transferred from the asylum, and she'd resolved to do whatever it took to ensure all six women would eventually look forward to the experience. Anything less would feel like a failure to Grace, professionally and personally.

"I agree, Angel. You know I spent much of my young life with my grandparents on their farm. Truthfully, it was the one place that felt most like home to me, but I realize now it wasn't about the house or the barn or the fields. It was about my grandparents and the sense of love and security they provided for me, there and anywhere else we were together. I can only imagine how your relationships with the others here have come to feel the same for you."

"Yes. You have described it perfectly. The people here are my family, every one of them. I don't know what I would do without them."

"I understand, Angel. And I promise I will find a home for you and the other women in this wing where you will be happy and safe and free to fully live your lives."

"But what about the others? What about James and Maria and Janna and Regina?"

"As you know, they require daily care. So they will have to move to a different home than the rest of you. The good news is that I have found a place with staff that will ensure their health and take care of their needs. And I am hoping it will be nearby to where you and the rest of the women will be living. So, you will be able to visit as you like."

With doubt still clouding Angel's crystal eyes, Grace felt compelled to reach out to this woman whose life experience had been so insular, so removed from the outside world. Enfolding the woman's frail hands within her own, Grace spoke carefully, doing her best to prevent her emotions from overwhelming her words.

"Angel, know you can trust me to do everything within my power to make sure all of you have the lives you deserve after so many years of being locked away here."

"Oh I've never felt as if I was locked away. In fact, I never had any desire to be elsewhere. You see, I am an orphan. I never knew parents or grandparents such as yours. The good sisters who took me in as an infant were the closest thing to family in my young years. Then when I came here, I learned to love the nurses and orderlies and the other people living here like me— all of them like family—and I am grateful for the love we have shared."

Despite her best intention, Grace could not control the emotions Angel's words stirred within her. As their power took hold of her heart, tears fell freely from her eyes onto their joined hands. And all at once, Angel became the comforter.

"Don't cry, sweet Grace. There is no need to feel sad about any part of my life. While it may not have been what others would deem good, I have been happy and enjoyed each day. Now as I enter the twilight, I am at peace with the world and all it has provided me, even this change you are suggesting. I have faith all will be well."

At that, Angel laid back onto the bed and, exhaling a deep sigh, closed her eyes. Carefully tucking the woman's hands under her cotton shawl, Grace drew close and brushed a kiss upon the woman's forehead. Rewarded with a gentle smile, she collected her files and quietly withdrew from the room, feeling as if she had just been in the presence of a true angel on earth.

Chapter Thirty-Three

GRACE DECIDED TO TAKE AN EARLY lunch break before her next Faith File visit. She'd been startled by the well of emotions stirred during her meeting with Angel and displeased by her tearful reaction. *Unprofessional, Grace, to say the least.*

At the same time, she knew her heart was one of the core reasons she'd become successful in her career. She genuinely cared about seniors and the quality of their remaining years. She'd built her reputation around understanding men and women at this life stage and finding ways to provide them all they deserved, on every level.

Seated in the staff lunch room, Grace grazed on the brown bag assortment of fruit she'd haphazardly packed that morning. What she was really craving was a bowl of tomato soup and a grilled cheese sandwich. It was a favored comfort meal that her nana would serve up in moments of childhood sorrow or teenage angst. At the moment, Grace yearned for such reassurance.

You're over 40 now and all grown up, Grace. You're supposed to be giving comfort, rather than looking for it. So get your head on straight and focus.

With a renewed sense of resolve, Grace opened her files to prioritize her final three patient meetings. Teagan Cormick, Maeve Mulherin Dempsey and Jane Bennett. All had spent most of their lives at Wood Haven. Each had her own set of problems. Each was deserving of a better life. As she became lost in thought, Grace was unaware of Jonathan's approach until he sat down beside her and spoke.

"Grace, I'm glad I found you. Got a minute?"

Tempering her reaction to jump off her seat in surprise, Grace forced a smile and replied.

"Of course, Jonathan. What can I do for you today?"

Moving her files and brown bag of fruit to the side, Grace pulled out a yellow legal pad and pen to take notes. As usual, Jonathan began straightaway, leaving out social niceties.

"I understand from Nurse Burke you are aware of the suitcases discovered in the attic of this building?"

"Yes. She told me about them last week, but between the board meeting, the state meeting and the upcoming town meeting, I've not had a chance to get back to her. She is on my list however."

"Understandable. All such meetings should take your priority right now. However, next week I'd like you to start going through the suitcases with Nurse Burke to try and find any belonging to the residents still with us. I think it's important to make sure their possessions are returned as whatever is in those suitcases may help ease the transition to their new residences. You know, mementos from their past to comfort them."

Before she could offer an opinion, her boss continued his one-way conversation.

"I realize it is a bit of a risk in that old memories may throw some of them into a depression or worse. But then, that is your specialty, right? Knowing how to help seniors adjust challenging situations.

Again, without waiting for a reply, Jonathan jumped up from the chair and turned to walk away.

"Oh and before I forget, Grace, Mayor Jenkins called to let me know the meeting on Friday is open to the public. He expects people on both sides of the issue to attend and speak."

Dropping that bombshell, Jonathan was off without further comment. Grace halfway suspected he'd saved the public meeting info for last, so as not to have to witness the terror in her eyes.

No matter, Grace. You know the legalities of this circumstance and you certainly know the needs of your Faith File seniors.

If those Midland Citizens she'd overheard at the Dew Drop Inn, or others like them, showed up on Friday, she'd be ready. The granddaughter of Duffy O'Connor was not going to turn tail and run. She was made of tougher stuff.

Jotting a note to call Mary Burke and find a mutual time to filter through the suitcases, Grace packed up her brown bag and her files and set off once again to the third floor. She had yet to decide which of the three women to next meet. The idea of flipping a coin appealed to her, barring the fact that she did not possess a three-sided coin. Instead she turned to the source of wisdom and guidance upon which she regularly relied.

Ok, nana. I need some help. Which way should I go? Who should I meet?

Turning right into the third floor hallway Grace's questions were answered with the approach of a solid built woman.

"Hello there, missus. I'm thinkin' you be the Grace Reid everyone 'round here's talkin' 'bout."

"Yes, I am Grace Reid, although I'm not sure if everyone has been talking about me."

"Beggin' your pardon, but t'is true. And you've been described as the woman goin' ta find us a new place ta live. Is it so?"

"Before I answer that question, may I ask with whom I'm speaking?"

"Sure'n, I'm Maeve Mulherin Dempsey. Shame on me fer not tellin' ya right off. I have a habit o'jumpin' in with both feet when I care 'bout something. And I care about makin' a new life away from this brutal kip of a place."

The woman's direct and friendly approach was a welcome relief to Grace.

Thanks, nana. You're the best!

Well, Maeve Mulherin Dempsey, it's a pleasure to meet you. I was actually just on my way to your room for a chat. Would you mind?"

"Not a bit. Follow me.

Maeve turned on her heel and proceeded to the very next door on the right side of the hallway.

"Here ya be. Tain't fancy, but t'is clean. Pull up a chair and we'll have a visit."

For the next half hour Maeve entertained Grace with tales of her life and her family, moving the two of them from laughter to sadness and emotions in between. Grace was particularly touched by Maeve's story of the death of her baby girl, Erin Maureen, and memories of her husband committing her to Wood Haven for being unable to manage her grief. The stalwart woman's description of her four children, whom she had never seen again, pushed Grace's emotions to the breaking point. Yet there was something about this dynamo-of-a-woman that demanded respect more than sympathy. Grace made sure that was what she offered.

"Maeve, as I listen to these stories of your life and all you have endured, I must say you are a remarkable woman. I also want you to know that my job at

Wood Haven is to help you, and the others here with you, to find new places to live. Hopefully to better lives."

"So's I've heard and ta tell the truth, I can't imagine actually walkin' out o'this place and ne'er lookin' back. Been dreamin' bout it since the day me husband left me here. And not a night has passed when I haven't gone ta bed prayin' fer a way ta get back ta me bebies. Do ya think that can happen as well, Missus?"

It was the first time one of the Faith File had asked about reconnecting with family. The question momentarily caught Grace off guard. She had no ability to promise such things. At the same time, she couldn't dim the woman's dream of one day being able to kiss and hug her children and perhaps her grandchildren. Not wanting to raise false hopes, Grace walked a tightrope in her reply.

"Truthfully Maeve, your records don't show an updated address or phone number for your family, so I can't foresee whether you will be able to find them or reconnect. What I can tell you is that once you and the rest are safely settled in your new homes, I will do my utmost to try and help you. No promises, but nothing to say it can't happen either. At this point, that's the best I can offer.

"That's grand and I understand ya not bein' able ta promise. After so many years—a number I don't even know—there's no tellin' what's happened to 'em and where they might be. Fer now, let's take one day at a time and see's where we get. That's the way Teagan and me have made it through and I'm here ta tell, there was days twasn't easy."

Pain shaded Maeve's eyes and filtered through her body, sapping her energy. Without thought, Grace knelt forward out of her chair in front of the Irishwoman who only moments ago seemed indefatigable.

"Maeve, I can't profess to fully understand the pain of your life and losses. What I can tell you is that my job is to ensure you will have a good future and you have my word that nothing will stop me from achieving that goal."

"I believe in all ya say, Gracie, and I'll be doin' whatever t'is ya need ta get us all outta here. Ya have me word in return."

Their closeness intensified their passionate words and the two became connected, soul to soul, their bodies blending in a heartfelt embrace. When at last they pulled apart it was clear, a special bond had been forged

"Alright, enough o'that now. Tell me who's left on that list o'yours ta visit? Have ya been 'round ta see Teagan yet?"

"Actually she is one of the last two I'm planning to see. She's on my list for tomorrow."

"Well then, I'll look forward ta hearin' the news as it comes, when we'll be moving and ta where. In the meantime, don't be a stranger, Gracie."

Grace had always hated anyone calling her by a nickname, yielding only to her grandfather's, affectionate, "Gracie Girl." Yet somehow when Maeve and Teagan uttered the singsong version of her name, it felt special, like a secret password shared by only the closest of friends.

"I will return as often as I can, Maeve. You take care."

Sharing one last hug, Grace took leave of the irish woman's room and headed back to her office.

Three o'clock already? Where did this day go?

Taking a seat at her desk, Grace summarized her visits with Angel and Maeve in her Faith File notes, making sure to write in a reminder to start a search for Maeve's children. While it certainly wasn't part of her job, Grace could not imagine leaving the caring mother in new surroundings, in a new community, without information or knowledge of the family from which she'd been separated almost half a century ago.

Grace sat back and let that reality settle into her brain. She tried to imagine Maeve's pain in losing a child at birth and, while grieving that loss, being taken away from the other children to whom she'd given life and nurtured It was insanity. But then, that was true of many of those who were committed to Wood Haven in the first part of the 20th Century. The reasons for locking them up were often a matter of convenience than true disability of mind or body.

Returning to her notes, Grace noticed the reminder to contact Nurse Burke about the suitcases. She picked up the phone and dialed the nursing services phone number. It took only one ring for the supervisor to answer in her usual efficient fashion.

"Afternoon. Wood Haven nursing services. Nurse Burke speaking."

"Hello, Mary. It's Grace Reid. How are you today?"

"I'm well, Grace, thanks for asking. What's up?"

"I'm calling to find a time when you would be available to take me to the suitcases we talked about in the attic. I'd like to get to them early next week, if possible. Once you get me situated, I imagine I will need a day to sort through them, however many there are, so the earlier in the week, the better."

"Oh you'll definitely need a day. More like a lotta days that will probably turn in to at least a month. The fact you're only looking for suitcases belonging to the current seniors should make it quicker for you. But still, there are hundreds of them stored away up there."

"Hundreds? I had no idea. Well, then I definitely need to start early next week. Could you take me up there on Monday, morning if possible?"

"Let me have a quick look at my calendar. Let's see, next Monday is the 17th of July. I am actually in Trenton that day to lead a forum for the New Jersey Branch of the American Nurses Association on proposed legislation to revise federal funding for mental health. Looks like Wednesday the 19th will be the earliest time next week I could meet. How about I come by your office around nine that morning and we'll get started?"

While disappointed at losing two days time, Grace was happy to get a date on the calendar. With any luck, she would separate out the suitcases of the remaining ten Wood Haven patients and in a few days, a week at the outside, be done.

"That would be wonderful, Mary. Thank you for accommodating my schedule. I know how busy you are with your ANA work and getting Wood Haven nurses settled in new jobs before the patients are gone. It will be like a morgue around here when there are only medical and dental researchers left in this building."

"Truthfully, Grace, it already feels like a forgotten place and makes me wonder how the last half century at Wood Haven will be remembered and judged? We've done our best to establish a hospital dedicated to caring for those with mental and physical issues using advanced medicines and expert care. I know that was not always the case, but I like to think we've made up, at least a little, for some of the sins of the past."

"I understand, Mary, and I feel the same about moving the ten remaining patients to new locations. I'm also hopeful that identifying their possessions in these suitcases will help in the process. I'll look for you next Wednesday. Thanks."

Grace finished up her notes from the day and read through the files of Teagan Cormick and Jane Bennett. Both were of sound mind, although Jane's health was failing and she was borderline in being assigned as an independent senior. Grace would have to carefully observe her actions and abilities when they met. Placing her improperly would be an injustice, especially to someone with a lifetime of nursing service.

When finally she'd finished her review for the next day, Grace glanced at her watch and saw that it was past 5 o'clock.

Good enough. Time to head home and grab some dinner on the way. This time, I'm going to make darn sure I'm driving the speed limit. No sense stretching my luck in dodging a ticket twice in one day.

Pulling out of the Wood Haven entrance Grace paid close attention to her driving speed, making her unaware of a car she passed, parked just off the road. And the fact that it eased out and followed her all the way home.

CHAPTER THIRTY-FOUR

TUESDAY ARRIVED GRAY and rainy, dampening Grace's determination to rise and shine.

Not exactly a morning to make a soul want to bound out of bed.

She had just convinced herself to roll over and delay the start of the day for a few minues when the telephone rang. The unexpected call knocked every bit of drowsiness out of her being as Grace jumped across the bed to answer the phone.

"Hello?"

"Good Morning, Grace. It's Jonathan.

"Is everything alright?"

"Relatively. I wanted to let you know that Jane Bennett fell last night. Apparently, she got up to go to the bathroom, lost her balance and was unable to get up. No one knew until one of the nurses found her at shift change this morning. She was disoriented and complained of pain in her right hip, so we have taken her to Good Samaritan Hospital in Midland for xrays and observation. I am out of the office today for meetings in Trenton, so I need you to be on top of this today while I'm gone."

"No problem. Jane was on my list today to meet about her upcoming transition. From all I've read in her files, it seems she is borderline between independent living and assisted care. This fall could end up making that determination."

"Exactly. So please check in on her today. See what the doctors have to say as well. We'll just take it one day at a time."

"Certainly. I will write up a full report and leave it on your desk."

"Appreciate it, Grace. The challenges of working with an aging population are difficult decisions that must be made in circumstances like these. I'll touch base with you tomorrow when I'm back in the office."

The adrenaline surge resulting from the early morning phone call energized Grace to shower, dress and head out the door in less than fifteen minutes. While she'd never met Jane Bennett, she suspected the woman's career could lead the former nurse to worrisome thoughts about her condition. The sooner Grace could get there and consult with the hospital staff, the better she would be able to reassure the woman.

Good Samaritan Hospital was utilitarian in appearance with its square, red-brick square highlighted by metal frame windows and doors. Walking into the large lobby, Grace headed to the information desk commanding the area.

"Good Morning. How can I help you today?"

The receptionist was dressed in a bright red blazer with a white nametag on her lapel, proclaiming the woman's name, "Jackie."

"Good Morning Jackie. I'm here to see a patient by the name of Jane Bennett. She was admitted early this morning."

"Well, let's see what my records show. Yes. I do have a Jane Bennett. Are you family?"

"No. I don't know that she has any family. Jane is a patient at Wood Haven and I am one of the administrators there. I've come to check on her condition and see if there is anything the doctors or nurses need regarding her medical history."

"Well, I have to call the nurses' station to confirm that I can allow you to see the patient. If you wouldn't mind taking a seat in the waiting area, I will let you know shortly."

Grace sat down on the bright orange vinyl couch flanked by low rise tables of scattered magazines. While airbrushed photos and fluorescent print promoted the latest celebrity gossip, Grace's mind wandered through thoughts of Jane Bennett and memories of her nana.

The last time Grace sat in a hospital waiting room had been just over a year ago. Nana O'Connor had been feeling tired, less than her perky self. After gentle urging from both papa and Grace, she finally agreed to see their family doctor. It was only a matter of weeks from that office visit to tests, a diagnosis, a hospital stay and the passing of her beloved nana. The stage four ovarian cancer had gone unrecognized for too long and done its mortal damage.

Grace had blocked all memories from that painful period, choosing instead to remember the lifetime of fun and laughter she and nana had shared. However, the sights and smells of Good Samaritan brought the impact of her loss flooding back. At the same time, Grace imagined the fear undoubtedly haunting Jane Bennett at the moment, with no family to offer comfort or assurance of her well-being.

"Excuse me, Miss Reid?"

The sound of her name brought Grace back to the hospital lobby where Jackie with the red blazer was standing.

"You can see Mrs. Bennett now. She is in room 359. Take the elevator to the third floor and turn left. You'll see the nurses' station in the middle of that hallway. Nurse Schwab is waiting for you to review Mrs. Bennett's chart before you go into her room."

Grace cleared her mind of her personal memories and refocused on the task at hand. Making her way to the nurses' station, she pulled out a notepad and pen from her purse in preparation for documenting Jane Bennett's medical data and prognosis.

"At this point, we have Mrs. Bennett scheduled for an x-ray this morning to verify if her hip is, in fact, broken. We started a pain med IV when she was admitted, which seems to be keeping her comfortable. The doctor will be in shortly on his rounds to do a more thorough examination. Unless it appears she has suffered a concussion or injury to her internal organs, the primary concern other than the hip is the patient's loss of balance. Obviously continued falls could be devastating."

Thanking the nurse, Grace moved on to Jane Bennett's room. Before entering, she again cleared her memory bank of all personal hospital experiences. Softly knocking, she pushed open the door to find the patient wide awake.

"Hello, Jane. We've never met, but my name is Grace Reid. I am part of the staff at Wood Haven. I heard about your fall and came straight away to see how you are feeling this morning."

Though frail in appearance, the woman in bed before her responded clearly and in strong voice.

"I am feeling reasonably well for a woman who laid most of the night on a cold, concrete floor and may have a broken hip."

"Well, that's one of the things I can tell you, Jane. The doctor will be here shortly to do an examination, and then you are scheduled for an x-ray on that hip. It won't be long before you know about your overall condition. In the meantime, the nurses will be checking in to make sure you're comfortable."

"Oh the nurses have been wonderful. We tend to stick together when the tables are reversed and we're the ones in need of care. I was a nurse at Wood Haven, as you may know."

"I do know you were a nurse. And I know from my career working in senior care facilities, where I became friends with a number of nurses, you take extra special care of your own. I'm also aware that nurses can make the worst patients, since they know too much for their own good!"

A knowing smile spread across the woman's face, which quickly downturned as Jane attempted to readjust her body in the hospital bed.

"Ouch! Judas priest that hurts."

Grace let out a burst of laughter, surprising both she and Jane Bennett.

"So did your nurse friends also teach you it's acceptable to laugh at people's discomfort?"

"Oh, I'm so sorry, Jane I am not laughing at you or your pain by any means. It's just I've not heard that expression in some time. My papa used to say it quite often, which always set my nana off on a tirade about how it was an inappropriate remark, especially in front of me. That usually led to my papa increasing his teasing and my nana becoming more flustered. They'd carry on like that for a few minutes until finally papa would make it all right by sneaking up and wrapping his arms around nana and saying how much he loved her. I hadn't thought about all this in such a long time, and truthfully, it brought me joy to hear you say, 'Judas priest'."

The former nurses' icy reaction melted into salty tears as she reached out a hand toward Grace.

"I completely understand, Grace. My mother was the one who taught me the phrase. Then she washed my mouth out with lye soap when I repeated it! Obviously it didn't stop me from continuing to use it, especially after my mother's death when it became sort of a comfort in difficult moments."

Joining hands, the two women sat in reflective silence, each recalling memories of their loved ones. It was only with the arrival of the doctor that they refocused.

"Good Morning. I'm Doctor Petersen," he said, not looking at either woman. Lifting the patient chart from the end of the bed, the physician began reading intently, voicing the words as his brain processed them.

"So, 75-year-old caucasean woman. Fell sometime last night. Went undiscovered. Complaining of pain in right hip. No other issues or problems.

On IV pain drip. Drank juice early this morning with a bit of toast. Ok, let's see what we can see."

As the doctor turned his attention to Jane he seemed a bit surprised to see Grace at her side.

"I'm sorry, and who are you?"

"Good morning, doctor. My name is Grace Reid. I am one of the administrators at Wood Haven, where Mrs. Bennett lives. I came by to see how she's doing and hear her medical assessment following your examination."

"I see. Well, you are not family and in most cases, I ask visitors to leave the room during a medical exam."

Before Grace could reply, Jane spoke up.

"I understand your rules and regulations, doctor, but please could Miss Reid stay? I have no family or friends any longer, at least of whom I am aware. She is the closest thing I have to someone who cares about me."

The raw emotion of the woman's plea touched the young physician as he rubbed his hand across his face to mask his watery eyes.

"Well, I suppose in a case such as this, I can allow an exception. However, I will need you to stand over to the side Miss Reid, where you won't block my light."

For the ensuing ten minutes, doctor and patient engaged in a litany of medical questions and answers, followed by the physician's careful pushing and prodding of Jane's body. While the exam clearly caused discomfort, Jane never once uttered so much as a low-level, "ow" or repeated her exuberant, "Judas priest."

"I'm happy to say that there do not seem to be any major injuries or problems, other than a possible broken hip. It's obviously very tender to touch and painful to move. It's also impossible to tell if it's a severe contusion or a break. You're scheduled for an x-ray at ten and I should have the results by mid afternoon. I will return later to let you know what they show. And of course, no getting out of bed and walking on your own until we know exactly what's going on with that hip."

Jane seemed a bit shocked by the doctor's prognosis and lay silent as he finished penning notes on her chart. Grace, however, had questions and decided it was her duty to get answers.

"Excuse me, doctor, is there any way to tell what caused Mrs. Bennett to lose her balance? She's been quite steady in her gait, so a fall like this raises a red flag.

"Well certainly there are any number of reasons she could have fallen. It was dark in the room and without light the mind and body can become disoriented. She may have tripped over an obstacle she didn't see in the dark. She may be weakening in her ability to keep her balance. First, let's determine what is going on with her hip and get that healed. Then we can start to address the reasons for her fall and set a course of treatments, if necessary."

Without waiting for acknowledgement or response, the doctor exited the room. Turning to each other, Jane and Grace took deep breaths and exhaled in unison.

"Well, that was an experience. Are you feeling alright after all of that poking around on your body?"

"I'm fine. Actually, he was quite gentle compared to the doctors who treated me when I was first committed to Wood Haven."

The expression on Jane's face left Grace little doubt of the cruel treatments that had been administered throughout the asylum's history. It also steeled her determination to ensure a better life for this special woman.

"So, let's talk a bit about the future, Jane. Once your hip is taken care of and you return to Wood Haven, I'll be helping you and the others on the third floor move to new places, new homes, where you'll be treated well. You'll be able to get outside regularly and enjoy fun activities like playing cards and watching tv. Perhaps they'll ever be a day trip here and there."

"I have heard Teagan talk about this. Truthfully, I wondered if she were imagining it. Now to hear you explain, it's a bit overwhelming. It's been so long since I've been a part of the outside world, I'm not sure I can return to it. Plus, I don't know if I can live alone anymore, or even with others on our own. My physical and mental strength is not what it used to be and after falling, I have concerns."

"I understand, Jane, and I promise we will work together in determining courses of action that will make you feel secure and safe. We're going to start with getting your hip healed. Then see if you need any therapies to strengthen your body. At the same time, you and I will talk about the life you want to live and how we can best achieve those goals. No pressure. Just well thought-out and considered options that will provide you with a good quality of life."

As she spoke, Grace saw the fear recede from Jane's eyes, the tension release from her body. Her reactions were reminiscent of the same ways nana would calm whenever papa said he loved her.

"Don't worry Jane, you are part of a family at Wood Haven. A family that loves you."

Chapter Thirty-Five

I T WAS LATE MORNING WHEN GRACE finally made her way to Wood Haven. Her day started unexpectedly with Jane Bennett's hospitalization and became further waylaid when she decided to stay at the hospital until the injured woman fell asleep. Feeling reasonably satisfied that the former nurse would awake with a comforted mind, Grace set off for the office.

Settled at her desk, she wrote a summary update about Jane Bennett for Jonathan and returned phone calls to staffers and board members regarding Wednesday's meeting. With the day slipping from morning to afternoon, Grace fended off her growling stomach with a trip to the nearby vending machine where she made the gourmet lunch choices of Lorna Doones and pretzels.

All my years of attention to healthy foods and good nutrition are certainly going to hell in a handbasket with this job.

At half past two, Grace swept away the crumbs and empty snack packages from her desk and packed up her Faith File notes. It was time to chat with the plucky Teagan Cormack.

Grace felt a sense of confidence going into this final deinstitutionalization meeting. The fact they had already spent time together raised her self-confidence. Also, knowing that she was moving all in her Faith File closer to new lives added a lightness to Grace's being.

Approaching Teagan's room, she saw the door was propped open. Still feeling an announcenment knock was appropriate, Grace tapped lightly as she called out.

"Hello. Teagan?"

Stepping inside, Grace looked around to find an empty room. Heading to the nurse's station, she introduced herself to the young woman at the desk.

"Hello. I'm Grace Reid. I'm a consultant here, working with Jonathan. I'm looking for a patient, Teagan Cormick, but she's not in her room. Might you have an idea of where I could find her?"

"Sure. Teagan spends every afternoon on the porch, at least that what she calls it. It's on the 4th floor. Turn left when you come off the elevator and go halfway down the hall. You'll come to a double set of doors on the right side that will lead you into a large room. It used to be a ward. On the far end of that room is a bumpout area, separated by a wall. It's a place where patients sat and enjoyed the view from a wall of windows. Teagan loves to sit there. Says she's done it for years."

Following the nurse's directions, Grace made her way to the wall defining Teagan's "porch." Cautiously, she stepped into the space and was immediately bathed in the warmth of the afternoon sun, filtering through leaves of the century-old trees adorning the building. At the end of the undersized room sat a line of weathered wicker chairs. In their midst sat Teagan, softly humming. While the room's walls were cracked, the paint peeling and the windows encased in rusty metal bars, there was no denying the room offered a certain comfort.

Grace continued on, moving further into the room, but it was only as she spoke that Teagan became aware of her presence.

"Good Afternoon, Teagan."

"Oh my! Afternoon, Grace. Whatever wouldcha be doin' here?"

"I came because I was hoping we could chat for a bit."

"Nothin' would give me more pleasure. I've spent many an hour on this porch. It holds memories o'me lifetime and people I come ta love, and those lost as well. Welcome ta ya."

Choosing a chair, Grace sat alongside the aged Irishwoman, still beautiful with her thick white hair and brilliant green eyes. It seemed to Grace that the wisdom of the world was held in those eyes and she looked forward to all that Teagan would teach her.

"We've talked a bit about your life here, Teagan, and I know it's not been easy all these years."

"Aye. T'is not the life I imagined when I left me home and me family. A time or two I wondered what might have been had I stayed in Ireland. But then, does a soul no good ta look back."

"You're a wise woman to understand living in the past isn't healthy for your soul or your mind. That's why I want to give you something new to think about. Something I hope will inspire you to look forward. As you may know by now, I was brought here to Wood Haven to help you and the others on the third floor move to a new place, a home. It will be in the nearby town of Midland, exactly where I'm not sure yet. But you and five of the others will live there with a full-time care giver and you will be free to come and go as you are able and desire."

Teagan remained silent, staring out the wall of windows before them. Grace was unsure of the woman's reaction and wondered if perhaps she was withdrawing from their conversation. While they had only interacted once, Grace hadn't noticed Teagan exhibiting mental instability. Still, she knew that even the suggestion of change from the lifetime this woman had come to know at Wood Haven could trigger fears that might manifest in withdrawal.

"In me homeland, t'is said the only sure thing in life is what ya make o'it. I've had me hard times and thought 'bout givin' up more than once. But at the end o' the day, 'twas knowin' the way me mam and da would have wanted me ta go on that kept me on the straight and narrow. So's I guess movin' ta a place aways from here will be a bit o'alright."

Grace sat for a moment and studied this woman whose thoughts were clearly formed by her family's love, as much as the suffering she had endured at Wood Haven. Noting her remarkable strength of character, Grace found herself wanting to make a connection with Teagan that would last a lifetime—however long that might be.

"Teagan, I can only imagine what leaving behind your family must have felt like, especially at such a young age. Then to lose the ability to stay connected or know if they are even still alive, all the while relying on your family memories for guidance, that's extraordinary. I hope you understand and realize the special nature of the love for your family you hold in your heart."

Teagan continued to sit, silently. Grace understood the woman's reaction as reflective and allowed her the needed time and space.

"'Tis always been a connection t'ween me and me family, stronger 'an most. Hearin' ya talk in such a way puts it firmly inta me mind and I'm grateful ta ya, Grace. Made up me mind long ago in this hell hole, the best way ta honor me family was by goin' on. Sounds as if makin' this move ya be talkin' 'bout is just that."

"I believe you're right, Teagan, and it's good to hear you speak about the move in such a positive way. However, nothing is going to happen overnight.

It's going to take some time to work through the laws of Midland regarding a group home like we're talking about. And of course, we have to find a suitable location. But I will keep you updated on everything as I work through it and anytime you have questions, I'm happy to chat with you. You know how to find my office, or you can leave a message with the floor nurses and they'll make sure I know to stop by and see you."

"Alrighty then, Gracie. I'll set me mind ta this move and keep good thoughts 'bout the future. But I have ta tell ya, it's a bit hard imagin' anythin' outside these walls. Been a lifetime here and I'm far from sure what the world'll feel like."

"I understand, Teagan, and you are not alone in those feelings. Others have said the same. The difference with you is that you have such a strong and positive spirit. I know once you have some time to think about the amazing life that lies ahead, you are going to be in my office everyday, asking when you're going to move."

"Me spirit has always been what's kept me goin' and alive. So's I'm guessin' you're right, Grace. Although I'll do me best not ta pester ya, as me mam would say!"

The rise of Teagan's humor and the smile across her face confirmed Grace's belief in the Irishwoman's strength. It also inspired her to make a request.

"That's the spirit Teagan! And while I'm at it, I'd like to ask a special favor. As I said, the rest of the patients on the third floor will be moving as well. A few will go to a place where they can receive full time care, while the rest, like you, will be living more independently with an aide. Either way, everyone is concerned about the change in lifestyle and worried about settling into the world outside of Wood Haven. If you could help them think about the move in the same positive way you just stated, it would be wonderful. I know they look to you as someone they can trust. What you say makes a difference."

"It's an easy thing you're askin', Gracie and I'll gladly talk ta all of 'em. But 'twould be good ta know which are going where?"

"Of course. James, Maria, Janna and Regina will move to a home with full-time care. You, Maeve, Liberty, Rebecca and Angel will move to an independent home with an aide. However, I would ask that you not spend much time talking about those details. Let's focus more on the improved surroundings and care that this move will bring to everyone."

"For sure'n I'll be missin' the company o''Maria, Janna and Regina. Bein' together as long as we have made us family. Truth be told, though, me days won't be the same without havin' a moment here or there with James."

As the man's name left her lips color rose through Teagan's cheeks. It was enough to catch Grace's attention and make her wonder.

Was there something about the Irish woman and the Greek man that she'd missed in reviewing their files?

As if anticipating the query, Teagan redirected the conversation.

"What about Nurse Bennett? Ya didn't mention her atal."

"You're right, Teagan. I didn't mention Nurse Bennett. That's because she took a fall last night and is in hospital to see if she has sustained any serious injury. Right now, we're only concerned about getting her well and back to Wood Haven. Then we'll know better where she'll move."

Grace watched Teagan carefully for reaction to the news about Jane Bennett. Jonathan had explained that the former nurse and the Irishwoman were closely connected, noting Teagan held Grace directly responsible for her survival in her early days of being locked away. Hearing that the former nurse had been hospitalized would no doubt be of concern.

"I"d heard the nurses talkin' 'bout Nurse Bennett's fall this mornin'. That's why I come early ta the porch. Ta pray ta Mary, Mother o'God fer help healin' the good nurse and makin' sure she returns. The woman is a saint and deserves ta be treated as one."

"I agree with you, Teagan. And I can tell you that I spent most of the morning with her and she is resting comfortably. She was actually sleeping when I left. So know your prayers are helping. If you like, I'll tell her you're thinking of her when I stop by the hospital on my way home today."

"Thanks ta ya, Grace. Me faith has always seen me through and I know God's gonna take care o'Nurse Bennett 'ccordin'ta his will. That's all I can ask."

"That's what my nana used to say, Teagan, and I think it's exactly right. You keep on praying and I'll keep you up to date on Nurse Bennett. Now I need to get back to my desk and write up a report about our visit. I have to say, I have enjoyed chatting with you and I look forward to spending more time together."

"As well, Gracie. Come visit me anytime on me porch."

Moving to the end of the room, Grace turned for a last look. Amid ruins of a space that had long ago provided a small slice of the outside world, Teagan sat like a queen among her realm. And Grace realized the remarkable ways in which men and women who'd been committed to Wood Haven managed to find ways to endure and exist.

Chapter Thirty-Six

THE WEEK FLEW BY AS GRACE balanced Wood Haven work with hospital stops to check on Jane Bennett. Thankfully, x-rays showed no break in Jane's hip, so she was scheduled for release over the weekend. In the more good news department, she successfully finished her Faith File meetings and Wednesday's board meeting went well. There was only one item remaining on Grace's to-do list—the Midland Town Board meeting.

What is it people say about saving the best for last?!

Grace felt fairly confident about facing members of the Midland Town Board. It was the community residents who might show up that concerned her. The meeting had been posted all around town, but there was no way to know if people would remember the date. Regardless, Grace was taking no chances. She was going "loaded for bear," as her papa used to say.

In the back of her mind, Grace was also contemplating her post-meeting dinner with Mike Healy. She had not heard from Midland's finest since Monday. Clearly he felt no need to communicate outside of his unusual method of pulling her over for speeding. That bugged her a little. He said he'd missed her and obviously wanted to spend time with her. It made sense to Grace that he also might like to chat more than once every five to fourteen days.

Save your energy for the town meeting. You can sort out your thoughts about Mike Healy later.

With her briefcase fully loaded with files and facts, Grace headed to her car. Easing her way from the employee parking lot, along the winding driveway and through the entrance pillars, Grace nosed her car onto the edge of the highway. Checking for traffic and seeing none, she pulled out onto the road toward Midland. It was only within a few seconds that Grace realized she was being tightly tailgated.

That's odd. There was no traffic coming from that direction, or I would never have pulled out. Wonder where that car came from?

As if sensing her curiosity, the driver hit the accelerator and flew past her, disregarding the speed limit and the double yellow highway lines. The action was startling and made Grace pay particular attention to the vehicle—a late model black sedan with New Jersey plate number 333-INN.

Had Grace not been on her way to the town meeting, she might have given the car and driver more thought. Instead, both were quickly replaced by a continuous mental loop of the presentation she was about to share with the board.

Nana and papa, I need your help. My presentation will set the tone for the Faith File project in this community. Please help me use my Irish charm and control my Irish temper.

Pulling into the town hall driveway, Grace drove to the end of the oversized municipal parking lot and backed into a spot where there were no other cars around. She'd learned at a young age that parking in uncrowded areas lessened the chances of those annoying car door dings that always seemed to happen.

Grabbing her briefcase and locking her car, Grace followed the signs to the Midland Community Room. What she found upon entering the ample space caught her completely off guard. The room was filled, wall to wall, with people. The immediate question in Grace's mind was were they for, or against, the Faith File group home?

They can't all be against it. There have to be some people in this town who will support seniors moving into their community. It's not as if they're a group of hardened criminals, for god's sakes.

Scanning the room for a seat, Grace could feel her Irish temper rising. Thinking it might be best to settle herself in the back of the room, her progress in that direction was interrupted by none other than Mike Healy.

"Good afternoon, Ms. Reid."

The unexpected appearance of her dinner date stopped Grace short. Seemingly amused by her speechless state, the Midland policeman gently took her by the elbow and guided her to a table in the very front of the room.

"Since you are the only presenter at this meeting, the mayor has asked that you sit here. There's a microphone on the table. Please use it in making your presentation, as well as when you interact with the board, so that everyone in the hall can hear you. When you are done, anyone in the audience who wants to speak on the issue will be asked to come up to the podium, over there to your right. It has a mic attached to it as well. That way everyone can hear and be heard."

"Thank you, Mi . . . er, Officer Healy. I must admit, I'm a little surprised to see you here."

"It's not my usual assignment, Sergeant-at-Arms at a town board meeting. The mayor just thought it would be good to have some reinforcements today, so he called me in. However, I'll still be ready for our date tonight, don't you worry."

With a wink and a dimpled grin, Mike left Grace to her own thoughts at the front of the crowded room.

What felt like a force field of eyes were trained on Grace and she realized her every move was being monitored. Taking a deep breath, she pulled her files and leather folio from her briefcase and flipped to her presentation notes. Although her brain was unable to process any of the words before her, to all appearances Grace appeared cool, calm and collected.

Never let 'em see you sweat, Gracie girl.

Doing my best, papa.

Suddenly the door behind the elevated dais at the front of the room swung open. Out walked Mayor Jenkins followed by four men, all of whom Grace assumed were board members. Taking seats across the raised platform, each individual was identified by a wooden plaque next to their microphone. The mayor sat center stage and was the first to speak.

"Good afternoon. I'd like to welcome everyone. It's good to know our citizens are engaged enough to turn out. I also want to take a moment to review the rules of a town board meeting. Since this is a special meeting, the protocol is a little different. We will begin with our presenter, Ms. Grace Reid from Wood Haven. She will have up to 15 minutes for her presentation. Next will follow discussion between the town board and Ms. Reid. Then I will open the meeting to the audience. If you have a statement or want to ask a question, come to the microphone up here at the podium. State your name and address and whatever it is you have to say."

A ripple of discord passed through the crowd behind Grace. She could feel her stomach knotting. The reverberation of Mayor Jenkin's gavel in concert with his booming voice only served to tighten that knot.

"I am only going to say this once. Outbursts of any kind, by anyone, will not be tolerated at this meeting. Should you ignore my warning, Officer Healy will escort you from the room and prevent you from re-entering. Further, anyone who speaks disrespectfully or inappropriately at this microphone will be fined for lewd behavior. Any questions?"

The ripple quelled to a silence as Grace sat in gratitude for the mayor's stern warning.

"Good afternoon and welcome, Ms. Reid, Whenever you're ready, please begin."

Hearing her name momentarily froze Grace's ability to form thoughts and words. Glancing over at Mike Healy, his encouraging smile provided her brain with a quick thaw.

"Thank you, Mayor Jenkins, and thank you to the town board for allowing me this opportunity to speak about the Wood Haven Deinstitutionalization Project. As you may know, there has been a movement across the United States calling for the closing of mental institutions and the mainstreaming of the individuals still residing within them. In some states, legislation calling for such action has been passed upon revelations of heinous stories of mistreatment and improper incarcerations of innocent men, women, and even children. Here in New Jersey, a plan is in place to assess individuals currently living in mental institutions and determine those capable of deinstitutionalization."

As she continued, Grace's nerves calmed while her passion for her Faith File seniors inflamed. What began as halting phrases exploded into non-stop sentences of undeniable facts and compelling story lines that she delivered without so much as a glance at her notes. From their expressions, it was clear the town board was engaged.

"So, I am here today with a request. I ask the Midland town board to approve the zoning of a house, the location to be determined, as a group home for six senior women, ages 54 to 78. Along with the women there will be one aide who will live there full time to ensure the resident's safety as well as the security of the neighborhood. In return, Midland will be enriched with six community members who will be respectful and most grateful for the opportunity to experience the wonderful quality of life the town has to offer. Again, I thank you, Mayor Jenkins and the Midland board members, for your time and consideration. I look forward to working together to provide new lives in your community for these six deserving seniors."

It took a moment for Grace to realize she had completed her presentation.

Did I tell them everything? Did I thoroughly explain the mistreatments the Faith File have suffered? How they're so deserving of this opportunity? Did I leave anything out?

Grace had only to look at the faces and read the body language of the mayor and the town board to know she had done her job.

"Thank you, Ms. Reid. Your presentation was thorough, informative and impressive. It's clear you know your profession and are dedicated to the Wood Haven seniors you represent. At this time I would like to open the discussion to the board members for their questions and comments."

Grace took a deep breath and waited. The man on the far right of the dais was the first to speak.

"I'd like to begin by adding my thanks to Mayor Jenkin's, Ms. Reid. You have informed us in a manner I believe is fair and balanced, and I appreciate that. There has never been a group home in this community and, as evidenced by the large crowd gathered here today, people are concerned. The story you shared about the lives these seniors have endured and the opportunity we can provide them certainly puts this issue in perspective. I do have two questions, though. Are any of these seniors mentally incapable and will there be regular testing to continually assess their mental stability?"

"Thank you Councilman Baer. I am grateful for your kind words and your positive perspective on establishing a home for the Wood Haven seniors. Regarding their mental acuity, I was hired specifically to meet with each one, get to know them and evaluate them physically and mentally. It is my job to ensure that we place them exactly where they should be, in situations they are capable of handling. It would be irresponsible of me to do anything other than deliver an honest and thorough assessment of each individual slated for deinstitutionalization. I owe it to them as well as to the residents of Midland. So, to answer your question, councilman, there are currently ten seniors residing at Wood Haven. Of those, four are in need of supervision at a level that categorizes them as skilled care patients. They will be moving to a skilled nursing facility. The remaining six, at this point, are all capable mentally and physically of an independent life style with an aide. The plan is to continually reevaluate all six twice a year and make new living accommodations as and when needed."

"Thank you, Ms. Reid. I yield to my fellow council members."

"Ms. Reid, how much will this deinstitutionalization cost Midland taxpayers?"

Grace looked into the hardened face of Councilman Johnson. The gray-haired man appeared to be in the age range of her Faith File. It was a statistic Grace knew she could use for her benefit.

"That's an excellent question, Councilman Johnson, but before I answer I'd like to ask you a question if I may?"

"Go ahead."

"Respectfully, sir, what is your age?"

A titter passed through the audience as the councilman's face turned beet red. Grace began to wonder about the wisdom of her strategy.

"I don't see how my age has anything to do with my responsibility as a council member to keep a close eye on town issues that can raise taxes."

"I apologize if I've offended you, councilman. I was only trying to make the point that should you, or anyone in Midland have celebrated their 65th birthday, you are costing taxpayers just as much as the Wood Haven seniors. You see, their social security payments will pay for their living costs and their medicare insurance will cover their medical costs, no different than you, sir. As for the cost of the house in which they will live, that will be covered under a federal government grant, already in place."

Still red-faced, the councilman yielded to Councilman Stager who took center stage.

"I would like to know what safety precautions will be taken to protect the neighborhood where these seniors might live."

Grace could feel her Irish rising as the negative innuendo of the councilman's words spread through the room. Fortunately, this was an area in which Grace had spent hours collecting statistical information.

"Actually councilman, I'm not quite sure what type of neighborhood security issues you think might arise with the presence of six women between the ages of 54 to 78."

Again a smattering of laughter passed through the audience, this time followed by a gavel-emphasized call from the mayor for quiet. Allowing for the full impact of the moment to settle, Grace proceeded.

"That being said, statistics show that people diagnosed with mental illnesses can exhibit behavior that the general public often deem as problematic and/or dangerous. However, the six seniors who will be moving into this community do not possess any mental instabilities to raise such concerns. They were committed to Wood Haven randomly, some simply by family members looking for ways to unburden themselves from providing care in stressful life situations. As I'm sure you understand, due to privacy terms, I cannot publicly reveal each woman's medical history. However, upon the signing of right to privacy documents, I will provide full medical reports on each woman to the town board so they can review and reassure the community."

"We'll look for those reports as soon as possible," Councilman Stager growled condescendingly. "Certainly, councilman. I have the right-to-privacy documents with me. If all of you are willing to sign them, I have five copies of the full reports on the seniors ready to distribute today."

Grace's preparedness cut short the councilman's demands. With nothing left to say, the remaining councilperson spoke up.

"Ms. Reid, your job is to advocate for these Wood Haven Seniors and to encourage us to vote for the rezoning of a portion of our town for group housing, isn't that right?"

"Primarily, Councilman Roberts. However, as a respected professional in the field of senior care, it would be foolish of me to try and force a living situation upon my seniors or upon your community. The only thing to be gained from that would be the ruin of my reputation and continued deprivation for the seniors. Trust me, sir, I desire neither of those outcomes. I have worked diligently, and will continue to do so, to ensure the success of this transition."

"Unless there are any further concerns, I am going to open this meeting to public comments and questions. Please keep in mind the rules of engagement I announced earlier. If you wish to speak, form a line at the podium."

Grace held her breath waiting for an onslaught of Midland citizens. To her relief, only one man stepped forward. She recognized him from the Dew Drop Inn. Bill, as she recalled, was his name.

"I'm William Marsh. I live at 596 Forest Avenue in Midland, in the same house where I was born and raised and where my wife and I are raising our son. I come here today to say my piece and for anyone whose been around me the last few months, there won't be any surprises. I'm against this group home and no sugar-coated talk is going to change my mind. I've been around these kind of people from nuthouses and they are crazy. Don't care what this woman says, they were locked away for a reason and that reason is that they could hurt others or themselves. Why in the world would we want to put people like that in the middle of Midland when we've all so worked hard to keep our town safe?"

Applause flowed like champagne from an uncorked bottle but was quickly quelled by the pounding of the mayor's gavel.

"Quiet! Quiet I said."

As the furor ebbed, the mayor exploded.

"I warned you people what would happen if you didn't control your reactions. Now this room is either going to get quiet and stay quiet or it's going to get emptied out, real fast. Bill, if you're done you can take a seat."

For a moment it appeared as if Bill Marsh wanted to say more. Whether or not it was the intense scowl on the mayor's face that discouraged him, he ultimately turned on his heel and returned to the back of the room. Grace found the courage to watch his progress to gauge if anyone commended the man in passing. Aside from a few nods from others in the crowd, the only real reaction came when Bill reached his seat and a teenaged boy jumped up and slapped him with a high five.

"Guess you told 'em, dad!"

"Turning a bright shade of red Bill tersely responded, "Sit down, son," and the parent child duo took their seats.

"Alright, since there's no one else lined up to speak, I'm going to call this meeting to a close. The town board and I will take all information presented here today under consideration and will schedule another public meeting to announce our decision."

With a strong rap of his gavel, the mayor stood up and walked out of the room, the four board members following closely behind. Grace suddenly felt a bit unprotected. Based on the reaction to Bill Jenkin's speech, she was pretty sure the majority of people in the room had no use for her.

Might be in my best interest to get out of here quickly as possible.

"Can I help you carry anything to your car?"

Grace was startled, but relieved, to see Mike standing close by.

"That would be great. Thanks."

Without hesitation, she packed up her files and portfolio into her briefcase and handed it across the table. Reaching out with one hand while placing his other hand across the small of her back, Mike guided Grace to the exit door.

"Thanks. I was starting to feel a little uncomfortable in there."

"They don't mean you any harm. They're just scared about having a group home in town. By the time you're done working with the town board, the people will understand it better and it'll be okay."

Approaching her car, Mike's words fell on deaf ears as Grace saw "Get out of Midland" scrawled across her windshield in a bright red tone.

A headless cat on her roof, the obvious source of the bloody ink.

Chapter Thirty-Seven

IKE HEALY LED GRACE up the stairs to her house, his arm protectively wrapped around her waist.

"Sorry we didn't get to Welcome Home, Grace."

"I hadn't even thought about it, Mike. Food is the farthest thing from my mind right now."

"I didn't mean the food part. I meant spending time together someplace other than a police station. Sharing a bottle of red wine and pleasant conversation instead of taking your statement. I truly am sorry about what happened tonight."

"I know. Thank you."

Approaching the door, Mike could see fear filter into her eyes and feel tension stiffen her body.

"Got your key? I'll unlock the door and take a look around before you go in."

Silently, Grace pulled a keyring from her purse and dropped it into Mike's outstretched hand. Then she leaned against the porch railing and closed her eyes.

"Just take it easy and wait here. I'll be right back."

Grace felt weak and incapable of anything, even the simplest conversation. Hours later, the memory of the cat on the roof of her car along with the bloody words scrawled on her windshield were still sending waves of nausea through her body. All she wanted to do was crawl into bed and pull the covers over her head. At this point, blocking out the world was the best she could manage.

"It's all good. Come on in. Let's get you settled."

Grace followed mutely, guiding Mike by hand signals as he supported her up the stairs and down the hall to her bedroom. Crawling under the bed covers fully clothed, Grace quickly faded off to sleep and into her patterened nightmares, these filled with dead cats, angry mobs and the tortured faces of her Faith File. Every time she woke up, Mike was right there, assuring her everything was ok and she was safe.

The cycle continued through to the early morning, until finally Grace could take no more of the frightening visions. Throwing back the covers, she stormed past Mike soundly sleeping in a chair and into the adjoining bathroom.

Reaching in to the shower, Grace set the water temperature to full-on hot. Peeling off her clothes, she stepped under the scalding spray allowing it to purify her body. She'd never thought of herself as weak, but the memory of that bloody cat on her car make Grace feel vulnerable in a way she'd never known. Part of it was that the vengeful person knew the car she drove and where she had parked it in the isolated end of the municipal lot. Did he or she also know where she lived? When she was home? Would they have the nerve to try to do something to her while she slept?

The possibilities became overwhelming. Slowly Grace sank down to the shower floor and started sobbing uncontrollably until she had no breaths left. Reaching up she turned off the water and with the last of her strength, crawled out of the shower onto the bathmat.

"Grace, are you okay?"

The last thing she wanted was for Mike to come in and find her exposed in body and soul.

"Yes. I'm fine. I'm just taking my time. I'll be out in a few minutes."

As she heard Mike's footsteps move away from the door, Grace curled up on the bath mat. Somehow she had to gather the strength to dry off and at least put on her robe before Mike returned to check on her again.

Just take a minute, Gracie girl. You've got all the courage and strength you need.

Papa, I don't feel courageous or strong right now. Please help me.

I'm here, Grace, but you can do this all on your own. Have faith.

Have faith. It was a phrase both of her grandparents had used to inspire Grace throughout her life and it had seen her through some dark days. It was just, at the moment, she didn't feel as if she had any faith to summon.

One step at a time. Start by getting a towel and drying off.

Massaging her body with the plush terrycloth gently invigorated Grace.

With deliberate care, she moved from the bathroom to the adjoining bedroom where she pulled her robe from the closet, slipped it over her body and belted it. With each motion, Grace felt energy building.

"You're looking good, Miss Reid. I've got some breakfast ready for you. You okay to walk to the dining room on your own?"

Grace knew she was on the mend when she felt her Irish temper rise to Mike's overly solicitous concern.

"I had a rough night, Mike. I'm not dying."

"With a laugh, he turned to the door and walked away.

"Well, I guess that shower did you good. See you at the table."

Grace used the time walking from her bedroom and down the stairs to the dining room to get a grip on her emotions. Mike didn't deserve to bear the brunt of her fear that was fueling her senseless anger Approaching the table, she reached out and took Mike's hand between her own.

"I'm sorry, Mike. I didn't mean to snap at you. I am so very grateful you were with me at the police station and stayed with me here through the night. I've never really had anyone to rely on but my grandparents. Since they both passed, I guess I've become pretty independent and not very good at accepting help or being able to express my thanks. On top of that, I was pretty freaked out at what happened and I'm just starting to sort all that out."

Mike stood and wrapped his arms around Grace. For several moments the two stood in silence. When finally they drew apart, Grace felt a renewed energy, no doubt drawn from Mike's strength.

"Come on let's eat. You have to be hungry. Even if you're not, you've got to get some food in you, especially after missing dinner last night."

"You're right, I'm not hungry, but I know I've got to eat. You've gone to so much effort to make a hearty breakfast. But, if you don't mind, I'm going to start with a bit of toast and see how that settles."

Passing her a piece of buttered toast on a plate, Mike picked up yesterday's edition of The Sun Journal he'd grabbed off the porch and started skimming it. The scene was much like breakfasts being shared in homes throughout the quaint Midland Township, except for the dark silence was overshadowing the couple. As it needed to be, Grace was the one to break that silence.

"Ok, this is not going to get any better unless we talk about it. I'll start. Last night was terrifying to me for a number of reasons. First, the violence of beheading a cat and then using its blood to write that message on my car. It's unimaginable that someone in this town would be that sick. Then there's the fact that someone knows my car. That makes me think they know where I live as well, and may even be following me wherever I go. Last but not least, there's the seniors at the core of this issue who shouldn't be maligned in any way and deserve to have a decent life, especially after all they've endured for so long."

The force of Grace's words brought Mike's law enforcement training to the forefront. With analytical precision, he addressed each of her concerns.

"No doubt the person or people who defiled the cat and your car are sick and need to be apprehended and treated. We completed the case report last night, and your car was impounded for fingerprints and fibers. All of that information went into the station's alert file and there is a full-out effort going on right now to find whoever is responsible."

The manner in which Mike explained the police department's investigation provided Grace a sense of confidence. She was not alone in dealing with the hateful act.

"As for anyone following you, I will be with you for the rest of the weekend. After that, I will be tailing you in my own car as you go to and from work. There will also be a regular patrol going past your house at various hours of the day and night. If anyone is following you or planning to leave any nasty suprises here, we are going to know about it and put a stop to it."

"Mike, you can't afford to take that kind of time away from your regular police duties. Besides, I would feel terrible if you got in trouble with your captain because of time you were spending with me."

"Mayor's orders, Grace. He is the one who called for police details on you and your home, last night before we left the station."

Grace sat in stunned silence. Suddenly she didn't feel so foolish about being upset.

"Finally, about your Faith File seniors. I need to tell you something that happened last night. Jonathan stopped by after you fell asleep. First off, he wanted to make sure you were alright. He also wanted you to know what a great job you did at the town meeting yesterday. He was there, in the back of the room, and heard every word you said. He asked me to tell you that he couldn't have done better himself."

"Why do I feel as if you are keeping the bad news for last?"

"Because I am. Jonathan came here to let me know that after our last month's board meeting someone drove into the Wood Haven grounds and threw bricks through the windows. They were tied with notes containing messages along the same lines as your windshield."

Grace felt her strength ebbing as she envisioned the sights and sounds of the hateful bricks crashing through the Wood Haven windows. What was wrong with people? How could the possibility of six senior citizens moving into a house in a community instill enough fear to lead to violence?

"I know this information has to be upsetting to you, Grace, but our police department is turning the town upside down to find who ever is behind these terrorizing acts. More than likely they are bullies with the courage to do these things only under the cover of anonymity."

"Do you think it could possibly be Bill Jenkins? After the way he spoke last night, I would think he would have to be on your list of suspects."

"I don't think it's Bill, but we haven't ruled him out. I spoke to the chief this morning and he's waiting for lab reports on the prints they found on your car. We should know more when that data is returned. At this point, it could be anybody. It could be someone you work with, someone you've never met, someone you've seen on the street, or when you're driving.

"Wait. Someone I've seen when I'm driving. There was someone, just yesterday. It was when I was leaving Wood Haven for the town board meeting. I pulled out of the complex and all of a sudden there was a car on my bumper. It appeared out of nowhere. The driver tailgaited for a mile or so and then hit the accelerator and blew by me. It was so odd that it made me pay close attention to the car and the license number."

"Do you remember them?"

"The car was a sedan. A black sedan. I don't know the make or model. The license plate was from New Jersey. Oh, what was the number? I remember it was odd, unusual. Darn, I'm so worn out right now, I just can't remember. Sorry Mike."

"Not to worry. If you remember it, that would be great. In the meantime, I'm going to let the chief know so he can post a notice about a black sedan with jersey plates. See if anything pans out."

As Mike moved toward the telephone, it rang.

Turning to Grace, he asked, "Do you want me to answer?"

"No. That's ok. I'm fine."

She got to the phone by the third ring and answered with a voice that belied her energy.

"Hello, Grace Reid speaking."

"If you know what's good for you, Grace Reid, you'll stop trying to bring those old people into this town, or the next time it will be someone, not a stupid cat, that gets hurt."

The slamming of the phone felt like a jolt of electricity through Grace's body. Once again she felt bile rise in her throat, as she had the previous night standing before her car. Her eyes began stinging with tears and somewhere in the distance she could hear Mike calling her name.

"Grace. Grace. Can you hear me? What is it? Who was on the phone? Grace talk to me."

With a fuzzy feeling at the back of her neck spreading through her spine, Grace's knees went weak and the room went black.

Chapter Thirty-Eight

GRACE AND MIKE SPENT the rest of the weekend together, shifting between discussions over the nasty turn of events and anything but. Despite the stress of the situation, the couple fell into an easy rhythm of life—cooking together, watching old movies on TV and managing the awkwardness of Saturday's sleepover with Mike on the couch and Grace upstairs in her bedroom.

The shock of the threatening actions against her all but shut down Grace's attraction meter toward the handsome police officer. However, she couldn't deny the bond developing between them as a result of the disturbing events. Nor could she ignore the comfort she found in the man's muscular arms whenever he wrapped them around her. By Sunday night, Grace felt like they were a couple, at least in their united plan against a common enemy.

The two agreed that Mike would monitor activity at Grace's home as well as her workplace and the direct driving route in-between. Grace had agreed to stay low key, going only to work and home, at least until Mike got information about evidence taken from her car.

"Mike, I want you to know how much I appreciate all you've done for me this weekend. But it's time for you to go. I have to be able to be here, by myself. It's important. If I am going to finish this job and take care of my seniors, I have to be able to stand strong against whatever comes my way."

"I'd like to disagree, Grace, but I respect your determination. I'll head out, on the condition you call me if even the slightest thing gives you any concern. I understand you want to handle things on your own, but everyone needs help, especially in situations like this."

"Don't worry, Officer Healy. If even a hint of something untold happens, I have a phone and I know how to use it."

Grace's light-hearted response failed to mirror her worries in sending Mike Healy home. She knew it was the right thing to do, but there was a part of her that wanted him to stay and protect her, like her very own knight in shining armor

"I get it. You're capable of taking care of yourself. I imagine you also have been around enough tough situations to know people don't always react the way they imagine at moments of stress. So, humor me, ok? I'm going to write my number on a piece of note paper and tape it on the wall beside your phone. You may never need it or use it, but it will be there for you, without you having to think."

Grace was on the thin edge of letting her resolve melt away completely.

Why not let him stay another night? After all, we've already eaten dinner and cleaned up the dishes. A couple of hours and we'll both be asleep. What difference could it make if he leaves tonight, or in the morning?

Before she could suggest a change of plans, Mike stepped toward Grace and pulled her into an affectionate embrace. Her body responded without thought, sinking comfortably into the curve of his chest and the comfort of his arms. Disappointment flooded through her when the law officer stepped back, exchanging her for his duffle bag.

"Make sure you lock the door after I leave and keep the curtains drawn as well. After I drive away, I'm going to circle back, just to be on the safe side that there's nobody hanging around."

Grace knew she had to break the cycle of need for Mike Healy that she'd developed over the last three days. Drawing her body up to its full height and snapping her hand to her brow in a smart salute, she responded.

"Will do, Officer Healy!"

"Ok, ok. I don't need to be hit over the head with a hammer. I'm outta here."

When the door closed, Grace found the silence of the room disturbing. Walking over to turn the lock, she realized how quickly she'd become used to sharing her house with someone.

Don't kid yourself. It's not about sharing the house with someone. It's about sharing it with Mike.

It was true. Through the ups and downs of the weekend, Grace found she was drawn to the easy-going policeman in ways that reminded her of times spent growing up on her nana and papa's farm. He was easy to get along with and had a great sense of humor. He also knew how to be respectful of her thoughts and feelings, something other men in her life had failed at miserably, except for her papa.

Grace wished her grandparents were still alive to meet Mike. They'd be able to tell her straight away if he was all that he seemed.

You don't need your nana and me, Gracie girl. You know well enough on your own when someone is special. You just need to trust your heart.

I'm not so sure papa. It's not that easy by myself.

With a sinking feeling, Grace realized she was exhausted as much as anything. Monday would come quickly and she needed to be ready to tend to her job at Wood Haven and her seniors. Even though it was only 8 o'clock at night, she decided an early bedtime was the perfect remedy for rejuvenating her courage and strength.

Moving room to room, Grace turned out the lights in the downstairs and made the climb to her second floor bedroom. Methodically, she raised the windows that encircled the room, allowing the cool night air to filter in and over her. As she faced the street, Grace paused to inspect the scene. Did anything look out of order? Was anyone unusual walking by? Anyone lingering around her house?

Each time, her answer was, "no."

Crawling under the covers, Grace offered an extra special rendition of her bedtime prayers, asking for protection from all nightmares as she slept. It was the last thing she remembered until the rising sun heralded a new morning.

Grace woke with an energy to get up and get going. She'd allowed too much time being intimidated by the cruel actions of others. That's why, despite her agreement with Mike to take it easy, she made up her mind that nothing was going to deter her from getting the Faith File settled into new living situations and better lives. The only way to do that was to get started facing the cowardly terrorists head-on.

By 7:30, Grace was showered, dressed, out the door and on her way to Cuppa Joe. Breakfast in one of the busiest places in town ought to send a message that she was not intimidated.

Breezing into the cozy diner, Grace could feel the eyes of the breakfast crowd following her as she headed for a stool at the counter. Grabbing a menu from the metal holders on the formica tabletop, she saw the morning specials were biscuits and gravy or fresh peach pancakes.

No choice. Fresh July peaches win out everyday.

"Hey, Grace. Long time no see. How are you?"

Looking up, Grace felt comforted by the fresh face of Suzy, the diner's stalwart waitress.

"Good morning, Suzy. I'm great. I'm also starved. How about an order of those fresh peach pancakes and a side of crisp bacon. And a cup of my chocolate coffee!"

"Good Choice. Those pancakes are A-MAZ-ING! Be right back with your special brew."

Suzy promptly placed a blended mug of hot chocolate and coffee on the counter in front of Grace. Taking a deep inhale of the choco caffeine-laden elixir, Grace relaxed into the welcoming atmosphere of the eatery. Regardless of what police discovered about those trying to intimidate her, she realized it was unfair to judge the the entire town by the actions of a few.

At least she hoped it was only a few.

"Here you go, Grace, hot off the griddle. And today you get the special treat of real maple syrup and fresh peach syrup for those pancakes."

The mingled smell of peaches and melting butter rising from the white china plate started her mouth watering. Deciding to splurge, Grace poured syrup from each pitcher over the bountiful dish and dug in.Her first forkfull was perhaps the most heavenly taste of food Grace had ever experienced. She savored the morsel with eyes closed and lips bonded in syrupy goodness.

"Well, I'm glad to see you've bounced back."

Grace recognized the voice without looking.

"Don't bother me, Mike Healy. I am in pancake heaven right now and want to enjoy this moment as long as I can."

"Well if they're that good, maybe I ought to try a stack. Hey, Suzy. How about a plate of those pancakes and some coffee?"

"Coming right up, Mike."

"Seriously, how are you this morning, Grace? I stopped by your place and was surprised to find you out of the house so early. Everything is ok, right? No nightmares, or phone calls? No one around last night or this morning?"

"Everything is fine. I went to bed right after you left and slept through the night. I feel reasonably strong, all things considered, and ready to get back to work. Thanks again for all you did for me over the weekend. I could not have gotten through without you."

"Here's your cakes, Officer Healy and, not to be an eavesdropper, but I heard what happened Friday night at that special town meeting. Any leads? Has to be some kind of lowlife to hurt an innocent animal like that."

"Nope, Suzy. Nothing yet, but we'll find who did it. That kind of behavior doesn't belong here in Midland. This town has a lot of good people in it and we're not going to let a few rotten apples ruin it."

"Well you know what I always say, Midland people have the biggest hearts. We're always looking out for each other around here and willing to help. That's why I can't figure out this whole fuss over some old folks moving in to town. It's just silly."

The conversation between the policeman and the waitress rekindled Grace's worries over the cat incident and all that had followed. Pulling money from her purse, she left enough for her bill and a tip alongside her plate of half-eaten pancakes.

"I've got to get to work. Thanks for the delicious breakfast, Suzy. Officer Healy, I'm sure I'll see you around."

"But wait, Grace, you didn't finish your pancakes or your chocolate coffee. Do you want to take them with you?"

"No, thanks Suzy. I don't think I'm going to be very hungry today."

As Grace made her way to the door, she again felt everyone in the diner watching her. Clearly news of what happened had spread through the town. Grace felt unnerved by the fact that people were no doubt talking about her and what they might be saying.

"Grace, wait."

Mike had dashed out the door and caught up to her as she reached her car.

"Mike, please. I just need to get to work and get focused on helping my seniors. I should have realized that everyone in town would know what happened and would be talking about it. Stopping here this morning was probably not the brightest idea I've ever had."

"You had every right to come here for breakfast, Grace, and anywhere else in this town you want to go. You haven't done anything wrong and most of the people in Midland will tell you that. It's just that this is a small town and people are connected to everything that goes on—good and bad."

Grace looked up into Mike's compassionate eyes and felt an easing of her anxiety. Maybe he was right. Maybe she just needed to trust that most people in town were good and caring, and eventually everything would settle down for

262 | *Beauty & Grace*

her and for her seniors.

"You go ahead to Wood Haven. I'm going to follow you to make sure you get there safely. When you're ready to head home, I don't care what time it is, promise you'll call me twenty minutes before you walk out the door."

"Mike, really, I don't need you following me around like some kind of child."

"There's no discussion about this, Grace. These are the mayor's orders and unless you want to be responsible for me losing my job."

"Ok. Alright. I promise. I'll call. But only today. I'm not promising any more than that."

GRACE WAS GRATEFUL TO ARRIVE at her desk without encountering anyone along the way. She definitly needed a few minutes in her office to clear her head—turn her focus away from decapitated cats and on to deserving seniors.

Now that she'd met everyone and organized the four seniors transferring to assisted care, Grace needed to brainstorm ways to bring together the six women who would be mainstreaming into an independent lives. It was important that they start forming into a group, with a sense of family.

Pulling out a blank yellow legal pad, Grace began making notes of ways to encourage the women to bond. As she wrote down bits and pieces about each one, she realized the lives they'd shared locked away at Wood Haven was a stronger connection than any program she could design. From the depths of her soul, Grace knew there would be few problems establishing a healthy home atmosphere among these women. Finding a home that would be safe and secure for them is what she now knew would demand every bit of her being.

Chapter Thirty-Nine

JONATHAN HUNG UP THE PHONE and pushed back from his desk. A conversation with the governor was not his usual way of starting off a work week. Then again, nothing at Wood Haven was usual these days.

When he'd accepted the directorship of the facility he knew there would be challenges, particularly when it came to the deinstitutionalization of the seniors. That's why he went out and hired a specialist in senior care. Someone compassionate enough to understand and handle the relocation of elderly patients who'd been locked away for so many years. And someone also able to manage the administrative duties involved in such a transition. Grace had been executing all levels of the job admirably. However, after Friday's turn of events, Jonathan questioned if she possessed the strength and determination to finish.

That's what the governor wanted to know as well in his early morning call. News of the beheaded cat and bloodied windshield traveled fast between Midland and Trenton. Likely, the police had shared the disturbing story statewide in an attempt to identify potential suspects.

Regardless, Jonathan assured the governor all was well and Grace was able and ready to carry on with her duties. The thing was, the Wood Haven administrator was not as confident as he professed. He hadn't seen Grace since he stopped by her place Friday night and Mike Healy brought him up to date on her frightened state of mind.

He understood her fears but, at the same time, he needed this job done. If Grace wasn't able, he would have to find someone else. It was business, plain and simple.

That's what set Jonathan walking down the hallway to Grace's office. He wanted to see if he could find files on the ten patients to get a handle on exactly what was remaining in their deinstitutionalization. It had been almost two months since Grace's arrival. In that time she'd met with all the patients, brought their files up to date, connected with the Wood Haven Board and

Staff and begun the necessary outreach to the Midland Community.

Stage two involved identifying several houses in Midland suitable for a group home, beginning the process of buying a house and completing any needed renovations. Since most real estate closings took four to six weeks, it was imperative Grace have a house under contract by mid September in order to meet the governor's state mandated end-of-the-year timeline.

Turning the corner into her office, Jonathan was startled to see Grace sitting behind her desk.

"What are you doing here?"

"This is my office, Jonathan. So I guess it's my turn to ask, what are you doing here?"

Running his hand through his short-cropped hair, the administrator took a seat across the desk from his employee, gulping a breath of air that forced out his words.

"I didn't expect to see you today, Grace. Well, maybe more than today. Actually, I was halfway expecting your letter of resignation. So I figured I better get started on assessing exactly where you are in the deinstitutionalization process and what steps need to be taken next."

"While I appreciate your concern, Jonathan, or perhaps I should say your concern for my job, as you can see I am here and working. If you would like me to update you on my progress and my plans for the remaining five months of my contract, I was just organizing that information and would be glad to share it with you."

A bit embarrassed by his concentration on the project more than the person, Jonathan paused to collect his thoughts.

"You know, Grace, what happened to you Friday night was inexcusable, unimaginable really. I've lived in Midland all my life and have never heard of such a hateful incident. In my mind the reason it happened is that you are doing a good job and people are scared you're really going to succeed at placing a group home in Midland. Your excellent presentation before the town board on Friday only served to strengthen that possibility. So I guess what I'm trying to say is, if you can, translate the nastiness to validation of your work and your dedication to your seniors.

"Thank you for your kind words about my presentation. I really have not been able to think about it or review it with all the furor. Good to know you felt it was effective. One thing from the meeting I would like to ask you about is Bill Marsh, the man who spoke against our senior home. What do you know about him? And was that his son sitting with him at the back of the room?

"I know Bill casually, mostly from the Dew Drop. Like he said the other night, he's born and raised here, still living in his childhood home. He's a member of the Midland Legion, not sure if and where he served. He's married to a real quiet woman. She's a stay-at-home mom and I'm pretty sure the Presbyterian Church is the only place outside the house she goes. As for their son, his name is John or Johnny. He's at the Dew Drop on weekends, busing tables and washing dishes. I heard he was in trouble not too long ago for driving with an open beer. Lucky for him, he wasn't drunk, so the judge let him off with a warning. Sorry I can't tell you anything more helpful, like why Bill is so opposed to our seniors moving into Midland."

"No problem. I was just curious as he was the only person to step up and speak out at the meeting, but as I watched him return to his seat, there were a lot of people smiling and nodding to him in support. And then there was his son. That whole high five thing was a little weird."

"I agree, Bill did seem to have a lot of support, but for the hundred or so people crowded into that meeting hall, I'd bet my right arm there are ten times that number in this town that will support our group home."

With the air cleared between them, the two began reviewing the necessary steps to locate and secure housing and continue to prepare the ten seniors for their transitions. Jonathan also laid out a plan of dealing with whoever might be the town's unknown protestors and any future protests that might be in store. Most of the provisos revolved around aligning with the Midland Police Department and the Mayor.

"The one thing the governor insisted was round-the-clock protection for you, Grace. I haven't spoken to the police chief yet, but I'm sure the governor's people have already been in touch with him. So, be prepared for that. There is too much at stake here to have a few unreliable people causing problems. And I do believe this is all the work of one or a few. With any luck, the police will figure out who it is and the whole thing will go away."

"You're right, Jonathan. I don't like the idea of having some police officer following me around. So I'm going to use it as motivation to find a house and get it approved for group housing and purchased. Once all those things are done, there won't be any use of people protesting."

"I hope you're right, Grace. I hope you're right."

Jonathan departed with a promise to check in at the end of the day, leaving Grace with a checklist of phone calls and a number of items to accomplish. She decided to start with the phone calls.

"Hello, Karen? This is Grace Reid. I work with your brother at Wood Haven. You helped me find a house to rent when I moved here in May."

"Hello, Grace. Good to hear from you. How's that charming Victorian working out? Are you enjoying it?"

"It's lovely, thank you. I would never have thought about renting it on my own, but you were right. It is a special place. That's why I'm calling. I wonder if you would help me find another house in Midland?"

"Are you thinking about buying?"

"Yes, but not for me. It's for some of the patients who have been living here at Wood Haven. Six of them to be exact. All women and all able to live independently with an aide. They are perfectly healthy in body and mind, so there is no danger or liability issue—no more than any elderly person moving into a home in a neighborhood. The only difference is that there will be six seniors, seven if you include the aide, who will be younger."

"Ah yes. I did hear about this over the weekend. I'm sorry for what happened to you, Grace. Please know that the people in this town are not mean-spirited and whoever did this does not represent the majority."

"Thank you, Karen, and I do hope you're right. That's why, rather than focus on the negative, I'm putting all my efforts into finding a house for these special women and making sure they enjoy a smooth transition into their new lives."

"Now that sounds like a plan and I'll be happy to help. Do you know the zoning that will be required?"

"Housing like this is considered residential, just like any other house in a neighborhood. So, there's no special zoning. The laws governing this kind of a home are set by the state and cannot be superceded by local municipalities. The only local condition we have to fulfill is to file paperwork that will allow the property to be assessed as a non-profit, eliminating the property taxes. That's what the hearing was about last Friday."

"Well then, that makes it easy. We can look in any neighborhood in Midland. I just need to know your size requirements and your price range."

"Ideally, I'd like a home with at least four or five bedrooms and the space to create more. Two bathrooms are a minimum and, of course, a kitchen, a good-sized dining room, a nice backyard and a basement or attic for storage. As for price, I have around $10,000 from the state and a commitment of a $40,000 grant to finance the rest, so I'd like to find something at no more than the mid to high $30,000 range so that I have money leftover for renovations and furnishings. A good-sized reno project in a nice neighborhood would be ideal."

"Got it. Let me go to work and see what I can do. What's your timing for the actual move?"

"I have to move all six seniors out of Wood Haven no later than mid December. So we've got four months at most."

"Ok. We can do this. Give me a couple of days."

"Thanks, Karen. You've been very encouraging. I feel as if we are on the right track."

Hanging up, Grace moved on to the next call on her list.

"Hello, this is Grace Reid from Wood Haven. May I speak to Mayor Jenkins, please."

Following acknowledgment from the secretary answering the phone and a few moments of Muzak, the mayor came on the line.

"Good morning, Grace. You were on my list to call today."

"Hello, Mayor. I wanted to touch base about my presentation last Friday and ask if you had any idea when you and the town board will rule on the tax exemption for the property for our Wood Haven seniors?"

"At this point, Grace, I have called a special board meeting for Wednesday and told the members to plan on making a decision then. I don't want this issue to drag on and cause more division in our community. I also want to minimize any further incidents like the one that occurred after the meeting. By the way, I'd like to apologize for the unpleasantness you encountered. I'm born and raised in this town, fourth generation. What happened to you is not in keeping with the character of this town or its citizens. I promise you, we will find those responsible."

"Thank you, Mayor. I have to say everyone I've spoken to since last Friday has expressed the same conviction and that certainly makes me feel better. What would make it all irrelevant, however, is if you and the town board decide to grant the tax exemption. Do you have any idea of how the board is going to vote?"

Grace knew she was pushing her luck, but her gut told her it was worth the risk. The mayor's hesitation let her know he was wavering.

"Now Grace, you know I can't give out privileged information. However, I will share that every board member called me over the weekend to express their displeasure over the incident you experienced and I would expect that support to impact their decision."

The fact that the mayor kept referring to the headless cat and bloody windshield as, "the incident" made it clear he had no stomach for the extreme form of intimidation. Grace recognized his vulnerability as an opportunity.

"Of course, Mayor Jenkins, I would never ask you to reveal a board decision unofficially. I am just grateful to know that the lasting image of a beheaded cat on the top of my car and a threatening message written in that cat's blood on my windshield is as offensive to all of you as it was to me."

The silence on the other end of the phone line let Grace know she'd hit her mark. She had no doubt when the mayor convened Wednesday's board meeting, he would serve as her advocate for the tax exemption. Though Jonathan had suggested calling each board member individually, Grace decided the mayor would do the job quite nicely.

That left only one call on her list—to the chief of police. According to Jonathan, the governor had asked she make contact with the chief to confirm her police protection. Grace also wanted to know if he had any leads from the fingerprints on her car.

Grace was just about to dial the number when she heard a noise, like someone clearing their throat. Sitting very still, she heard it again, this time identifying the sound as coming from the hallway outside her door.

Silently making her way toward the hall, Grace peered around the entry to find Teagan standing shyly along the wall.

"Good morning, Teagan. It's nice to see you. Would you like to come into my office?"

"Good morning, Missus. Twasn't meanin' ta bother ya. It's just me and some of the others was talkin' 'bout this movin' and we was wonderin' a bit."

"Of course. Please come in and sit down."

Grace motioned for the woman to enter her office, and followed as she did.

"Have a seat here in this chair, Teagan, and I'll bring my chair around so we're next to each other. I don't like having a big desk in between two people when they're trying to enjoy conversation, do you?"

"Truth be told, don't pay much attention. Most times them's I'm talkin' with are sittin' next ta one another. No big offices or fancy furniture."

Grace felt a sting of embarrassment as Teagan's words reminded her of the stark reality of her life and the lives of others from the Faith File. What soothed Grace was the thought that soon they would be enjoying better lives.

"Are ya ok there, Missus? Ya had kinda far away look on yer face. Sorta like you was dreamin' o'somethin' real pleasant."

"You're absolutely right, Teagan. I was dreaming of something very pleasant. Something I deeply want to make happen, which is moving all of you into a new home. So let's talk about concerns and questions you and the others have so we can begin figuring everything out."

In the company of Teagan and amid their conversation, Grace realized she had the strength and courage to do whatever was needed to ensure a better future for the Faith File and in some way, for herself as well.

Chapter Forty

GRACE DASHED DOWN THE HALL to Wood Haven's third floor common room. She had a standard of being on time, infused through her years of Catholic school education. At the moment, that standard was in jeopardy due to a phone call from Midland Chief of Police, Bob Reynolds.

"Hello Ms. Reid. This is Chief Reynolds. I wanted to let you know the latest on our investigation into the incident with your car."

Again with "the incident". Can't anyone call it what it was? At least name it the bloody cat scandal. The poor feline deserves to be acknowledged.

"The finger prints we lifted from your vehicle came back with several identiites. One is yours. Another is Officer Healy, which he attested happened when he stopped you for speeding earlier in the week and rested his hand on your car door and roof. The third is a Midland citizen. Jack Beatty. So, I need to ask, Ms. Reid, can you verify Officer Healy's statement and have you met, or do you know of, Jack Beatty?"

Grace's thoughts immediately divided. In one part, she reimagined Mike pulling her over and asking for a date rather than writing her a ticket, and the problems that could cause if the sheriff knew the truth. Her other thoughts spun around like a rolodex of people she'd met in Midland over the last four months searching for a Jack Beatty.

"Yes, chief, Mike Healy did pull me over last Monday to warn me about the reduced speed limit on the outskirts of town. So, his prints are very likely on my car. As for Jack Beatty, I'm sorry, I don't recall meeting anyone by that name. I have met a lot of people through my work here at Wood Haven and people I have never met seem to know who I am, because of my job. Perhaps if I could see a picture, I might recognize him."

"Sure thing. I'll make sure Officer Healy has a photo with him when he resumes your surveillance detail later today. In the meantime, if you think of anything that might help, don't hesitate to call. I believe you have my direct line."

"Yes, I do, thank you. I will certainly stay in touch. Oh, and chief, one thing. I am grateful for your professional concern, but everything seems to have settled down since the town board meeting. It's been over a week and nothing else has happened. Do you think we could drop the surveillance?"

"Ms. Reid, I've been in this business a long time. One thing I've learned is just because you can't see the danger doesn't mean it don't exist. What happened to your car and that cat may seem like a minor act to you, but in a town like Midland, it's serious and it's not gonna be tolerated. I appreciate you'd like to have your privacy back, but until we catch whoever did this, there's going to be a member of the Midland Police Force with you at all times."

Grace was surprised to realize that as frustrated as she was by the chief's answer, she was also relieved. The residual effect of the bloody cat apparently took more of a toll than she understood or was willing to admit. Just this morning, she realized that everywhere she went she was looking over her shoulder or proceeding with caution, just in case. Fortunately, other than her Wood Haven co-workers, the only other person she saw was Mike Healy. Perhaps police protection within the immediate sound of her voice was a security she should value and accept.

"Now, if you would like me to switch your detail to another officer, just say the word. I know sometimes personalities can clash in situations like this, so it's not a problem to make that change."

Grace did her best to hold in her laughter as she envisioned the look on Mike's face if he were to hear she was unhappy with her surveillance detail.

"Not at all, chief. Officer Healy is terrific and I appreciate the ways in which he respects my privacy while doing his job."

"Alright then, but if you find you need a change, don't hesitate to speak up."

"The only request I have, chief, is that you find the person who did this so my life can go back to normal."

A normal life. That seemed to be a shared goal these days, not only for herself but for the Faith File.

Arriving at the door to the third floor common room, Grace paused. This was her first time gathering all six women together. Her first attempt to begin quilting them into a family instead of a random group forced together in a shared time and space. It was a moment vital to the success of Wood Haven's deinstitutionalization and a responsibility Grace felt deeply.

Nana, I know if you were here you would have just the right words to help me guide these special women to their new lives. Please, if you would, inspire me with those words as I begin this journey.

Shoulders back and taking a deep breath, Grace entered the room. Teagan, Maeve, Angel, Gabrielle and Rebecca were gathered around the table with two chairs unoccupied. One for Grace and one for Jane Bennett.

Sitting down, Grace's heart skipped a beat over the empty chair beside her. Jane's absence from the gathering underscored the uncertainty of her future. It also intensified Grace's determination to do anything possible to help the former nurse recover her health and remain part of the Faith File.

Looking around the table, Grace spoke to each woman, greeting them by name. They responded individually at varying levels of warmth. Teagan then took the lead in launching a group conversation.

"So's missus, are we goin' ta be movin' from here anytime soon? We've all been talkin' since ya come ta us one at a time and we'd like ta be knowin' your plan."

"Teagan, that's a great question and I can see from the looks on everyone's faces that, even if you may be looking forward to leaving Wood Haven, you have concerns. The good news is that as we work through your concerns and draw closer to moving, I am going to be with you every step of the way. Any problems, any worries, even questions, even if you think they're silly, I am here for you and we work through this move together. I sincerely mean that and hope eventually each one of you will feel the same way. We are a family and it's important that we all think in those terms and support each other."

"Well, me brothers and I used ta scrap all the time. Thinkin' ya not be meanin' family quite like that, I'm guessin'!"

Teagan's comment brought laughter around the table, lightening the mood of all.

"Well Teagan, I think we'd all be less than honest if we didn't acknowledge that we're not always going to agree, or even get along. At the same time, I have no doubt that after all you have gone through living here at Wood Haven, the future is going to be much more enjoyable. So let's start working on that future.

"Excuse me." Angel raised her hand as if a student in a classroom.

"Angel, please, feel free to speak when ever you wish. The same goes for all of you ladies. Our gatherings are not business meetings or school events where you must sit in certain seats and can only speak if you are spoken to."

"Oh, yes, Miss Reid. Thank you. What I would like to ask is about Nurse Bennett. I have visited with her since her return from the hospital and I am hopeful she will be moving with us, but I also see how weak she has become. It would be so sad without her. She has been a trusted friend to each one of us, and so many others."

"Well, first, I'd like to ask that you all call me Grace instead of Miss Reid. And Angel, I understand exactly how you feel. I have spent quite a bit of time in the company of Jane since her fall and I've come to know her as all of you do—a special woman with a heart of great kindness. At this time she's recovering from the effects of her recent fall but it has definitely taken a toll on her overall health. The good news is that the doctors and nurses are doing everthing possible to rebuild her strength and at this point, she is still on my list to move with you to independent living. I have every hope she will remain there."

The faces around the table registered equal expressions of concern. Grace wanted to console them with positive feedback on Jane Bennett's health, but she had to be honest. Jane's continued lack of mobility was a growing issue and, since the fall, her appetite was decreasing. Equally concerning, she was exhibiting occasional bouts of disorientation. The latest report from the doctor was that Jane's health and her chances of moving with the rest of the Faith File were declining.

"Thank you, Miss Reid, I mean Grace. If I could ask one more question? If Nurse Bennett is not well enough to move with us, what will happen to her?"

Again the women sitting around the table felt like one force behind Angel's question. While Grace was pleased by the unity among them, it made her feel like an outsider, which would be a liability if she could not break through that invisible barrier and into their circle of friendship.

"Angel, thank you for giving voice to a question that I think is on all of our minds. If I can share a little secret, I have been worried about Jane's future myself and I've lost sleep wondering what I could do to help her regain her health. Also, as I have gotten to know all of you, it is clear you are a special group of women and it would be a shame for any one of you to be left out of this move. So, there are a couple of things I would suggest for all of us. First, when you have a few minutes, stop by and visit with her. Talk about the new home, when you're going to move. Talk about the new life you're going to share. Tell her that she is a part of that new life and you want her to be there."

"That may all be true, but won't we be makin' the poor woman feel worse? What if she ends up not well enough ta come? Seems like sorta mean thing ta do."

Grace looked to Maeve as she answered. While Teagan appeared to be the leader of the group and Angel the heart, Maeve was clearly the voice of reason among them. As such, she would more than likely sway the group's collective mindset.

"Maeve, I would never encourage you to do anything cruel, especially to the women in this group. As I said, going forward you need to think of each other as family. Despite Teagan's tales of brawls with her brothers, I think we can all agree that in this particular family we are about love and support and throughful consideration of each other."

Grace's reference to Teagan's description of her family brought smiles all around.

Good. They're engaging. I need my next words to inspire them to become involved in Jane Bennett's recovery.

"Keeping that in mind, I will tell you the doctors believe it is possible for Grace to recover from this fall and be able to live independently. In fact, they have told her those very things. The problem is that, being a former nurse, Jane has her own ideas about what's going on with her health and her outlook is not so positive. The more we spend time with her, encourage her, let her know we are a family, the better she will be. We also need to start sharing positive messages of health and healing with her, the more often the better. We can help Jane Bennett be well enough to move with us. Our positive thoughts and physical encouragement can make a difference."

"I can make a schedule for us." Liberty spoke up. "Something simple like draw a calender on a piece of paper and leave the days blank. I can hang it on the door of my room so everyone can mark the day and add in the time they can visit. It's sort of the way I used to organize the suffragists for marches when we were fighting for the vote."

"I will make sure every day to visit Nurse Bennett, as it was she who did the same for us."

Rebecca's voice was soft but forceful as the others nodded in silent agreement. This was exactly what Grace had hoped for and why she was sure the spirit of these women would serve them well as they settled into a society that once turned a blind eye to all they were suffering. Choking back her quickly emotions, Grace glanced down at her Faith File. Suddenly her nana's words formed in her heart.

"Ladies, thank you. I am touched by your compassion for Jane and I have faith that with your support she will be with us when we walk through the door of your new home. Faith has always been a strong part of my life. It's something I learned from my nana and papa and it guides me still today. In fact, when I reviewed your file—-all of you here today, and Jane—I prayed for guidance so that I would be able to help each one of you make this transition in the way that best suits you. In the midst of that prayer, I was inspired with a name for you, as a group."

Casting a glance at the women, Grace could see they were also struggling with their emotions, some on the verge of, and beyond, tears.

"So did ya name us the six musketeers, then?"

Their soft, shared laughter comforted all, as Teagan once again did her best to bring smiles.

"Cause ya know missus, we'd be all fer one and one fer all!"

"Yes, Teagan, I can already tell you are going to be a formidable group of women and that makes me burst with pride. It also justifies the name I've given you—-The Faith File. You are amazing women. Each time we speak and get to know each other more, you inspire me to have faith in your ability to survive and sustain yourselves and each other, no matter what challenges may come. That's what has given me the faith to believe that I can do my job, and by the end of December we will be sitting in a lovely home in Midland raising glasses of champagne and toasting your freedom and your new lives.

As the women applauded Grace and cheered themselves, she fought to ignore nagging reminders of the headless cat and the bloody car windshield message—and thoughts of the Midland Citizens who might turn her every word into lies.

Chapter Forty-One

GRACE STACKED THE DAY'S paperwork neatly on her desk and packed her planner and portfolio into her briefcase. It was only halfway through the week and her to-do list was still lengthy. Glancing at the clock, she estimated there was just enough time to stop for a quick lunch before meeting Karen at her real estate office for an afternoon of Faith File house hunting.

As she set off to the Wood Haven parking lot, Grace was deeply immersed in thoughts of the upcoming house search.

"You're leaving early. Got a hot date?"

Mike's unexpected appearance startled Grace out of her mind.

"Mike! What are you doing scaring me like that? That's not funny,"

The expression on the policeman's face proved equal surprise.

"Gee, Grace, I'm sorry. You were walking right towards me. I had no idea you didn't see me getting out of my car. I'd never scare you on purpose. Especially after all you've been through lately."

Though Grace's heart still felt like it was pounding out of her chest, she knew Mike meant no harm. Plus his sad dog expression made it impossible to be mad at the guy.

"Sorry, Mike. I suppose I am a little preoccupied. I'm on my way to meet Jonathan's sister-in-law, Karen Spencer. We're going to start searching for a house for the Faith File."

"Ok. I'll follow you."

Grace had to catch herself from rolling her eyes at Mike's immediate reply. She knew it wasn't a fair reaction, especially after her earlier conversation with Chief Reynolds. He was only doing his job. Plus, if she were being honest, she was starting to enjoy Mike Healy's regular part in her life.

"I'm sorry you're still following me around, Mike. It must be wearing thin. Tell you what, I was planning to stop for a quick sandwich. Let's have lunch together. My treat."

The look in the policeman's eyes left no doubt about his desire to accept Grace's offer.

"Sorry, but I'm supposed to be undercover on this assignment. If we go to lunch and then people see me drive away following you, we'll be tipping our hand."

The dimpled smile accompanying his reply made Grace feel weak in the knees.

Good grief, this man is getting to me and we haven't so much as shared a kiss.

"You're right. Sorry, I'm still not used to this whole surveillance thing. In fact, I actually asked your chief to call it off today."

"I can imagine what he had to say."

"Well if you are imagining a big fat, 'no,' you've got it right. However, he did say that if I didn't care for the officer assigned to my surveillance detail, he would make a change. All I have to do is say the word."

Mike's eyes communicated the insulting impact of her statement. Feeling badly that he misunderstood her gentle teasing, Grace stepped closer and touched her hand to his cheek.

"But of course my response to the chief was full-out praise for the wonderful officer who has been watching out for my safety, with absolutely no desire to replace him."

The blush across his face encouraged Grace to stretch up and plant a soft kiss on Mike's cheek. That, in turn, caused the man's blush to deepen, charming her even further. She wasn't sure if it was legal to kiss your body guard, but at the moment she really didn't care.

"Ok, Officer Healy. I'm off to the Dew Drop for a sandwich at the bar. From there I'll be heading straight to Karen's office. Feel free to follow me in whatever mode you choose. And thank you for your protection. It is much appreciated."

"I'm not sure it's such a good idea to go Dew Drop, Grace. We still don't know who's harassing you and after the way Bill spoke at the town meeting, he is a possible suspect. You really don't need to be in close proximity to him until we get this thing straightened out."

"I hear you and I respect your opinion, Mike. At the same time, this guy stood up and vehemently spoke out against my seniors moving in to the community, as if they could present a danger. I can't let that go and I'm also not going to let him think his actions intimidated me, in any way. I'm going to the Dew Drop and I'm going to sit at Bill's bar and I'm going to order lunch which, as far as I know, is not illegal.

Mike ruffled his hand through his hair in his frustration. It was a reaction that was becoming very familiar to Grace. Shooting him one of her Irish charm smiles in return, she climbed into her car and set off for the Dew Drop. No matter what Mike had to say, Grace was determined to face Bill and look him straight in the eyes. Whether he was the cat killer or not, she wanted this guy to know who he was up against."

Pulling in to the Dew Drop parking lot, Grace noticed the unmarked police sedan drive on. She wondered how Mike would keep tabs on her in a public restaurant without seeming obvious.

However he does it, you're on short time. Get in and get your lunch ordered.

Since it was almost 1pm, the daily lunch rush was over. Those still at tables were finishing up their meals and preparing to pay their bills. Then there was a group of men at the far end of the polished bar, with no bartender in sight.

Grace planted herself on a barstool and waited. It was just a few minutes before Bill appeared at the far end of the dining room and slid behind the bar. His eyes sparked as they focused on her.

"Afternoon. What can I get you?"

According to plan, Grace looked straight back into his eyes.

"I just stopped for a quick lunch. I've got 25 minutes. Can I get a burger and fries and be out in time?

"Yeah. I'll get your order in right away."

"Thanks. And I'll have an iced tea when you have a minute."

Their exchange appeared like any other at the bar, but the staredown left Grace a little shaky. Taking a deep breath she moved her attention around the restaurant and felt renewed confidence seeing Mike tucked at a corner table. Despite her earlier display of bravado, she was glad to know she wasn't there alone.

"Mind if I sit here?"

Swiveling her barstool, she came face-to-face with an older man dressed in overalls and a flannel shirt. On his head was perched a well-worn New York Yankees hat struggling to tame an unruly head of white hair. Scanning the length of bar and the lineup of empty seats, Grace wondered why he was choosing to sit next to her.

"Feel free to sit."

"My name's Charlie Johnson."

"Hello. I'm Grace."

"Don't believe I've seen you in here before. You new in town?"

As she considered her answer, Bill appeared with her iced tea, setting it down without so much as a glance.

"Hey Charlie. The usual?"

"Yep. I'm here for the game."

Immediately Grace became aware of a television positioned on the opposite wall, above the extensive display of liquor bottles. The screen was featuring a preview of the upcoming game between the Yankees and the Boston Red Sox and had captured her bar buddy's attention. Grace was grateful for the interruption that allowed her to ignore the man's question. Not knowing if he was for or against the Faith File house, she didn't feel like exposing herself to that conversation. Yet she was interested to find out more about the man and perhaps get him to share his take on Wood Haven's deinstitutionalization plan.

"Do you watch all the ball games here?"

"Yep. I come here everyday the Yankees play to have a little lunch and a beer. I've even got my own beer mug on the wall over there.

As the man spoke, Grace noticed Bill move to a collection of glass steins on shelves to the far right of the bar. Choosing one, he filled it with a foamy brew and put it in front of Charlie.

"Each one of the mugs got a name engraved on 'em. See this one's Charlie Johnson. If you come here enough, Bill will keep a mug with your name on it and anytime you come in, you can get a beer served up in your very own glass.

Grace was fascinated by the expansive wall of glassware defining the backbar area. She hadn't noticed the line-up of mugs during her first visit.

"That's amazing. There have to be over a hundred mugs."

"One hundred and ninety eight, to be exact. There's more, but there's no more room on the shelves. Bill keeps the overflow underneath the bar and move mugs up as a space clears."

"With the start of the baseball game, the man turned his attention to the

TV. Grace, on the other hand, more fully considered the beer mug wall. The fact that more than more than two hundred Midland residents had their own Dew Drop mugs made it clear they considered the watering hole somewhat of a home away from home. It also provided evidence that the town valued traditions.

Grace was willing to bet that the people who had a Dew Drop mug would not want things in Midland to change. They'd probably even be inclined to stand up against the something like a group home coming into their community.

"Excuse me, Charlie. You mentioned something about moving mugs to the wall as space clears. I don't mean to sound silly, but how does a space clear?"

"Eh, it varies. It can happen when people die, but most often it happens when they move away. Not many who're born here leave, but when they can't get around so easy, they got no choice but to go to one of them senior homes. We don't have any in Midland, so they have to go to other towns."

"I bet people would like to be able to stay right here in Midland as they age. It's too bad there's no senior housing."

"I guess. Not something people talk about much. At least not until lately. That Wood Haven place has decided to put some of their old people into a house here and it's causing quite a stir."

"But if the town could create housing for residents who are aging and unable to live on their own, wouldn't people want that? Wouldn't they like to be able to stay in the town where their families have lived for generations?"

"Can't say, lady. I'm just an everyday guy. Not one of them movers and shakers who makes things happen around here."

"You can say that again."

Bill served up his comment with Grace's burger and fries and a cold hard stare. Not willing to give any edge she returned the look, challenging his gaze. Grace was adept at stare downs having perfected her technique in college competitions where she was the campus champion for four straight years. However, their war of will ended without a victor, as Charlie intervened.

"Hey Bill. I could use another beer and where's my grilled cheese?"

Ignoring Grace's smug grin, Bill refilled the Charlie Johnson mug and headed off to the kitchen. Looking at her watch she realized she needed to wolf down her food or she'd be late meeting Karen.

From that point lunch became enjoyable as she and Charlie became caught up in the Yankees-Red Sox game and the excitement that the long-running rivalry always delivered. By the end of the first inning, Grace and Charlie had become friends and she agreed to return for another go-round sometime during the season.

Putting a five dollar bill on the bar, Grace said good bye to Charlie and wished his Yankees good luck. Looking around for Bill, he was nowhere to be found. Somehow that gave Grace the feeling of a moral victory—over what and whom she wasn't sure. She just knew that by coming to the Dew Drop and facing the man, she'd taken a stand for her Faith File and put him and any who stood with him on notice that she and her seniors were not going away.

Heading out of the restaurant, Grace used all of her self-control to ignore Mike, still sitting at his corner table. Despite all of protests, she really was glad he was keeping tabs on her. No matter how much courage she might have, twenty-four hour police protection was definitely a nice bonus when it came to dealing with people who thought killing a cat and writing with its blood was a good way to deal with a community issue.

Driving off to Karen's office, Grace turned up the radio and rolled down the windows. Perhaps it was going to be a good day after.

Chapter Forty-Two

KAREN PUT TOGETHER A list of 5 homes for the two women to inspect. Grace was excited over the prospect of so many potentials to consider, until the experienced realtor added a caveat.

"Truthfully, Grace, these are the best of the bad lot. I don't hold out a lot of hope that we're going to find anything today, but we have to start somewhere."

As it turned out, Karen's forecast was spot-on. The five options were faulty in varied ways from size, to price, to location. Driving back to the real estate office, Karen launched into her practiced realtor's pep talk.

"I know today was discouraging, Grace, but truthfully, it's going to take some time to find a property to suit your needs, in your price range. The other issue we need to consider is location. Midland zoning laws are strict. If we find something in an area zoned single family- residential, I don't know if the town will grant a variance, particularly after what happened after the town board meeting last Friday."

The reminder of the headless cat incident whipped Grace's mind to attention. She'd been so caught up touring the five houses that all thought of the incident had faded. Glancing in the passenger side rear view mirror, she saw no sign of Mike Healy's unmarked black sedan. Only a red pickup.

"I understand, Karen and I appreciate your time in getting started. Based on the houses we saw today, I'm going to talk with Jonathan to see if there is any way we can increase our purchase price. I'm also going to ask him to talk to the mayor for clarification on the zoning issue. Then, we've got to know where the townspeople stand. Their support is crucial and obviously is in doubt."

"I know we haven't discussed the cat thing, Grace, and we don't have to. I can only imagine how you must have felt that night, and how you probably still feel. The thing is, I've lived in Midland all my life—fifth generation. I've also sold houses to most people in this town. I know them. From everything I've heard about that town board meeting, what you're dealing with is no more than one or two random morons. And I'm willing to bet they are the same few who always rail against any kind of change in this town."

The strength of Karen's words broke through Grace's lingering fears, bringing her to the verge of tears.

Absolutely no crying. It won't help. I need Karen to think of me as in control. The Faith File needs to be represented by someone strong and capable.

"I guess what I'm trying to say is there are a lot of people in Midland who are absolutely fine with seniors from Wood Haven starting new lives here. I know it's hard, but you've got to set aside whatever nastiness this small minority is throwing at you and rely on the rest of us to support you and help make this group home a reality."

Karen's suggestion that the town would support Wood Haven's senior residence caught Grace off guard. That the community would rally around the Faith File was nowhere in her thoughts. In fact, Grace had already resigned herself to battling through every step of the process. Could Karen be right? Was it possible that the Midland community-at-large would support the establishment of this special home?

"Karen, I'm beyond thrilled to hear your take on the community's mindset. I have struggled since the special town board meeting wondering I would ever be able to accomplish my job. Hearing you say most people are not opposed to our group home is a relief. My question is, how do I reach those people to get them onboard and silence the nasty minority?"

"My best advice, Grace, is to keep doing what you're doing. Focus on your seniors. Make sure they are ready to make the move into an entirely different living situation. Then, let the people of Midland do the rest. I have a hunch this community will find their own way of taking care of any potential nastiness that may try to rise up again.

As Karen guided her car into the office parking lot, Grace felt revitalized. Rather than allowing fear to overshadow her work, she was going to follow the realtor's advice and keep moving all aspects of her Faith File project forward. Come hell or high water she would meet the timeline of moving her six seniors into a new home by Christmas.

A check of her watch made Grace's next decision easy. She was going straight home. The afternoon had long passed and she was tired and hungry.

Sharing a quick good bye and a pledge to stay in touch with Karen, Grace set off.

Driving through the center of Midland, the thought of Mike suddenly popped into her head. Scanning her rear view mirror there was still no sign of the black sedan. But that red pickup was not far behind. Suddenly, Grace was uncomfortable.

It's probably not the smartest thing to lead whoever that is to my house. Since it's a truck, maybe I can lose it by speeding up.

Grace hit the accelerator and detoured away from her house, heading toward the northern outskirts of Midland. Whenever she approached an intersection, she turned, trying her best not to slow down in the process. But none of her drive exploits mattered. The damn red truck stayed right with her.

Ahead, Grace saw an entrance to the Interstate ahead with signs for New York City.

How much better could it get than to be caught up in traffic headed for Manhattan?

With a quick turn Grace was caught up, weaving in and out of highway traffic. Continuing to check her rearview mirror, she finally saw no sign of the red pickup. Miles down the road, Grace felt confident that she was finally safe. Taking the next exit, she stopped at a gas station for directions back to Midland.

An hour later, as she pulled up to her house, Grace was stunned to see a red truck parked out in front. The very red truck she'd spent the last ninety minutes trying to loose. Deciding it might be wise to head to the police station, Grace went to punch her car's accelerator when a man jumped out of the truck's driver's side door.

Mike?

Grace hit the brakes and swerved to avoid hitting the Midland Police Officer dead-on. Before she could put the car in park, Mike was at her driver's door.

"What in the world are you doing driving like that?"

Rolling down the car window, Grace did her best to stay calm.

"I don't know why *you're* upset Mike, but if you'll let me pull into my driveway and get out of the car, perhaps we can discuss whatever this is calmly, like mature adults."

Stepping aside Mike stormed toward the house, giving Grace room to guide her car off the street. With her blood pressure rising, she knew it was going to be a toss-up, which one of them would be more unreasonable. As it turned out, Mike took the hot-head honors.

"Would you mind telling me exactly what you were doing back there, driving like some kind of maniac?"

"Would you mind telling me about this red truck? Was that you following me all that time?"

"Yes, it was me. Who else would it be?"

"Well, considering for the last week you've been driving a dark sedan, I had no idea who might be following me around in a truck."

As Grace spoke, the adrenaline that had fueled her body's aggressive driving skills reignited into raw emotion. Bursting into tears, she turned away and headed into the house, slamming the door soundly behind her.

Moving through the living room into the kitchen, Grace grabbed a large glass and a bottle of red wine sitting handily nearby. Pouring a generous amount into the glass, Grace took a healthy swig. Closing her eyes, the wine flowed through her body in warming fashion.

Enough. I've just had enough.

A strong knock at the door invaded her thoughts.

"Grace, open the door. We need to talk."

Grace's heart was determined to remain as closed to the man as her front door. Yet she knew this misunderstanding between them was equally shared. She could have been less accusatory, calmer. Then again, the pace of her life these days kept her pretty wound up.

Another strong knock let Grace know Mike was not going to give up easily. All things considered, opening the door might be the wisest move.

"Mike, I'm not up for arguing or anger. If you are capable of leaving both outside, you can come in."

Without waiting for a reply, Grace moved to the kitchen and retrieved another wine glass. Turning around, she found lawman standing steps away. Extending the glass, she nodded to the wine bottle on the kitchen shelf.

"Help yourself."

"Look Grace, I know I was a jackass out there just now and I apologize. But for the love of god, what were you doing driving like that?"

Standing completely still with his eyes drilling into hers Grace could feel Mike Healy's passion. What she couldn't understand was his apparent inability to comprehend his role in her driving escapade.

"It's simple, Mike. For the last week you have been driving around town, following me in a non-descript, black car. This afternoon that car, and presumably you, dropped out of sight, and a red pickup suddenly appeared. I had no idea who the truck belonged to, or who was behind the wheel. I just knew in the last week, my safety had been seriously threatened and I was not about to let whoever was in that truck follow me home."

Grace's words had a profound impact on Mike as his facial expressions morphed from angry to frustrated, to humbly-enlightened. The reality of changing vehicles without informing Grace became clear.

A wall of silence blocked off communication between them. Grace took another healthy sip of her wine while Mike desperately searched for some sort of intelligent reply. The pause gave Grace reason to assume that nothing worthwhile was going to come from engaging in further conversation. And truthfully at this point, she was too tired to care.

Rising and walking into the kitchen, Grace drained her wine glass and rinsed out the dregs with cold tap water. Setting the glass in the sink, she began making her way upstairs to her bedroom.

"I'm tired, Mike. Beyond tired. You can let yourself out. Please make sure you turn the lock on the door handle as you leave."

Stunned, the policeman watched his special assignment walk up the stairway and out of his sight. Grace's forceful closing of her bedroom door set loose a torrent of thoughts in his mind, all of them ready to stream from his mouth. The problem was, without Grace, there was no one to hear them.

What quickly became clear to Mike was that this misunderstanding was mostly a lack of consideration on his part. He switched vehicles without telling Grace. It was that simple. However, in his defense, it had all happened so quickly.

While following her from the Dew Drop, Mike realized his car was dangerously low on gas. Rather than take time to fill the 25-gallon tank he decided to stop at the police station, which was on the way to Karen's real estate office. There he could quick-swap out the car for his truck and catch up with Grace before she and Karen got started on their house hunting. He was so focused on not failing in his assignment that he failed to think of anything other than keeping Grace in his sights.

The question now was, what was he going to do about it?

Clearly Grace was in no mood to listen or discuss anything with him. She'd as much as thrown him out of the house, in her own classy way. At the same time, leaving felt like giving up too easily. If he didn't make more of an effort, would Grace interpret that as a lack of interest or care?

So are you admitting you're interested in her? That you care?

That thought sent Mike's mind into a whole new tailspin as he struggled to sort out his professional dedication from his personal feelings. Minutes later, while still debating he came to one clear conclusion. He might not be completely clear about his feelings for Grace versus his professional responsibilities for her safety, but he wasn't walking away from this situation without giving every part of his being to making it right.

Striding to the front door, Mike turned the lock on the handle and slid the deadbolt as well. Touring the kitchen, he turned off all the lights and moved into the living room. Grabbing the oversized blanket Grace kept draped over the couch, Mike turned off the nearby floor lamp, wrapped himself in the soft woolen coverlet and lowered himself onto the cushions. It was a sleep setting he'd become familiar with over the previous weekend.

Grace might not be happy to see him in the morning, but he was going to be sure she knew he cared enough to be there and try to explain. That's if he didn't scare her to death when she came out of her bedroom.

Chapter Forty-Three

RESTLESS.

That was the word streaming through Grace's mind as she awoke. Actually, she wasn't sure she'd really slept. The less-than-successful house hunt with Karen played on her mind throughout the night. Then there was the big glass of wine she'd gulped down when she finally got home, coupled with the fact that she went to bed hungry. Topping it all off was the ridiculous encounter with Mike Healy. No wonder she felt like she'd been hit by a truck.

Arrrgggghhhhh. The damn truck. That's what started the whole thing.

Refusing to spend any more time angsting about Mike and his truck, Grace peeled herself out of bed and headed for the kitchen. While she didn't drink coffee often, today was one of those days she definitely needed to get a pot brewing. The funny thing was, she could swear the scent of fresh coffee was already drifting through the house.

As she neared the stairway, Grace noticed light beaming up from the first floor.

I gave Mike explicit instructions to lock up. Apparently he didn't think that included turning off the lights.

Then she heard a voice calling out.

"Good Morning, Grace. Don't be startled. I'm here in the kitchen."

The enticing coffee scent coupled with Mike Healy's familiar voice twisted Grace's already foggy brain. Was she awake, or was she hallucinating smells and sounds? The sight of the Midland cop at the bottom of the stairs only served to ramp up her confusion.

"What you are doing here, Mike?" The words shot out of her mouth like rivets.

"That's a good question. How about I pour us a couple cups of coffee and we sit down and talk?"

Coming down the stairs Grace could feel her Irish temper toughening her mindset.

"I don't drink coffee. I drink tea."

"Okay, tea it is."

Grace sat down at the kitchen table and took some deep, calming breaths.

Nope. That didn't help. You're going to need something stronger than breathing techniques to avoid taking this guy's head off

Mike set a mug of tea before her and Grace hung her head over the rising steam, inhaling deeply. This time the combination of the brewed elixir within her breath tamped her temper down. She was able to raise her eyes toward the man without shooting daggers.

"So, you're wondering why I'm here. The truth is, I never left last night. It felt wrong the way our conversation ended, actually the way the whole afternoon and evening went. When you basically told me to get out last night, my stomach twisted and I was worried if we didn't straighten out this misunderstanding it could do some serious damage to our friendship. Now, I don't know about you, Grace, but I don't want that. In fact, I'd like just the opposite, but you were clear you had no intention of talking to me last night. So, the only thing I could figure was to camp here on your couch until you got some sleep and hope that you'd be willing to let me try and explain my way back in to your good graces this morning. And here we are."

Two good swallows of tea and Grace still couldn't manage intelligent conversation. The other thing she couldn't manage was her anger. She had clearly told Mike to leave and yet he disregarded what she wanted and did exactly as he pleased, *in her home.*

Regardless of his professional assignment as her bodyguard or protector, or whatever the hell he was, he had no right to ignore her wishes in her own house. With her temper at a boiling over point, Grace knew she needed time and space to get a grip on her emotions.

"Let me get a shower and get dressed for the day. Then we can talk before I leave for work. That's the best I can do right now."

Mike nodded and Grace took her tea upstairs to the bathroom, praying for patience and a dose of compassion. Twenty minutes later she was back in the kitchen feeling as if she had managed to reset into a reasonably considerate human being. Not wanting her temper to stoke again, she began.

"I have no idea what happened yesterday, Mike, other than I took action in my best interest and safety and you didn't like it. There may be more to the story from your perspective, but for me that's it in a nutshell. And at the end of the day, even if you are supposed to be protecting me, you have no rights over me, or ownership of me. And you certainly have no rights when it comes to what goes on in my home.

"Fair enough Grace. I appreciate you sharing your view. For what it's worth, now I'd like to share mine."

With precise language, Mike detailed his switch of vehicles and the confusion that resulted. With a softened tone he concluded.

"When I lost you on the interstate I had no idea what to do, how to find you. So, I came back here, hoping you'd eventually return. When I finally saw your car coming down the street, I couldn't help myself. The hours of worry and waiting had built up inside me and pretty much exploded as soon as I jumped out of my truck. The next thing I knew I was ranting and raving and pretty much everything went downhill from there."

Grace had no desire to continue on this conversation. At the same time she was drawn to this man who cared so passionately about others—about her. What was it he said earlier? Something about not wanting to damage their friendship? Like it or not, she knew she felt the same way.

"It's my turn to thank you, Mike, for telling me your side of the story. While it doesn't erase the bad feelings created by your overreaction, it does allow me to understand how it happened. Truthfully, I am grateful to have you on my side of this nightmare situation. I know you're protecting me and doing all you can to ensure my safety."

Grace could see the effect of her words as she observed Mike's body visibly relax. Taking a breath, she did the same. Walking over to the tea pot she poured a hot refill and took a deep sip. The caffeine was restoring her to the land of the living and she was grateful for the energy boost. Glancing at the clock on the kitchen stove, she knew it was time to go if she was going to get a jump start on her day.

Not only did she have work to do regarding the purchase of a house for her Faith File, she needed to follow up with the mayor on last night's town board executive committee meeting regarding tax exemptions for the house. Then there were those suitcases in the Wood Haven attic that she really wanted to dig through and return to their rightful owners. Grace could only imagine the emotional impact of all of those moments.

"Grace? You ok?"

"Yes, sorry. I was thinking about my list of must-dos for the day. I really have to get going."

The look on the policeman's face reminded Grace of the bassett hound her nana and papa owned when she was a child. Floppy was his name, because of his long ears, and Grace loved that dog as if he was her own. The two wandered her grandparent's farm together as the best of friends and Grace was heartbroken when Floppy "crossed the rainbow bridge" as her nana explained his passing.

"Mike, please don't look at me like that. Look, let's just chalk up yesterday to an unfortunate series of circumstances following a very disturbing incident. Truthfully, I think we're doing pretty good considering all that's gone on in the last five days."

A smile radiated across the man's face and settled deeply into his eyes. It was a look Grace had seen pass between her nana and papa many times and had come to know as love. Unexpectedly, it brought warmth to her heart.

Love? Is Mike Healy falling in love with me? Am I falling in love with him?

The suggestive moment caused Grace to grab her briefcase and head towards the door. With space between them, she would be better able to manage her emotions.

"I know you'll be following me. What vehicle should I expect—or are you going to surprise me again?"

The devilish tone to her question led the two to share another smile, this one pretty much smoothing over the previous day's turmoil.

"I was thinking about a stretch limo."

Shared laughter ensued as the couple prepared to walk out the door, just as the telephone rang. Grace was tempted to ignore whoever it was, but the look on Mike's face reminded her that the call could be important. Setting down her briefcase, she headed to the phone, dreading what might await.

"Hello."

"Good morning, Grace. It's Chief Reynolds."

Grace recognized the man's distinctive gravelly voice as soon as he began to speak."

"Good morning, chief. I'm assuming you're calling with some news or update on my case?"

Hearing her words, Mike drew closer, making sure Grace could felt his support.

"I was hoping you could come down to the station. We have Jack Beatty here and I'd like you to be present when we question him."

Images of narrow, windowless rooms and bright overhead spotlights sprang into Grace's mind. While the setting sent chills through her body, in her mind she wanted to be there to find out if this was the guy responsible for terrorizing her.

"I can do that, Chief. What time do you want me there?"

"Is Healy there with you?"

"Yes, he is. We were just leaving as I have to get to Wood Haven."

"Ok. Have him explain to you how it works when you observe a suspect being questioned. Then I'll expect to see you both at the station in 15 minutes. It won't take long. I'm sure Jonathan will be fine with you being a few minutes late in order to cooperate on this case."

With that, the chief hung up, leaving Grace holding a silent phone receiver against her ear.

"What did he say, Grace?"

"I'm supposed to ask you how it works when a suspect is being questioned and then he ordered us to be at the station in 15 minutes. He's holding Jack Beatty for questioning."

STANDING BEHIND THE ONE-WAY GLASS, Grace felt the anxiety in the interrogation room through the oversized window pane.

"I'm going to get a cup of coffee. Do you want anything?"

Mike's words short circuited her thoughts.

"No. Thanks."

"Ok. I'll be right back. You'll be fine here. No one else will come in."

Despite his assurances, Grace moved into a far corner of the room where she had full view of both the door and the imposing one-way window. That way she could monitor everything going on.

Don't be ridiculous. You're in a police station for goodness sake. How much more protected could you be?

Breathing deeply to settle her nerves helped until voices from the interrogation room suddenly blasted through a hidden intercom above her head. Then the door of the viewing room blew open.

"Hey Grace, what's wrong? You feeling ok? You're pasty-white pale."

Grace knew she was bordering on a full-out fainting spell. It was something that started when she was a teenager. The doctor said it was related to the hormonal changes raging through her body, and once they settled down she'd be fine. For the most part he was right, but there were still moments when intense emotions could cause her body to flare and lose consciousness. The good news was that Grace was aware of the signals that telegraphed an impending faint and could usually short circuit the causes and prevent the ultimate effect.

"I'm ok. Not great. I just need to breathe and stay quiet."

Concerned, Mike brought over a chair and wrapped his arms around Grace as he lowered her onto the seat. Standing behind her, he gently massaged her neck and shoulders as she purposefully inhaled and exhaled. Slowly the stars floating before her eyes disappeared and the perspiration that had drenched her body cooled into a clammy shroud.

Feeling a shiver run through her, Mike removed his jacket and placed it around her shoulders. Silently, she thanked him, knowing any movement could tip her body into unconsciousness.

"Ok, Mr. Beatty. Where were you on the night of Friday, October 13th?"

Chief Reynolds sat across a worn wooden table from a man of slight build and thinning hair .

"Like I told you, I was home."

"Was anyone with you?"

"No. I live alone. My son stopped by earlier in the day and we ate supper together, but then he left."

"So there is no one who can corroborate that you were in your home that Friday?"

"No."

"Mr. Beatty, what do you do for a living?"

"I'm a janitor at Midland High School."

"How long have you worked there?"

"Going on twelve years."

"What do you do in your spare time?"

"What do you mean?"

"You know, hobbies, things you like to do for fun."

"I'm interested in science. I do experiments in my basement sometimes."

"What kind of experiments?"

"I dunno know. Mixing up minerals and liquids. Using rotted garbage and recycled stuff to make energy, like for flashlights. Stuff I read about in science magazines.

"Do you like animals, Mr. Beatty."

"Yeah, I guess you could say that."

"Ever own any pets?"

"Dogs when I was a kid. Nothing since."

"No cats?"

"Nah, hate cats."

"Mr. Beatty, have you heard about the senior citizen group home that may be coming to Midland?"

"Yeah, I've got a friend works at Wood Haven and he's talked about it."

"What do you think about it? Do you think it's a good thing?"

"Don't know. Don't care."

"Mr. Beatty, did you happen to hear about an incident outside town hall last Friday involving a cat?"

"Can't say as I have. I don't get into town gossip much. Pretty much do my job and go home."

"You're saying you didn't hear anything about it at school? "

"Actually, I've been out sick the last two days. Today is supposed to be my first day back and I'm late because of being here. Can I go now?"

"Not yet. I have a few more questions. Do you know a woman by the name of Grace Reid?"

"Never heard of her."

"She works at Wood Haven. She's new in town."

"Nope. Don't know her."

"Do you ever have reason to go to Wood Haven?"

"Not really. Sometimes I give my friend a ride home. His wife is a nurse there and their schedules aren't always the same. Every once in a while he'll ask if I can pick him up and drive him home."

"Have you done that favor lately?"

"Now that you mention it, I did a week or so ago."

"Tell me about it."

"Nothin' to tell. I pulled into the parking lot like always. I was early so I got out of my car and smoked a cigarette. Walked around a little. My friend came out with some of the other guys who work at Wood Haven. We all went to high school together. We hung out and shot the shit for a while. Decided to go the Dew Drop and have a couple beers. That was it."

"While you were in the Wood Haven parking lot, did you touch or get close to any of the cars there?"

"Whaddya mean?"

"Just what I said. Did you touch any of the cars there, other than your own?"

"What's this all about? You know you can't just keep me here asking me questions. I know my rights."

It was about this time that Grace began to feel woozy again, feeling the rising tension from the interrogation room permeating the one-way glass. Keeping a firm hold on her shoulders, Mike kept her body solid.

"You're right, Mr. Beatty, I can't keep you here, but if you refuse to answer my last few questions, it's going to make you look bad. And trust me, you don't want to look bad. Now, one more time, did you touch any car that was not your own when you were in the Wood Haven parking lot last week?"

The scowl across the reed-thin man's face suggested an impenetrable wall between the two men. At the same time, Sheriff Reynolds puffed out his barrel-shaped chest with a deep breath and slowly exhaled directly into Jack Beatty's face, casting an intimidating eye as he did.

For a moment, no one moved, nothing changed. It appeared to Grace like a Mexican standoff, from one of those spaghetti western movies that were so popular. Finally, after a few moments, Jack Beatty cracked under Sheriff Reynold's practiced intimidation.

"Ok, maybe I did touch a car, but I didn't do any damage or anything. So sue me."

"What kind of a car?"

"One of them fancy European jobs. I'd never been around one up close before and I just wanted to see it. I didn't open a door or anything, just leaned around and peeked in the windows, that kinda thing."

Blowing out another round of air, Sheriff Reynolds stood up and shoved his chair back under the table.

"You're free to go, Mr. Beatty. If your boss gives you any trouble about being late, have him call me. I'll let him know that you were cooperating on a police investigation."

The bony man wasted no time in escaping from the interrogation room, slamming the door behind him. At the same time Mike Healy opened the door from the viewing room, leading Grace into the adjoining space.

"So that clears up that mystery," the sheriff spoke in frustration. Since Miss Reid here has the only foreign car in Wood Haven's staff parking lot, the guy's prints are legit.

"So back we go to Friday night to try and find someone, anyone, who may have seen something," Mike responded.

Both men turned toward Grace and from the lack of color in her cheeks, realized it would be a good idea to get her out in the fresh air.

"I'll make sure Grace gets to Wood Haven. Then I'll come back to the station and we can make a plan."

"Sounds good, Healy." He nodded at Grace, "Miss Reid."

With a pivot, Sheriff Reynolds exited the room, leaving Grace and Mike behind.

"Well I can't say I enjoyed being here, but I guess it's good that we found out Mr. Beatty was not involved. One less suspect."

"In some ways it's good, Grace. In others it's tough. We really have no solid leads in this case and so far no one has stepped forward to tell us they saw something that night. That's the frustrating part. That parking lot is a busy place where people walk all the time. I find it hard to believe not one person in this town saw someone putting a dead cat on the roof of your car and writing on your windshield with its blood."

The hardened cop's graphic description of the incident ramped up Grace's woozy feelings. Seeing her sway, Mike grabbed her around the waist and whooshed her out of the station into the sunlight and fresh air. Doing her best to stay steady Grace's mantra from the previous day ran through her mind.

Enough. I've just had enough.

CHAPTER FORTY-FOUR

GRACE BOUNCED BACK FROM THE rough start to her day. While it took some effort to drive from the police station to Wood Haven, she knew Mike was following and would be right with her if she faltered. Then when she got settled in her office, Teagan stopped by for a chat. Conversation flowed easily between the two women and Grace was invigorated by their exchange.

"So's missus, how's the search comin' fer that new place fer us ta live?"

"Well, I was out yesterday and saw a few homes, but none I thought really suited you lovely ladies."

"Aw, go on with ya now. That's a bit o'blarney. Can only imagine tryin' ta find someplace where's we can all fit. On top o'that, makin' sure the folks living 'round be likin' us."

Grace was surprised to hear the sheltered woman mention a concern about neighbors. The comment was out of character, so much so that Grace concluded Teagan had probably overheard gossip in Wood Haven's hallways.

"Now Teagan, what would ever possess you to say something like that about your future neighbors? Of course they are going to like all of you. Why wouldn't they?"

"Listen here, Gracie, I may be old, but I'm no fool. I hear what the nurses are sayin' 'bout them people in town not wantin' us. I heard too 'bout the dead cat on your car. So's don't be wastin' time tellin' me any different."

Grace was disturbed by Teagan's awareness of the senior housing controversy. She was equally concerned over who else among the Faith File might have heard the same stories.

"Alright, Teagan. I'm not going to shield you from the truth. There are a few people in Midland who don't want their community to change, in any way. However, that is not just about you and the other women moving into town. It's about any way in which Midland might change from exactly as it's been for the last 200 years. Can you understand that?"

"Course I can, missus, but t'is no matter. Right now, we'd be the change they're not wantin'and t'is not a good thing."

Grace couldn't argue with the woman's logic. She was right. While resentment against a home for seniors seemed to be the mindset of a few, if the flames of their discontent were not doused, the fire could rage and make Midland relocation an impossibility.

"Teagan, do any of the other women know about this?"

"Not ta me knowin'. Been keepin' it ta meself, not wantin' ta discourage the rest, don'cha know."

"Good. That's perfect. Let's keep it that way, alright? You and I will work through this and find a way to overcome those few Midland naysayers and the rest of the ladies won't have to know anything about it."

"I'm with ya, Gracie, but gotta be on me way right now. 'Tis time fer me visit with Nurse Bennett and I'm not wantin' ta be late."

With that the plucky Irishwoman was gone, leaving Grace to wonder about Jane Bennett's condition. She needed to stop by and see her as well, but not today. Her afternoon was blocked out for Wood Haven's head nurse, Mary Burke.

Grace was looking forward to working through the attic full of suitcases Mary had described. As she explained, each one was filled with personal items belonging to people who'd been committed to Wood Haven over the years. Her estimate was that there were almost 400 suitcases stored among the dusty rafters. The two women agreed that their first priority was to try and locate the ones belonging to the ten seniors still within Wood Haven's walls.

As Grace considered the impact of restoring the suitcase possessions to each senior, her office phone rang.

"Good Morning. Grace Reid speaking."

"Hello Grace. I guess it is still morning, barely. This is Mayor Jenkins. I'm calling to update you on our committee meeting last night regarding the property tax exemption for your senior home."

In the turmoil of the morning, Grace had lost track of the all-important meeting. The tenor of the mayor's voice provided no advance clues.

"We discussed the factility at length last night, and, as I told you in our last phone conversation, I was determined to get this decided. When we finally voted, the count was 3 to 2, with me casting the tiebreaker."

"And which way did you vote, Mr. Mayor?"

"Oh right, it would help if I told you that, wouldn't it? The tax exemption passed. So if and when you find a home that suits your needs, you will have to appear again before the town board and submit the paperwork for the exemption, including blueprints and any proposals for renovations and needed variances."

"About variances, do you have a feel for what the town board might be willing to approve and what would be a hands down no? I'm just trying to keep this process simple by being aware of structural changes that might go against the town's building codes."

"I would suggest you get with our town engineer and building code officer, Mark Halperin. He's been doing the job for twenty years now and knows the code book inside and out. In fact, he helped the state write the code book, so he knows the rules and regs. If you consult with him as you work through this process, I would say that the town board will approve your requests."

"That's great, mayor. Thanks so much. I'll be in touch."

Grace's day was looking up. All she had to do was write a summary of her phone meeting with Mayor Jenkins and drop it off in Jonathan's office. Then she could be on her way to Nurse Burke and the suitcases.

FOLLOWING MARY BURKE UP WOOD HAVEN'S attic stairs, Grace found herself wondering about others who had climbed the same steps. Nurses and orderlies storing away belongings of people locked away in this asylum, in effect stripping them of their personal identities.

Grace found these thoughts heart breaking, and as the two women continued their climb, she made a silent promise to do everything within her power to discover and restore the belongings of her seniors.

"Watch the tread there, it's loose."

Mary Burke was a kind woman. Grace was grateful they were sharing this search through the private lives of so many displaced men and women. As they reached the attic door, Mary retrieved an old-fashioned skeleton key from her pocket and inserted it into the aged metal lock. With a click, the door swung open.

Grace stood in awe of the sight before her. It was a room like most attics, defined by exposed rafters and ceiling beams, unfinished walls and a rough wood floor. A single window at the end of the room provided a tunnel of daylight. What mesmerized Grace were the rows of crudely constructed racks with shelving, lining both sides of the cavernous space for the full length of the room. A wide walkway between the racks allowed for access to the shelves on both sides.

Mary stepped back and allowed Grace to more fully enter the room. Cautiously, she moved along the walkway to the first section of shelves. Stunned, she stood starring at haphazardly stacked suitcases of all shapes, sizes and materials, each one offering an unspoken suggestion of the person to whom they once belonged.

"How did this happen? Why were all these people's belongings thrown up here and left, as if none of it—or them—mattered?"

Mary moved supportively alongside Grace. In silence the two women stood in rembrance of those connected to the hundreds of suitcases before them.

"As emotional as it is to see all these suitcases, Grace, it's even more compelling when you start to open them and discover what people brought with them. Bits and pieces of their lives that held such meaning and were discarded into this attic as worthless."

Hearing Mary's words, Grace stepped over to the closest shelf and carefully pulled out a small brown valise bound with leather straps. Looking to Mary and receiving a nod of permission, Grace tugged at both fasteners until they gave way to the possessions they'd been protecting for so many years. Pulling apart the valise and laying it flat, a treasure trove of books came to light.

Grace was breathless as she fingered leather bound volumes of words written in French. The pages were yellowed and brittle with faded black script both front and back. On some, artistic drawings added beauty in the form of flowers and trees. On the front page of each book the same name appeared in an elegant handwriting. Emeline D'Chantre.

"These appear to be the diaries or journals of this woman. They're so beautiful, works of art really. She must have missed them when they were taken away."

"I'm sure most who lost their suitcases were heartbroken, Grace. Then there were those who were so mentally unstable they had no idea if they arrived with a suitcase or not. Today, there would be help for such patients. Back then, they were locked away or given medical treatments that made them worse, guaranteeing their lifetime in asylums like Wood Haven."

Taking in the full scope of the shelves before them, Grace's strategic mind kicked into gear.

"How do we go about finding the suitcases of our ten seniors? Do we have to go through everyone? And do you even know if they all have suitcases up here?"

"The good news is that we do know each one of our seniors downstairs has a suitcase somewhere here. There were records kept of the bags stored away in this attic. We came across that paperwork recently in one of the rooms on the fifth floor that has been locked up for years. The notes in the paperwork varies widely, I imagine based on who was entering the information when each person was committed."

"So where do we begin?"

"There are a group of volunteers who have started the process for us. They have been matching suitcases and bags to the paperwork and then sorting them into groups according to the years in which people were committed. They have also added name tags on the outside, when possible. However, they've only just begun so not many have names. I would suggest for today is we start by working through the suitcases already sorted into years, making notes of those groups as we complete them. If we find some of our seniors, great. If not, we can return in a few days and go through those that have been newly sorted."

The two women moved to the end of the attic where stacks of suitcases and bags were neatly organized behind placards ranging from 1869 to 1945. Lowering themselves onto the dusty plank floor, Mary set the list of the ten Wood Haven seniors between them. They divided up the names and the years in which to search, each woman being responsible for trying to find five of the ten suitcases. Sorting through the stacks, they eliminated any suitcase or bag with a name that was not one of their ten. From there they began working through the luggage by years.

The work was painstaking and emotional as Mary and Grace respectfully worked through the personal belongings of men and women who'd been forced and forgotten behind the impenetrable asylum walls. Sorting through faded photographs, tattered pieces of ribbon and lace, table settings of silverware, fine china cups, journals and jewelry, guns and knives, pots and pans, dolls and blankets, each individual came alive. Yet after three hours, the women had not discovered one suitcase belonging to their Wood Haven seniors.

"I don't know about you, Grace, but I'm getting pretty stiff sitting on this hard attic floor. Plus the light is fading. What do you say we call it a day?"

"I hate to give up without finding at least one suitcase, but I can't really feel my backside anymore and my one foot is asleep! What do you say we each do one more suitcase and then we call it good for today?"

Nodding in agreement, each woman pulled an item off one of the shelves. Mary chose an oversized, rectangular suitcase with an exterior of woven natural bamboo highlighted with dyed bamboo accent stripes. A Lucite handle of transparent ochre and brass latches completed the stylish piece of luggage.

Grace reached for a small bag hand sewn from swatches of cloth, each different in design and material. The bag was closed with a double drawstring of purple braided velvet that was finished off with fringed purple tassels.

A hobo bag. That's what nana called this kind of sack. She said the name came from the way hobos placed their possessions in an oversized piece of cloth, then tied the cloth with braided rope and onto a long pole to carry over their shoulders.

The memory of her nana's description made Grace wonder if the person who'd brought the bag to Wood Haven had actually been a hobo, or perhaps more accurately, someone without money and unable to care for themselves. Grace knew this was the standard in America following the economic crash of 1929.

Carefully, she worked to part the drawstring, battling against years of tightly-knotted closure. When at last she was able to pry apart the braided velvet, she steadily pulled open the mouth of the bag and turned it over to dislodge its contents. To her surprise, a cascade of marbles came tumbling out, rolling across the attic floor.

Laughing in delight, Mary and Grace scrambled to round up the errant marbles placing them into a nearby, empty cardboard box. Returning to the bag, Grace cautiously slid her hand inside, hoping more treasures might await.

Moving her fingers throughout the velvet, doing her best to feel every inch of the quilted fabric it was only as she reached the very bottom that Grace felt something. Giving out a small cry of excitement, she carefully latched on to the object and pulled it out, into the light.

"What did you find?"

"I'm not sure yet. It's a paper of some kind."

In her fingers Grace held a brightly colored blue paper. Turning it over, she could see it had been folded in thirds to form a note card, with a bright white cross striping the area where the folds met. Pulling the card open Grace discovered a handwritten verse in a language unfamiliar to her.

Αυτά τα μάρμαρα δίνονται στον Δημήτρη Κρίστο *Ardonis* από τον παππού του Δημήτρη Μαξιμούμ *Ardonis* με την ευκαιρία της ονομασίας του. 26 Οκτωβρίου 1913. Looking over Grace's shoulder, Mary immediately defined the writing.

"I can't tell you what it means, but I can tell you it's written in the Greek language."

The woman's analysis of the words sparked a thought in Grace's mind. Slowly reviewing the script again, she found exactly what she hoped.

"You are brilliant, Mary! This *is* Greek and I know who the bag and marbles belong to. Look closely. In the middle of the first line and at beginning the second line, what do you see?"

"Ardonis?"

"Exactly."

Turning to Mary, Grace could see the realization flood her mind as they both shouted.

"James!"

Chapter Forty-Five

THE DOG DAYS OF SUMMER ROLLED into autumn with trees throughout Midland transforming into gorgeous hues of red, orange and gold. Fall was Grace's favorite time of year. She looked forward to September's kickoff to the season, shedding summer's humidity for crisp, sun-filled days and cool blanket nights. The blend was perfect.

On the downside, the advancing calendar also meant time for finding a Faith File House was running short.

Karen had been holding up her end of the bargain, touring Grace through at least five houses a week through August. The main stumbling blocks were the number of special requirements for the group home combined with the budget they could afford. Grace and Jonathan brainstormed regularly about ways to lower their costs and increase the state monies to help them purchase a home. In the end the best they'd been able to manage was a $5,000 swing. Helpful, but still not quite enough.

While the ticking clock ramped up Grace's stress level, she was also still dealing with the unsolved dead-cat-on-her-car issue. The only progress on that front had been Chief Reynolds' agreement to call off her round-the-clock police guard.

Grace was relieved not to have a shadow all the time, though Mike was less than thrilled that she was now on her own. After one particularly intense night of debate on the topic, the couple came to a compromise. They agreed Grace would put together a weekly calendar of her meetings and events so Mike knew where she was and could find her at any time. Since then, the two had been doing their best to revert from police officer and crime victim to a dating couple getting to know each other better. Making the transition definitely had its challenges.

The bright spot for Grace these days was the Faith File. She tried to get up to the third floor at least three times a week. She loved checking in on her ladies and encouraging positive conversation about their upcoming move. As promised, Teagan had not shared a word about the townspeople opposing the Wood Haven relocation and for that Grace was grateful. She didn't need that problem added to the mix right now.

Grace also spent time at the other end of Wood Haven's third floor, with the seniors slated to move to St. Augustine's. While their relocation offered few challenges, James, Maria, Janna and Regina still needed assurances that their new home would be a safe and comforting place in which to live.

When she discovered James's hobo bag of marbles in Wood Haven's attic, Grace excitedly wanted to immediately present them to the sweet man. Thankfully Mary prevailed with calmer thoughts.

"Hang on a minute, Grace. Let's play this out. If you go to James and return this bag he brought with him, but don't have the same to return to the other nine seniors, that could be terribly disappointing to them. It could even put them into a mental tailspin, depending on what they remember of their suitcases and what was in them. I know finding this bag with the marbles and the note is exciting and hopefully it will thrill James as well. All I'm suggesting is that we let the volunteers keep sorting and we keep searching at least for a few more weeks. With any luck, we will find the suitcases and bags of all ten seniors and send them all off to their new lives with a good start."

Grace knew in her gut Mary was right. Following the head nurse's direction, Grace cleared a space at one end of the attic shelving and tacked a paper sign to the edge reading, *Property of Wood Haven Seniors. DO NOT TOUCH by order of Wood Haven Director of Nursing, Mary Burke and Wood Haven Director of Senior Services, Grace Reid.* On the shelf behind the sign, Grace placed James's bag of marbles, offering a silent prayer for their protection as she did.

Grace had not been able to return to the attic since that initial day with Mary. Between keeping up with house hunting appointments, attending Wood Haven meetings and carving out time with her seniors, there weren't enough hours in her day. Realistically, she was going to have to come in on weekends to continue the suitcase treasure hunt. She also knew if those nine suitcases were in that attic, she was going to make sure they were found.

Pulling out her calendar, Grace added an attic search on every Saturday in September, knowing she'd extend it into October, if need be. Maybe she could convince Mike to help her. They were together most weekends anyway and when she told him about finding James's marbles, he became fascinated with the suitcase story. She'd mention it to him at dinner on Friday.

Looking at the clock, Grace realized she'd worked through lunch again. By now the cafeteria was closed and thoughts of a vending machine snack did nothing to soothe her growling stomach. The question was could she tough it out until dinner time, or should she take a run to Midland for a quick sandwich? As she was about to flip a coin, the phone rang.

"Good afternoon. Grace Reid speaking."

"Grace! So glad I caught you."

The excitement in Karen's voice stirred an enthusiasm in Grace.

"Hi, Karen. You sound chipper today. What's going on?"

"I am chipper. I think I may have found you a house. A friend of mine just called to tell me about it before it's officially listed. It's got some drawbacks, but nothing that can't be managed and it's close enough to your price range that I think we'll be able to swing a deal. The only catch is that we need to see it right away, before anyone finds out about it and makes an offer."

"I'll be at your office in twenty minutes."

"Actually, Grace, this house is located between Wood Haven and my office, so why don't we just meet there to save time. The address is 633 Brookside Lane. Take the main highway from Wood Haven heading towards Midland. Drive past the Welcome to Midland Sign and as you come into town you will see South Grove on your right. Turn there and the first street on your left will be Brookside. The house is at the end of the road, last one on the right. I'll meet you there in ten minutes."

Guess I'll be having that vending machine lunch after all.

Grabbing her purse and car keys, Grace flew down the stairs to the main floor where she exited directly across from one of the vending machines sprinkled throughout the building. Rummaging through her change purse, she decided to splurge on a bag of chips and a Three Musketeers Candy Bar. Shoving them both in her briefcase, Grace gave a wave to Pete at the security desk and zipped out to her car.

Karen's directions proved to be pinpoint. Grace pulled up in front of 633 in eight minutes. Tearing into the bag of chips, she launched a visual inspection of the house from her driver's seat.

Good sized. Looks older. One floor, which is crucial. Neighbors only on one side. Nice open area on the other side. Looks like room to expand there and maybe into the backyard as well? Lots of trees. Porch looks a little saggy. Roof might be iffy. Needs a coat of paint. Lots of nice windows, although I don't see screens or storms.

Crumbling up the empty potato chip bag, Grace was just about to dig in to her Three Musketeers when Karen pulled up behind her. She exited her car to meet the realtor, brushing chip crumbs from her dress.

"Hey, Grace. Have any trouble finding the place?"

"None at all, Karen, your directions were excellent. And you're right, it would have been foolish for me to drive all the way to your office just to turn around and come back here."

"No problem. It's tough when you're not that familiar with the area. Now before we start, remember this house has some drawbacks, but I think overall it's the closest we've come to something that can work. Would you like to start outside, or in?"

"Well I've had a few minutes to do a quick visual of the outside and I'm encouraged. So, let's go inside and see how it looks."

As Grace noted from her road side view, the porch leading to the front door was in need of repair, possibly replacement. Grace's second thought was that removing it might be the best solution. Stepping inside, Grace was stunned to find that every wall and all the ceilings had been peeled down to the studs. Seeing the shock on her client's face, Karen began talking as fast as her words would form.

"OK Grace, hear me out before you say anything. Yes, this house is in need of a lot of work. Every room—the living room, dining room, kitchen, family room, all the bedrooms and baths are just like this. But the beauty of this house is that you can easily make renovations and pretty much create the floor plan you want. That's a huge cost savings."

Gauging that her words were having a positive effect, Karen continued.

"The other thing you're going to see as we walk through this house is that there is room to expand. Since there is already a good-sized basement underneath the existing house, if you add an addition you won't need to dig for a full foundation and pour concrete to create more basement space. You can just build the new section on concrete blocks, with a crawl space for air circulation. And that will lower your expansion costs substantially.

Karen could see the wheels turning in Grace's brain, so she kept going.

"The property itself backs up to a federally protected wildlife preserve, so there won't be any new construction going on. You won't have any additional neighbors other than those already on the one side of the house and across the street. It's basically a semiprivate lot with a wildlife preserve as your backyard."

At this point, Karen had one card left to play and it was an ace.

"Last but not least, the owners are selling because the rehab job they started has become too much for them and they can't afford to hire someone to finish the job. They just want out. So, they've priced the house to sell and are willing to entertain offers in order to make a quick deal."

Finally, Grace spoke.

"What are they asking?"

With an appropriate pause to raise the drama of the moment, Karen smiled as she spoke.

"$35,000."

"Sold."

"Wait, Grace. You can't say sold. You haven't seen all of the house yet. There are some issues we need to discuss, like the roof and the porch and the windows. Those are all big ticket items you need to take in to account."

"Ok. Let's finish the walk through and take all the big ticket items into consideration. Then we'll offer $30,000 and make the deal.

Karen was slightly stunned by Grace's matter-of-fact assessment, but a quick calculation led the experienced realtor to think the lowball offer might have a chance. For the next half hour, realtor and client went through the house and around the property, listing every potential problem and worst case scenario. True to her word, when all was said and done, Grace authorized Karen to submit a $30,000 offer on behalf of Wood Haven, tagging a 24 hour time limit on the deal.

Grace returned to Wood Haven concerned over how Jonathan was going to react to her news. At the same time, after more than six weeks of searching, she knew the challenges of finding a suitable property in Wood Haven's budget. The house on Woodside was a solid fit in both categories.

Making her way to the executive director's office, Grace paused outside his door for a quick prayer and a deep breath.

Nana, I remember how papa always teased you about your retail therapy habit but I have fond memories of special times that we shared shopping. I know you are always with me, listening and helping. If you could guide me through buying this house for my special seniors, I would be so grateful.

With a sense of calm settling into her bones, Grace entered Jonathan's office, bypassing the unoccupied secretary's desk and knocking directly on his door.

"Come in."

"Hi Jonathan. Got a minute?"

"For you, always."

Grace appreciated the director's kind response as it strengthened her courage in sharing news of her purchase offer.

"I have something exciting to tell you. I've found a house for the Faith File that is going to be perfect."

"That is exciting, Grace. Where is it located?

"On Brookside Lane, right in the town. It's on a piece of property with a wildlife preserve that starts on one side and wraps around back of the yard, so it should be a protected space for years to come."

"And what about the house itself? Does it meet our list of specifications for a group home?"

"Well that's the thing, Jonathan. The current owners bought it to renovate, but as they got into the project they decided it was too much to manage. So, all the walls and ceilings are down to the studs. We can pretty much make the existing space into any configuration we want. Additionally, there is space on the lot to expand the house into the bedrooms we'll need, but we won't have to dig a full foundation since there is already a basement under the existing house."

"And the mechanicals?"

"The furnace and hot water heater are fairly new, but we'll probably have to add another hot water heater to manage the demands of seven people. No question the roof and porch are going to have to be replaced and the windows needs storms and screens."

"Those are all big ticket items. I can't imagine being able to afford the buying price and then adding on five thousand dollars for those items in addition to renovation and construction costs. You know as well as I do, the top limit of our budget is $55,000.

"Normally I would agree with you, but that's the beauty of this house.

Because the owners want out, they have priced it $35,000. After a walk-through inspection with Karen, I took into account the major repairs needed and figured that $30,000 would be a strong offer. We've already been promised that money from the state and should have pretty immediate access to those funds. And from what Karen said, it sounds like it could work, as the owners are interested in a quick deal."

"I do trust Karen. She's been in this business a long time and knows the market. If you think this house will work for us and if Karen thinks $30,000 is a good faith offer, then shall I sign the paperwork?"

"Well, here's the thing. Karen called me about this house before it was officially listed. She's pretty definite it will sell quickly and, if not, a bidding war will probably happen once people see it."

"All the more reason to get an offer signed then."

"Glad you think so because Karen drew up the contract right on the spot and I signed it. As far as I know, it's been submitted with a 24-hour time limit to accept."

A jolt passed across her boss' face causing Grace to hold her breath in anticipation of his angry response.

"I'm a little surprised you would take such action without consulting me first, Grace. At the same time, we have talked through this project ad nauseum and I know you're adept at your job. I'm just going to have to trust that you've made the right decision."

The adrenaline coursing through her body pushed a stream of words from her mouth.

"Thank you, Jonathan, for your confidence in my decision. You're right, we have reviewed ideas for this house for months and I have no doubt we are of one mind. And, like you, I believe Karen is expert at her job. She is also a strong advocate for the Faith File and wanting to do all she can to help find them a home. As soon as I hear anything from you will be the first to know and I promise, nothing else in this deal will move forward without your full knowledge and permission."

"I hope not. After all, if anything goes wrong, it will be my head on the govenor's chopping block."

Heading to her office, Grace felt a combined sense of relief and fear rippling through her from head to toe causing a loud growl to rumble through her abdomen up into her chest. Between a glance at her watch and a look in her briefcase, Grace realized it was almost dinner time and she'd never even finished her Three Musketeers lunch. She decided to treat herself to a take out order of rigatoni del curaso from Welcome Home.

The thought of the hand made pasta luxuriating in a rich cream sauce laced with garlic and rosemary and blended with thick-sliced mushrooms and smoky bacon made Grace's mouth water. Grabbing the phone receiver, she ordered her dinner and then packed up her briefcase. She would work on a checklist of renovation and construction jobs for the Brookside house over a glass of red wine and a plate of pasta. It would only take thirty minutes at most before she would be comfortably settled at home.

Now all I need is some of nana's retail therapy magic to come my way.

Chapter Forty-Six

I T TOOK 23 HOURS AND 35 MINUTES before Karen called about the Brookside purchase offer. The lengthy time lapse kept Grace in nightmares through most of the night. Finally giving up all hope of sleep, she headed to her office in the early morning darkness.

Once at her desk, she went to work reviewing the lists of construction, renovation and repair projects she'd created the night before. Making margin notes and wholesale edits, she then formed the lists into a comprehensive scope of work.

Looking at the clock and seeing it was past starting time for most construction businesses, Grace placed a call to Gary Adams, owner of Adams Builders. He was suggested as a trusted resource by Jonathan. After explaining the project to him, the two spent almost a half hour discussing preliminary renovation and building cost estimates for the Brookside house and property. She was in the process of evaluating those numbers until a phone call demanded her attention.

"Good Morning, Grace Reid."

"And a good morning it is, Grace Reid. This is Karen."

"Karen, thank goodness. I was beginning to wonder if you were ever going to call. What do you know?"

"Well, they didn't say no. They countered at $32,000 and added on a closing date of 30 days. If you can manage to come up with that $2,000 knowing what I do about the governor's determination to have your seniors out of Wood Haven by the end of the year, I feel confident we can manage a 30-day closing."

The pit in Grace's stomach tightened. She and Jonathan had worked the financials for the Faith File house everyway possible. They had a $55,000 limit, period. Based on the $20,000 building and renovation estimates from Gary Adams and the furnishings costs, Grace was going to need every penny left from her $30,000 purchase offer.

Yet she wasn't going to lose this house over $2,000.

"Any chance you think they might accept a counter to their counter?"

"Well, I never say never, but all things considered, I don't think I'd waste too much time trying to make a deal. This listing is now live in the realtor's directory statewide. It's only a matter of time before people start going through it and I really don't think it will last on the market once that happens.

"Ok. I hear you. Give me an hour and I'll get back to you with an answer."

Grace knew there was no wiggle room in her purchase offer. She also knew there were always ways to move things around in a budget. It was about prioritizing and being willing to compromise. Unfortunately, there was no compromising on the house's room requirements, as required by New Jersey's Department of Senior Affairs and Housing. There had to be one bedroom for each person living in the house, a minimum of 8 x8 in size. There had to be a fully equipped kitchen and a dining room capable of seating the number of people living in the house. There had to be at least two bathrooms with double sinks and shower/tub enclosures, as well as a large room for group activities. A fenced and protected yard and storage in the form of a basement and/or garage finished the checklist of the state's non-negotiables.

Once the rooms were roughed in, there was drywall and painting, carpeting, wiring, and lights, plumbing and kitchen/bath fixtures and cabinetry to be completed. Add to that curtains and furniture for every room, dishes, glasses and silverware, linens and bedding, equipment for cutting the lawn and yard maintenance and outdoor furniture. Grace knew that there needed to be an emergency fund as well for unforeseen construction issues that would undoubtedly arise. Somewhere in this list there had to be ways to find the money she needed to make the deal.

Turning her brain upside down and inside out, the name Henry Driscoll popped into her mind. The distinguished Wood Haven board member had become a valued supporter, since their first meeting. These days he stopped by her office regularly, asking for progress updates on the ten seniors and their housing needs, ultimately always sharing his best advice. Grace had come to lean on him for his wisdom, as she had with her papa.

Picking up the phone. Grace dialed the board member's number. She wasn't sure what she expected from the conversation, but she knew instinctively

Henry would improve the situation.

"Henry Driscoll here"

"Good morning, Henry. It's Grace Reid. How are you today?"

"Why I'm doing just fine, Ms. Reid. And yourself?"

The smile in the man's voice re-enforced Grace's confidence.

"To be truthful, I'm in need and hope you can help me."

"I'll certainly try my best. What's the problem?"

Detailing the events of the last 24 hours, Grace finished with a plea that unfolded as she spoke.

"After torturing myself trying to figure out a way to come up with this $2000, I decided to call you. I know there is a way to make this deal, but for the life of me I can't envision it. Can you please help me?"

The silence on the phone line between them lasted a bit too long for Grace's comfort. She was just about to ask Henry if he was still there when he finally spoke.

"The amount of money you need is relatively insignificant compared to the gain of finally finding a house that meets your requirements. While I understand the state's budget for this purchase is tightly defined, there are always ways to massage such finances to reach your ultimate goal. What I would suggest is the formation of an alliance with the contractors on this project, asking for a 10% discount on their materials and services. In return, I know the state will provide a tax rebate to those contractors equal to that discount. Based on the $20,000 you have projected for your construction and renovations, you will make up the $2000 you need for your deal."

"You are amazing! But do you really think the state would authorize such a tax rebate?"

"They already have. There is a home renovation incentive program for special needs groups. I'm experienced with it from some of the not-for-profit board work I've done. While your seniors may not fit the typical profile of those who've previously received funds from this program, they are definitely people with special needs."

"I knew you would have a solution to my problem! Thank you, Henry. Thank you so much! What do I need to do to get this program set up?"

"Leave that part to me, Grace. I'll talk to Jonathan and explain what we've discussed. Then I'll set the wheels in motion with the state. I have some friends in positions of influence with the governor. I'm sure I can get this rebate program organized in no time."

Grace could hardly contain her excitement as she flew down the hall to Jonathan's office. Without pausing to acknowledge his secretary or knock on his door, Grace burst into the room.

"Jonathan, wait 'til you hear what I have to tell you"

"What's going on, Grace?"

"I contacted Gary Adams first thing this morning to get a handle on the building and renovation costs. He gave me an estimate of $20,000, which includes a 10% emergency fund, in case of overruns, which keeps us in line with our budget. Right after I spoke to him, Karen called. The owners countered with a price of $2000 more than our offer."

"Well if that's why you're so excited Grace, I hate to burst your bubble, but we absolutely do not have and extra $2,000 to spend. We've talked about this and you know it."

"You're right, I do know it. But what I just learned is that the Faith File house is eligible for a state home renovation tax incentive program. If we can get all the contractors who provide materials and services for this project to give us a ten-percent discount, there is a state program that will give them that amount in a tax rebate. And if Gary's estimate of $20,000 for the construction and renovations is right, then we'll be able to make up that $2,000."

"I don't know where you heard about this state program, but even if it's true, it can take months to get something like that set up."

"That's the exciting part. I learned about the rebate from Henry Driscoll. He is going to call you later today to fill you in on the details and he has promised me that he can get this program set up and operational for our Faith File home project."

Looking skeptical, Jonathan let out a huge sigh. Just as he was about to speak, his secretary knocked on his office door.

"I'm sorry to interrupt, Jonathan, but Henry Driscoll is on the phone for you. He says it's important that he talk to you right away."

Twenty minutes of conversation later, Jonathan was onboard with Henry's plan and he gave Grace the go ahead to meet the counter offer. By midafternoon, Karen presented Jonathan with the completed contract, ready to sign and at day's end, the deal was complete, pending the Midland Town Board's approval.

The next board meeting was scheduled in three days. Grace wasn't familiar enough with the governmental process to know if she could even get on the meeting agenda in such a short time.

Dialing the mayor's number is the quickest way to find out.

"Mayor Jenkins office, how can I help you?"

Hello. This is Grace Reid from Wood Haven. Is it possible to speak to the mayor?"

"What's it in reference to?"

"I'm working on a project related to a group of Wood Haven seniors and the mayor asked me to call him when I had an update."

"One moment please."

As Grace listened to the irritating " hold" muzak, she calculated the best way to approach the mayor about the upcoming meeting. She didn't have long to ponder as he quickly clicked in to the call. "Hello, Grace. My secretary says you have a Wood Haven update for me."

"Yes, I do. Jonathan has signed a purchase offer on a house, pending approval by the town board. I was hoping I could present the contract before the board at the upcoming meeting, as you stated you want to move this forward as quickly as possible.

"I'm going to have to consult with the town attorney about this. Usually it wouldn't be a problem, but considering it's the first of such projects in our town, I want to be sure we allow for adequate public notice. I'll get back to you as soon as I have a legal decision on the matter."

With that the mayor was gone, leaving Grace with a dial tone buzzing in her ear.

She had no more than placed the receiver back on the phone base when she heard a chirpy voice calling her name.

"Top o'the morning' ta ya, Gracie. How ya be?"

The site of Teagan standing in her office doorway immediately lifted Grace's mood. The woman was indominable in her spirit and she and the others in the Faith File were what kept Grace working to make the dream of their home come true.

"Teagan, you are just the person I hoped to see at this moment. Won't you come in and share a cup of tea?"

"That's kind of ya, Missus. Be happy ta do so."

The women moved to the special seating area Grace had created following their first meeting in her office. She'd added another oversized chair to compliment the one already in place and found a small wooden table at Jewel's attic that perfectly completed the setting. The Irish hand-knit shawl that Teagan favored was draped over one of the chairs where Grace gently guided her. She proceeded to set the table with china cups and saucers alongside linen napkins and silver spoons. Bringing water to boil, Grace warmed her ceramic teapot and set two bags of Irish tea to steep.

"I have to say, Gracie, ya set a lovely tea. Me mam used ta do the same on special occasions. She'd call us kids ta the table and make us sip from the cups, just so. Me brothers hated it, but me and me sisters thought it a bit o'magic."

Teagan's words reminded Grace of a package of wafer cookies she'd stored in her desk drawer to add to their tea tradition.

"Excuse me just a moment, Teagan."

Lifting a saucer from the nearby bookcase, Grace moved to her desk and retrieved the cookies from the bottom drawer. Carefully opening the package, she placed a small handful of the sweet treats onto the china plate. Returning to the comfy seating area, Grace set the plate alongside the tea pot and cups.

Teagan's eyes lit up like candles as she reached for one of the cookies. Taking a bite, her face filled with a joyous smile.

"Oh missus, these are like the cookies me mam would make fer us on Sundays. 'Twas always a special treat eatin' 'em fresh and warm from the oven. Thanks ta ya."

As the women sat and sipped tea and shared conversation Grace felt that she had to tell Teagan about the house. She was sure she could keep the news secret until the deal was finalized and she wanted to give this special woman a sense of security about her future in a way that had been missing for so much of her life.

"I have some exciting news that I'd like to share with you, but I need you to keep it just between us for now. Can you do that?

"Aye, I'm a good secret keeper. When you're one among eight, ya learn ta mind yourself!"

Sharing in a moment of laughter, Grace could feel her heart connecting with Teagan beyond the boundaries of Wood Haven and the Faith File. The Irish woman was becoming a significant part of her life in a way she'd not known since her nana.

"So's what's the news, Gracie? I'm hopin' it's somethin' ta make me smile."

With great delight, she shared details about the house and the plans for making it the Faith File home, monitoring Teagan's face closely as she explained the timing of the project, making sure to emphasize that it all depended on the town board's approval.

"Well now, we both know there's them in town not wantin' us. Can't say as I blame 'em, doncha know but t'is a shame we can't sit down ta a cup o'tea with 'em. Me mam always said, there's nothin' can't be solved over a good strong tea."

"Teagan, that's it! Exactly!"

Grace wrapped her arms around the astonished woman and raised her up off the chair. Together they began dancing around the room like a pair of leprechauns. It was only when she felt the older woman gasp for air that she carefully returned her to her seat.

"Saints be praised, I haven't jigged like that in a month of Sundays. What ever's gotten inta ya, Gracie?"

"Your idea of letting the town meet you is exactly what needs to happen. How would you feel about attending the town board meeting with me and telling people why this house matters to you and the rest of the Faith File?"

Her uncharacteristic silence surprised Grace. Had she gone too far? Did she speak too quickly, without thinking of the challenges Teagan would face in stepping out into the real world? Perhaps she should withdraw the idea all together. As she was about to speak those very words, Teagan stood and raised Grace up alongside her. With a knowing smile and the ever-present twinkle in her eyes, she answered.

"Ya know Gracie, I think the two of us together, we oughta have a go at this town board."

Chapter Forty-Seven

GRACE TOOK A FINAL LOOK at the notes on her index cards. She'd spent the last 48 hours agonizing over her presentation for the Midland Town Board, editing details on the house, the lot and the purchase terms into easily accessible bullet points. She also formulated all the information into comprehensive presentation folders for each board member and made a few extra copies, just in case.

Jonathan and Henry Driscoll were also going to attend the board meeting, and would be joining her at the presentation table. Grace was comforted by that knowledge.

And then, there was Mike.

She really hadn't seen much of Officer Healy lately. He'd added a new part-time community position at the Midland High School to his regular police duties. It was aimed at building relationships between teens and the police. Mike was giving a lot more to the job than required, and he was still trying to figure out the balance. That's why the couple agreed to a late dinner at Welcome Home, to try and reclaim their dating life. Unfortunately, the evening went south in short order.

The problems began when Mike explained that Chief Reynolds had once again assigned him as Grace's security guard, beginning immediately, for a three-day period in and around the board meeting. He continued that Mayor Jenkins had ordered a special patrol for the same three days, to keep watch over the municipal parking lot outside the town hall. Clearly, neither official wanted a replay of the dead cat on the car incident from the last meeting.

While Grace understood the security precautions, she was frustrated that no one had taken the time to consult with, or even inform her about any of the safeguards. Since Mike Healy was the closest target, he received the full brunt of her frustrations.

"Really, Mike, I do think that as the target of the past nastiness, someone in this town would think to inform me of what's happening. Or, God forbid, ask what I might prefer when it comes to my personal security. The fact that you're supposed to be someone who cares for me and never once mentioned any of this until it was all decided is infuriating."

The stunned look on the cop's face led Grace to understand he'd never once thought about communicating any of the special security measures until after all the decisions had been made.

"What if I tell you I don't want you trailing around after me and to go away? What if I unilaterally made that decision for you? How would that feel?"

Grace knew she was boiling over unnecessarily. Getting a grip, she took a deep breath followed by a gulp of red wine. When she looked into Mike's eyes, she saw a blend of confusion and annoyance. Working to stay focused on the fact that the chief, the mayor and Mike were just doing their jobs, Grace swallowed her pride, along with her frustration, and tried to salvage the evening.

"I'm sorry for my outburst. I've been dealing with a lot of stress the past week trying to get this house deal done. Now there's the town board meeting and all the pressure of getting the house approved for occupancy and the town tax break. It's not an excuse, just the reality of my life these days. I know you and the chief and the mayor are doing your jobs as well. It's just insulting that no one thinks to actually talk to me. After all, I'm the one in the cross hairs here. Wouldn't it make sense to plan a protective strategy together so that I could be a supportive part of your plans?"

This time when Grace came up for air, Mike was ready and waiting.

"First off, Grace, I completely understand the pressure you're under right now. The whole town is talking about this board meeting and there is a definite community divide over the suitability of this house. It's a lot for everyone. Second, you're right. Chief Reynolds and Mayor Jenkins and I are doing our jobs when it comes to staying on top of this case and protecting you. We're determined that what happened last time will not happen again. Apparently, where we've gone wrong is putting all these plans together without you. Not the smartest tactic for three pretty intelligent guys. While I can't speak for the others, I apologize for not considering your thoughts and feelings about the security surrounding you and this meeting."

For the next few moments the couple ate and drank in silence, each allowing the impact of their words to take full effect. The thing was, Grace was no longer interested in her food. Her hunger had been replaced by the cumulative effect of the week's roller coaster of emotions, especially her worries about bringing Teagan to the board meeting.

While the Irish woman had shown no fear about stepping outside of Wood Haven's walls, Jonathan and Nurse Burke expressed major reservations over Grace's plan. Jonathan went as far to say that he feared Teagan's attendance at the meeting could cause the woman emotional harm. Thankfully Mary Burke sided with Grace in her belief that the 65-year old was both physically and mentally strong enough to take on the experience. The head nurse did however acknowledge concern over Teagan's safety should something unpleasant occur. In the end, Jonathan reluctantly gave his permission and Grace began preparing Teagan by taking her on short trips outside of Wood Haven's walls.

Their first excursion was to the Dairy Isle on its last day before closing for the winter season. While Teagan admitted to once sampling a bit of ice cream during her work with the Englers, she thrilled at the taste sensation of the hot fudge sundae Grace ordered for them to share. Accordingly, each trip they took marked a new experience in an unknown world for the aged woman, as well as for Grace who was seeing it all through Teagan's fresh eyes.

"Grace, aren't you hungry? You've hardly touched your dinner."

Mike's words brought her back to the restaurant. While she knew he was trying to shore up the mood of their dinner, Grace was past the point of no return. She wanted to go home and get a good night's sleep. She was going to need every advantage in order to ably face the town board and anyone from the town who showed up tomorrow night.

"I'm sorry, Mike. I know you planned this lovely dinner for us, but I am past exhausted. I've got to be sharp and ready to go tomorrow. If you don't mind, I'm going to call it a night. But feel free to stay—head over to the bar or whatever. Just because I'm leaving doesn't mean you have to go as well."

As soon as the words left her mouth, Grace knew she was wrong. Of course Mike wouldn't stay. He couldn't stay. He was back on Grace Reid patrol. Smiling meekly, she gave her bodyguard her best offer.

"Right. Sorry. I'll leave the door unlocked. You're welcome to bunk on the couch. You know where everything is. Help yourself."

Sharing a half-hearted hug, Grace turned and dragged her weary body out to the municipal parking lot. Standing amid a collection of cars, she scanned the rows, searching. No sign of her car. Nervously, she started walking in between the rows of parked vehicles. Still, nothing. The more she searched, the more she panicked until finally giving voice to her fears.

"Gone! My car is gone."

Abandoning her usual sensible nature, Grace began imaging all sorts of stolen car scenarios, even connecting her missing auto to the dead cat nightmare.

Mike. I need to find Mike.

Whipping around, Grace bounced off of Mike Healy's rock-hard body. Grabbing her in his arms, the sturdy man pulled her close and held her tight.

"It's okay, Grace. I drove us here tonight."

Appreciating the warmth of Mike's body and the soothing tone of his voice, Grace stayed wrapped in his embrace for several minutes. When at last her breathing calmed, Mike opened his arms and gently lifted Grace's face. Tenderly he matched his lips to hers in a kiss that sent chills through her body.

"What do you say we get you home and into bed?"

"After that kiss, Mike Healy, I'm not allowing you anywhere near my bedroom!"

AFTER A FITFUL NIGHT'S SLEEP, Grace drove to work in the gray dusk of dawn. The days were growing shorter as September was winding down. Next week would be the first of October. Time was flying and December 31 was looming.

You can't worry about that right now. Stay focused on the town board meeting and making sure Teagan is ready and able to handle it.

Grace slipped into her office and extracted the stack of reports and index cards from her briefcase.

Wouldn't hurt to make one last review.

Scanning the the pages and reading through the cards, Grace was confident she was prepped and ready to go. Glancing at her watch, the time was 8 am. There was a full day ahead before the 7pm board meeting. She needed to create a task list to keep her mind occupied and away from any imaginings of what could go wrong tonight.

"Mornin' Missus."

"Teagan, how did you sneak up on me? I didn't even hear you out in that hallway.

"Been there fer a bit, but you was workin' still-like and I dinna want ta disturb ya."

"You're not disturbing me at all. In fact, I was just thinking about you. How are you feeling today?"

"Ta be sure, I've a bit o'nerves flippin' 'round in me belly."

"Me too! Guess that makes us two of a kind! But I've just reviewed all my notes and I know I'm ready. And if you decide you want to say something tonight, we can go over the things we've discussed about moving into your own home and becoming part of the Midland Commuity and how much that will mean to all of you. And if you don't want to speak you don't have to. Just being there with me is enough.

"Right, Gracie girl. Don'cha worry. I'll be ready."

THE MIDLAND COMMUNITY ROOM continued to fill behind them as the two women sat quietly at the long table set at the front of the room. Grace didn't want to turn around and see how many people were in attendance. She was nervous enough. Just before 7pm, Jonathan and Henry Driscoll took their seats alongside her, all the while Teagan sat with her eyes locked on the dais before them.

"You ok, Teagan?"

A nod was all she gave.

Worried about the woman's nerves, Grace reached for her hand, entwining their fingers. Giving a soft squeeze, Grace was relieved when she returned the same.

With a rush of air, the door behind the dais opened and the Mayor and four Town Councilmen strode to their respective seats. A quick rap of the gavel and Mayor Jenkins called the meeting to order.

"Good evening everyone. In consideration of the large number of citizens present, we are going to move through the general business items of our meeting in a little different manner. I would ask that, *tonight only*, all department heads submit their monthly reports in written form for our review, which we will do later. If anyone in the town wants a copy of these reports we can make them available."

Pausing, the mayor placed his hand over the microphone before him. Turning right and left, he spoke to his four fellow law makers. As the quartet nodded in apparent agreement, Mayor Jenkins continued.

Regarding old business, there is only one item on tonight's agenda and that is Jack Sebastian's application to sell Christmas trees on his farm this year. The issue is that the area is strictly agricultural and according to Midland zoning laws that prevents the establishment of a customer service business. Our town attorney Anthony Charles is working with our building and zoning commissioner, Gary Appleton, to resolve the issue. If there are any protests agains this potential business, please stop at the town clerk's office tomorrow and file the appropriate paperwork."

Stopping to regard his notes in front of him, the mayor took several minutes before resuming.

"In accordance with Robert's Rules when discussing a special issue within a regular scheduled town board meeting, the meeting must be temporarily suspended before the special session can begin. So, at this time I would like to call for a motion to temporarily suspend the regular session of the Midland Town Board Meeting."

"I move we temporarily suspend the regular Midland Town Board Meeting."

"Councilman Baer with the motion. Do I have a second?"

"I'll second."

"Councilman Roberts seconds."

Rapping his gavel, Mayor Jenkins then called to order the special meeting on the Wood Haven Senior Group Home.

"Before we get started, I'm going to set some ground rules. If you want to speak, you must come to the podium at the front of the room. Before you start, you have to state your name and address. You will have two minutes to speak. No more. Disresptful or inappropriate language will be not tolerated. And finally, if you cause any trouble you'll be escorted out of the town hall by Officer Healy."

As the crowd whispered about the mayor's rules, Grace pulled her index cards and her presentation files from her briefcase. Her movement gave Teagan a start and Grace again reached over and laced together their hands. This time the Irish woman turned towards her and shared a tender smile.

Not bad for her first time in a community setting like this. Not bad at all.

"I'd like to start by asking Grace Reid, Director of the Wood Haven Senior Group Home to give us an update."

As she rose from her seat, Grace leaned toward Teagan and whispered, "I'm just going to stand up. I'll still be here, right next to you."

Grace was heartened when she spoke in return.

"I'm doin' fine Gracie. Don'cha worry."

Seeing a twinkle return to Teagan's eyes inspired Grace. Tonight was her chance to make sure the Faith File would have better lives. All she needed to do was present the details of the proposed house renovations in a manner that would encourage the townspeople to understand the importance of the project and the need for it.

Nana and papa, please help me find the words.

"Good evening Mayor Jenkins and Midland Board Members. Thank you for this opportunity to update you on the Wood Haven Senior Home. I'd also like to acknowledge all members of the Midland Community who have come out tonight."

As she spoke, Grace turned to address those gathered. Instantly she was set off balance by the crowd overflowing the room into the adjacent hallway. At the same time, she realized they weren't necessarily all naysayers. Many could be supporters. Wasn't that what Karen told her? That there were a lot of people in Midland in favor of the senior residence.

"This kind of turnout is the mark of a caring community. I look forward to answering your questions and earning your support for our Wood Haven Seniors."

Turning back around, Grace glanced at the front row to check on Teagan. The sprightly woman gave a quick wink and a nod of her head that let Grace know all was well. Feeling her confidence build, Grace continued.

"Before I begin, I'd like to distribute these presentation folders to the board. They are an in-depth report of what I am going to present tonight.

Mayor Jenkins nodded to Mike, who took the folders from Grace to distribute across the dais. The brief break provided her time to lay out her index cards in organized fashion on the table. Taking a deep breath and putting a smile on her face, she began.

Ten minutes later, Grace had succinctly laid out all details of the house, the renovation plans, the security measures that would be taken once the seniors moved in and planned programming to integrate the six women into the Midland Community.

At the end of her presentation, Grace detailed the finances of the project, making it clear all costs would be fully funded by a coalition of federal and state agencies. That left only the small requests of the Midland Town Board's zoning approval for the house renovation and construction permits along with the granting of the property tax relief, already approved at a previous meeting.

When Grace flipped over her last index card, she looked up at the five men holding the fate of her Faith File in their votes. Right to left, three were fully engaged, one appeared annoyed and the last seemed on the verge of boredom. Whatever was about to unfold at the Q&A would undoubtedly seal the deal. Grace was going to have to rely on her passion for the project and her quick Irish wit to win this battle.

"Seeing as so many of you have come out to this meeting, we are going to open it to public comment right away."

The words had barely left the mayor's mouth and people were lined up behind the microphone. Grace stood up and motioned for Teagan to slide over onto her chair so that she could serve as a protective buffer against negative remarks or actions that might be directed their way. Knowing she would be called on for information she decided to remain standing.

For the following thirty minutes, townspeople spoke their minds and asked questions. Most were respectful, a few were frustrated. All in all, Grace felt as if her answers kept the momentum going her way.

As the last speaker departed the podium, Mayor Jenkins announced a final call for comments. Whispers rippled through the room as Grace waited in hopeful anticipation.

"I wanna speak."

Grace felt her heart drop to her stomach. Without even turning, she recognized the voice as belonging to Bill Marsh. Looking over at Teagan, she summoned her best smile and reached out to give the woman's hand a caring touch. Teagan answered back with another of her sassy winks and a, "No worries, Gracie."

"I'm Bill Marsh. I live at 596 Forest Avenue in Midland. I come here tonight to say my piece again about this group home. This woman here has reeled off a lot of numbers and fancy ideas about setting up these crazy old ladies in the middle of one of our family neighborhoods. I still say they were locked away for a reason and that reason is that they are dangerous and could hurt people."

The mayor started banging his gavel when the words, "crazy old ladies" caused a stir in the audience. He was still banging when Bill accused the Faith File of being dangerous. This time, however, the mayor could not control either the speaker or the listeners.

Bill kept on, pounding his fist in emphasis on the podium, which invoked audience calls of support. As the room became more raucous, Grace looked to Mike in hopes that he would provide she and Teagan safe passage from the room.

Reaching out a hand to Teagan, Grace helped her stand and started guiding her forward, away from the crowd. But as strongly as she pushed, Teagan resisted. Suddenly Grace realized the woman was moving away from her and towards Bill Marsh. Grabbing at the collar of Teagans' dress, Grace held her steady in wait.

As the pint-sized Irishwoman and the ranting man drew close, silence fell across the room. More suprising, Bill stepped back, whether in fear or out of respect, Grace wasn't sure. Taking her place at the podium, Teagan nodded to the town board and spoke.

"Evenin' gentlemen."

She then pivoted to face the full room of Midland citizens.

"And evenin' ta all, ladies and gentlemen."

Turning back to the microphone, Teagan continued.

"Me name is Teagan. Teagan Cormick. 'Twould be 68 years old I am and 'twas born and bred in County Cork, Ireland. I come ta this country some fifty years past, on me own, so's I could find me way as an artist. 'Twas me life dream ya might say. Right off, I got a job and earned me own way, but like many, the crash stole ev'ry bit o'it. With nothin' and no one, I took ta livin' 'neath a bridge usin' cardboard fer me bed. Then one day come the constables, throwin'me in a truck and takin'me ta a place unknown. Locked away inta a concrete cell I was, with no bed nor toilet and little ta eat or drink. Fer days I lie in me tattered clothes, stains o'pee and poop markin' me. Not a soul knew or cared whether I be livin' or dead."

Teagan's words hung in the air, raining down stark images of her life upon the entire room. Without pause, she continued.

"Come a day I was drug ta a room where's a doctor stuck a needle in me and said I'd be forever locked away in the hell hole o'a place they'd been keepin' me. True ta his word, since me seventeenth year this is me first time bein' out with townfolk like yerselves. T'is way different from bein' chained ta a cot in a room o'human rot and stank."

Teagan's words tumbled from her trembling body spuring Grace to move closer in support. Yet as she turned around to address the crowd, Teagan stepped away, into her own space.

"I know's some here don't think people like me belong. Ya don't want us 'round 'cause we might cause trouble. Well I'm here ta say, have a look. Have a look at me, Teagan Cormick. Hear me words and the words o'others been locked away most o'their days, fer no good reasons. We coulda rotted and died like many at Wood Haven who was treated so bad. But we dinna. We survived in spite o'it all. Now all we're askin' is ta be able ta live whatever time is left us in a real home, like ya'd want fer your own mothers don'cha know."

Revolving around to the dais of town officials, brave woman stared down each man as she spoke.

"Grace here has told me each one o'ya has a vote on decidin' where me and the others from Wood Haven will be livin'. Ta me own mind, that's a bit o'power. Then again, others been lordin' power o'er us for more years than I'd be knowin'. 'Tis hard countin' time when you're locked 'way from the world and all ya care fer and love, for no good reason. And if that makes me a crazy woman, so be it."

In the stunned quiet of the meeting room, Teagan turned slowly to Grace and gave her a wink and a smile . . . and fainted into her arms.

Chapter Forty-Eight

AFTER FAINTING INTO GRACE'S ARMS, Mike rushed over and grabbed the lifeless woman, ordering Grace to follow him. Jonathan preceded the trio, clearing a path through the crowded room to the nearest exit. Once outside, Mike set Teagan onto the ground as if she were a valued treasure. Loosening the collar of her dress, Mike moved his hands to the pale woman's limp wrist, tracking her pulse.

"Her heartbeat is fairly strong and her color is coming back a bit. I would guess her system overloaded in the excitement of the moment. That's probably what caused her to blackout. I'm still going to call for an ambulance and have her checked out at the hospital, if that's alright with you two?"

Jonathan and Grace nodded in immediate agreement.

"Alright then, Jonathan, would you go back inside and make sure a call has been made to the emergency squad for an ambulance to take Teagan to the hospital. In the meantime, I'll stay with her and track her vitals."

Jonathan sprang to the nearest town hall entrance while Grace remained alongside Teagan, opposite Mike. A sense of guilt traveled through her as she thought back to Jonathan's warning over the meeting being too much for the 68-year old. If Teagan suffered lingering effects as a result of Grace encouraging her attendance, she would bear the responsibility—and the guilt.

"Hey, Grace. You need to take some deep breaths and relax. I don't need another woman passing out on me."

Realizing she'd been holding her breath, Grace followed Mike's instructions and began fully inhaling and exhaling.

"That's the way. Just keep breathing nice and easy. We need you to be in good order when Teagan comes around."

As if on command, the Irishwoman's eyes flickered apart and just as quickly closed. Grace was desperate for Teagan to recover consciousness and say a few words to prove her stability. Once more her eyelids parted and then drooped. If she didn't know better, Grace would think Teagan was playing a deceptive game. The grayish tint to her skin told otherwise.

Screaming sirens announced the arrival of the rescue squad. Grace jumped up to flag down the ambulance as it came flying through the parking lot. Within minutes skilled EMTs had Teagan safely tucked into their emergency room on wheels. Before closing the doors, a technician called out if anyone wanted to ride along to the hospital. Grace flew into the tight treatment space and wriggled herself alongside Teagan. With a slamming of the ambulance doors, the driver sped off amid a burst of sirens and flashing lights.

The rest of the night became a blur of dark corridors, intensely lit exam rooms, incessant medical personnel, endless hospital forms and, to Grace's relief, Teagan's return to consciousness. Doctors determined a drop in blood pressure to be the direct cause of her fainting spell. To be safe, they decreed an overnight stay and monitoring.

As the sun curled around the plastic blinds in the window of Teagan's room, Grace stirred in the bright green plastic chair that had served as her bed. Unable to get comfortable, she became more fully awake as the ache of a sore neck and a stiff back set in. Yet when she opened her eyes she saw Teagan, looking healthy and resting peacefully. Nothing else mattered.

Acknowledging strong need to pee and infuse her body with caffeine, Grace set off for the hospital cafeteria. While waiting in line to pay for her tea, she noticed the morning edition of The Midland Journal. There across the top of the front page in bold type she read the troubling headline.

Wood Haven Group Home
Continues to Stir Controversy

Frustrated by the tone of the title, Grace decided to ignore the attached article. What did catch her eye was an emboldened block at the top right of the page, set prominently above everything all else.

Time to Wipe Clean the Slate of Shame—
Today's editorial on the Wood Haven Group Home. **Page 23**

Grabbing a copy, Grace paid for both the coffee and the newspaper and hurried to a nearby table. Flipping to the noted page, she began reading. The editorial was written by the owner of the newspaper, Steven Bradlee. In straight-forward style, Bradlee told the story of his grandfather, Jacob, who'd founded the Midland newspaper.

My grandfather was an immigrant who came to this country from England in June of 1893. Upon his arrival at Ellis Island, he decided to make his way to the state of New Jersey, where he'd heard of job opportunities in the wake of the Industrial Revolution's second wave across America. Meeting up with fellow Englishman, Marcus Henry, the two decided to settle in the town of Midland, where they were immediately hired to work at the local grainary, today the building that houses Jewel's Attic.

Midland at this time was a lively town with a strong blend of immigrants and block upon block of thriving businesses. Marcus and my grandfather settled in easily, sharing a flat over the town butcher shop. While they toiled shoulder-to-shoulder six days a week, on Sundays they parted ways—Marcus to explore Midland's available ladies. My grandfather to explore the local landscape.

It was during one such outing that my grandfather discovered a sprawling collection of buildings on the edge of town, their boundaries defined by an imposing iron fence with pillared gates. Intrigued, the next day my grandfather inquired of his fellow workers what they knew of the complex. Every answer returned the same: "That's Wood Haven, where they lock up crazy people." It was only when my grandfather met a young woman at a church social, following Sunday services, that he received a different reply.

Jean Marie Kerrigan was a Galway girl. She'd come to America with her family in 1889, but now was on her own, working as a nurse's aide at Wood Haven. As my grandfather always told the story, he was immediately drawn to the young woman's azure eyes, set off by her coal black hair and lightly freckled cheeks. Her kind disposition further entranced him as she agreed to spend the rest of her Sunday afternoon sharing her favorite spot in all of Midland. You can imagine my grandfather's surprise as Jean Marie snuck him through Wood Haven's gates and proceeded around the outer edge of the property, to a beautiful crystal lake.

As the story goes, the couple passed the afternoon along the shore of that lake with Jean Marie sharing stories about her work at Wood Haven and my grandfather asking questions along the way. My father often quoted my grandfather about that day, saying he was both, "compelled and horrified" by the Irish girl's descriptions of the animal-like treatment and abusive medical therapies. The additional tragedy in my grandfather's opinion was Jean Marie's stories of women locked away for years despite, in her judgement, being of sound mind and body.

As time passed, my grandfather fell in love with Jean Marie and within a year's time they were married. During that same time, he became obsessed with Wood Haven and those trapped within its walls. His intense interest eventually led my grandmother to smuggle him inside, where he spoke to those unjustly locked away. The experience was life-changing and inspired my grandfather to write in-depth stories about the facility. When he couldn't find a publisher willing to print his work, he launched the Midland Journal and showcased his stories of torturous treatments going on behind the asylum's dark gray façade.

While his work did not significantly change or improve Wood Haven's medical protocol, he never stopped writing about the injustices going on at the state-run facility. Upon his death in 1924, Steven's son, (my father) Michael, became the Journal Editor. Through his vision, he expanded the newspaper in advertising revenue and award-winning staff. He also continued his father's Wood Haven crusade, to little acclaim and no change.

Fast forward twenty-seven years and yours truly started working at The Journal as a wet-behind-the-ears reporter for the small town newspaper my father has grown into a respected, state-wide publication. Along the way, I learned about the Journal's Wood Haven cause, started so long ago by my grandfather.

Like these two men before me, I became a standard bearer for improved treatment for Wood Haven "patients." Only this time as I employed the power of my pen, America was changing. People were listening. Powerful people with a knowledge base to understand the scope of the asylum's deplorable conditions and the abilities to change them.

I'm proud to note that The Journal became a respected nationwide voice regarding this topic and paved the way for the national de-institutionalization bill passed only months ago. I carried memories of my grandfather and father with me when I traveled to Washington, DC, at the invitation of the President, to witness the bill signing in the Oval Office. All of which brings me to the recent town board meetings regarding the establishment of a Wood Haven group home in Midland.

For more than three quarters of a century, this newspaper has held a spotlight on the inhumane treatments administered at Wood Haven, often by residents from our own community. Equally as shameful are the long list of men and women who were committed to this asylum for reasons that could qualify most any of us to be locked away. Right now, we have a chance to wipe clean that slate of shame. We have the opportunity to welcome into our town six women, ages 54 to 78, whose lives were robbed from them by people and circumstances of no appreciable merit.

These women are not insane. They have never been diagnosed with any sort of mental imbalance. In fact, if you were able to read their medical charts, you would find they are just as normal as anyone in this town. But for decades, they have not had a home, by any definition of the term.

These women could be your grandmothers, your mothers, your aunts, your sisters. And all they're asking is for a decent place to live out the remainder of their lives. For the government and the people of Midland to allow anything less is as criminal as every abusive action administered at Wood Haven in its 115-year history.

By the time she read the last line, Grace's tears were smudging the newsprint. She had never met Jacob Bradlee. She didn't even read the Midland Journal, except for an occasional news clipping Jonathan would leave on her desk. But at that moment she wanted to go to The Journal office and give the man the world's biggest hug.

She wondered if Jonathan had seen the editorial? Or Mike? Looking at her watch, it was just before 7am. Still a little too early to go calling around town. She'd just have to control her excitement, go back to Teagan's room and wait for someone . . . anyone . . . to show up.

Tiptoeing into the room, Grace was just about to slip back in to her green chair when Teagan popped up like a jack-in-the-box.

"Morning there Gracie. Was wonderin' where ya'd gone?"

"Gracious, Teagan, you scared the life out of me. I thought you were still sound asleep."

"Ay, I heard ya sneakin' out and been waitin' since. Did ya happen ta bring a cuppa tea?

The bubbly spirit of the woman brought laughter from Grace's heart. Clearly she was feeling better and hopefully would be released soon.

"I did not, Teagan, as I'm not sure what the doctor will allow you this morning. Let me go and check with the nurse."

"Ah, don't bother. I'd rather have ya here with me. So's tell me. Did I do ya proud last night?"

"Oh my goodness, proud isn't the half of it. You were amazing. Every word was perfect and when you turned around and spoke to the crowd, there wasn't a dry eye in the house. Next time I'm just going to let you do the presentation all on your own."

"They'll be no next time, I'm tellin' ya that right now. Once speakin' up like that 'twas enough fer this Irish lass! Just good ta know I did ya proud."

As she spoke the last words, Teagan's eyes filled with tears. Seeing her emotional response, Grace moved to the hospital bed and lowered the metal side rail. Bending forward, she wrapped her arms carefully around the sweet woman's shoulders and gave a gentle hug, causing her own eyes to fill. "Well, good to see my two best girls are up and awake."

Mike Healy's entrance into the room caused Grace to quickly straighten and Teagan to smile.

"Well now, Officer Healy, what would you be doin' in a hospital on a fine day such as this?"

Moving closer, Mike took hold of Teagan's hand and lifted it to his lips for a kiss.

"Did you really think that I would let the morning start without checking on you? "

With a wink, he planted another quick kiss on the blushing woman's hand before turning his attention to Grace.

"And how are you feeling this morning, Ms. Reid?"

"I am beyond grateful, thanks for asking. Did you see the morning paper?"

"I did. That's one of the reasons I stopped by, to make sure the two of you saw it as well."

Seeing confusion pass across Teagan's face, Grace gathered the newspaper and proceeded to read the editorial aloud. When she finished the final sentence she was again in tears, as were Teagan and Mike.

"Beautiful. Just beautiful. Does ya know this writer, Gracie?"

"I don't but Mike may."

"Yeah, he's a good guy and almost always on the right side of issues in this town. What's really important is that people read his stuff and they respect what he has to say. This editorial may be all you need after last night's Academy Award Winning performance by Miss Teagan here."

Mike's words caused the Irish woman to blush beet red. Grace wondered when the last time so much fun and laughter had been part of Teagan's life. She *had* to make the group home happen so that all the Faith File could start to enjoy this kind of normalcy.

"Good morning everyone. Miss Cormick, how are you feeling this morning?"

As Teagan gave a positive reply, the nurse cranked up the hospital bed and wrapped a blood pressure sleeve around her patient's arm. Listening intently as she released the air valve, the nurse declared the pressure to be perfect. Taking her temperature and registering her pulse rate completed the nurse's check list.

"Breakfast will be here in just a few minutes. The doctor will be along shortly. Based on your vitals and the good night's sleep you enjoyed, I would imagine you'll be going home soon."

The next two hours passed with a steady stream of people coming and going. Teagan managed the activity well, eating a full breakfast, answering questions from nurses and orderlies and not showing any signs of weakness from her fainting spell. Mike left in the middle of all the activity, needing to get to the middle school by 9 am. He brought another blush to Teagan's face as he gave her a kiss on the cheek and a promise to look in on her later at Wood Haven.

Finally the doctor arrived. He reviewed her patient chart and remarked on her strong vitals. Then he eased Teagan out of bed to check her reflexes and balance, all of which were perfect.

"Well, young lady, I think you are well enough to be released. However, I want to see you in my office for a check up next month and I'm going to write a scrip for the Wood Haven nurses to monitor your blood pressure. If there is any change we're going to have to make some decisions about possible surgery for a pace maker."

"Don't ya be worryin' there, doctor. I'm fit as a fiddle and have no intention of bein' anything else. But if it's a chance ta visit you're wantin', ya can always come by the new house when we're moved."

Grace almost spit out the sip of tea she'd just taken when she heard Teagan so shamelessly flirt with the doctor. Thankfully he was good natured and flirted right back.

"Well now, I may just take you up on that offer, Teagan. It's not often I get to meet a lovely Irish Colleen such as yourself. You take good care and remember to call my office if you need anything."

With a wink and a smile, the doctor was gone, but not before Teagan boldly winked back.

I'm starting to wonder if all those years locked away may have created a flirtatious monster.

"Ok let's get you dressed. It will take the nurse a bit to process your discharge papers, so we can go slow and easy."

"I can do meself, Gracie, thank you very much. I'll just take me clothes inta the loo and be back in a jif."

Grace kept a close ear to the bathroom door in case of a slip or fall. All she heard, however, was Teagan's happy humming of Irish eyes, an old Irish folk tune. The woman's quick recovery was a blessing and Grace could not imagine the day getting any better. She remembered that thought as Jonathan came by to check on the patient and to talk to Grace about two phone calls he'd received from Mayor Jenkins.

Grace's heart jumped at the mention of the mayor. She didn't expect a decision on the Faith File home for at least a week, until the regularly scheduled board committee meeting. She knew the town and the board were split on whether or not to approve the house and she was sure those opposed were doing their best to sway that decision. The only reason she could imagine the mayor calling twice in less than 24 hours after her presentation was an across the board refusal to approve the project.

Just as Jonathan launched into his conversation with the mayor, Teagan exited the bathroom perfectly dressed and groomed.

"Good morning ta ya, Jonathan. Have ya heard the good news? They're letting me outta here."

"I'd not heard that, but I'll be glad to drive you back to Wood Haven as soon as you are ready. In the meantime, I was just starting to tell Grace about some conversations I had this morning with the mayor."

"Go right ahead. Don't let me be stoppin' ya."

"So, let's see, where was I? Oh yes. The mayor called last night and said that after Teagan was taken away in the ambulance, a lot of people in the audience came up to talk to both he and the council members. In fact, it got to be a fairly sizeable group. They were all commenting on what a sweet woman Teagan seems to be and how they couldn't imagine her life, being locked away at Wood Haven since she was seventeen. They agreed clearly that she wasn't any more crazy than their own mothers and grandmothers—which was meant as a joke, Teagan, don't be offended."

"Taken as such, don'cha ya know, Jonathan."

"Anyway, after the people dispersed, the board decided they wanted to sit down then and there and hash out all the particulars about the group home. When they were done, they were two for and two against with the mayor holding the tiebreaker vote. He told them he wasn't comfortable making that decision for the town, so he asked everyone to go home and sleep on it and they would conference call in the morning."

Grace felt sick with anticipation. She wished Jonathan would just get to the point.

"I have to tell you I didn't sleep very well after that call. In fact I was up at 5am trying to figure out what we could do to resubmit our proposal should the town board reject it. In fact, when the mayor called this morning, I was ready to hit him hard with a counter proposal."

"That's the way Jonathan! No need ta be takin' it lyin' down."

"Thank you, Teagan. I thought the same thing. Then the mayor told me about Jacob Bradlee's editorial in today's Journal. Said it was a damn good piece and that he'd started getting phone calls about it at seven this morning. So he called the board together at his office to poll them and they voted unanimously to approve . . . everything. The Faith File is going to get their home."

CHAPTER FORTY-NINE

L IFE WAS TRAVELING AT A HEADY PACE and Grace was doing her best to keep up.

It had taken a month for all the paperwork and financing to be completed for the Faith File house. True to his word, Henry Driscoll had arranged the incentive tax program for all contractors on the project. When the time came to close the deal, Grace paid the extra $2,000 without worry.

Work on the house started in mid-October with Jake Russell on board as the project manager for Adams Builders. Jake drafted a two-phase construction plan that began with a focus on exterior renovations and construction of the addition. Miraculously, no unexpected problems arose during the work and all went according to schedule. By early November the new roof was completed, the porch removed, the storms and screens replaced and the addition constructed and made weather tight. Phase two called for completion of the interior over the ensuing month, allowing for the house to be furnished and ready for occupancy by December 20th.

While the building schedule kept Grace busy coordinating construction progress and ensuring that group home regulations were being met, it was primarily her ten seniors who were commanding the majority of her time. The transition of the four in need of skilled care was proving a bit more difficult than Graced anticipated. To try and minimize their individual and group issues, she was doing all she could to fully engage them in the excitement of moving on to their new lives.

After signing their contracts for St. Augustine's, she took photographs of all three of their living suites so she could share them with James, Maria, Regina and Janna. Grace also picked up some of the facility's glossy, color brochures that showed off the comfortable community spaces. Now she was trying to figure out the best ways to present the information to each one.

She decided to start with James. The Greek man welcomed Grace to his room whenever she stopped to visit, which was frequently. From the start she found him charming and enjoyed his company, but the more they spoke about moving, the more he proffered reasons why his room at Wood Haven was all he needed. In each conversation, no matter how Grace approached the topic, he offered a different reason to stay put, none of which rang true.

In trying to figure it out, one thing kept returning to Grace's mind. It was something James shared in their first conversation—about a woman he loved and claimed was still part of his life. Grace checked with the nurses in charge of the third floor and all stated they had no knowledge of such a relationship, but he'd been so convincing in speaking about it. She wondered if possibly the woman only existed in James' imagination but she also had a gut feeling that there was something more to the story that was fueling his reluctance to move.

Standing outside his room, Grace took a moment to compose herself and clear her mind so she could focus only on James.

"Good morning, James. You're looking very handsome today."

The distinguished man lay on a hospital bed with his upper body slightly raised. Years of hand digging Wood Haven graves that had caused irreparable damage to his spine made just about any body position uncomfortable. That's why Nurses provided around-the-clock adjustments of his moveable bed that delivered some relief. Despite the constant pain, James's outlook was always positive.

"Ah, Miss Reid. The sun follows you wherever you go. Thank you for bringing it into my world today."

"I come bearing gifts and news. Are you up for some conversation?"

"Conversing with you is something to which I always look forward. Please bring a chair and make yourself comfortable."

Sliding a nearby chair to the side of James's hospital bed, Grace sat down and nestled the St. Augustine photograph and brochure on her lap. Over the last five months, she'd learned that engaging James first on a personal level was key to successful interaction.

"When we talk, your words are often so poetic they paint pictures in my mind of what you're describing. The other day I was reading through a magazine and came across photographs of Greece. They were so beautiful and made me want to talk to you about your homeland. Are there memories of your life there that you would share with me?"

"Ah Miss Reid, you have discovered one of the greatest gifts we Greek have to offer. That is our deep sensitivity to the world around us and the ability to express those thoughts and feelings. That is why words of Greek philosophers from centuries past are still considered and revered. I am honored my words touch you in such a way."

For the next half hour, Grace sat mesmerized as James spoke of mountainous cliffs holding tightly to crowded masses of whitewashed buildings, all of it immersed in shrubbery scents of thyme, rosemary, oregano, and bay. He described the reflection of the island across the aqua blue depths of the Aegean, Ionian and Mediterranean Seas, and beaches of white sand cradled by imposing limestone cliffs. Through each narrative, Grace's senses were fully engaged, as if she were actually experiencing the man's homeland. When it was clear that James could go no further, she experienced profound disappointment.

"James, your love of Greece poured from your words. Thank you for giving so much of yourself in sharing those memories. Now I'd like to return your kindness by having you sit back and listen while I share stories that I hope you will enjoy.

Standing for a better angle, Grace raised the photograph of the St. Augustine's suite to a level where they could view it together.

"I am not an accomplished storyteller, like you, so I have some photographs to help me. This is a picture of the suite, your suite, at St. Augustine's. I know we have talked about your moving there, but I thought it would be helpful if you could see where you will be living, so you can better imagine your new life."

Silently James studied the image Grace held before him. His stoic face gave no indication of his thoughts, making Grace wish for mind reading skills. Just as she was about to describe the layout of the room, the usually-engaging man spoke.

"This suite, as you call it, appears like a room with much size, more than is needed by one man who cannot move from his own bed. I have no need of anything more than I have here.

Grace had anticipated James's reaction and again suspected his protest to be a ruse. Trusting her instinct, she decided to question him about the secret love he had professed. She knew it was a calculated risk, but with less than six weeks before Wood Haven's nursing facility closed down, she had to take to do something.

"I respect your thoughts, James, but have you considered how nice it would be if the woman you told me about when we first met, the woman you say you love, if she would have space to spend time with you in your new home."

"Ah, Miss Reid, you are a wise woman reaching into my heart, the most sacred of a man's spaces. But you must understand, should I choose to turn to this new life you are offering, the woman to whom you refer would only be able to be with me in my heart. Circumstances would separate us and allow no more."

Grace felt as if she were struggling with a puzzle made up of real people and real life situations and not enough of the frame to piece them all together. She needed to entice James to share key pieces of this relationship.

"James, I hear what you are saying, but when it comes to love I believe all things are possible. If you would share with me the reasons why moving to St. Augustine's will keep you apart from this woman, perhaps I can change that. At least give me the opportunity to try, because Wood Haven is closing and no one, not the nurses, the patients or even myself, can stay.

"Ms. Reid, the Greek have a saying, kánete tin kalýteri dynatí chrísi tou ti eínai stin exousía sas kai párte ta ypóloipa ópos symvaínei. It means, make the best use of what's in your power and take the rest as it happens. I understand the decision to move to St. Augustine's is not in my power and though my deepest wish is to remain here, sadly I will have to take the rest of my future as it happens. So now, if you will excuse me, my eyelids and my heart are both heavy. I must rest."

Leaving James, Grace understood he had just agreed to move. However, her intuition told her that he might die in the process . . . perhaps of a broken heart.

Grace had two more stops to make with the St. Augustine pictures and brochures. After the emotional drain of her visit with James, she decided to undertake the interaction she anticipated being the easier—Janna and Regina.

In previous visits with the women, Grace found them sweet, almost childlike. Most of the time Regina dozed while Janna spoke of her life in Poland and her parents. Despite the trauma the woman had endured from a young age, she sustained an innocence that allowed her to see only the goodness in life. Going to St. Augustine's was simply another change which, when Grace presented it to her in the form of the picture and brochure she agreed to accept. As for Regina, her only concern was that she and Janna be together.

With an hour left in the morning, Grace turned to the last person on her list. With dread, she knocked and pushed through the door.

"Good morning, Senorita Rodriguez."

The youngest of all the Wood Haven seniors, at age 54, the diminutive woman was seated in a rocking chair, expertly knitting a tightly rolled ball of yarn into a beautiful blanket. As was their routine, Maria ignored Grace. In turn, Grace pulled up a chair and sat down directly across from the woman.

"Your knitting is beautiful. My nana tried to teach me to knit, but I was forever dropping stitches. She was such a love though. She always stopped whatever she was doing to help me pull the knitting apart to where I'd dropped the stitch and get me back on track again."

The sweet memory touched a chord deep within Grace's heart, swelling into a teardrop down her cheek. Moving to catch it before it flowed from her face, her sudden movement attracted Maria's attention. Halting the smooth motion of her knitting needles, she sat and scrutinized Grace.

"I too had an Abuela who taught me things. She was a wise woman who never judged me, always held me. When God took her, I lost my world."

Like Grace, the memory of her Abuela swelled a teardrop that slowly slid down Maria's face. Yet rather than brush it aside, she let it drop onto the blanket she had resumed knitting. For the first time since meeting, Maria allowed a kindness to pass between them. It was the opening for which Grace had prayed.

"I was raised by parents who were always working. In the summers, to make it easy on themselves, they sent me to my nana and papa's farm. That's where I learned what it was to be loved. I miss them so, but I am grateful we had each other for as long as we did. I talk to them everyday about whatever is going on in my life. I've talked to them about you. Asked them to help me find a way for us to talk."

Again pausing her knitting, Maria looked at Grace with a small grin.

"So you talk to dead people and ask them about me, eh? And I'm the one locked up for being loco!"

The irony of her words made both women laugh. If nothing else, Grace had cracked open a small space in the tough woman's veneer.

"Yes, I suppose I do sound crazy, but I would bet a bag of yarn that you have the same kind of conversations with your Abuela."

Another smile crept across Maria's face as her knitting needles moved at lightening speed.

Be careful where you go next, Grace Remember, easy does it. One step at a time.

Ok nana. I hear you.

"Well, Senorita, I will leave you to your knitting. Thank you for this visit. I am grateful to have shared memories of our loved ones. You brought my nana closer into my heart today."

Standing to leave, Grace willed the woman to say something, anything, but silence reigned. It wasn't until she reached the door that the woman's will gave way.

"Miss Reid, I hear from Teagan about this place to which we are supposed to move. She tells me it is good and I will be safe there. I still have not decided if I am going to go."

"Senorita Rodriguez, if your Abuela or my nana needed to go to a place to be taken care of, I would take them to St. Augustine's without worry. You will have to make up your mind yourself, but I will leave this photograph of your suite they have ready for you and a brochure where you can learn about the rest."

Returning to the woman, Grace placed both items on the small table next to the rocking chair.

"Hasta pronto, Senorita."

As she exited the room, she heard the woman's whispered reply.

"Good bye for now, Miss Reid."

Returning to her office, Grace was ready to take a lunch break before jumping back into the myriad of construction issues stacked on her desk. Grabbing her purse, she was almost out the door when her phone rang. The temptation to ignore the call was strong, but she knew she would pay for delaying whatever issue was on the other end of that receiver.

"Grace Reid."

"Hello Grace. It's Chief Reynolds. I wondered if you could come down to the station?"

"I can try. When?"

"Right now would be good. It's important."

"Care to give me any hints, chief?"

"Let's just say that the sooner you get here, the sooner we can simplify all of our lives."

Realizing she was being stonewalled, Grace gave up asking and agreed to come immediately.

Pulling in to the Midland Police parking lot, Grace noticed Mike Healy's pickup in the back where on duty officers left their personal vehicles. Grace wondered if he was at the middle school or out on patrol, or if she might run in to him at the station.

Walking into the single level brick building, Grace got her answer as Mike was standing in the entryway.

"Hey! Fancy meeting you here, Officer Healy."

"Actually, I was sent to meet you and bring you to the chief. Right this way, m'am."

The wink and smile he shared made Grace feel slightly more comfortable about being summoned to the police chief's office. Still, she wondered if this was about the dead cat on her car, or if she was in some kind of trouble of which she was unaware. These days, anything was possible.

Following Mike's lead, she walked in to the office and sat down on a chair opposite Midland's head law enforcement officer.

"Hello Miss Reid. Thanks for coming in on such short notice. I think you'll be glad you did when you hear what I have to say."

"You've certainly got me intrigued, Chief Reynolds."

"I'm going to get straight to the point. We are closing the case on the dead cat incident. There haven't been any more nasty episodes or threatening phone calls that I know of, unless you haven't reported them?"

"Absolutely not. If anything had happened, you and Officer Healy would have been the first to know.

"Good. And now here's the big news, we're closing this case because we have arrested the person responsible."

Grace's ears began ringing as her blood pressure rose.

Did she hear right? Was the chief saying that who ever had stalked her, threatened her and tried to intimidate her with a dead cat was in custody? Was she finally going to be able to drive down the street without looking in her rear view mirror for someone following her?

Turning to Mike, she saw the validation of the chief's words in his eyes. It was finally over.

"Who is it you arrested?"

Giving a nod to his officer, Chief Reynolds relinquished the answer. Eye to eye, Mike held her steady as he replied.

"Johnny Marsh. Bill's son."

CHAPTER FIFTY

SUNLIGHT STREAMING THROUGH the window illuminated dust showers tumbling through the golden rays. After decades untouched, powdery layers coated every suitcase and bag Grace and Mike were extracting from Wood Haven's attic shelves.

This was the third Saturday the couple had dedicated to sorting through the abandoned suitcases. Other Wood Haven staffers were equally dedicated, working nights and weekends to catalogue the contents and identify the rightful owners of each piece of luggage. Yet for Grace, her focus was on finding the specific suitcases belonging to her Wood Haven seniors.

The luggage existed. Record keeping of the hundreds of suitcases proved that the possessions of all ten were taken when each was committed to the asylum. The problem was the assorted pieces of luggage were then locked in the attic and permanently forgotten

Just like those women and men, locked away and forgotten.

As someone who cherished her family's possessions that has been handed down through generations, Grace experienced a melancholy each time she immersed herself in a suitcase of displaced keepsakes—a set of seasoned pots and pans tucked away with cards of hand-written recipes titled, "From the kitchen of Hannah Brown,"—a small, neatly-packed collection of leather journals dating back to 1883, written by a young girl named, Alice, chronicling her journey from Poland to the coast of Spain and eventually safe passage to America.

For his part, Mike was captivated by the suitcases of men's shaving kits and knife collections and women's beauty items and kitchen aprons—items that personified each unknown owner.

Yet all who gave time to sorting through the suitcases were most deeply impacted by the letters and photographs that chronicled the people and places from which Wood Haven patients had been forever disconnected. Were it not for the tragic circumstances, the suitcases could easily have been documented as historical artifacts from the world at that time.

"Grace, come here. Check out what I've found."

Looking over her shoulder, she saw Mike holding up a piece of rectangular fabric. Moving towards him, she could see more clearly that the fabric was a sash made from satin and banded on either side in faded colors. Centered between the bands were black letters that read "Votes for Women."

Cautioning herself, Grace's heart began bubbling with excitement.

"Mike, I think you might be in Liberty's suitcase."

Kneeling beside the functional leather case, she carefully began sorting through the remaining items. The Women Suffrage Cookbook, a small round green pin with the letters, "WPU" stenciled in gold, a collection of photographs of women in hats and full-length dress wearing sashes resembling the one from the suitcase, most carrying signs demanding, "Votes for Women."

At last the suitcase revealed the possession for which Grace had been silently praying. In a side pocket, protected away, Grace extracted a handful of postcards. Hoping the collection would identify the owner, she slowly studied the photos on the front side of each card. The first showed a cartoon image of a woman actively resisting two police officers as they arrested her. Above the image, a title proclaimed, "The Wild Rose, Which Requires Careful Handling."

The next card showed a woman speaking in front of a group of men who were disparaging her in balloon remarks such as, "Go home and wash the baby." The title above the spirited woman read, "SUFFRAGETTES. Beauty & Intellect Are Superior to Brute Force."

Continuing to read through the collection, Grace came to the last card. Turning it over, she discovered a handwritten message in faintly readable ink.

September 12, 1920
Dear Liberty,

I must tell you that your name is truly reflective of the powerful spirit you bring to the suffreage movement and to our National Women's Party. We would not have achieved earning women the right to vote without your tireless efforts. I pray you continue to help carry us forward as we fight for passage of the Women's Equality Amendment.

In Sisterhood,

Alice Paul

Opposite the note was a mailing address. Miss Liberty Filipek 97 Orchard Street New York City, New York.

While Grace was not a student of the sufferage movement, she knew enough to recognize Alice Paul as the woman who had founded the National Women's Party and helped American women win the right to vote. It was also clear that this card was written to Gabrielle "Liberty" Filipek.

This is Liberty's suitcase.

Grace wrapped her arms around Mike offering a hug and a kiss fueled by the passion she felt at that moment for her seniors. Mike met Grace's intensity, folding her into his arms and caressing her lips within his own. The two became centered in the moment and their shared desire for more. It was only a loud cough and an awareness of another presence in the attic that drew them apart.

"Ah, excuse me, Grace, could I have a minute?"

Quickly disengaging, the two looked like high school kids busted by the principal.

"I apologize, Jonathan. Mike just found another suitcase belonging to one of the ten seniors and I guess I let my excitement carry me away."

"Nothing wrong with a little excitement to spice up a day, Grace. However, I just came from a meeting with Mayor Jenkins and Chief Reynolds. I knew you were up here sorting through the suitcases. I figured I'd make a quick stop to review and get these things off my mind."

Grace stood and smoothed away the imprint of Mike's body from her sweater. Taking his cue, Mike began gathering the vestiges of Liberty's mementos and returning them to their rightful place within her suitcase.

"Certainly, Jonathan. Do you want to go to your office, or mine?"

"No need. This will just take a few minutes. Then you can get back to looking through these suitcases. I know you're trying to find the last few to be able to return all ten before the seniors move."

Flipping open his leather portfolio, Jonathan began working through his check list.

"To start, the mayor and the chief and I reviewed the police investigation of Johnny Marsh. As you know he has admitted to following you, harassing you on the phone and leaving the dead cat on your car. Since he is a minor and this is his first offense, the prosecutor is willing to give the kid a break. If you agree, he will be sentenced to 500 hours of community service, which if completed within six months will allow for the charges to be dropped. At the same time, the judge on the case is recommending both Johnny and his father undergo counseling to get a handle on their anger and their shared, inappropriate behavior regarding our seniors moving into the community. While Johnny and his father are clear that the kid acted on his own, without awareness or support from his father, obviously Johnny takes his cues from Bill. The judge thinks it's important for the two of them to work on their problems together."

"I think a sentence of community service is a good solution, Jonathan. At seventeen, I would not want to see Johnny sent to any kind of reform school or prison. Plus, I believe helping others can teach important life lessons to people of any age. Who knows, maybe his father will benefit from the counseling experience as well. If I might make a suggestion. Perhaps assigning Johnny to community work with senior citizens at hospitals or in care facilities would be effective."

"Actually, Grace, I came up with an idea that all three of us endorsed, and I hope you'll agree as well. Johnny is going to fulfill his community service by helping finish our senior home. Then he'll have to perform maintenance and upkeep as well as any specific chores the seniors may have after they move and settled

Mike immediately spoke up in response to the proposal.

"Sounds like a good plan in theory, but are there safeguards to make sure he doesn't act out in anyway against the seniors?"

"Good point, Mike. We did discuss that very concern and the chief is going to work something out with the prosecutor and Jake Russell to make sure that Johnny is supervised at all times and held accountable."

"As long as there is accountability, Jonathan because I have the same thoughts as Mike. I don't want to disrupt this kid's life, but at the same time he's got a wicked streak that I don't want our seniors to directly experience. It needs to be made clear to both he and his father that there will be strong and punitive consequences should Johnny undertake so much as one cruel or underhanded action in that house, against the seniors or any staff that serves them."

"Agreed. I will make sure that stipulation is included in the final court paperwork. Moving on, I have read through your latest reports and everything seems in good order. I know that this suitcase project is eating up a lot of your time and you still have not found the ten pieces of luggage you are seeking. You're going to have to set a deadline, Grace, and come to grips with the fact that you may not be able to return everyone's possessions."

Grace felt a flare of anger rise up in her chest. Jonathan may be her boss, but he had no right assessing her suitcase goal as potentially unreachable. If she had to stay nights after work and weekends for the next month, she would find all ten of her senior's possessions. She was sure of it. Taking a calming breath, Grace did the thing her papa always advised.

Smile nice and say what people want to hear . . . then do what you want. It's usually easier to ask for forgiveness than permission.

"Thank you, Jonathan. I appreciate the advice and will make sure my suitcase search does not interfere with the senior's moving plans. That being said, I am happy to tell you this suitcase we just discovered brings the total to 8 that we now have in hand. The last two will hopefully turn up soon."

A sound of footsteps pounding up the attic stairs stopped conversation and diverted everyone's attention. Marge Davern, head nurse on the weekends, flew into the room at a frantic pace.

"Jonathan, it's Jane Bennett. Her temperature has spiked and we can't bring it down. She's not complaining of pain anywhere, but she never does. According to her chart, she hasn't really eaten for the last two days and they haven't been able to get liquids into her today. It's like she's decided she's not going to live and is purposely shutting down.

The prognosis moved Jonathan to the stairs with Nurse Davern close behind. Grace went the opposite way, to a shelf at the end of the attic where her senior's suitcases and bags were sitting in wait. The previous Saturday she had discovered Jane Bennett's valise filled with a leather bound album of pictures of the woman in younger and happier times and a matted, stuffed bear with a missing right eye.

Grace grasped the light weight bag and motioned to Mike.

"You can come or you can leave, but I have to give Jane Bennett her suitcase."

Instinctively the Midland cop understood the emotional drain Grace would experience in returning the woman's long lost possessions. Without hesitation, he followed her downstairs to the third floor, where he protectively remained as her shadow.

Grace stopped first at the nurse's station for the lastest update on Jane Bennett's condition. They told her pretty much the same details Nurse Davern had shared. Moving down the hallway, she quietly entered Jane Bennett's room, recalling only weeks earlier when she had done the same at Midland Hospital. This time however, the former nurse appeared dwarfed by her Wood Haven bed, her blankets barely rising and falling through her shallow breaths.

Jonathan stood with Nurse Davern on the far side of the bed A younger man, unknown to Grace, stood on the near side. Remaining just inside the door, Grace decided to observe and listen and be aware of all that was said.

It was the man who spoke first.

"To be honest, she is out of our medical control. I see it quite often with people this age. They decide they no longer want to live and there is no medicine that can change it. I'll write a prescription for pain killers, should she need them, and will check in later tonight."

Nodding to the man as he left the room, Grace turned her attention to Jane Bennett's stagnant body. Quitely moving to her bedside, she placed the small valise on a nearby tray table.

"Jonathan, if you have no objections, I would like to speak to Jane and tell her about her suitcase."

"I have no objections. Nurse Davern?"

"It's fine. I just don't know if she will respond. She has been slipping in and out of consciousness all afternoon and her body is showing signs of shutting down."

The impact of the nurse's words enflamed Grace. Over the last seven months she had come to know and love Jane Bennett. No doubt, following her recent hospitalization, the woman's body had declined, but her mind was still sharp. On a number of late afternoons the two women had enjoyed conversations ranging from books to favorite foods to God and religion. Grace felt as if she had been gifted with a second nana and Jane told everyone that Grace was family. She couldn't let this special woman slip away without hearing how much she was loved and valued and needed.

"Jane, it's Grace. I know you're feeling sleepy, but I'm hoping you'll open your eyes to see what I've brought you. It's a suitcase. Your suitcase. The one you had with you when you were committed to Wood Haven. Would you like to see what's in it? Shall I open it?"

With no recognition for her efforts, Grace determinedly continued. Releasing the two brass locks on the front of the valise, she raised open the lid. Choosing thoughtfully, she exhumed the photo album.

Turning back the cover, Grace began describing the various pictures forever captured on the brittle, yellowed photo paper. Images of Jane Bennett through the years were easy to identify. Other than some gray streaks and a few wrinkles, the woman's beauty had not faded. As for the rest of the people and the places, Grace simply made up stories as she told them.

None of it mattered. Jane never moved.

There was, however, motion beside her as Teagan entered the room and stepped alongside Grace, pressing solidly against her in support. Looking at the slowly fading person of Jane Bennett, Teagan reached out and lifted the woman's lifeless hand. Stroking from her fingers to her wrist, Teagan began humming.

Grace stood in amazed witness as the former nurse stirred slightly, her eyelids fluttering. As Teagan continued her healing actions, the comatose women opened her eyes and spoke in recognition.

"Grace. Teagan. I am so happy you are both here and we have this moment. I want you to know that I love you both. Always remember that."

Wanting desperately to sustain the woman's consciousness, Grace picked up the stuffed bear from the valise and held it where it was easily visible. Within Jane's momentary confusion blossomed a full reconnection with this remnant from her past.

"Where ever did you find it, Grace? That bear was the favorite stuffed animal of each of my children. As one outgrew it, the next would adopt it. Such sweet memories that make it feel as if they are here, right with me, after so long apart. Thank you for bringing them back to me Grace."

Encouraged, Grace exchanged the bear for the photo album and again began reviewing the images. Yet as quickly as Jane had engaged, she faded back into herself.

"Jane, look. Look at these photographs of you and your family, your children. Can you tell me who they are and where the pictures were taken? Jane? Jane!"

"You're goin' ta have ta leave her go Gracie. T'is her time and she's made up her mind."

Grace wanted to tell Teagan to be quiet and shake Jane to wake her up, but in her heart she knew the truth. Jane was near-death.

Retrieving the one-eyed teddy, Grace nestled the well-loved bear into the crook of Jane Bennett's neck, leaning in to kiss her on each cheek and across her forehead.

"I love you, Jane."

Then leaning back into the comfort of Teagan's body, the two women held vigil through the night, honoring their friend as she peacefully drew her final breaths and died.

Chapter Fifty-One

JANE BENNETT'S FUNERAL TOOK PLACE on Monday. Jonathan and Grace agreed the immediate scheduling was key to the wellbeing of the Wood Haven seniors, all of them deeply connected to the dedicated nurse.

The service was simple. Rev. Johnson from the Midland Congregational Church offered prayers, and Jonathan spoke briefly about Jane and her lifelong connection to Wood Haven. It was held in the common room on the third floor, allowing all nine seniors to attend, some with nurses guiding their wheelchairs, some walking independently, each carrying their own private memories and sorrows.

For Grace, the loss of Jane Bennett fueled her desire to discover the still-missing suitcases and return all nine to their rightful owners. Yet the timeline for the Faith File move was growing shorter, forcing Grace's work schedule to grow longer. More and more she could only carve out attic time during late night hours, leading to overnight stays in her office, when she was too exhausted to drive home.

Mike continued to partner with Grace in exploring the suitcases, often setting aside his own priorities. As they worked, the two shared memories of their own families, friends and growing up years. With the telling of each story the couple became more closely entwined, with each other and with the suitcase lives they were discovering.

"Did you always want to be a cop?"

It was a question Mike had asked himself lately, but he was caught off guard by the query coming from someone else, particularly Grace.

"I knew that I always wanted to serve my community. My work as a policeman is the ultimate definition of that goal. At the same time, I'll be able to retire when I'm fairly young and I have thought about what I might want to do then. To be honest, I'm not 100% sure."

"That's what I love most about you, Mike Healy. Your honesty. Even in those moments when I don't want to hear it, I love that you are always honest."

Wait, did I just say I love Mike Healy?

Grace didn't have to wait for an answer to her question.

"So, you love me, do you Grace Reid? Good to know."

Grace knew she was trapped in a quagmire of her own making and there was only one way out.

"That's the thing I HATE about you Mike Healy. Your obnoxious, arrogant attitude."

Laughing heartily, Mike left the suitcase he'd been investigating and moved to Grace. Taking hold of her arms he gently pulled her up, off the floor.

"Wait! What are you doing? Stop it, Mike. We have work to do. It's late and I'm tired."

Folding her into his chest, Mike gently massaged the small of Grace's back, nuzzling his cheek against hers. While she wanted to rail against him, the touch of his hands dissolved her mind into thoughts far removed from the Wood Haven suitcases.

"I'm sorry for teasing you, Grace. I know you weren't saying that you love me. But here's the thing, I *do* love you. I've come to love you with all my heart."

Grace's ears burned with the glow of Mike's words. While her mind began flashing warning signals, her body ignored them as she reached her lips to his in passionate desire for this special man.

When at last they pulled apart, Grace again ignored her mind and spoke.

"I forgive you Mike Healy, not because you deserve it, but because . . . I love you. So be careful with my heart."

In baring her true feelings, tears welled directly from within her.. Understanding, Mike spoke words from his heart as well.

"Sweet Grace, one thing you can forever trust is that I will always be true to you."

Sealing their love in a tender mingling of tears and kisses, the couple finally drew apart. Returning to their suitcases, the space between them filled with a heightened sense of each other. Quietly they continued their work within the resolute hope of restoring the memories to those who had lost them, at the same time creating their own.

Moving to select a new piece of luggage, Grace became particularly intrigued with a satchel pushed far to the back of a middle shelf. Like a true treasure it lie hidden, easy to miss. Scrunching face down on the shelf, she wriggled her body into the tight space and extended her arm to its maximum reach, determined to grab an edge of the satchel's leather straps. Finally, on her third try, Grace managed to give a good tug on one of the straps and the bag popped loose.

Extracting both herself and the satchel, Grace gently shook the oversized bag until, amid a cloud of dust, she could see the artful stitching used to craft the hand sewn piece of luggage. Unloosening two brass buckles, more suited to a belt than a satchel, Grace pushed back the flap and discovered a satin-lined interior.

The fabric was torn away in spots from its outer shell, and its rich burgundy tone had faded, but at the top edge, where lining and bag were still bound, a small pink rectangle caught Grace's eye. Turning closer to the overhead light, she pushed the flap further back and bent the satchel, allowing more illumination onto the pink shape. All she could see was delicate embroidery thread, the same pink as its background, in the shape of a word too pale to define.

"Mike, can you try to read this? Even under the lightbulb I can't make it out."

Moving beneath the singular light, Mike took the satchel and examined the inner lining, to no avail. Tucking the bag under his arm, the veteran cop reached into the deep side pocket of his vest, retrieving a mini black flashlight. With a grin, he acknowledged Grace's look of surprise.

"I was a boy scout. We're always prepared."

Shining the intense beam onto the fabric strip, Mike began calling out the embroidered letters as he could read them.

"The first one is an R. Then there's one that could either be an O, or a zero. And the last one is. . . ."

Grace spoke before Mike could finish.

"W. The last letter is a W. For Washington. Mike, this satchel belongs to Rebecca Odera Washington."

GRACE TRACKED THE CONTINUED rapid passage of November, not by the calendar but by the completion of the rough plumbing, wiring and drywall installation at the Faith File house. According to the latest update from project manager, Jake Russell, the walls and ceilings would usually be sanded and ready for paint in a matter of days, but with time off for Thanksgiving, they wouldn't be done until next week.

Thanksgiving.

Grace had received a few invitations to turkey dinner, one from Jonathan who was going to his sister, Karen's, and was sure she would be welcome. Another from Mary Burke, who was cooking for a housefull of her Irish relatives and extended family and kindly offered, " one more is no problem."

The thing was, Grace had a real yearning for a sense of place and family for the holidays this year. Realistically, she was not living in her own home, or in a town where she had roots. Plus the only family she could count were her parents, and they'd already let her know they were flying to DC to celebrate with some high profile attorney friends. The realization of just how isolated she was launched a gloom over Grace's mind that was descending upon her body.

Don't be sad, Gracie girl. You're not alone. You just need to count your blessings to realize how thankful you should be this year.

Oh papa, I know. You've always told me I need to count my blessings. It's just at this very moment, I feel a little lonely. I miss you and nana and the holiday traditions we always shared.

Make your own, sweet child. Don't be down in the dumps. Get out and have some fun.

Not wanting to be disrespectful, Grace adjourned the inner dialogue with her papa, but her heart was cleary communicating it wasn't in the mood for fun. Maybe she'd call Mike and see if he wanted to have dinner together.

Grace hadn't seen much of him lately. She knew he wore a lot of hats, but after their "I love you" moment the previous weekend, she thought he'd be around more.

As if responding to some kind of mental telepathy, Mike Healy appeared in her office doorway.

"Excuse me, Miss. I'm looking for Grace Reid."

"Feeling happiness rise from her heart, Grace smiled and joined in the game.

"I'm Grace Reid. What can I do for you officer?"

Striding toward her, Mike stepped around the desk and placed his hands on her office chair, spinning her fully into him.

"I received a complaint that you've been working too hard and need time away from the job. I've been assigned to take you into custody and ensure that happens."

Leaning into her, Mike offered his lips in a sensuous kiss that Grace received and returned. Without parting, he raised her body from the chair and bound them together. Coming up for air, Grace locked into Mike's eyes and saw the same expression she remembered her nana and papa sharing when they hugged.

Love.

"So, Miss Reid, where would you like to go for dinner? I'm here to whisk you away to the place of your desire."

The joy flooding through her body reminded Grace of her papa's advice to count her blessings. Suddenly she knew exactly how she wanted to celebrate Thanksgiving.

"I want to go to the P&C."

"The grocery store? Well, I guess I can cook if that's what you really want."

"No silly. I'm not talking about cooking tonight. I want to cook for Thanksgiving—a good old-fashioned turkey dinner with stuffing and gravy and mashed potatoes and green beans with French fried onions on top. Oh, and pies. Pecan and pumpkin with real whipped cream."

"Whoa, whoa little lady. Just who is going to eat all that food, cause it's way too much for the two of us."

"Of course it is. We'll be cooking for 11."

"And just who might those other nine people be?"

"My Wood Haven seniors, of course!"

It took Grace most of the following day to lay the groundwork for her Thanksgiving plan, but she managed to get everyone on board. Jonathan gave his permission for the celebration to take place in the third floor common room. Mary Burke agreed to allow nurses to rotate in and out of the dinner to ensure all seniors would be taken care of. In turn, Grace promised turkey suppers for all the nurses on staff that day. Joe Bush agreed to set up tables and chairs. Janine Skelley gave Grace carte blanche in the kitchen. Now all that was left was inviting the guests and preparing the food.

Invites first.

Grace left work early so she could stop by Schulz's Fine Paper and Exquisite Cards before they closed. Moving to the greeting card department, she did her best to stay on task amid cards of all materials and styles for every holiday, occasion and imaginable life moment. The beautiful array was overwhelmingly tempting to the greeting card junkie.

Determinedly moving to the end of the row, Grace found a collection of cards dedicated to Thanksgiving. Considering the late date, the display was pretty-well picked over. Grace worried if she would even find invitations for her turkey day feast. Finally, behind a stack of "This Season of Blessings" note cards, Grace discovered the last package of invites. Checking the price, she saw that there were ten cards and they were on sale.

Perfect!

That night, nestled in her bed, Grace wrote out nine invitations for Thanksgiving Dinner to all of her seniors. The thought of all of them gathered together around a table giving thanks in the place where so many had been hurt and destroyed sent chills up and down Grace's body. She was going to do everything within her power to ensure this dinner turned out perfectly.

Thanksgiving morning found Grace knee deep in potato peelings before the sun rose. The good news was that Janine had prepped the stuffing, squash and green beans the day before and Mary Burke had fashioned a centerpiece from mums and floral bits and pieces leftover from her own table. Additionally, Mike laid claim to professional turkey roasting skills taught to him by his mother, which he was exhibiting at the nearby sink where he was expertly rinsing and drying the 28-pound bird before "dressing and tenting it," whatever that meant. Overall, Grace felt confident that her turkey dinner would be a feast for the eyes as well as the stomach.

Her hand-scribed invitations had been delivered to each senior by Jonathan, along with a chocolate turkey sucker and his wishes for a Blessed Thanksgiving. Grace had purposely asked her boss to hand out the invites to involve him more in the celebration. While he couldn't attend the dinner, she thought it important for the seniors to know he was part of the planning. Grace was touched by his idea to include chocolate gifts with the written invites. She was equally heartened by the gift Jonathan gave her on Thanksgiving Eve, just before she left Wood Haven for the night.

He entered her office carring a black rectangular case, which he set on the desk before her with a dramatic flourish.

"Miss Reid, in the time you have been here you have given all of yourself and more in helping discover and establish homes for our Wood Haven Seniors. To say everyone here appreciates your diligence, your fortitude and your heart would be short-changing all you have accomplished. That's why tonight, I want to give you something in return. Something I know you have worked hard to discover, pushing yourself beyond ordinary limits. I humbly offer it to you as a result of my own efforts on your behalf. Happy Thanksgiving, Grace. I speak for everyone at Wood Haven when I say we are most thankful for you."

The sincerity of Jonathan's words rolled emotions from deep inside her that spilled out in tears of gratitude. With the merry-go-round of emotional happenings going on these days, it was becoming a regular event for Grace to break down and cry at work. Professional or not, she didn't even try to hold back anymore.

Standing up, Grace moved to the other side of the desk and encircled this man, more friend than boss, into an embrace of like hearts.

"Now you've got me tearing up, Grace. We've got to put a stop to this love fest before we're both crying like babies."

Stepping apart, Grace turned to her desk for a closer inspection of Jonathan's gift.

"Aren't you going to open it?"

"I am. I'm just trying to figure out what it is and why you're giving it to me."

"Let's just say it's something you've been struggling to find and I got lucky and found it for you. Now, would you please just open the darn thing!"

Releasing the metal levers that locked the lid to the base, Grace slowly raised the top of the case. Inside she discovered sketches, varied seascapes of shorelines like those she recalled from the trip to Ireland with her nana. Choosing one for closer inspection, Grace felt an awareness of the artwork, as if she'd seen artwork like it before. In a spark, she imagined the unframed canvas she'd purchased at Jewel's attic. The two artist's styles were remarkably similar, only unlike the unidentified painting hanging over her fireplace, the sketch in her hand bore a small signature in the lower right corner. Raising the paper closer, Grace stood in stunned silence as she read the name.

"Teagan?"

"Yes, Grace, Teagan. This is her suitcase from the attic. I spent the day up there yesterday determined to find it, and by the grace of God, I did. Now you have all nine suitcases and you can return them to each senior to help them move forward into their new lives."

Soaking up the full realization of Jonathan's words, Grace understood these suitcases offered a sense of place and family long ago stolen from her seniors that she could now restore—and perhaps somehow rediscover herself.

Chapter Fifty-Two

WITH ONLY A WEEK UNTIL CHRISTMAS, Grace was a bundle of nervous energy, all of it related to the relocation of her Wood Haven Seniors.

Today she was focused on ensuring the safe transfer of James, Maria, Janna and Regina to their suites at St. Augustine's. In two days, on December 20th, she would be immersed in moving Teagan, Maeve, Angel, Liberty and Rebecca to their new home, exactly on schedule.

Since Thanksgiving, Grace's life had become a blur of construction delays, permit deadlines, state inspections, board meetings and financial reviews. Yet in-between she'd managed to carve out meaningful time with her nine seniors—answering their questions, calming their moving fears and, more than anything, talking about their long-lost suitcases she'd returned to them on Thankgiving.

After Jonathan had presented her with Teagan's luggage on Thanksgiving Eve, Grace dragged him to the attic to help transfer the eight additional senior's cases down to her office. When all was in place, she made a point of locking her door to secure the valuable baggage. That night when Grace arrived home, she called Mike to update him on the turn of events. Together they agreed their Wood Haven Thanksgiving dinner would be the perfect time to return each suitcase to its rightful owner.

As it happened, the couple could not have scripted a more perfect plan, as Jonathan showed up at the holiday dinner unexpectedly, just as Grace and Mike were serving pie and coffee. While the seniors enjoyed dessert, the three conferred and agreed that Grace would undertake the formal presentation while the two men would hand-deliver the suitcases and bags.

Standing at the head of the dinner table, Grace began carefully explaining the attic discovery of the 400 suitcases, earlier in the year. She continued with details about the focused efforts of Jonathan, Nurse Burke, Officer Healy, herself and so many members of the Wood Haven staff, in searching for the suitcases belonging to the nine special individuals seated before her.

With a nod to Jonathan and Mike, Grace continued her speech while the two men began distributing the various pieces of luggage. The irony of the moment was not lost on Grace, as she observed the heartfelt reactions of those who had withstood so many years of mistreatment within the very walls where they were now gathered. Their reactions made the moment almost undefinable, as each senior became lost in emotional rediscoveries of their former lives.

There were Liberty's suffragist mementos and postcards packed with an assortment of letters and a leaflet of medical instructions following "female surgery." Janna's dresses were still neatly packed in tissue paper alongside a pair of worn leather shoes, a heavy knit sweater and a collection of hand made cards bound by a blue ribbon—signed by all six of her children.

Maria's valise was brimming with a family bible and prayer book, both printed in Spanish, a crucifix with a sliding front revealing a small white candle and a vaporized bottle labeled, "Holy Water," a black lace mantilla and carved ivory peinta, all protectively wrapped in a multi-layered floral skirt embroidered with beads and tiny gold bells.

Angel's collection included children's books tied with a thickly woven brown cord and attached by a clothespin to a raggedy doll with no clothes. Beneath were a book of poems and a bookmark prayer card featuring Mary, Mother of God.

James' simple leather luggage contained jacks and marbles along with a Greek Bible and a tooled leather wallet containing two dollars, a New York State driver's license expired in 1926 and a tattered photo of his wife and his children.

Maeve's possessions numbered a matched set of a hair brush, clothes brush and comb tucked away separately from a china teapot, a hand painted tea cup and a tin of black tea, all of it overseen by a photo of her four children taped to the suitcase lid.

Regina's satchel produced picture frames filled with the smiling faces of her three children and drawings on torn pieces of butcher paper, signed with professions of love for their mother. The layers of artwork kept hidden a midnight black velvet envelope safeguarding a triple strand of pearls and teardrop pearl earrings.

Rebecca's hand sewn bag was filled with gold coins stamped in German, a worn baby blanket and a stuffed animal of indeterminate shape and color all part of her childhood, while a deep blue velvet dress with her name hand stitched into the neckline evidenced her adult life as a seamstress.

Then there was Teagan's suitcase packed with canvases of Irish landscapes, a man's tweed cap, wooden rosary beads nestled into a woven pouch, a postcard of the Titanic and the Olympia ships and a photograph of the woman as a young girl, perched on the knee of a handsome man wearing the same tweed cap

Tears and laughter were in constant supply as the mementos were unveiled and the meaning of each keepsake revealed. The moment was inspirational and overwhelming and, as Grace began to notice, tiring. The emotional toll of the day was beginning to show on the faces and in the spirits of her seniors.

"I know we have all enjoyed the end to this special day, but it's time to give final thanks for all of us gathered around this dinner table and get some rest. So if I could ask the nurses to help our seniors return everything into their suitcases and secure them. While that's being done, I'd like to ask Jonathan to offer a closing blessing.

"Beggin' your pardon, Gracie, t'would it be alright ta add a bit o'somethin' ta the prayer?"

Recognizing the voice as Teagan's, Grace smiled and nodded at the sweet Irish woman who had become the unspoken leader of the Wood Haven seniors.

"Of course Teagan, you are all welcome to add any prayers you wish."

"Then I'd be wantin' ta add a prayer fer Nurse Bennett. T'is sad she's not here with us tonight, but I've not a doubt she watchin'o'er and smiling as we go sortin'through our bits n'pieces. May God have mercy on her soul."

A chorus of "Amen" echoed through the room in benediction for the woman who had cared for so many as both nurse and friend. Jonathan completed the Thanksgiving celebration with a simple grace.

"Lord, bless us all as we celebrate these special memories of the past and allow them to guide us through the future. Please help us always to remember the love that has surrounded us this Thanksgiving, uniting us forever as family."

* * *

DAYS AFTER THE HOLIDAY DINNER, the impact of the discovered suitcases continued to reverberate through Wood Haven's rooms and halls. Nurses and staff were mesmerized by the return of the belongings and what each person had packed so many years ago, or what their families had packed for them.

As for the seniors, they were grateful to again be in possession of their heirlooms, which most believed were forever lost and a few had even forgotten. Now, weeks later, the time had come to gather the four St. Augustine seniors along with their suitcases and begin the journey to their new lives.

Janine Skelley organized a farewell party in the third floor lounge. There, Jonathan and Wood Haven administrators gathered with the seniors and the nurses attending them. Glancing around the room, Grace noted the appearance of many as forlorn. In fact the mood of the entire room felt gloomy. She absolutely could not let this departure break down into tears and sadness.

"Teagan, can you sing us one of your special Irish songs?"

"Gracie, 'twas just thinkin' a bit o'music would give us all a cheer. I'll do a ditty me da would sing ta make us kids smile."

Teagan lifted her voice and encouraged everyone to clap along. Within minutes the gathering was transformed into a spirited party with a few of the nurses dancing their own version of an Irish jig. When at last Teagan sang out the final verse, the room erupted in racous applause and cheers. It was a perfect send off.

Before the good cheer diminished, Grace called on the nurses to transport the four seniors to the waiting van in the parking lot. Within minutes all were safely tucked in place and on their way to St. Augustine's.

Upon arrival, it took the better part of an hour to settle James, Maria, Janna and Regina into the care facility. The St. Augustine staff immediately took charge of escorting the seniors to their new homes, while Grace met with the facility's administrator, Marcus Johnson.

The two reviewed the required paperwork to ensure all was in order. Grace then handed over files she had meticulously created based on information in each senior's asylum paperwork, as well as from the times and talks she had shared with them over the last seven months. It was a task she'd felt driven to accomplish in hopes that the compilation would smooth the transition for all involved. When at last Grace felt sure every detail was complete, she set off for a final check on her seniors before leaving them. She decided to start with

Maria, knowing the woman would be the most difficult to engage.

Knocking on her door and announcing herself, Grace was taken aback when Maria called out an invitation to enter. Cautiously, Grace poked her head into the room anticipating a nasty remark, or worse, stone silence.

"Buenas tardes, Senorita Reid. I hope the end of this long day still finds you well. You must be exhausted with all you have done to make this move good and safe for us."

Instinctively, Grace responded.

"Buenas tardes to you, Maria, and yes, it has been a long day. I am tired. But I didn't want to leave without making sure you are settled in and if you have any needs or questions."

As Grace stepped fully into the sitting area of the suite, she noticed the prayer book and bible from the woman's suitcase set out on the main table, and the crucifix already hung on a nearby wall.

"My needs are few and, as you can see, an attendant came by and hung mi madre's cross in a place of honor. It has been a lifetime since I felt her spirit. Now I have her prayer book and her bible, I can be at peace here and again celebrate the religious traditions we once shared."

Pausing in thought, Maria turned her gaze fully to Grace.

"Senorita Reid, I have been not friendly since your arrival at Wood Haven. But tonight I thank you for bringing me to this new place and returning to me my mother's possessions. I will forever keep you in my prayers."

The months of struggles between the two women faded in the warmth of Maria's words. Grace moved closer and entwined their hands.

"Thank you for your kindness, Maria. I am grateful we have come to a better place and I pray your life at St. Augustine's will be a good one. The nurses will keep Jonathan updated on how you and James and Janna and Regina are doing and I will be sure to stay in touch."

Leaning in, Grace kissed away a tear slowly sliding down the woman's cheek.

"Dios bendiga. God bless, Grace."

The surprisingly poignant exchange caused Grace to take a moment before moving on to Janna and Regina. Standing in the hallway outside their room, she felt her emotions from the last month compounding—not just the frustrations and challenges of organizing the relocations, but the realization that completing her job meant the end of her Wood Haven relationships.

Certainly, it was the nature of her work—short time frames with specific goals which, when achieved, moved her along to the next assignment. That didn't mean this particular leaving was easy.

Grace never became overly involved in any of her consulting work. She made friends and formed relationships that continued through yearly Christmas cards and occasional phone calls, but they were just that, long distance. She'd been fine with that for years. However, thoughts of never again sharing tea with Teagan or flirting with James, or being lectured on women's rights by Liberty were all painful and a bit disorienting.

"Are you alright, Miss. Can I help you?"

The queries from the St. Augustine nurse nudged Grace from her reflections.

"Thank you, I'm fine. Just taking a moment before I visit my friends."

Friends? When did these seniors become more than another work assignment? When did they become part of the fabric of my life?

Shaking off her melancholy, Grace summoned a positive mindset and a smile as she entered Janna and Regina's suite. The scene before her caused true joy to embellish her smile. The two women were cozied up in oversized recliner chairs, furniture Grace had ensured would be part of their new home. On surrounding tables, pictures and artwork of their children rediscovered from their suitcases were prominently displayed. The effect made the room overflow with the presence of their families. Drawing close to the two women, Grace realized they had donned the jewelry and clothing from their suitcases as well—Janna's pearl necklace and earrings handed down to her from her grandmother and Regina's heavy knit sweater crafted by her mother with love.

"Well ladies, I don't know what to say. You've hardly been here a day and already your new home is beautiful. I love the photos and the artwork. It's as if your children are right here with you. How do you feel? Are you comfortable? Is there anything you need?"

As always, Janna spoke first, with Regina smiling contentedly.

"Oh my, Grace, our new home is lovely. Everyone has been so nice, stopping by to check on us and putting our children's pictures and artwork around. We feel so blessed, don't we, Regina?"

Through a shy smile, the seventy-six-year old woman reached up and caressed the luminescent string of pearls encircling her neck.

"I am happy to once again wear my grandmother's pearls. It was the last time I saw my mother that she gave them to me, on my wedding day. Her mother had given them to her, the same, and she told me that no woman should live without one fine piece of jewelry."

"I understand your passion for your pearls, Regina, as I have my grandmother's and wear them whenever I have the chance. It makes me feel close to her, as if we're together again, like when she was alive."

With the women expressing no needs or wants, Grace gave them each a warm hug and a promise to stay in touch before moving on to her final St. Augustine's stop.

Of all the Wood Haven seniors, James Ardonis held a most special place in Grace's heart. It wasn't solely his flirtatious charm, it was the heartfelt stories he told of his life in Greece, in America and at Wood Haven. The man had a way of engaging her no matter the narrative or its circumstance.

With a knock, Grace cautiously pushed open the door. There in the middle of the room, on a bed designed to support his fragile back, James lie lay in smiling welcome.

"Miss Reid. Please enter in to my home. I am honored to welcome you as my first visitor."

While the charming Greek would never have full need of his spacious living quarters, Grace was glad Marcus Johnson had agreed to place him in the suite. After surviving in a one-room cabin beside a graveyard for so many years, she felt a responsibility to settle James in a space that was gracious and felt welcoming, like a true home. She knew it would only be a matter of time before James would need to be transferred to long term care, but for now he would wake up each morning in a place that made him feel special.

Looking around, Grace recognized James' Bible from his suitcase on a table within his reach. Taped to the edge of that table was the photograph of his wife and children.

"James you look right at home in this fancy suite. I think you will really enjoy living here."

"Let us be honest, Miss Reid. I will be here only a short time as the demands of my dwindling body will continue. But today, I am most grateful for all you have done to give me this time and place. It is my fondest hope to live fully here each day and, God willing, welcome my love."

Of all the mysteries surrounding Wood Haven, Grace found James and his professed love the most intriguing. Who was this woman of whom he continually spoke? How was it they managed to develop a relationship within the stringent confines of an asylum?

"James, your honesty is one of the things I find most appealing about you. Out of respect, I acknowledge your prognosis of the time you may be able to remain in this suite. What I cannot fathom, however, is this woman whom you call your love. Who is she, and how have you managed to forge a relationship over these many years?"

"Miss Reid, I too have enjoyed the integrity of our words and thoughts. Such things are too often set aside as unimportant, but I know them to be the foundation of relationships. That is what attracted me to the woman I call my love. That and her beauty, of course."

Within the playful nature of his remark, Grace recognized the truth James was openly sharing. Yet she could still not imagine how a love affair could thrive within the toxic Wood Haven atmosphere. As she went to question him again about the woman's identity, James spoke.

"For more time than I know or can count, the very thought of this woman has given me reason to rise each morning, even on days when sadness and pain were my sole companions. Our time has been slight, for many years only when outside working and, now moving freely through the third floor, together in my room where we talk of so many things and sit in silence as well, grateful to be together. But no matter where or when, this woman and I are bound by one night many years ago in my cabin when we pledged ourselves, mind and body. It was a moment almost inconceivable, but worth every risk. And although we continued to be separated, from that night we have been bonded, as if husband and wife."

Grace was astounded by the story James was sharing, to the point of being unsure if she truly understood his words. Did he and a woman consummate a relationship in his cabin by the cemetery? The logistics of such a thing happening were almost impossible to consider. Yet James had no reason to tell her such, other than truthful revelation.

More than anything, Grace was driven to know the identity of the woman. Since James continued to refer to her in the present tense, she had to believe, "his love" was still alive. Whoever she was, the woman had to be one of the Wood Haven seniors. As if reading her mind, James spoke through a tearful smile.

"My memories of that special night continue to move me to tears, as you can see. My heart overflows for this woman, which is why I am speaking to you. It is my deepest hope that by sharing our story, a secret for so long held, you will help find a way that we can still see each other now that I have been moved here. Trusting, I am asking if you will do us that kindness, Miss Reid."

Stunned again, Grace responded simply.

"James, I have to ask, who is this woman you speak of as your wife?"

Looking calmly into her eyes, James spoke the name.

"Teagan, Ms Reid. The love I hold so deeply in my heart is Teagan."

Chapter Fifty-Three

GRACE AWOKE WITH A pounding in her head. Rolling over to try and escape the noise only compounded it with the sound of ringing bells. As she was about to plop a pillow over her head, her brain decided to engage, forcing her awake. Quickly she identified the coupled ringing of her alarm clock and telephone, with what sounded like someone vigorously knocking at her front door.

Tackling the closest first, she clicked off her clock. Then she grabbed the phone and asked who ever was calling if they could hang on a minute. Belting her robe in place, Grace ran down the stairs to answer the still-insistent knocks at her door.

"Grace. Are you ok?"

Mike Healy stood before her, backed by morning sunshine outlining his body like a sainted halo.

"Mike, what are you doing here and why are you pounding on my door?"

"Well, first of all, it's December 20th. Moving day for your Faith File and we had early morning plans for breakfast at Cuppa Joe. I know how hard you've been working and how tired you are, so when you didn't show up for breakfast, I figured you'd overslept and. . . ."

The rest of the policeman's words were lost midsentence as the realization of the day dawned on Grace.

"Oh my gosh, I gotta go."

Turning on a dead run, Grace took the stairs two at a time and slid down the hall to the bathroom. Flipping on the shower faucet, she made a quick turn to her bedroom to grab clothes for the day. As she sped past her bed, she saw the receiver sitting alongside the phone.

"Hello. Hello. Are you still there? Grace, is everything ok?"

Recognizing her boss's voice, Grace was not about to let him know she'd overslept on moving day.

"Of course, Jonathan. I'm sorry. Someone was knocking at my door at the same time you called."

"Alright. I was just calling to remind you about our review meeting before you transport the seniors to their house. After all we've gone through I don't want there to be any last minute hold ups or complications. Also, there's something I need to discuss with you."

"Of course, Jonathan. Nine o'clock in your office. I'll be there."

Steam from the shower was wafting through the hallway as Grace finally got herself and her clothes into the bathroom. Flipping on the fan and cracking open the window, Grace jumped under the steaming water and allowed herself a few minutes of luxurious relaxation.

Where had the time gone? Was she really prepared to move the Faith File from Wood Haven? Had she covered all the details well enough to satisfy Jonathan? Equally as important, had she put the furniture and decorating touches in place well enough to transform the house into a home for these women who deserved all that and more?

In her mind, Grace knew the answers to all the questions were yes. It was trusting herself that was the challenge. Grace wanted beyond all measure to ensure the future comfort and care of Maeve, Liberty, Angel, Rebecca and Teagan. Her fierce dedication to the women expanded her project goals beyond any she had ever accomplished. Added to that was Grace's intense desire to permanently preserve the memory of Jane Bennett. The end result was an extensive project checklist requiring extraordinary attention to detail and coordination of services. Being late on moving day was not any part of that list.

Dressing and giving her hair and make-up a once over, Grace headed downstairs to the kitchen to brew a pot of tea. Entering the kitchen, she laughed as she realized that, despite leaving Mike at the door, he'd come in and made his own coffee and was standing in wait, offering her a thermos of tea to go.

"Thought you might need this today."

"Mike, you are the best. I'm so sorry about missing breakfast. I know I've been out of the loop for the last few weeks and it's not going to get any better after in the next few days. I'll be completing all the final Wood Haven paperwork and packing up my things in the office as well as here in the house to move back to Buffalo."

Grace's words gave rise to emotions that choked off her voice. The couple had not really discussed their relationship since their attic declaration of love. Sensibly, Grace felt as if the end of the Wood Haven project would lead to their parting of the ways. Long distance relationships just weren't feasible. They were both adults and needed to be reasonable about their futures.

"That's what I was hoping to talk to you about at breakfast, Grace. I know your schedule has kept you beyond busy since Thanksgiving and we've had no time to really talk. And while there may be roadblocks to continuing our relationship, what we've found is special, not like anything I've ever known. So before you get your mindset on packing and moving, can we please find time for us to sit down and see if we can figure out how to make this work?"

Grace felt her stomach knot with the words her throat was choking down but she knew needed to be spoken. Mike was a romantic. She was a realist. The relationship they'd developed was based on the intense experiences of the last seven months, which was not a true barometer of their compatability. He had to understand that. She would make him understand it.

"Mike, I've come to love you and the time we've spent together while I've been in Midland, but the truth is, my home is in Buffalo and yours is here. Add to that the fact my career is all about travel. I am on the road for months at a time. I love what I do and don't envision myself being a stay-at-home wife or mother anytime soon, if ever. I think we need to be realistic about our chances and pehaps agree to part on good terms now rather than in hurt or anger down the road."

Grace could see in Mike's eyes the pain caused by her words.

Better now, before it gets harder.

The silence between them felt like an impenetrable wall and Grace knew the responsibility for the moment was hers.

"Mike, I'm sorry. I'm not trying to hurt you. This is painful for me as well. I just don't see any other way. And right now I have got to get to Wood Haven."

Without a word, Mike picked up his police hat and strode out the door, closing it firmly as he left.

Grace wanted to run after him. She wanted life to be simple and easy that way. But she couldn't and it wasn't and she had to go to work. The Faith File was waiting for her to help them begin again and that's where she would focus.

That's what would get her through. That's how she would finish the job and move on.

REACHING HER OFFICE WITH AN hour to spare, Grace pulled out the day's check list and began making notes. After her meeting with Jonathan, she needed to reach out to the media to ensure their attendance at the special ribbon cutting ceremony, check with the Midland government officials to remind them of the 2 pm ceremony time, call Suzy at Cuppa Joe to follow up that they were delivering and setting up the refreshments, and check in with Jake Russell that the punch list of items in and around the house she left after her final walk through had been completed.

It was a going to be a busy day and Grace wanted to be sure she didn't lose sight of the most important element—making sure Maeve, Liberty, Angel, Rebecca and Teagan were all safely and comfortably settled into Bennett House.

Bennett House. I like the sound of that and I love that Jane Bennett will be a part of the home, as a member of the Faith File, as she deserved.

Grace came up with the idea after one of her afternoon teas with Teagan. It was clear from the Irish woman's conversation that the seniors missed Jane Bennett and were struggling with her absence. Wanting to soothe their pain, Grace came up with the only way she could imagine to keep the caring nurse connected in a real way. She made the suggestion to Jonathan to name the Faith File home Bennett House and host a ribbon cutting ceremony in honor of the remarkable woman. She was thrilled when Jonathan approved the idea without hesitation and could hardly keep from sharing the secret with her seniors everytime they were together. She couldn't wait to see their reaction at the ribbon cutting.

"So's you're lookin' pretty happy with yourself, Gracie girl. Is it bein' rid o'us puttin' that smile on your face?"

"Teagan. I'm happy because you're here and we can share a cup of tea. Come and let's catch up."

Grace had been trying to spend time with Teagan since James had revealed their relationship. While she initially found the information startling, she decided to discuss the situation with Jonathan to see if there would be any problem with a regular visiting schedule for the couple. After consulting with Mary Burke regarding the couple's interactions while at Wood Haven and reaching out to Rebecca Whitford from the state's office of senior services and Marcus Johnston at St. Augustine's, Jonathan agreed. At this stage in their lives there was no reason to prevent James and Teagan from spending time together. A calendar was drawn up and a ride system organized with St Augustine's van service that provided a weekly time for the two to share lunch and visit.

"So Teagan, how is James?"

Grace was tickled to see a pink blush cover the almost 70-year old woman's face.

"I'll be sayin' he's fine, Gracie girl, thanks ta you. Not him nor me ever thought we'd be spendin' time together like a normal couple. Ta be able ta share a meal and chit chat without worryin o'someone catchin' us, or punishin' us, 'tis as good as any miracle God's performed."

With a breath that turned into a longing sigh, Teagan softly added, "Truth be told, I'm thinkin 'tis a miracle only meant ta last fer a bit. James isn't eatin' all that much these days and he's sleepin' a fair share. I've seen it many a time o'er the years and know there be only a number of days we'd be havin' left."

Grace wanted to tell Teagan she was wrong, that she and James had years ahead. Sadly, that wasn't the case and both women knew it. Searching for the right words, Grace found herself sharing details about her own love life.

"Loving someone is hard. You have to be realistic and not let the impractical, romantic side of your heart overly influence you. Otherwise you end up in poorly matched relationships with no future. And for my nickel, that's more painful than not being in a relationship at all."

"Now Gracie girl, would we be talkin' 'bout me here, or 'bout you?"

The honesty of the question grabbed Grace's heart.

I guess if I'm being honest, I'm talking about me. I know I was completely logical in what I said to Mike about moving back to Buffalo—that it's the best thing for both of us. But I'm starting to wonder if anything could be worse than the heartbreak I'm experiencing right now.

"There's a bit of advice I'm goin' ta share with ya Gracie. I'd a lifetime locked away with people missin' love in any form. 'Tis not good, not normal. Like keepin' sun and water from the soil. So many in this God forsaken place withered up and died in their hearts. I hear what ya say 'bout makin' sure love makes sense, but at the end o'the day, nothin' 'bout love is sensible, don'cha know. 'Tis all about the heart and without that, true love can't survive. If ya love him, Gracie Girl, ya best think 'bout it. Now I'm off ta finish packin' me things and makin' sure the others is ready ta go as well."

As Grace gathered her notes for her meeting with Jonathan, Teagan's words kept replaying in her mind. Was the woman right? Was love solely about the heart? Were logic and good sense the antithesis of true love? Thinking about it hurt her head and so she stopped, needing all of her brain power to focus on the day's full schedule of moving and ribbon cutting.

Reaching Jonathan's office, Grace found the secretary's desk unoccupied and her boss's door open. Making her way to the doorway, she gave a rap on the solid oak frame.

"Morning, Grace. Have a seat."

For the next half hour the two reviewed the day's schedule along with the final details of the press conference and ribbon cutting. Grace had everything in place and ably presented all details to Jonathan in an orderly fashion. When they completed their shared check list, Grace packed up her notes and prepared to leave.

"Grace, there's one more thing I'd like to discuss with you, if you've got a minute."

"Certainly."

Opening his desk drawer, he withdrew a beautifully wrapped box finished off with a perfectly tied bow. Handing it across the desk, Jonathan spoke.

"Grace, I know it's been a long seven months for you here at Wood Haven and you have endured experiences none of us ever anticipated that were unquestionably above and beyond the norm. But I have to say you managed the challenges with a professionalism that earned the respect of the Midland Community as well as New Jersey State officials, from the governor's office to the department of senior services. Most importantly, you became integral to our seniors in listening to them and understanding their needs and wants when it came to the relocation process. Every single one of them love you, truly. So, on behalf of all of us at Wood Haven, I want to give you this gift to thank you and keep us all forever close to your heart."

Again, with no ability to control her emotions, Grace carefully unwraveled the ribbon and wrap to discover a small gold box. Opening the lid, Grace discovered a gold heart locket with a photo of her Wood Haven Seniors inside. On the back, the words, "Love you Gracie" were engraved.

"This is beautiful, Jonathan, and means more than you will ever know.

Thank you."

Hoping to escape before breaking into a full out barrage of tears, Grace started to leave and was again stalled by Jonathan.

"One more thing, Grace. Rebecca Whitford called me yesterday. She'd just come out of a meeting with the governor and wanted to talk to me about you. Seems your work here has not gone unnoticed by state officials and they want us to discuss a new position they are creating within the senior services department. The title is Director of Deinstitutionalization and it would involve working with former asylums across the state, just as you have here. It would be a pilot program in New Jersey that could serve as a prototype for the rest of the country. If that happens, there's a very good chance you would be asked to oversee the program nationally."

This day seemed intent on delivering shocks to Grace and it wasn't even lunchtime. Taking a couple of deep breaths, she did her best to collect her thoughts and reply intelligently, despite feeling as if her brain was quickly turning to mush.

"Jonathan, I'm at a bit of a loss for words. That is a lot of information to process, especially today when I need to focus on moving the Faith File and the ribbon cutting. I truly appreciate that the governor and Rebecca think so highly of my work. I'd ask that you give me a couple of days to think it through."

"Absolutely. And when things here have calmed down and you have some time to clear your head, know that I'm here to talk about any of this. I've been around the state for more years than I want to admit and am happy to share my experiences, if you think it would be helpful."

Grace retreated to her office and closed and locked the door. Her head felt like it was going to explode with her conversations with Mike, Teagan and Jonathan, each one pulling her heart in a different direction.

Looking at the clock, she had a half hour before Janine Skelley's celebration for the Faith File. Then she had to focus on getting all five of her seniors transported to Bennett House in time to get them settled and ready for the ribbon cutting.

Nana, I am so worn out by today with emotional moments yet to come this afternoon. Please help me find the strength to do what is needed to support my seniors and get them settled in ways that will make them feel as if they are truly home.

Chapter Fifty-Four

TEAGAN LED THE GROUP WALKING up the steps and through the front door. As the five women entered into the freshly painted and decorated living room, the space was filled with a deafening silence.

Cautiously they began moving through the house, each one drawn to a different aspect of the layout and design. Along the way, a word was spoken, an observation murmured, but for the most part the procession was reverentially quiet.

When they reached the bedroom wing, Grace became a tour guide, assigning each woman a room she had decorated specifically for them. That's when the dam broke. Conversation and laughter began spilling through the house, transforming it into a home.

When they were settled, Grace summoned all five to the dining room where she introduced them to Rosemary Koch, the woman in charge of the house. Rosemary was a mother of six grown children and she had cared for both her parents until their dying days. She loved to cook and clean and enjoyed the company of others. In effect, she was the perfect person for Bennett House.

As the women took seats around the table, Rosemary served a lunch of tomato soup and grilled cheese sandwiches. She topped off the meal with a plate of fresh-from-the-oven chocolate chip cookies that disappeared like snow on a sunny day. Conversation traveled around the table in an energy sustained by the women's excitement. Grace wanted to send them to their rooms to rest before the ribbon cutting, but first she had to update them on the house dedication.

"Ladies, I'm thrilled to look around this table and see your smiling faces. It is the best Christmas gift I could receive. I know you're looking forward to the ribbon cutting this afternoon. I'd like to suggest until then, you take a little rest in your rooms. But before you go there's some news I would like to share with you about today."

"Truth be told, Gracie, there's nothin' ya say could be givin' us anything better than this house and our rooms."

"Well, Teagan, I'm glad you feel that way, but I think you and Angel and Maeve and Rebecca and Liberty are all going to want to hear what I have to tell you. Jonathan and I talked at length about the need for a name for your new home. We thought it was important not only for you, but for the people of Midland to have an identity for this special place that would distinguish it. After much thought, we decided to name your new home, Bennett House, in memory of Jane. Today when the ribbon is cut we will unveil a plaque at the front door in Nurse Bennett's honor."

Grace's announcement was met with a combination of applause, cheers and a few tears. Angel was the first to speak.

"I will always be grateful for Nurse Bennett bringing me back to life after being raped in the storage closet. Living in a home in her name and honor will continue to make me feel safe."

Looks passed around the table, wordlessly communicating all each woman had endured and managed to survive. Without a sound, Teagan stood. Reaching out her hands to each side, the rest of the women followed until they were connected in a circle. Raising her voice, Teagan began singing the words to her mother's favorite hymn, "Amazing Grace." It took only a few notes before the rest of the women joined in the singing, delivering their own benediction upon the spirit of Bennett House.

Over the next hour, Grace worked outside, attaching the plaque to the house and setting up the ribbon across the doorway, leaving an oversized pair of gold scissors to the side for the official ribbon cutting photograph. Inside, Rosemary prepared the dining room table with refreshments Grace had ordered from Cuppa Joe and set out planters of poinsettias, donated by Karen's real estate office. Grace added the final touch by turning on a tape recording of Christmas music. The instrumental tunes drew the women from their bedrooms, walking in wonder throughout the space.

When the invited guests and media arrived, the ribbon cutting and dedication of Bennett House took place. While the five women began the ceremony as unfamiliar participants, by the time the ribbon was cut and food was served, they were fully engaged in the celebration, giving interviews to reporters and posing for photographs with the mayor. Watching the merriment unfold. Jonathan approached Grace to congratulate her yet again.

"Something tells me we are not going to have to worry about these women enjoying their life at Bennett House."

"I agree, Jonathan. It's been amazing to watch them settle in and be immediately comfortable. I thought it might take a bit of time, but I do believe dedicating the house to Jane gave them a sense of belonging."

"It was your brilliant idea, Grace. Again, job well done. And by the way, I hope you seriously consider our conversation from this morning. You have a real talent for this work. I believe you can make a difference across America helping seniors, as you have done here at Wood Haven."

While Grace politely acknowledged Jonathan's words, she felt a strong tug at her heartstrings when he mentioned Wood Haven. She'd worked and consulted at a number of senior care facilities, but neither the staff nor the seniors had ever impacted her so deeply. And if she wanted to be honest, Mike Healy played a part in her strong feelings as well.

Finally, Bennett House emptied of all but those who belonged, and Grace. Rosemary had cleared away the refreshments and was preparing to serve up a dinner of salad and spaghetti with meatballs. The smell of her homemade sauce permeated the house.

All five women assembled in the dining room, animatedly talking about the day and the interviews and the photographs, all within the background of Christmas carols. It was perfect. It was home.

Moving through the group, Grace bent and gave each woman a hug and kiss, promising to stop back often over the next few days. When she came to Teagan, the sturdy Irish woman pushed away Grace's hug and instead stood alongside of her.

"Ladies, if you'd all quiet down just a minute, we need ta give Gracie here a proper thanks and good night."

With a descending noise level, Teagan continued.

"Grace Reid, ya come ta us a stranger, but you'll be leavin' us a daughter we couldn't love more were ya our own. There's not enough thanks in the world ta repay ya fer what ya give us, but know that we'll love ya forever and keep ya in our prayers always."

As the women applauded and cheered her name, Teagan turned and folded Grace into a hug that connected the two women through generations. It was a place Grace longingly remained, imprinting the feeling deeply into her being. When at last the two women drew apart, they understood they were forever bonded. Reaching her hand to Grace's cheek, Teagan whispered to her.

"Be good, Gracie girl, and remember life is all about love. Without it, nothin' else matters."

GRACE SPENT THE DAYS LEADING up to Christmas as planned, completing the necessary Wood Haven paperwork for the state and the Midland Township during the day and packing up her house at night. When she found herself a bit at odds, missing her seniors and Mike, she would make a stop at Bennett House for a quick fix. So far, she had dropped by every day since the ribbon cutting.

Today's trip was different, however. Grace was driving to Bennett House with a gift in the form of the painting she had discovered in Jewel's Attic. The canvas seascape sketches in Teagan's suitcase reminded Grace of the artwork she purchased when she first arrived in Midland. Rather than ship it back to Buffalo, she thought it might please the women to have it displayed in their home.

Pulling up to Bennett house, Grace saw a police car parked on the street just beyond the driveway. Concerned, she left the painting in the back of her car to accelerate her entry into the house. Taking the front steps two at a time, she swung open the door and landed in what appeared to be a holiday party, complete with Santa Claus seated in the center of the room.

"Gracie girl, close the door and come in. We're just finishin' up a Christmas party, don'cha know. Santa here has been handin' out presents. Sure'n he's got somethin' in his sack fer ya."

Glancing at Santa, Grace tried to get a better look at the jolly old elf's eyes shaded beneath his fur bordered hat and gold frame glasses. She knew those eyes. She'd looked into them recently during some pretty memorable life moments.

"Ho-ho-ho, Gracie girl is it? Come over here and sit on Santa's lap. Tell me what you'd like for Christmas."

"No, that's ok, Santa. I really don't need any presents."

Grace's refusal launched Maeve and Rebecca into action. Before she could avoid them, they were doing their best to push and pull her toward Santa's chair. Worried her resistance might hurt the women, Grace acceded and gingerly deposited herself on the edge of Santa's legs. Deciding the best way to get through the situation was to play along, Grace turned toward Santa and gave him an ear full.

"Ok Santa, you want my list, here it is. I want everyone at Bennett House to be happy and healthy. I want the people of Midland to welcome these women into the community and make them feel as if they matter. And I want you to promise to keep them all safe. And I don't think any of those things are in your pretty red sack, so I'll be getting up now."

Grace felt Mike Healy's eyes burning into her back as she moved away from him.

"Aw, Gracie, that was a lotta good wishes fer us, but nothin' fer yourself. Is there nothin' you'd be wantin'?"

"Actually, Teagan, I have something I want to give to all of you but it's out in my car. I'll be right back."

As Grace struggled to extract the oversized painting from the back seat of her car, Santa Mike came out of the house followed by the fond farewells of the Bennett House seniors. Walking down the driveway, he dropped his sack alongside her car and opened the opposite back door. Gently he freed the artwork and guided it into Grace's grasp.

"Thank you."

"Consider it Santa's parting gift."

"Mike."

"Save it, Grace. I get it. You had your fun while you were here, but now you're leaving and I'm just part of what you are leaving behind. Disposable."

"That's not fair. I never said anything like that and you know it."

"You know what's not fair, Grace? That you unilaterally decided for both of us what should happen and why. You never even tried to talk about it together, or give us a chance to figure something out. That's what's not fair. So, Merry Christmas, Grace, and good luck where ever you go."

With that, Mike whipped off his Santa hat and beard, picked up his sack and put it all in the police car. Making a tight u-turn he drove off without so much as a glance Grace's way.

Well, I guess I deserved that. And it certainly makes it easier to leave.

Turning to the house, Grace saw all five women standing in the windows.

Clearly they had been watching her Santa encounter. Grace was going to have to adeptly dodge their questions and concerns. Hopefully the painting would serve as a distraction.

Re-entering the house, Grace asked the women to gather around the dining room table. Once they were all seated, Grace shared the story of her first weekend in Midland and the Saturday she spent strolling through the town. She described in detail Jewel's Attic, her excitement in finding the hidden painting and learning the store owner had purchased it at a farm auction in New York State. Finally, Grace explained that with all of the Wood Haven seniors settled at St. Augustines and Bennett House, her work was now complete. She would be returning home to Buffalo. Rather than pack up the painting and risk shipping it, she wanted to give it to Bennett House and share its beauty, which she'd loved from the moment she saw it.

Turning the canvas toward them, all the women oohed and aahd, except Teagan. The Irishwoman slowly stood and moved to the painting, taking it from Grace's hands and setting it onto the dining room table. The room fell hushed as everyone watched her lightly run her fingers over the seascape, as if tracing the image. After several minutes, Grace decided to try and engage her.

"Teagan, is everything alright?"

Smiling through her tears, the woman answered.

"Yes, Gracie girl. It's just I've not seen this paintin' since I was a young woman livin' with Mr and Mrs. Engler, the people who hired me ta nanny their beibis. When the Crash come they lost their money. Couldn't afford ta keep me. But they'd been good ta me, the Mister even payin' fer me art lessons. So's I give 'em this paintin' afore I left. They packed it along with their own as they were leavin' their home ta go live with the Missus' family on their farm. Twasn't quite finished so's I hadn't signed it, but it made no never mind. 'Tis the only one of me paintin's left, as when the rotten police locked me up, they threw 'way the rest. 'Twas only the suitcase of me sketches survived."

Grace was stunned by the story and the coincidental nature of the moment. Imagining the impact of the painting, she stepped next to Teagan and supportively wrapped her arm around the woman's shoulder. In response, Teagan cradled her head into Grace and the two women became lost in the endless emerald shore of Ireland.

Chapter Fifty-Five

THERE WAS NOTHING LEFT. Her Wood Haven paperwork was completed. Her office cleaned out. Her keys returned to Jonathan. The two shared a few moments before she drove through the massive stone pillars one last time. He reiterated his admiration for her accomplishments and support for her potential collaboration with the state. She thanked him for both and promised to keep him updated. Then, just like that, Grace was officially unemployed.

All she had left to do was return to the house and put her suitcases in her car. Then she would drive to Buffalo and figure out how to get through Christmas Eve tonight and Christmas tomorrow, all on her own.

She decided not to stop at Bennett House again. The good bye she had shared with the Faith File when she dropped off the painting had gone well. Grace had managed to keep her tears at bay, relying on her nana's firm belief in making the best of life, no matter the pain. She shared a moment with each of the five women, soaking in their sweet wishes and loving thoughts. Seeing them settled in Bennett House made leaving them manageable . . . except for Teagan. No amount of inspirational thought soothed Grace's heart as the two embraced one last time.

While the Irishwoman was hearty, in a few weeks she would celebrate her 70th birthday. While Grace knew that life could end at any moment, her job reinforced the fact that aging raised the odds. It was that thought that compelled Grace to hold on to Teagan just a little tighter, just a little longer.

"Aw, go on with ya now, Gracie Girl. I'll not be dyin' anytime soon if that's what you're thinkin'. So be gone now and get ta livin'. You're young with a long road ahead. And I'll always be with ya, right there in your heart."

Ok. You have got to get your mind clear. There's a long drive ahead and looking backwards the whole time won't be good. It's Christmas Eve and you can make it fun or sad, your choice.

Grace decided she was going to make it fun, beginning with a stop at Cuppa Joe for a Grace special.

Last minute shoppers were clogging every Midland street in the downtown area, but she lucked out in finding a parking space right across from the local diner. She was in-between the morning and lunch rush, so the place was only partially full. Settling into her spot at the counter, Grace ignored the menu and instead looked around the cozy diner. What she saw were families and friends and the spirit of Christmas inspiring them all. What would she do back in Buffalo? Her nana and papa were gone, her parents away on their annual Greek Island cruise, her friends married and in the full-blown stages of parenting.

When did this happen? How did I become so isolated in my world?

"Hey Grace. Merry Christmas. I've missed seeing you."

Suzy's warm smile and kind words comforted her. The woman had a way of talking to Cuppa Joe customers that made each one feel that they were special. It was a talent, a gift really, and Suzy shared it every day from behind her counter.

"Merry Christmas to you, Suzy, and thanks for missing me! I've been busy the last few weeks moving all the Wood Haven seniors to their new homes. Kept me off the streets for sure."

The women shared a laugh as Suzy took Grace's order.

"What can I get you? Pancakes? Eggs and toast?"

"No thanks. I'm not really hungry. I just stopped for a Grace special."

"One half and half, coffee and hot chocolate coming up."

Sitting with her mind unoccupied, Grace's thoughts again returned to Christmas. Her favorite memories were attached to a parade of beautifully lit and decorated Christmas trees passing in mental review. Grace's parents were always too busy for the holidays, so her best Christmas memories revolved around nana and papa coming into the city to take Grace to pick out a tree and then taking it home and decorating it.

Nana had stringent standards when it came to tree decorations, beginning with the lights. They had to be mixed colors and inset on the tree branches to fully illuminate the evergreen from within it's triangular shape. Next, decorations had to be spaced out evenly and artfully, followed by tinsel placed one strand at a time. Finally, in the finest of traditions, papa pulled up a dining room chair snug to the tree and boosted nana to a standing position on the seat. Holding tight to her legs, papa provided the balance that allowed nana to reach higher and farther than she was able in order to perfectly center an angel on the very tiptop branch.

"Grace, I'm sorry, I forgot to ask. Is your special for here or to go?"

"To go, thanks, Suzy."

Grace's thoughts immediately returned to her envisioned Christmas trees and the traditions that followed the decorating. There was the manger complete with ceramic figures of Mary, Joseph, the shepherds and sheep, the three kings, the angel, a donkey and a cow, along with a bag of straw. It was Grace's job to artfully display all beneath the tree, arranging them on tiered shoe and cake mix boxes covered with angel hair. As was the Irish Catholic tradition, she hid away the baby Jesus until Christmas morning, when he was actually born.

"Ok, here you go. One Grace special. And I added just a spot of whipped cream. After all, it is Christmas Eve."

Suzy's gesture touched Grace and, again, she thought about spending her Christmas in an empty apartment without any person-to-person interaction. The scenario sparked a need within Grace to be known and belong. As she pulled out her wallet to pay the bill, Grace asked Suzy for a favor.

"Sure, Grace. Whatever I can do."

"Today's my last day in Midland and, truthfully, I'm finding it a bit harder to leave than I anticipated. I feel like I'm leaving a part of me here and that's never happened before in my other consulting jobs. I wondered if maybe I can reconsider and say yes to your offer to add the Grace Special to your drink board?"

With a grin that spread from her lips to her eyes, Suzy leaned across the counter and gave Grace a sweet hug in reply.

"Grace, nothing would make me happier this Christmas Eve than to make you a permanent part of this town, right here at Cuppa Joe. It'll be up on the board this afternoon."

It was silly, Grace knew, but having her chocolate coffee featured on the menu of Midland's most popular eatery somehow mattered.

Grace left the diner and began driving up and down the business district while enjoying her mocha treat. The merchants were perfectly decorated and lit, music of the season was playing throughout the Main Street shopping district. At the far end of thoroughfare, a bright red trailer was parked on a grassy area, safely set apart from traffic. A banner draped across the side heralded, "Santa's Wonderland." Children corralled by their parents were standing in wait for the chance to enter and whisper their Christmas wishes in Santa's ear. It was picture perfect in every way.

Jazzed by the double shot of caffeine and boosted by the town's Christmas spirit, Grace returned to her rental house, humming, "Deck the Halls." Room by room, she swept through the classic Victorian, checking for left behinds and finding none. Carrying her luggage to the door, she took one last look around the space she'd called home for the last seven months.

From room to room, one vision continually came to her mind. Mike Healy. He was in the kitchen making her coffee. He was in the living room listening to her talk about her seniors. He was in her bedroom protecting and comforting her after the dead cat on her car. He was at the front door, walking out after she broke his heart.

She'd told him what she thought was best for both of them and he was hurt.

Exactly, **you** *told him what was best for both of you. How would you have felt if he tore apart your relationship based solely on what he thought?*

Grace didn't necessarily want to hear what her brain had to say. The fact that it was Christmas Eve and she was set to drive 8 hours to a home where no one was waiting and no one cared was depressing enough. She just needed to pack up her car and get on the road.

Dragging the first suitcase out the door, Grace set it down next to the car and opened the trunk. With a heave-ho motion she lifted the bag and launched it into the empty space. Watching it topple into place, reminded Grace of Teagan's description of her paintings tumbling away from her as the police grabbed and tossed them.

How did she ever survive all those heart-breaking moments? How did any of my seniors find the strength to go on? And what have I learned from them in these last seven months?

Retrieving her second suitcase, Grace used the car as a brace in lifting the fully packed bag and wedging it into the trunk. Her muscles strained from the effort, reminding her of the night she and Jonathan brought the eight suitcases down from the attic and the director's gallantry in insisting he be the one to take the heavy bags.

It was nice that people at Wood Haven cared about me and wanted to do things for me. In all my years of consulting, not one of my supervisors ever gave a thought about my professional struggles or what my needs might be. Not like Jonathan.

Saving the lightest for last, Grace picked up her third bag and transported it over the threshold. Setting it down on the porch, she reached around to the inside of the door, turned the lock on the handle and pulled it shut. Since the trunk was full, Grace opened the back-passenger side door and slid the bag onto the seat. Slamming shut both the car door and trunk, Grace walked to the end of the driveway to check her mailbox one last time. Finding it empty, she looked up to where her imagination envisioned a red pickup truck parked on the street with Mike flying out the driver's door, steam blowing from every inch of his body.

At the time I thought he was such an idiot, but when I think now about the turns I took and the red lights I ran to get rid of him, he risked his life to try and protect mine. He could have been killed.

Taking a last look at the ornate Victorian home and its white picket fence, Grace slipped into her car and started the engine. The quartz clock embedded in the dashboard read 1:28. With any luck, Grace would be parked in her underground garage and riding the elevator to her condo by 9:30, enough time to unpack and fall in to bed.

So go. What are you waiting for?

Grace was unaware of waiting for anything or anyone. Still, she wasn't putting her car's gear shift in reverse and pulling out of the driveway. Was she having some sort of mini-stroke where her brain was unable to clearly communicate with the muscles and nerves in her body? Was there some latent fear in her mind immobilizing her? Had she reached some turning point about her life and future?

Bingo! You finally got it. After months and months of working with people who have seen the seamiest side life has to offer, you, Grace Reid, have learned something—an important life lesson about yourself and the people in your life.

Really? Important life lesson? I don't feel as if I have changed in any demonstrable way since May. And if I have, how does that come in to play with my leaving Midland and going home to Buffalo?

Grace's inner voice failed to answer, which generally meant she needed more time to consider. That was one thing she did have, time. There was no one pushing her return to Buffalo, and nothing setting a deadline she had to meet. She was the one who had arbitrarily set December 24th as her departure date and Buffalo as her location. At this point, she could put the car in reverse and set out for anyplace in the world.

Yet you're still sitting in this driveway. What's stopping you?

Stymied, Grace turned to the one source she knew she could trust, even above herself.

Nana, I need your help. I feel so lost right now. No guidelines, no goals to push me in any direction. Just a sense of different life values based on all I learned from my Wood Haven Seniors. All that was stripped away from them. The physical and mental punishments they endured through most of their adulthood. The time stolen from them for reasons of no just cause. Relationships with people they loved that were completely destroyed. The compromises they had to make to survive. The simple pleasures they value now as a result. And here I am with the ability to go anywhere and be with anyone and I am choosing to leave this place and these people and return to a life of solitude and fulfillment achieved only through my work. I'm not sure that's who I am anymore, nana, but I think I'm scared to find out.

As if expecting a miracle or a ghostly appearance by her beloved grandmother, Grace remained fixed in the driveway. It was only as a light snow began dusting her windshield that she was reminded of the challenges of winter driving, especially when headed to Buffalo. Putting the key in the ignition, Grace backed out of the driveway and began heading out of town.

Desperate to hear anything but her inner voice, she turned on the radio. Christmas carols were playing from one end of the dial to the other. She really was not in the mood. Finally, she flipped to a station featuring a new Christmas song by The Eagles, which meant there were no memories or people attached to the song. Listening to the bluesy beat, Grace honed in on the unfamiliar lyrics.

> *Friends and relations send salutations*
> *Sure as the stars shine above*
> *But this is Christmas,*
> *Yes Christmas my dear*
> *The time of year to be with the ones you love.*

Like a lightening bolt, Grace was immersed in the last words Teagan had shared with her.

"Remember, Gracie, life is all about love. Without it, nothin' else matters."

Grace knew what she had to do, what she wanted to do.

Hitting the accelerator, she raised her car's speed over Midland's lawful designation. Zoooming out of the business district she began to approach the town limits and the back side of the billboard that read, "Thank you for visiting Midland Township, Where History is a Way of Life." If luck was with her, it would only be a minute or so.

Increasing her speed, Grace was beginning to question the wisdom of her plan. And then she saw it. The red gumball whirring in her rear-view mirror.

Applying the brakes, she navigated her car onto the shoulder of the road and pulled out her license and registration.

Please let it be him. Please let it be him. Please, please, please let it be him.

Rolling down her window Grace could see, it *was* him.

"Afternoon, Officer Healy," she whispered, doing her best to control the happiness she felt.

"Afternoon, Miss Reid. I'm sure you're aware that you were driving significantly over the speed limit. In a hurry to get back to Buffalo, no doubt."

"Actually no, Officer. More I'm in a hurry to get back to you-—and start our new life."

AUTHOR'S AFTERWARD

IN MY AUTHOR'S EXPERIENCE, writing a book begins with a combination of blessed and torturous inspiration. An idea that becomes so powerful it haunts me until I have to tell it in a story.

The inspiration for Beauty and Grace came to me from another writer. A remarkable woman by the name of Mary Jo Hodge. I came to know Mary Jo when she asked to meet over a cup of tea and a chat about our shared writing craft. Always happy to spend time with fellow writers, I agreed. We set a date.

What I learned at our tea and talk was that Mary Jo was the author of four books, three of which were novels featuring inspiring and strong women as the main characters. I liked this woman right away!

More significantly, Mary Jo shared with me that she had been diagnosed with Parkinsons, which was gradually challenging her writing abilities. The thought of this lovely woman struggling to do the thing she loves most sent waves of sadness through my heart. At the same time, there was not an ounce of, "woe is me" in Mary Jo's words or actions. I not only liked this women, I now held her in awe.

As our afternoon became immersed in storylines and characters, Mary Jo shared a story from her earlier career as a nurse. She told of an assignment at a facility that had been repurposed from a mental institution / asylum to a long term care facility. Some of the asylum patients were transferred over to the care facility, being deemed sound enough of mind. As a result nurses charged with caring for those patients were provided an insider's view of their asylum life.

As Mary Jo told the story, she came to this facility years after its repurposing. When she was hired, a core of nurses from the transition period were still on staff. As their time together evolved, the veteran nurses began sharing stories from earlier days, the most compelling of which centered on Irish women who had immigrated to the United States in the early 20th Century.

It seems that these women came to America in search of new lives and new opportunities as they'd heard about from family members already settled across the ocean. With grit and deteminiation these independent women packed small bag of belongings and set off, traveling in the filthy depths and disease of steerage class ships. Like so many others, they believed once arrived in New York Harbor they only had to make their way through Ellis Island to begin their new lives.

However, their stories ended much differently than the women ever imagined.

When the they arrived, unmarried and with no man meeting them, they were immediately deemed as liabilities, American Immigration Officials unilaterally determined that without a man as head of the household, these women would never be able to make their way financially. eventually becoming a drain on the nation's economy.

Choosing the simplest solution, the officials institutionalized the Irish women without notice to anyone who loved them or knew them. These women became invisible, unknown, and slipped through the cracks of medical or government inspections that could have righted these egregious wrongs, remaining institutionalized as much as 50 years later.

The details of Mary Jo's story swirled within me for months. Even when life did it's best to distract me, my stubborn Irish mind continued to return to those women and the unjust treatments they endured. Needing to do something to clear my head I turned to the most reliable tool in my writer's repertoire—research.

Over the ensuing year I spent time investigating, reading books, attending lectures and visiting actual asylum sites, anything I could do to verify the nurses's story. Sadly, I could not find any exact history of such incidents. Tragically, I found reams of stories about women and men locked away in degrading lunatic asylums across the United States for reasons beyond my comprehension.

Death of sons in war	Political excitement
Feebleness of mind	Religious enthusiasm
Novel reading	Uterine derangement
Overaction of the mind	Women troubles

The sampling above is what eventually drove me to write Beauty and Grace.

While the book you have just finished is a novel, it is based on the horrific and undeniable acts of cruelty administered to people of both sound and unsound minds in lunatic asylums and mental institutions across the United States. It was in response to courageous mental health advocates like Dorothea Dix and Nellie Bly that the heinous asylum treatments came to light and the medical profession and the United States Government gradually began to change their ways, beginning with the creation of the National Institute of Mental Health in 1949 through to the 1980 passage of the Mental Health Systems Act. Yet the challenges of mental health treatment in our nation remains.

According to a recent report, there is a critical nationwide shortage of psychiatric beds in America, forcing many mentally ill patients with severe symptoms to be "boarded" in hospital emergency rooms and jails as they wait, sometimes for weeks, for an available bed. Estimates are that an additional 123,300 psychiatric hospital beds are needed to alleviate this shortage. It is my hope that Beauty and Grace will help bring light to the struggles of all who face mental challenges and encourage humane and thoughtful means of dealing with those struggles.

Beauty and Grace was not an easy book to write. There were days when my spirit was so burdened by the stories that I was forced to tuck the book away and allow my mind to escape Wood Haven and its cruelities. The blessed relief of those escapes also instilled in me an undeniable awareness of the oppressive nature of such asylums and the desperate feel of being trapped with no release. Thankfully, encouraging support from family and friends provided me with strength to continue. And to those special I owe great debts.

To Holly Lorincz, editor extraordinaire and the first person to tell me she believed in this book, when it was but a mere idea rattling around in my head.

To Kate McGregor who courageously read through Beauty & Grace before it was really ready and found ways to encourage me to continue.

To Daniel Middleton, for making sure my words look good and read well and for breathing life into my vision of Beauty and Grace as a book cover. You are a creative force.

To Marion, Emily, Jocelyn and Cindy, for grinding through test reads of

Beauty and Grace, even when they dragged on for over two years.

To Claudia for tutoring me on how to transform what sounded like Yoda-talk into a German dialect.

To my children, Lisa and James, for the ways in which you show respect for my writing craft.

To Bennett and Ella Rose, for inspiring me to work at my craft so that you will have a family legacy and an example to follow. No matter who you become or what profession you choose, nana will always be proud of you.

Last but not least, to Mary Jo Hodge, you are a woman of strength and courage, and I am inspired by your detemination to carry on despite life's challenges. Thank you for sharing your story and for giving me permission to write it. I hope you feel I did justice to all in the pages of this novel and that you recognize yourself in the character of Teagan—a woman determined to live life, no matter.

—Christina

75781944R00244

Made in the USA
San Bernardino, CA
04 May 2018